Blo
Beers &
Burritos

JO BLAKELEY

MIJOMA
BOOKS

Published in 2017 by Mijoma Books

ISBN Paperback: 978-0-9957305-0-2
Ebook: 978-0-9957305-1-9

A CIP catalogue copy of this book
can be found in the British Library.

Published with the help of Indie Authors World

IndieAuthors
World

Note From The Author

I am really excited that you have picked up Blokes, Beers & Burritos, and are about to read it. I don't want to spoil things for you so I won't reveal too much, but I would like to say that I am an ordinary woman with no special talents, apart from a passion to help others. I wrote this book to help women to be happy in every area of their lives, but in a much shorter timespan than it took me. When I was younger, I wasn't willing to admit to anyone - not even myself - that I needed help, so there was no way I would have turned to a traditional self-help book. To help women in a similar situation, I decided to put the Steps to Bliss within the pages of fiction so that they could have fun while learning about themselves too. With this in mind, you can either do the Steps to Bliss alongside Cath as she learns them, or you can finish the story and then go through the Steps with your own life in mind. There is a summary of the Steps to Bliss at the end of the book.

Dedication

To mum and dad, without whom I would never have had the dogged determination and drive to succeed in life. I thank you and love you with all my heart.

Acknowledgements

So many people influenced this book that it would be impossible to mention them all. Most of all, I would like to say a special thanks to my husband who has been my rock throughout the long and often frustrating process. As I am not a professional writer, it was a steep learning curve for me and I had to fit writing in-between being a mum and being a bread-winner, which was a huge challenge! With this in mind, I would also like to thank my son for putting up with me when I was sometimes lost in my thoughts in a far-away world. In addition I would like to thank all my wonderful friends and family – you know who you are – who have supported me and stuck by me in my darkest days. Also, a big thank you to all my teachers along the way who have taught me everything I know. On a practical note, I would like to thank my editors, Jane Goodfellow and Keidi Keating aka Your Book Angel for a wonderful job on helping get my book to this stage, and finally, a huge thank you to Indie Authors World for all their help (and patience!) in turning my goal into reality.

Prologue

West Hampstead, London - 28 March 2015

A slice of glistening light beamed through the crack in the mocha curtains, creating a mystical grey-blue haze in the room. Cath blinked her eyes open while stifling a yawn with one hand and stretching out the other. A smile tugged at the corner of her mouth as she observed Brian's upper arm muscles tensing as he ripped the duvet from his naked body. 'What are you doing?'

Brian sat up and placed his elbows on his taut thighs, clasping his head in his hands. 'Sorry.'

Cath shunted across the bed like a caterpillar to move closer to him. 'Don't worry about not getting me a present – it's not a big birthday.' She flicked her long chestnut-brown hair so it fell provocatively over her left shoulder, revealing the delicate flesh of her neck, before reaching across to caress Brian's tanned back. But, as her fingers made contact with his skin, he recoiled. Leaning forward, she peered up at him with her piercing grey eyes, hoping they would mesmerise him, and at the same time she kissed the cusp of his lower left hip, a place she knew turned him on, but he shifted away.

'No, that's not what I meant. Sorry. I can't do this anymore.'

Cath felt the temperature in the room plummet.

'What did you say?' Cath grabbed for his elbow but he snapped his arm away. She burrowed her finger in her ear and rattled it in the hollow. 'I can't have heard you correctly after what happened, three times, last night?'

Brian stood up, eyes scanning the floor. 'You heard me.'

'But... you can't... break up with me today.' Cath bit her bottom lip in an attempt not to cry. The room was so cold, she feared her tears would emerge as icicles. 'It's my birthday.'

Brian leant over and picked up his boxers, hauling them on quickly. After hesitating for a few seconds, he delved into his overnight bag, producing a crumpled HMV bag. He tossed it onto the bed, where it landed as far away from Cath as possible. Anger engulfed the sadness she felt as it rose from the depths.

He continued to scoop his shorts and t-shirt off the floor. 'It's a present.'

'I can see that. Is it a consolation prize?'

'No.' Brian was about to say something further but nearly toppled over in an attempt to put his shorts on too hastily. Cath suppressed a snigger. When Brian regained his balance, he continued getting dressed, still avoiding eye contact. 'Things haven't been right for a while. I didn't think it fair to string you along. I bought you the present because I felt bad.'

Cath registered the use of the past tense then snatched the HMV bag, tipping out *Insurgent*. She threw the DVD at him. 'So you bloody well should!' Realising that this action had left her flesh fully bared, she grabbed the duvet to cover up her exposed body. 'Take your poor excuse of a present and get out. Now.'

Brian grabbed his overnight bag, wrenched open the bedroom door, then slammed it hard enough behind him to make the framed black and white photograph on the wall tremble. She cursed Brian for disturbing her favourite picture in the world: a photo of her dad kissing her when she was four years old.

Vibrating with anger, Cath fell back into bed and bashed the pillow with her bare fists. *Why is this happening again? And on my birthday? What's wrong with me?* She curled up into the fetal position and hugged the pillow tightly. The faint smell of Brian's aftershave provoked spasms of emotion but she swallowed back the tears. Although she could feel the familiar hurt clambering up from the depths, she would not allow herself to cry. Instead, she plunged her unwelcome feelings further into the abyss, leaving them to fester.

The previous night's rampant activities together with the morning's emotional drain were taking their toll on Cath and she couldn't keep her eyes open, so she fell into a deep sleep.

As she woke up, she felt a streak of saliva dribbling down her chin and it had soaked the pillow. She wiped her chin with the duvet and then registered the time on the bedside clock, which told her she had been asleep for a couple of hours. She downed a pint of water then fumbled for the *Insurgent* DVD, inserted the disc into the DVD player, and pressed play. She saw the pictures but the storyline wasn't registering. All she could think about was what could be wrong with her. *Why doesn't Brian want to be with me? Am I boring? Ugly? Fat?* She came to the conclusion that if she dieted and made more of an effort with her appearance, perhaps he would want to be with her. But that wasn't the only thing bothering her. Not only did she have another failed relationship to add to her growing collection, she also had a pending bullying charge hanging over her at work.

She had always wanted to go travelling, so maybe it was time to take the plunge. Resolving to go to Trailfinders on Kensington High Street the next day, Cath returned to watching the second film in the Divergent series.

Chapter One

Mexico City, Mexico 25 August 2015

Uh oh, something's wrong. Adrenalin raced through Cath's veins as she watched the taxi driver disappear into the darkness of the tunnel a few metres ahead. *Don't follow him anymore. Get away from him!* She couldn't ignore her internal screams for a moment longer so she turned around and headed back towards the airport. *I only landed an hour ago. How have I managed to get myself into trouble already? Idiot!*

She heard footsteps behind her, so she figured the driver must have noticed she was no longer following him. He was now pursuing her instead and yelled something in Spanish but, as she didn't understand what he was saying, she sped up as fast as her legs would carry her. Well, as fast as possible with a 20-kilogram backpack bobbing up and down on her sweaty back. Ahead, she spotted a queue of tourists underneath an over-sized, glowing neon sign that said, 'Taxi'. *Idiot!* How she had managed to miss this enormous sign on her way out of Departures, and had instead decided to follow a complete stranger claiming to be a taxi driver, she would never know.

She reached the queue and stopped suddenly next to two short, dark-haired guys with backpacks resting against their legs. She side-stepped to be even closer to the boys in an effort to feel safe, aware she was invading their personal space.

She peeled the backpack off her melting back, trying not to whack anyone in the process. 'Hi.'

'Hi.' The two boys took a couple of steps back but, as they did so, they collided with a six-foot natural blonde standing in front of them.

'Sorry, I didn't mean...' Cath wasn't sure if she was apologising for causing the boys to embarrass themselves or because they had to speak to her instead of the Nordic beauty.

The shorter of the two spoke first. 'No problemo, eet okay.'

In normal circumstances, Cath would have savoured the sound of English spoken with an Italian accent, but she was still getting over having been almost kidnapped by a Mexican taxi driver. She scanned the vicinity and sighed deeply when she couldn't see him anywhere. Turning her attention back to the two Italians, she felt the need to explain why her skin was coated in a fine glaze of moisture. 'I've just narrowly escaped being raped, killed, or sold into a life of slavery.'

Ignoring her comment, either through incomprehension or embarrassment, the boys offered her a full-strength Marlboro cigarette. A cigarette was the perfect antidote for calming her nerves, but if she succumbed, it would mean throwing away a year of kicking the habit. She shook her head slowly as she watched the boys enjoy every inhalation of nicotine, tar, and carbon monoxide. Coughing on their second-hand smoke, Cath answered their barrage of questions: 'What's your name? Where are you from? Where are you going? How long are you away for?'

Asking the same questions back, Cath learnt that their names were Alessandro and Matteo, they were from Milan, they were on holiday for two weeks, and they were heading to *Chiquita's* in the centre of Mexico City.

Cath grabbed the bottom of her t-shirt to mop up the globules of sweat on her forehead until she realised the boys were staring at her exposed flesh, so she quickly replaced the material. 'What a coincidence, that's the same hostel I'm going to.' With her backpack between her legs, Cath waddled towards the front of the queue like a penguin. As the boys bundled into the next available taxi, Cath stood with her mouth open. *Surely you're not going to abandon me?*

Alessandro, the taller Italian, held the taxi door open and gestured for her to get inside.

'Come.'

Is he asking or telling me? Cath didn't care and climbed into the taxi before it could drive off without her.

Forty-five minutes later, the clock on the wall behind the reception desk at the hostel told Cath it was midnight. A quick calculation in her head meant she had been awake for over twenty hours. A yawn slipped out of her mouth involuntarily.

Matteo gave her a sympathetic nod, 'You, bed?'

If you were four inches taller, I might be tempted. Cath was about to giggle at her own joke when Alessandro reached for Cath's hand like it was a delicate flower and kissed it. 'Buona notte.'

Before she had time to blush, Matteo elbowed him out of the way playfully, positioned himself in front of her and kissed her on both cheeks softly. 'Buona notte, bellissima ragazza.'

Then, as if they were in a hurry, the boys smiled and marched up the stairs arguing. Even when they had vanished round a corner and were out of sight, Cath could still hear them quarrelling in the distance.

After following basic directions in pidgin English from the receptionist, she found herself in a labyrinth of corridors. After double-backing on herself three times, Cath eventually found her dorm room on the second floor. As she pulled open the door, she was hit with a stench of blue cheese and an oppressive heat as stifling as a sauna. Beads of sweat clung to hair follicles she didn't even know she had. *Yuck! How can anyone sleep in this?* A beam of light shone in from the corridor, and illuminated two bunk beds lined up along either side of the wall. It was as inviting as a prison cell. There was a narrow strip of floor, a little wider than the walkway on a Boeing 747, covered in random trainers, flip flops, t-shirts and shorts, as well as various toiletries labelled in different languages. Every one of the bunk beds contained a comatose body except for the top one to her right. *That'll be my bed then.*

As soon as she closed the door, a nightlight launched into action, leaving the room in a dull shimmer. She peeled off her t-shirt and tracksuit bottoms while keeping an eye on the sleeping bodies, to ensure no-one was taking a sneaky look, and pulled out a sheet sleeping bag and an over-sized bright pink t-shirt. She put on the t-shirt and undid her bra's catch, pulling it out expertly through the armholes.

Having found a small area behind the door for her backpack, she climbed up the wonky ladder timidly. When she'd made it to the top, she had to manoeuvre herself horizontally onto the lumpy mattress or risk colliding with the over-sized fan positioned inches from where she was supposed to sleep.

Cath counted the straining rotations of the aged fan, which was barely creating a disturbance in the surrounding air. She reached one hundred and seventy-nine when a pressure forced down on her bladder. *No. Not now!* She got halfway down the ladder before her foot slipped off the bottom rung and she fell onto the floor with a thud. *Idiot!* No-one moved. She was more irritated that no-one had noticed her stunt worthy of a scene in an action movie than at having hurt herself. Steadying herself to her feet, she warily placed one foot in front of the other, avoiding the obstacles on the floor until she reached the bathroom door. Sighing with relief that she had made it without further injury, Cath closed the door and switched on the light. As soon as the brightness finished assaulting her eyes, bile advanced into her throat. The room looked and smelled like a public toilet following a *Delhi belly* outbreak.

To avoid the billions of germs, wet urine splashes, and 'pebble dashes' on the seat, Cath used every ounce of muscle strength in her thighs to hover over the toilet while trying not to throw up. She cradled her head in her hands. *What was I thinking? Why did I think travelling would solve my problems?*

With an absence of toilet roll, Cath had to drip-dry. She washed her hands three times and hoped she wouldn't develop Obsessive Compulsive Disorder over the following year. She switched off the light and precariously climbed through the semi-darkness and back into bed. At two-hundred and ninety-three counts of the fan, she eventually drifted to sleep.

Riley, Cath's latest love interest back home, whom she'd become involved with after being dumped by Brian on her birthday six months earlier, was spooning her in a four poster bed with sheets that felt soft and silky against her skin. There was a gentle rocking motion while Riley's fingertips shadowed the contours of Cath's naked waist and then moved towards her breasts suggestively, almost touching her already aroused nipples, before retreating leisurely to the top of her thighs. He repeated his preferred form of torture until Cath was writhing so much she couldn't take it anymore. She seized his hand and positioned it on her wet mound. She moaned as her erogenous zone rushed signals throughout her body. 'Oh Riley, you turn me on so much!'

She was about to slip her hand underneath the waistband of his boxer shorts when she froze and opened her eyes. It was a matter of seconds before she realised where she was. Face burning, she peered over the edge of her bed, careful not to engage in a fight with the fan, and saw that the rocking motion had been created by a giant Nordic-looking bloke on the bed beneath her. The enormous man was sitting on the lower bunk bed while trying to dress himself, causing the entire bed frame to shudder in greater degrees as they expanded away from him like ripples from the epicenter of an earthquake. Cath breathed an exaggerated sigh. When she had finished expressing her annoyance at her rude roommate, and had woken up everyone else in the process, Cath slunk back under the fan. Closing her eyes in the hope she would float back into her dream, pangs of hunger screamed from her stomach to her brain, making sleep impossible. She got up, flung on some clothes, and followed her nose through the labyrinth of rooms to find the cafeteria. She gave up and stopped a Tom Cruise lookalike for directions. 'Excuse me, where's breakfast?'

'Basement. I'm going there, follow me.' He marched ahead without waiting for her.

When they arrived, Cath was nearly level with her guide and was about to engage him in conversation when he disappeared into the sea of bodies.

The cafeteria was a heaving array of mismatched tables and chairs reminding Cath of a school canteen. She spotted an area at the top of the room where a throng of people were buzzing around, so she joined them in the hope they were at the food station. After several minutes of being jostled from side to side, Cath reached a few slices of anaemic looking bread before deciding she wasn't hungry after all. Next up was a large metal drum of boiling water, which made her think of a church hall coffee morning. She grabbed the last sachet of Lipton tea along with a chipped mug and filled it with boiling water. Then she broke free from the swarm and scanned the room for her two Italian saviours from the night before. Every table was crammed full of backpackers of varying shapes, sizes and degrees of cleanliness, but no sign of her lovely Italians. *Damn!* Cath didn't know what to do so she took a deep breath, pushed her shoulders back, held her head high, and walked defiantly towards the door through which she'd entered.

Cath weaved through the maze of corridors to relocate the reception area. On the way, she passed a yellow-tinged computer that looked like something out of the 1980's and a fridge full of soft drinks that lit up the otherwise drab surroundings. Cath reached the reception counter and rifled through a jumble of leaflets – all in Spanish – about local attractions, tours, and activities while she waited for the two receptionists to stop talking to each other. The pictures were all she could comprehend so she replaced the leaflets, tapped her fingers on the wooden surface, and looked at her watch. *How rude! Customer service in this country isn't up to much.* As if one of the receptionists could read Cath's mind, she turned and looked at her like she was a piece of dirt. Cath was about to ask if she could use the internet and buy a cola lite, when she stopped and asked, 'You speak English?'

The olive-skinned receptionist used her finger and thumb to demonstrate how much. 'A *beet.*' Then shot a smile to her colleague.

'How – use – internet?' Cath asked, pointing at the lonely computer. 'How – much – cola lite?'

Smirking, the receptionist answered with perfect English in a broad Yorkshire accent. *Cow!*

With cheeks burning, Cath paid for half an hour's internet access and a drink and marched over to the computer, collecting an ice cold cola lite on the way. The can of drink opened with a hiss while the computer thought about working. Cath was hit with a cool sweetness which provided momentary joy while the aged modem dialled-up to the World Wide Web. It took five minutes before Cath could view the ten spam emails in her inbox. Cursing under her breath, she decided to use the remaining twenty minutes to send emails and write her first blog.

First, Cath wanted to let Riley know how much she was already missing him. Having randomly met him at a party via a friend, they'd had a whirlwind romance akin to something out of a *Mills and Boon* novel. Even though he was originally from Liverpool, he lived and worked in London so they saw each other every day of the six weeks before Cath flew to Mexico City. While Riley showed signs that he adored her, Cath wondered if his feelings were so intense because he'd always known their relationship had an expiry date. She decided to find out how committed he really was.

All I can think about is how much I miss you, and worrying that it will be a full year before I see you again – unless you come and visit me of course!!! I'd love it if you could

PS. I had a very rude dream about you last night...!!!

Cath was apprehensive about what his response might be, and then wrote her first *Brown on Tour* blog, which would be read – hopefully – by the friends and family to whom she had provided the link a few days ago.

Brown on Tour
Day 1: Mexico City

After an uneventful but long flight, I arrived safely and am loving Mexico City – it's so vibrant, hot, and the people are friendly. The hostel is plush and, even though I'm in a dorm, we've got our own en-suite bathroom. Not what I was expecting for the equivalent of £5 per night!

I haven't tried any Mexican food yet but I'm looking forward to sampling my first nachos, tacos and fajitas and washing them down with a Tequila Sunrise. Can't wait.

I can't tell you what I've got planned for the day because I haven't organised anything yet but I'll keep you updated!

Finally, she emailed her best friend, Rosie.

Please ignore what my blog says. It's true that I arrived safely – just; after nearly getting led down a dark alleyway by some bloke pretending to be a taxi driver - but the rest is rubbish. The hostel is hideous and I'm surrounded by stinky, loud backpackers. What have I done? If I wasn't

*so stubborn, I'd turn round and come back tonight! But I
left for a reason so I must force myself to stay for at least
a week.*

Cath still had ten minutes of online time left so she
scanned her inbox to see if there was anything worth
reading. She wasn't in the market for a 'hot, sexy, young'
Russian bride. Delete. Nor was she interested in pills to
enlarge her penis. Delete. Nor did she want to give an
imprisoned Prince her bank details in exchange for a
share of his $2 million fortune. Delete. Next, there was an
email from The Bliss Expert entitled, 'Cath, do you want
it all?' Goosebumps raced through her body and she felt
compelled to open it.

- *Do you want to be happy?*

- *Do you want to be in a long-term relationship with a man
  who loves and respects you as much as you do him?*

- *Do you want a close relationship with your family?*

- *Do you want to be fit, slim and healthy?*

- *Do you want a job you feel passionate about, and a
  career that fulfils you and earns you a lot of money?*

Of course I want all those things. Who doesn't? But she was
intrigued how the email could be specifically addressed to
her and how it knew to pinpoint all the things she wanted
in her life. In fact, how did it know the very reasons why
she'd come travelling in the first place? Despite being
tempted to read on, she assumed it must be a scam so
pressed the delete button. No sooner had she done so than
another email popped up from the same address. She
opened it.

I wouldn't delete emails from me if I were you. I am offering you everything you could ever want.

Over the course of your trip, I will give you advice, useful tips of where to go, who to travel with and who would be best to avoid. Here's a taster of what you can expect if you decide to trust me:

- *It was a good decision to not go with the taxi man last night; it wouldn't have ended well*

- *Go with the two Italians when they ask you. They'll help you to settle into travelling*

- *Don't use Riley to make you feel better about yourself*

- *Be open to people who you would normally judge harshly. They could be of immense help to you if you'll let them*

Then, when you are ready, I will give you The Ten Steps to Bliss that will help you create positive changes in your life.

The world stopped moving. Cath scanned the room for anyone suspicious-looking but she could only see the two receptionists chatting at a million miles an hour, so engrossed in their conversation that Cath could have stripped naked and performed a rain dance in front of them and they wouldn't have noticed. There was not a single other person around, suspicious-looking or otherwise. *How could The Bliss Expert know about the things I want most in my life? How could he know that I'd deleted his email?* She had assumed The Bliss Expert was a man. *How come his email contains my name? How does he know that I followed the taxi driver and met two Italian boys last night? And judgemental? How dare he!* One plausible answer was that the Italian boys had somehow got hold of her email address and were playing a prank on her. Maybe, like the receptionist, their English was much better than they'd made out and they had guessed a girl travelling alone in Mexico might be searching for something. But then she reasoned it couldn't be them because she hadn't told them about Riley. Before she had time to reread the email, the screen flickered and went black. Her thirty minutes was up.

Now what? Swallowing her pride, Cath approached the receptionist from Yorkshire and asked where she recommended visiting.

'There's a minibus taking a few guests on a day trip to a cathedral and some pyramids. They're worth seeing and only an hour away. It's leaving in thirty minutes outside the front here.' She pointed at the revolving door behind Cath.

'Sounds great!' Cath paid the receptionist for a ticket and returned to her room, which smelled like someone had died. She had enough time to shower, eat three packets of biscuits, two oat bars and a mini cheese sandwich that she'd pilfered from the plane before researching where she was about to visit. Her *Lonely Planet* guide book confirmed that the receptionist was indeed recommending a 'must see' sight on the outskirts of Mexico City.

Cath checked her watch. It was six minutes past ten and she couldn't see a minivan anywhere. *Maybe the receptionist sold me a fake ticket?* She was about to charge into the reception area and complain when she heard a succession of deafening short beeps followed by flashing lights and a loud skid as a clapped-out bright green minivan screeched to a halt inches from where she was standing.

The door slid open and the Tom Cruise lookalike from breakfast leant forward and beckoned her inside. 'Get in!'

Chapter Two

Cath climbed on board hoping the smiling, waving Mexican driver would return her to the hostel in one piece. She sat on a seat held together by more duct tape than material and looked at her fellow passengers. There were Tom and three other boys who looked so young she thought they should be accompanied by a responsible adult. One had acne that looked slightly better than it would have had he not had a healthy tan. Another was short but buff so the sleeves of his rugby shirt were stretched to their limits, while the third boy was tall but so thin he looked like he could snap in half at any minute.

Tom interrupted her thoughts. 'Sorry, I needed a cashpoint so we persuaded the driver to take us to one before picking you up. Claire told us there was another person on the tour.' At least Cath now knew the receptionist's name. 'Thought one should do that before picking you up. I'm Fitz.' He held out his hand.

She shook his hand. 'Cath, nice to meet you.'

Fitz then introduced his friends. 'Meet Edward,' *acne,* 'Harrington,' *rugby,* 'and Charles,' *stick thin.* Then he pointed to the driver. 'Meet Julio.'

With his right hand, Julio put his fingers and thumb together and placed them to his lips, kissing them as if he'd just eaten something delicious. '*Moi Linda.*'

'No, it's Cath.'

The boys erupted into laughter.

'What's so funny?'

Edward clarified. 'Linda means "pretty" in Spanish. Julio was paying you a compliment.'

Cath's cheeks blossomed pink. 'Oh, right.' She faced Julio but with eyes zoned in on the floor. 'Gracias.'

'De nada.' Julio flashed a mouth of yellow stained, uneven teeth. 'Vánamos!'

The four boys erupted in a lively cheer as if they were off to a rugby match. Cath stayed quiet but managed a smile. She was determined not to let the email from The Bliss Expert or feelings that she was gatecrashing an upper-class stag party plague her enjoyment.

An hour of kamikaze driving later, they arrived at The Basilica de Guadalupe. The Cathedral was not what Cath had expected. It looked more like a football stadium than St Paul's. There were hundreds of people buzzing around, which was more akin to rush hour at King's Cross station than a place of worship. She had not expected a service to be taking place either and, for the second time that day, she felt like she was intruding. The priest's voice boomed through Cath as the microphone amplified his voice above the low whirr of whispers. A faint musty smell made her feel queasy. Or maybe it was Julio's driving?

'Oh, I get it!' She nudged Fitz.

His nose remained in his guidebook. 'What do you get?'

'Why they built this building circular.' Cath considered her use of grammar, and couldn't be bothered to rephrase it, so continued. 'No matter where you stand, you can see that. There.' She pointed at a giant picture of a praying lady hanging over the altar.

Fitz looked up and followed Cath's finger. 'You mean the image of the Virgin of Guadalupe? The most visited Catholic pilgrimage site in the world?'

'Yes. Apparently, in 1531.' Cath said a silent thank you to her short-term memory. 'She appeared to a local and identified herself to him as the Mother of the True God. She instructed him to have a temple built on the site and left an image of herself imprinted miraculously on his tilma, which roughly translated is apron, to prove who she was.' She stared boreholes into his eyes to show that she had a brain too and smiled.

'I see one's read up.' He returned to his book. 'Says it's in a low-oxygen atmosphere and covered in bullet-proof glass.'

Not wanting to be outwitted, Cath spouted more knowledge. 'Many believe she can cure almost any illness. Rather than going to Alcoholics Anonymous, they vow to the Virgin they will never drink again and, most of the time, they fulfil their promise.'

They continued to walk towards the picture when Fitz stopped. 'By George!'

'No, really. It's true. I can read you know!'

Fitz rolled his eyes. 'No. Look!' he pointed ahead. 'Come on!' and charged towards a conveyer belt below the image of the Virgin of Guadalupe.

The pair stepped aboard the walkway, which took them and the stream of other tourists and pilgrims past the image as if they were on their way to their designated gate at Heathrow airport. They glided by the image, admiring the holy relic, and then caught the conveyor belt back again.

Cath felt confused. She didn't know if it was the clash of the modern world with ancient artifacts, or the mysterious emails from The Bliss Expert, or the conflicted feelings she had over Fitz, or the noise of hundreds of people clashing with religious serenity. Whichever it was, Cath needed to be on her own, so when Fitz wandered off in search of his friends, she stared fixedly at her book, pretending not to notice him disappear into the crowd. Now that she was alone, she could concentrate on what was really bothering her: it was the emails from The Bliss Expert. She wanted to know who he was, how he knew so much about her, what he wanted from her, why he said she was using Riley to feel better about herself, and judges harshly? *I don't judge people!*

As she didn't have answers to any of her questions, she felt irritation gripping her lower intestines and there were other uncomfortable feelings there too. Cath had assumed that travelling would give her a break from herself but it was the opposite; she felt even more insecure, sad and lonely because she was in an unfamiliar place surrounded by strangers who didn't care about her. Swallowing back the lump in her throat, Cath glanced at her watch and remonstrated with herself when she realised that she was ten minutes late for meeting Julio and the boys at the main entrance.

When she got there, they were already waiting for her and Fitz made sure she was aware of his annoyance by tapping his watch and shaking his head. *What? I'm only a few minutes late, what's the big deal?* 'Sorry, got lost.'

Julio raced them to the next site, the Teotihuacan Pyramids, as if he were Michael Schumacher. When they arrived, Julio held up four fingers before disappearing in

a flurry of dust. Cath registered that they should recon-
vene at the same place at four o'clock before turning her
attention to the swelling crowds funneling their way into
the Avenue of the Dead. It reminded her of the theme park
she'd visited years before in the summer holidays where
the sheer volume of people had sucked all the fun out of
the day. She hoped the same would not be true here.

The four boys bumped their way through the mob like
balls in a pinball machine, leaving Cath in their wake.
Usually she would have been upset at being abandoned
but on this occasion she was glad because she didn't want
to fight her way through the other tourists, and the locals
selling food and merchandise. When she finally made it
through, she stood at the foot of the Avenue and gasped
at the magnificence of the ancient site. The Avenue was as
wide as a motorway with both sides lined with perfectly
aligned pyramid structures. The atmosphere felt alive, as
if the ghosts from a once-vibrant city were still wandering around attending to their daily lives. She saw the boys
in the distance approaching the base of the Sun Pyramid
with youthful enthusiasm as if it were a minor hill to climb.
They scrambled up the pyramid easily, by the time Cath
got to the base, she was bracing herself for the pain she was
about to endure. There were two hundred and forty-three
intimidating steps in front of her.

By a quarter of the way up, Cath's legs were burning in
agony. Hauling herself up and over each giant step she recollected that it was the third largest pyramid in the world, and
wondered why she'd listened to the receptionist.

Cath reached the top and collapsed into a heap before
draining the dregs of water left in the bottle. It did nothing

to quench her raging thirst. Her cheeks were on fire, she felt sick and her t-shirt was drenched. Fitz came over while the other boys rugby tackled each other. 'You okay?'

'If I die, my parent's details are in the back of my *Lonely Planet*. Let them know will you?'

Fitz's face creased with laughter. She felt like she'd arrived at the summit of Everest – but in forty degree heat – and her body was about to give in to exhaustion. He handed her his bottle of water. 'Finish it, I've another.' She thanked him with a nod, finished it and sat quietly for a few minutes while Fitz rejoined his friends. When she'd cooled down, she stood up and gasped when she saw the magnificent view for the first time. It was breathtaking, and now she understood why this had been named one of the most impressive sites of the Aztec World. From up high, she saw symmetrical, vast stone structures lining the avenue on either side of a wide dusty road. She could not comprehend how an ancient civilisation could have built such enormous, perfectly proportioned constructions with the technology available to them at that time. *Have the historians got it wrong and the ancient civilisation were far more advanced than anyone gave them credit for?* Before Cath had time to develop the thought, in her peripheral vision she caught sight of Fitz sauntering towards her. 'Feeling better?

Cath couldn't peel herself away from the visual feast in front of her. 'Just about. Your water was a life-saver, thanks.' She turned to face him. 'Can you feel the energy too?'

'Of course, but don't tell the others.' He smiled and Cath was momentarily sidetracked by the full extent of his good looks: smouldering brown eyes, long, thick eyelashes, and full eyebrows. He even had a misshaped nose just like Tom Cruise's. She could have sworn his eyes twinkled when he smiled. 'They'll think it's piffle.'

Cath was disarmed. Just an hour ago, Fitz had been an arrogant twit, whereas now, he was being, well, nice. *Perhaps it's the heat? Perhaps he's feeling sorry for me?* Whatever the reason, he was far too film-star-handsome for her, so she dismissed the smutty thoughts that were charging through her mind. 'Legend has it that if you stand at the centre of the pyramid and make a wish, it'll come true.' Then, before she had time to stop herself, she touched him lightly on his arm. 'What wish will you make?'

He whipped his arm away as if he'd been stung by a bee. 'Crikey, I'd best go and join the others.' With that, he scurried off to be with his friends.

Cath hoped he hadn't read too much into her touching his arm; she hadn't intended to add to his over-inflated ego. Moving to the queue, she waited in line for the centre to become free, and when it was her turn, she stood quietly, closed her eyes and made her wish. 'I want to be happy.' Then she screwed her eyes even tighter, 'Perleeeeeeeease.' When she opened her eyes, she still felt sad and the boys were still frolicking about like posh juvenile delinquents. *Maybe tomorrow things will be different. Maybe The Bliss Expert is the answer to my prayers. Maybe pigs really can fly.*

Chapter Three

It was seven o'clock and Cath was on her own again after the aristocratic boys had gone out without inviting her. Hunger was now ripping out her insides; she'd only managed a mouthful of food at lunch before the spiciness of the food had stung her mouth. She needed to find an establishment where she could trust that the food wouldn't corrode her mouth. Her eyes lit up when she noticed in her guide book that there was a burger bar close by.

It only took her five minutes to walk from the hostel, and another three to have her dinner in her hands. She'd never felt so happy and relieved, all rolled into one. She tucked into her fish burger, and within seconds, the last morsels of fish and bun had disappeared. Cath was about to start on her fries when the two Italians walked through the entrance. Cath was glad she didn't have any food in her mouth or she might have choked.

'Hi. What you do today?' It was Matteo, the shorter of the two, who asked.

'I went to the cathedral and ruins outside of the city. How about you?'

'Walk in City. We go Oaxaca Tomorrow. You come?'

Cath was speechless while her stomach was flipping

pancakes. *How could The Bliss Expert have known they would ask me to join them?*

Cath nodded before she had a chance to consider her answer and they arranged to meet in the reception area at 4.45 a.m. the following morning. On the walk back to the hostel, Cath's mind was overflowing with questions: *Who was the mystery emailer? How did he know about the Italians and that they would ask me to go with them? Was he a stalker or a psychopath? Was he part of a sophisticated scam?* It occurred to Cath that The Bliss Expert and his emails were like a storyline from a scary film where the main character doesn't understand how much trouble she's in until it's too late. *Should I be ecstatic or scared?* She had no idea.

Chapter Four

Cath leapt out of bed to log on to the hostel's computer. Talk about slow. The ice in her cola lite had melted by the time she accessed her email account. There were ten new messages waiting for her. After deleting six spam messages, there were four remaining, from Riley, Rosie, her mum, and The Bliss Expert. As she was too nervous to open those from Riley and The Bliss Expert, she updated her blog first.

Brown on Tour

Day 3: Oaxaca

After my first instalment, I went with some 'spiffing' chaps on a day trip to just outside Mexico City. It was weird spending the day with complete strangers, getting to know them, and then never seeing them again. I guess I'm going to have to get used to that. I 'm now in a small place called Oaxaca. (By the way, why is everything so noisy in Mexico? I came away expecting time for some quiet reflection but all I can hear is loud traffic, loud talking, loud music, and loud rain. It's driving me mad!).

I'm travelling with a couple of lovely Italian guys who are helping me get by with my non-existent Spanish skills. We visited some temples and ruins at Monte Alban yesterday and we are heading to Puerto Escondido later, which I'm really looking forward to because it means I'll get some beach action.

Now onto what you know I love: Mexican food. Forget what you'd order in a Mexican restaurant in the UK, there isn't anything like that here. I've found tacos but they're unsalted and served with refried beans (no flavor or cheese). Then there are tamales, which can only be described as a steamed dumpling. No thank you. Everything else is smothered in mole, which is a thick dark brown sauce that tastes like bitter chocolate. Yuk! Every dish contains blow-your-head-off chillies so I'm living on burritos filled with refried beans, which have no yummy cheese, guacamole or sour cream as you'd get in the UK. Bland is the key word and I'm tiring of them already after having them twice yesterday!

Being British, it would be remiss of me not to mention the weather. I wish it would make up its mind! It's either burning hot sunshine or peeing it down with rain. I never know whether to wear my bikini or raincoat! Maybe I should just be done with it and wear both.

Next, she took a deep breath before opening the email from Riley.

I'm made up with your email and want to hear about your dream!

Got West Ham at the weekend, might head back to watch the game and visit the folks whilst I'm there.

Work's doing my head in. I want to tell my boss where to stick it. I'm his top earner - he'll regret being a dick to me when I hand in my notice.

Not much else going on - you only left a couple of days ago.

Hope you're having a good one. If not, I'll come out and sort you out myself. Saying that, I hope you are having an awful time!!!

PS. Miss you too

Cath had hoped his response would be positive but she hadn't expected him to hint at coming out to see her. With a beaming smile, Matteo walked past on the way to break-fast, so she waved good morning to him. Then she returned her attention to the computer and hit the reply button.

Poor you. I'm sorry you're having a miserable time at work (but I'm secretly pleased because it means you're missing me as much as I am you). I am having a terrible time so you'd better get over here to sort me out.

Then she opened Rosie's message.

Yes, you should definitely give travelling a bit more of a chance, i.e. longer than a day. Be safe and stop following random men into dark places. Miss you. Rx

And finally, her mum's email.

Glad to hear you got there safely. Keep in touch.

Cath braced herself before opening the email from The Bliss Expert.

I'm glad you listened to my last piece of advice. Here's some more:

- *Follow the guidance you'll get from Travels*

- *Don't eat the spaghetti*

- *Don't be tempted by a Riley lookalike*

What?! This can't be real. Who is he? What's he talking about? Travels? Spaghetti? Riley lookalike? It doesn't make any sense! Cath was shaking after she had finished reading the message. She wished she could talk to someone about the stranger emailing her but the Italians' English wasn't fluent enough and they might think she was strange. Instead, she hit the reply button and typed with defiance.

Thank you for your advice, but who are you??? What do you want? How do you know me? How did you know about the taxi driver, the Italians and Riley?!!!!

Feeling slightly better, she logged off and joined the Italians for breakfast.

Alessandro and Matteo beamed at Cath when they saw her coming. Alessandro was slightly taller and thinner than Matteo but the less attractive of the two. Not that either of them was particularly tall – or good-looking – but what they lacked in stature and looks, they made up for in personality. Despite a lack of English, they made Cath laugh with their facial expressions and constant bickering. They were like an old married couple and it was dawning on Cath that she was the source of their squabbling. It also struck her that both boys were wearing the same jeans and denim jackets they had worn since she'd met them at the airport. But at least they had on clean t-shirts, which demonstrated their senses of humour: Matteo's was dark blue with *Breakfast Included* written in white, while Alessandro's was red with *110% Italian Stud* written in white.

As Cath approached the table, Alessandro stood up, pulled a chair out for her and waited for her to sit down before sitting down himself. Feeling like a princess, Cath shunted herself forward in the chair. 'Alessandro, you're a gentleman, thank you.'

'Any-sing for you.' He picked up a pot of tea, tipped it forward and hovered it over her cup. 'You want?'

Cath knew he'd ordered the tea especially for her because both Italians drank only coffee. She smiled directly at Alessandro. '*Gracias*. You're very kind.'

Matteo turned to Alessandro and said something in Italian. Alessandro didn't look pleased and barked something back. With their passionate, sing-song dialogue, Cath could only tell when they were arguing by their facial expressions. Their faces said that neither of them was happy.

Alessandro turned to face Cath. 'Matteo want you know he get tea. Not me.'

This must have been the cause of their disagreement. She touched Matteo's hand. '*Muchas gracias*.' Matteo's grin was so wide, his face should have cracked.

Alessandro put the teapot down at the far end of the table so Matteo had to stretch over to reach it. Tutting, he picked it up and poured the brown liquid into Cath's cup as expertly as a waiter. 'You look 'appy'.'

Cath helped herself to milk. 'I've just received an email from my boyfriend. He might come out and see me.'

The teapot clattered on the table as Matteo set it down too forcefully. The two boys looked at each other, seemingly able to communicate telepathically. It was Matteo who broke the silence, almost spitting out the words. 'You never say you 'ave boyfriend.'

Cath swallowed the urge to giggle. It was like being in a soap opera with Ant and Dec. She assumed her announcement about her boyfriend had ruined their gallant play for her, which was a competition between the boys. She had better put them right otherwise they'd sulk all day.

'Strictly speaking, he's not my boyfriend. I only met him six weeks before I came away.'

Matteo said something in Italian to Alessandro and then the boys relaxed back in their chairs and grinned at each other. The play for Cath was back on.

Chapter Five

Brown on Tour

Day 6: Mazunte, Mexico

I'm starting to get the hang of Mexico: whatever the locals tell me, I don't believe them.

I decided to fly from Oaxaca to Puerto Escondido while the Italians took the scenic route by bus. When I booked my flight, the travel agent said that I had to book straight away because there was only one seat left on the plane. I booked it. She advised me to arrive at 6 a.m. as the flight left at 7 a.m. so I did what I was told. When I arrived, I was the only person in the entire airport apart from the cleaner! When the pilot arrived two hours later, I was the only passenger on the six-seater plane!!! Still, I was glad I'd flown because the Italians said their bus journey was 7 hours of stomach-twisting hell on treacherous mountain roads.

I'm sure Puerto Escondido would have been lovely but the weather was so atrocious (more rain) that we quickly moved onto Puerto Ángel. During one scorching day there I burnt my back on a boat trip where we saw dolphins and a turtle. The next day, we decided to go to a beautiful emerald beach called Buais de Huatulco. We were told by the taxi driver that the journey would cost 200 pesos but when we arrived, he asked for 400 peso. Grrrr! We hired kayaks but the weather turned from glorious sunshine to torrential rain in seconds so we hurried back to the hostel and tried to outrun the rain by moving to Mazunte, where we've just arrived.

Cath ran out of internet time so joined the Italians who were in the café next door, enjoying their third expresso of the morning in the sun. They jumped up as soon as they saw Cath, placed themselves either side of her, and linked arms with her while crossing the road to the beach. As Cath stepped onto the glistening golden sand, she felt the warm granules envelop her toes. The rustic hostel they'd chosen as their accommodation for the night had a hippie vibe that wasn't to Cath's taste but the exuberant owner, Eduardo, made them feel so welcome that she soaked up the chilled ambiance. She even smiled when he pointed to their beds for the night: a few hammocks swinging from a central wooden post, like spokes on a wheel, two metres from the turquoise sea's edge.

'Perfect! But what if it rains? Where will we sleep?' Cath pointed at the charcoal clouds bubbling up on the horizon, looking as ominous as a doberman about to attack.

Eduardo was short, thin and had dark eyes that radiated kindness. Laughter lines etched his tough olive skin like lines carved in wood and intensified when he smiled, which was often. He announced proudly in a booming voice and smile worthy of a winner on Oscar night, 'It never rain at night in Mazunte!'

Cath shrugged her shoulders; she knew better than to contradict a man in Central America. Machismo was very much alive and well in Mexico.

After some sunbathing and a few games of Rummy, it was dinner, so the trio joined a couple of other backpackers in the café, which was nothing more than a wooden shack and a few weathered tables and chairs. Cath positioned her chair so she could admire the sun as it set over the horizon, only to discover that the clouds had multiplied, so there was no sun in sight. Still, Eduardo reassured them again it never rained at night in Mazunte. The boys were hungry and seemed more intent on studying the limited menu than the weather while Cath asked if it were possible to have a burrito with refried beans, and chips.

Eduardo winked. 'Anything for you. Moi Linda.'

She was about to correct him that her name was, in fact, Cath when she remembered he was paying her a compliment. Her cheeks flushed red and she pretended to admire the waves now lashing forcibly at the water's edge. That was one thing about Mexico: the men certainly knew how to make a woman feel special. Even if they were thirty years her senior and missing most of their teeth. Alessandro rubbed Cath on the hand lightly to get her attention. 'What you sink of oméless?'

'The homeless? Ummm, it's really sad. Despite having a Welfare State in England, there are still many homeless people.' Alessandro looked confused so Cath tried a different tack. 'It's crazy that there are still homeless in Europe in the twenty-first century.'

He continued to look perplexed. 'Yes, but don't you think they're, how you say, stinky?'

'Some are, a little I guess. Why?'

Holding his nose and looking accusingly at Matteo, 'I sink they very, very stinky.'

Alessandro continued, 'I weesh people not 'ave them.'

Now Cath was completely lost. Just in the nick of time, Eduardo came over to take the boys' orders so the conversation came to a natural end. Alessandro asked for the burger while Matteo ordered a cheese omelette.

Alessandro gestured at Matteo wildly. 'Why you order that? You know I 'ate them. They very stinky!'

Cath erupted into raucous laughter as she understood the confusion. 'You,' looking at Alessandro, 'were talking about omelettes but I thought you were talking about the homeless. Priceless!' Matteo and Alessandro smiled politely while Cath continued to giggle when she felt the first drop of rain fall on her head. Then it was followed by another and another until the skies tore open for a torrent of water to fall down on Mazunte. At night. On them. Cath looked up and saw the roof was a patchwork of driftwood littered with various-sized holes. Cath didn't like to remind Eduardo of his earlier promise but she did want to know where they were going to sleep.

Julio gave his trademark toothless smile and pointed to the café floor. 'Here.' Cath was not impressed at having to spend the night on a dirty wooden floor and her face must have communicated as much.

Alessandro rubbed Cath's arm. 'No worry, Cath. We sleep 'side you. We keep you warm.'

'And safe,' added Matteo, as he stroked her other arm.

My Italian heroes. How will I cope without them when they leave?

Chapter Six

Brown on Tour
Day 21: Playa Zipolite, Mexico

It's Independence Day today! Last night, the receptionist at our hostel told us we had to go out to celebrate as there'd be a hive of activity of fireworks, parties, food, dance and music. So we went out full of excitement and expectation. Granted, there were flags, flowers and decorations lining the main street and one passer-by threw some confetti over us shouting, 'Viva Mexico' as a single carnival float drove past, firing off three fireworks. Disappointed, we went back to the hostel to ask the owner where the party was at, and he told us to go to a particular 'happening' bar which would be full and only open to the 'best people.' When we arrived, we were the only customers in the entire place! Still, it wasn't raining.

Tonight is my last night with my lovely Italians. We're going to see if we can have a slightly more exciting night tonight to celebrate and then I'm going to head off to San Cristobel while they go back to Mexico City to fly home. Boo hoo, I'm feeling heartbroken.

Cath logged off, disappointed that The Bliss Expert hadn't replied. She was about to go to the room to search for the Italians when she spied them sitting in the lounge area. It was no longer a surprise that they were waiting for her nearby, however, what was strange was that they were silent.

'You okay?' She looked at them both.

Alessandro answered. 'No, we sad. We no want to leave. You.'

Cath grasped Alessandro's hand and when she saw the disappointment on Matteo's face, she took his hand too and squeezed it tightly.

The three friends then adopted their usual way of walking together: Cath in the middle of the two boys with her arms linked through their arms. They wandered through the dark, deserted main street until they found the only restaurant open in town. If she'd thought last night was tranquil, tonight was a ghost town. The three friends sat down at a table in a corner, and ordered three beers.

When the waitress returned with three bottles of ice cold beer, Cath thought she would spice up the night and ordered three shots of tequila too. The restaurant was as empty as a dried up well. As Cath didn't want to embarrass herself in front of the Italians, she suggested getting something to eat.

Alessandro acted immediately by joining the outside edges of his hands together and flapping them like wings to indicate to the waitress that they wanted some menus. She shouted her answer from behind the bar, 'Solo menu del dia.'

Cath now knew what these four words meant. 'Looks like it's dish of the day or nothing then.'

'It okay for you? What if meat?' said Alessandro.

'Don't worry. I'm used to it now; Mexicans don't do vegetarian. I'll pick any meat out. I'm more concerned if it's too spicy!'

By the time their food was positioned in front of them, Cath was drunk and the boys' eyes were glazed. Cath looked at the plate of food. It was spaghetti with blood red sauce splattered over it like a scene in a horror movie. Cath remembered something The Bliss Expert had said about not eating spaghetti. But she didn't care; since he'd not replied to her questions, she had dismissed his emails as spam. Besides, she needed to eat. Dipping her tongue tentatively onto a strand of creamy soft string, she smiled when it didn't explode her taste buds. And it didn't seem to have any meat in it either. The food did what it was supposed to and soaked up some of the alcohol. The three friends laughed about their adventures together and how unlucky they had been with the weather.

Matteo took a gulp of his drink. 'September not good time visit Mexico.'

Cath agreed. 'Especially when you have to sleep in a wooden shack with more holes in it than a sieve. I got a total of...' she pretend-counted her fingers, 'zero hours sleep.' She paused before continuing. 'I feel sorry for you both. At least I've got time to find some sunshine. You,' she pointed haphazardly at the boys, 'have to go home.'

The mention of the word *home* forced Cath to feel miserable again as she knew she would never see the two Italians again.

An hour later, Cath felt odd. Her stomach ballooned as if she were six month's pregnant and then a sharp pain stabbed her from within, followed by an urgency to go to the bathroom.

On her return to the table after an explosive experience in the toilet, Matteo pulled an exaggeratedly sad face. 'You look... how you say? White?'

'But *steel* beautiful,' added Alessandro.

'Thank you! Shall we get...' But she couldn't finish her sentence. More pain stabbed repeatedly deep inside her stomach and she had to run to the bathroom again.

When she re-emerged, she looked a shell of her former self, as if all life had been sucked from her. 'Sorry boys, going back to room. Feel awful.'

'Let us 'elp you.'

'No. Stay. Enjoy. Drink more.' She wasn't sure at what point she had started to speak English like the Italians, and dashed off before they could join her. She wanted to be on her own so there wouldn't be any ears listening to the squelching noises or noses to smell the nuclear waste being expelled from her nether regions like sulphur spurting from a pipe.

Cath darted back to the hostel convinced she wouldn't make it back in time but she did. *How can I be feeling this bad, and this quickly? It must have been from lunch or the boys would be sick too.* Before she could finish her thought, the boys stumbled into the room looking as pale as she was.

'Oh no, not you too?'

Matteo nodded. 'Feel bad.'

With that, Alessandro almost knocked him over in a race to reach the bathroom first. *Oh no!* Cath had left a terrible smell in there and had used up most of the toilet roll. When Alessandro eventually came out, he didn't say a word but crawled into bed instead. *Perhaps he was too ill to notice.* She hoped that was the case.

'*Eet* spaghetti,' Alessandro whimpered from beneath the covers. As if in agreement, Cath's stomach sent out urgent messages to her brain that she needed the bathroom, but Matteo beat her to it. In desperation, she ran into the corridor and found a communal toilet. She made it just in time. While she was sitting there, she spotted several toilet rolls piled neatly on a cobwebbed shelf above the door. After the pain in her stomach subsided, Cath hobbled back to the room and awarded the boys two toilet rolls each. They accepted them like Christmas presents, managed feeble smiles, pulled the sheet up over their fully-clothed bodies and bunkered down for the night.

After a very long night, Cath pitied the poor cleaners and the next guests. Matteo and Alessandro still looked drained, lifeless and pitiful but, like Cath, they too had to make their onward journey. She shared out her diarrhea relief tablets like sweets while the boys packed in slow motion and silence.

The time had come. Cath hugged each boy in turn and gulped back the tears as she watched them climb on board their bus. She slumped down on a bench and waited for her bus feeling empty and numb. It was as if her insides had been hollowed out, taking all her emotion with it. The thirty minute wait seemed endless, but when it arrived, she managed to secure a vacant seat with no-one next to it, rolled up her fleece, buried it behind her neck, rested her head on the glass window, and closed her eyes. She fought back the urge to cry every time she thought about never seeing the two Italian boys again. As she drifted in and out of sleep, fear started to overtake the sadness. She didn't know if it was because she was going to be alone in an unfamiliar town in a foreign country thousands of miles from home. Again. Or because The Bliss Expert's prophecy had come true. *How had he known to warn me about the spaghetti? Was it a lucky guess or is there really a stranger out there who is able to predict my future?* A shiver coursed up and down Cath's spine as her incredulity at the mysterious emailer gathered pace. While she was now intrigued to know what he meant about the *Travels* and *Riley lookalike* comments, she was also petrified.

Chapter Seven

Two days later Cath awoke with a throbbing headache, this time due to a hangover and not food poisoning. Staggering to a café next door to the hostel where she was currently calling home, she opted for toast saturated with butter and lashings of strawberry jam, with sweet tea on the side. It made her feel marginally better. Even though San Cristóbal was colder than anything she'd experienced so far, she was glad she'd come because she'd met a nice group of people at the bar last night, who were partly the reason for her feeling so tired and hungover. As she ambled back to the hostel, she didn't want to be inside on such a beautiful day so she scanned the hostel's overgrown garden, found an upside-down bucket and sat on it, hoping the plastic wouldn't collapse under her weight. There wasn't a cloud in the sky, the sun was shining and radiating a hint of warmth. If it hadn't been for the underlying coolness, it could have been a summer's day. Debs, a girl she'd met the night before from Chelmsford, approached her. 'Alwight, babe?'

'Not really. I'm hung over.'

Debs looked distracted as she searched for something to sit on. She found another bucket and sat down too close for Cath's comfort. Debs didn't seem to understand the concept of personal space. She also needed to learn that less is more when it comes to make-up. A brassy-orange film covered the majority of her face until it reached her jaw-line and then, abruptly, stopped. Her eyelashes were thick with lumps of mascara and her cerise lips shouted 'Look at me!' and would have been more at home on a blow-up doll.

Cath moved on from Debs's face. She would need to find a hairdresser soon to attend to her inch-long black roots that were merging crudely into peroxided blonde hair. Oversized hoop earrings sparkled in the sun when it caught them at the right angle, while black leggings clung to her stick-thin body as snugly as her skin-tight vest top. The look was finished with gold-coloured flip flops.

Despite her harsh appraisal of Debs, Cath felt jealous. She did a quick self-assessment: no make-up, over-sized baseball cap covering lank, greasy hair, long beige waterproof trousers that strained at the seams around her bottom, hiking boots covered in dried mud, and a baggy t-shirt.

'How are *you* feeling?'

'Crap, babe. Last night, we were right on it, weren't we?'

'I know what you mean.' Cath sounded as posh as the Queen compared to Debs. A giggle tried to escape but she contained it before it reached her lips. 'What are you doing today?'

'Going to a local village, innit. Chamula or summat. What's that party fing called in Mexico?'

'A fiesta?'

'Yeah, right. You're dead cleva, ain't ya? Wanna come, babe? Debs wriggled her boney bottom on the upside-down bucket to get comfortable.

Assuming she'd just been invited to go to the fiesta, Cath nodded.

About five people from the hostel joined them and, together, they caught a minibus which dropped them at the main square. Considering it was only midday, the party was in full swing. 'Livelier than the Independence Day celebrations I experienced a couple of days ago.'

Debs looked at her quizzically. 'Eh?'

Cath smiled as she wondered what Alessandro and Matteo were doing. 'Don't worry, just reminiscing.'

'Remi what?'

Before Cath could reply, a horde of children headed their way holding their palms up, shouting, '*Un peso, un peso!*'

Before the girls could respond, there was an almighty bang as a firework exploded in the air a few inches from where they were standing. Involuntarily, Cath and Debs crouched down and covered their ears while the children giggled.

Debs shouted, 'What the 'ell waz that?!'

'I guess that's the Mexicans celebrating! At least it distracted the kids from asking us for money!'

Cath regained her composure and stood up, waving the children off as kindly yet firmly as possible. She looked around and drank in the buzzing atmosphere. People were everywhere, from babies to octogenarians - dancing, swaying, chatting, laughing and cavorting around on horses. Then Cath noticed bodies lying on the ground, scattered in-between groups, in corners and underneath trees. It wasn't until one of the guys from the hostel handed Cath a cup of clear liquid that she understood. The fumes were enough to disintegrate her eyebrows.

'Wow. What is this?'

The guy – she didn't know his name – grinned. 'Posh. It's the local brew. Try it.'

Cath shook her head as she listened to her headache and tasted stale alcohol on her tongue. 'I think I'll have some food first. Thanks.'

The guy looked like he was going to say something else but shrugged his shoulders and turned round to talk to his friend.

Cath bought a bowl of soup, hoping that the lady was telling her the truth that it was vegetarian, but halfway through she spotted something black and hard. 'What's that?' Cath tilted her bowl to one side so Debs could see what she was pointing to. Debs prodded it with her spoon and flipped it over.

'Cockcoach, innit,' as if Debs was speaking about an everyday occurrence.

'Yuck!' Cath flicked it out of the bowl on the dusty ground, narrowly missing a local snoring loudly on the floor. Even though she didn't intend touching another morsel of cockroach soup, Cath stirred the remnants to see what other delights she might find. 'I don't believe it!'

'What, babe?'

'There's a chicken bone!'

'Shhhh. Don't shout or they'll…' she indicated the passed out locals on the ground, 'all want one.'

Ignoring her friend's sarcasm, Cath continued to complain. 'But I asked if the soup was without meat. In my best Spanish. Three times.'

Debs rolled her eyes and alternated between slurping her soup and sipping her Posh.

Cath threw away the rest of the soup and devoured a burrito she'd bought from a more reliable seller. Hunger satisfied and hangover cured, she noticed that every-one, including Debs, was inebriated. Feeling left out, she decided she would join them so she bought a cup of Posh and found that, if she held her nose while chucking it down her throat, she could tolerate it. It wasn't long before Cath was suitably drunk too. She turned to Debs, 'Why you travelling, Debs?'

Debs' legs wobbled slightly before she answered. 'Found out me man had been banging me mate. Told him where to stick it but I went back to 'im. He did it again. Proper mug, weren't I? Best fing was to get away. And 'ere I am! What 'bout you?'

'I wanted to find out who I am. I haven't been happy for a long time. And I do too much of this,' she pointed at her Posh.

'Na way! Yous proper confident, babe. And gorgeous. Don't you see all the men are after you?' She pointed in the direction of the guy who had offered Cath some Posh when she'd first arrived.

What's she talking about? He was just being nice. The men are staring at her, not me! 'Thanks, but my confidence is just a front. I need to do some internal excavation work but it scares me. I'm afraid of what might be lurking underneath. A bit like in my so-called vegetable soup earlier!'

'Not sure what yous talkin' about but, cheers to that!' Debs threw up her cup and held it midair.

Droplets of liquid flew everywhere as Cath clinked her cup with Debs's. Behind blurry eyes, Cath knew there would come a time when she needed to stop partying and start digging. *But not yet.*

Chapter Eight

Cath's head felt like someone had let off fireworks and was having a New Year's Eve party in there. She fumbled around in her bag for painkillers but the packet was empty. Before there was enough time to find Debs to ask her if she had anything to ease the throbbing, Cath felt woozy and her body trembled, while a rising queasiness built up from her gut. *Oh no, I'm gonna puke.* She dashed to the sink and threw up, which helped her to feel mildly human again. As she lurched back to her bed, she noticed the girl from the bed next to her watching her as she was fumbling in her bag for something. *How embarrassing, I didn't know anyone was there.* But the girl seemed concerned rather than judgemental as she found what she was looking for and handed Cath an unopened packet of tablets. 'Here, looks like you need these.'

Cath detected a slight Eastern European accent as her cheeks burnt cerise from realising the girl had seen her throw up. 'Er, thanks. Sorry about that,' said Cath, indicating the sink and wiping her mouth clean with the back of her hand.

'No problem. I was party girl once.'

Cath wished she could speak a foreign language as well as this striking girl did. She also wished she was as naturally beautiful as she was to be able to look as amazing as she did with such a severe haircut, which consisted of a curly mass of pink locks flopping over a closely shaved area above both ears. 'Russian?'

She tightened the straps on her backpack and heaved it onto her back. 'Polish. But I live in UK many years now. I must get bus to Cancun but I finish this,' holding up a book with her free hand, 'so I leave here if you want to read it.' She placed it on her unmade bed.

Cath thanked the girl, said goodbye and wished her a safe journey, not taking any notice of the book she'd left behind. It was a matter of minutes before she was asleep again.

After coming to and downing a litre bottle of water, Cath felt mildly human again. She was about to take a shower when she remembered the book the beautiful Polish girl had left so she grabbed it and almost dropped it like it was red-hot metal. No way! It was *Travels* by Michael Crichton. Spine-tingling goosebumps raced up Cath's back. That's what The Bliss Expert had meant by following the guidance I'd get from Travels. But had The Bliss Expert paid the Polish girl to give Cath the book? It seemed a bit far-fetched to believe this but the alternative – that a random girl had left her the exact book that The Bliss Expert had prophecised – was crazy. Cath thought that either he had to be part of an international ring of scammers who were following her every move or he could predict the future. The former seemed too ludicrous to be true but so did the latter. If it was the latter, she wondered whether he was trying to help or harm her? Whatever the truth, there was no way she could not read the book so she got back into bed and turned to the first page.

After a long day of reading, Cath had finished the book and she knew what The Bliss Expert was hinting at: find a retreat, somewhere that would take her away from external temptations so she could focus on herself and reflect upon why everyone abandoned her, why she felt so lonely, why she attracted men who rejected her, and why she felt so much negative emotion inside. While she knew this was sensible advice, she couldn't stop wondering who The Bliss Expert was, how he knew so much about her, and what he wanted.

Chapter Nine

Feeling refreshed after a night off the booze, Cath had a nagging sense that she had to follow the advice from *Travels*. She headed to an internet café where she accessed her *Hotmail* account after just twenty minutes. She searched for *Retreat Central America*, and found one result: *Los Cuadrados*, a retreat in Guatemala. After clicking onto the website and reading about the month-long course that ran every four weeks, goosebumps charged up and down her spine like stampeding buffalo. She sent the retreat a message asking when there was availability on the course in the next couple of months. Then it was time to update her blog.

Brown on Tour

Day 26: Chiapas, Mexico

I'm in the Central Highlands region of Mexico, which is cold, but I'm enjoying travelling with an Essex girl called Debs. I've been to local villages and fiestas, riding horses and checking out local markets. We then went to Palenque, where I saw even more ruins and stayed in a basic resort in the middle of the jungle. I tried some interesting yoga classes where we had to spend 15 minutes shaking, then 15 minutes dancing, then 15 minutes bouncing, and

*then 15 minutes shouting, and then 15 minutes clapping.
It was beyond weird but I enjoyed the 15 minutes of meditating (i.e. sleeping) at the end.*

*Later on today, Debs and I are planning to head to Isla
Mujeres, which is an island in the Caribbean Sea.*

Then Cath turned her attention to her inbox. When she
saw Riley's name, she couldn't resist clicking onto it immediately.

Haven't heard from you in a while, you okay?

*Bad week for the Reds. Lost to the Hammers at home
(last time that happened was 1964!), then the Mancs beat
us, and rounded off with the mighty Bordeaux, where we
grabbed a late draw. Not looking forward to the Norwich
game at the weekend either. At least me Ma's roast dinner
should sort me out!*

*Good news, though, I've finished my dissertation! As
soon as I know I've passed, I'll be looking for a new job
- which means I should be able to visit you. Let me know
when would be a good time.*

Cath hit the reply button as over-the-moon as if he'd
asked her to marry him.

*I'm really glad to hear that you've finished your disserta-
tion. When will you get your results? The sooner you hear,
the sooner you can tell John you're leaving. I bet he'll be
gutted to lose his best biller!*

*I really want to see you so anytime is good for me! But
make it soon.*

There were a few messages from other friends but
still nothing from The Bliss Expert. She even reread his

previous messages to check that she wasn't going insane but there they were in black and white, predicting her life. Part of her was scared to receive another email, but another part was irritated that he hadn't written to her again. *Perhaps the third prophecy about the Riley lookalike tempting me needs to come true before he'll get in touch again?* Cath shivered.

Chapter Ten

Brown on Tour
Isla Mujeres: Day 31

Wowee! I've finally found heaven. Isla Mujeres (Island of Women) is amazing, as is the weather, finally. It's the epitome of beach paradise; white fluffy sand and turquoise sea. I'm still with Debs and we've been sunbathing, swimming, snorkelling and cycling loads. I'm bronzed and feel wonderful. The only downside was seeing a caged tiger in the middle of the island yesterday, which I think had gone mad. He kept pacing up and down with a glazed look in his eyes. Poor thing. I can't stop thinking about him and his desperate situation. I was ready to rip open the bars to set him free. Then I decided that he might be hungry and I would be the first thing on his radar, so didn't.

When I'm not out enjoying the sun, I'm playing pool, dancing, and drinking until the early hours with a fun group of like-minded travellers. Sun, Sea and lovely people. Happy days!

Cath logged off and headed to the pool bar to meet Debs who was already on her fifth beer. 'Get a drink, yous got some catching up to do!'

After downing a couple of tequila shots at the bar and grabbing a beer, Cath racked up another game of pool, sipped her drink and absorbed the jubilant vibes generated by the hive of activity in the bar. She turned towards the open window and smiled as she felt the sun's warmth on her face. As she turned to take her first shot, Cath stopped in her tracks as she saw a tall guy with a chiseled jaw and shaved head walk through the door. Tingling exploded up her spine as The Bliss Expert's third prediction came true. A bronzed version of Riley was standing in front of her. A gasp escaped out of her mouth before she could stop it.

'Watch 'im,' Debs warned as she used her elbow to push Cath playfully out of the way so that she could break instead.

Cath wanted to know why she needed to watch him but she was too shocked to speak. Not only had The Bliss Expert known she'd meet a Riley lookalike but he was right to warn her against him; she was hugely attracted to him. She didn't think it possible but she would even go as far as to say that he was better-looking than Riley. *Or have shots of tequila at lunchtime given me beer goggles?*

'His name's Jack. Met 'im in Mexico City.' When she didn't get a response, Debs waved her hand in front of Cath's face. 'Erf to Cath!'

Cath blinked to stop herself from staring. 'He's gorgeous.' She didn't want to explain to Debs that, in addition to finding Jack incredibly tempting, she was freaking out that a mysterious stranger's third prediction had come true.

Debs wagged her finger and shook her head. 'Babe, you wanna stay clear of 'im.'

Yeah, I know I should, The Bliss Expert told me to. But what could be so dangerous about him? As she thought this, she knew she was in trouble: telling Cath she couldn't have a particular man was like a magnet being told it shouldn't attract metal. 'Why?'

Debs looked pleased as she potted one of her own balls for a change, then lined up her next shot, aimed and missed. 'Awmygawd.' Then turned to face Cath. 'On my life, he's a player. Keep away. He's bad like my ex.'

Cath took a lingering glance at Jack before refocusing on the pool table. She saw an easy shot and was about to take it when Debs interrupted. 'Aven't you got a bloke back 'ome?'

Cath potted the black by accident and lost the game. 'Oi, you did that deliberately!' She threw her cue on the table in recognition of her defeat. 'Not really, we were only together a few weeks. Anyway, I've been good so far. Besides, I'm only admiring the view.'

At that moment, Jack came over with a tray full of shot glasses containing a yellowish liquid. He placed them on the pool table and greeted Debs with a peck on the cheek. He turned to Cath and introduced himself before handing out the shot glasses. After downing three shots in quick succession, Cath felt a surge of confidence soar through her body while in the back of her head The Bliss Expert's warning was setting off earsplitting alarm bells but the alcohol was dampening them to a minor tinkle in the far distance.

Jack removed the tray from the pool table. 'Fancy a game?' He directed his question to Cath as if Debs didn't exist.

Cath looked at Debs to check she didn't mind. She shook her head. 'Sure, why not? But you can rack them up.'

While Jack was doing as he was told, Debs approached Cath and whispered in her ear, 'What you doing, babe?'

Cath glanced at her like she was a fly that needed swatting away. 'You sound just like Rosie. I'm having fun. Try it sometime.' She turned away and sauntered towards the pool table to gracefully pose for her shot. She stood with her back straight and bottom wiggling provocatively. She missed. Jack grabbed the cue from her and stroked his free hand up and down Cath's back. She momentarily flinched at his touch but, after too much alcohol, she felt like the sexiest girl in the world. 'Are you always this forward with girls you've just met?'

'Only ones I like.' He patted her bottom like it was a drum.

She grabbed his arm playfully, removing it from her behind. 'So tell me, what do you like about me?'

He twisted her around so their faces were inches from each other. The electricity between them was palpable. Then, as quickly as he had pulled her towards him, he pushed her away playfully. 'It's not my job to big you up.'

If it hadn't been for the pool table being in the way, Cath would have lost her balance. She steadied herself and approached Jack, caressing her hand up the side of his leg. 'Oh, come on. Tell me.'

Why has my eight year old whining-self just emerged?

His killer half-smile came out to play and, with it, a twinkle in his eye. 'Pretty face, great curves and confident. Just how I like 'em.'

Did he really just say that?! Cath positioned herself for her next shot. 'Tell me about yourself, Jack.'

He took a swig of his beer. 'What is this? Twenty questions?'

She potted one of his balls and nodded. 'Your turn. But you have to tell me about yourself before I hand over the cue.'

'Okay, okay. I'm twenty-five, a broker, and from Hackney.' He grabbed the cue from Cath and took his shot.

It registered somewhere in Cath's consciousness that he hadn't asked her any questions about herself.

As the clock struck eight, the horizon dragged the sun into its vast void. Cath and Jack staggered to the next bar, *Brit's Abroad*. Cath was sober enough to order a large bowl of chips in an attempt to soak up some of the alcohol but Jack had other ideas and bought another round of tequila shots. Cath couldn't remember when she'd lost Debs. *Oh well, she's a big girl and can look after herself.*

Cath and Jack stood at the bar facing each other with only an inch between them. For the first time, she noticed a small metal object in his mouth. 'What's that?'

'Tongue-piercing.' He stuck his tongue out and waggled it at her, the silver ball so obvious now she knew it was there.

'Does it hurt?'

'You should only feel ecstasy when I use it to make you come.'

She was half repulsed by his vulgarity and half turned on, wondering what additional pleasure he could give her with a tongue-piercing. Jack stroked the small of Cath's back and nuzzled his nose on hers while tantalising her with a brush of his lips. 'Wanna go back to mine to find out?'

Cath nodded as Jack grabbed her hand and led her to his room, which was in the building next door to the bar. Cath had only just registered that there were two unmade beds on opposite sides of the room before Jack pushed her onto one while falling on top of her purposefully. He stroked her hair away from her face, staring into her eyes with apparent tenderness. Cath couldn't tell if this was just lust but she didn't care. She wanted him to kiss her. He leant forward, but this time she turned her head to one side. He laughed, 'Well, if you don't want to.'

Irritated that her tactics hadn't worked, she grabbed his face with both hands and plunged her tongue into his mouth. A thrill charged around her body as the hard metal ball brushed across her tongue and ignited every nerve-ending like Oxford Street's lights at Christmas. She wanted him inside her *now*. Jack's free hand disappeared under her top and he pulled her bra up and over her breasts. She moaned as his fingers expertly squeezed and pinched gently, causing her to spread her legs involuntarily. Grinning, Jack rolled onto the bed propping himself up with one arm and replacing his fingers with his tongue. The mixture of smooth softness with solid metal striking her erect nipples sent her to another stratosphere. Cath felt herself getting moist down below as the warm sucking sensation and gentle jabbing worked its magic. She couldn't hold back any longer and fumbled around his waist to find an entrance to the place where she could pleasure him.

Just as she had found a button, she heard the sound of a key unlocking the bedroom door. Cath saw a white light prancing in the dark with the silhouette of a person standing behind it. The torch was replaced by the brightness of the main light to reveal a tall, thin guy standing in the doorway. Jack didn't seem alarmed so Cath assumed it was his roommate. The guy ignored them as if they weren't there, switched the light off, stripped and climbed into his bed.

Jack whispered, 'Let's go to yours.'

Outside, the fresh air sobered Cath up. It was at this point she realised how drunk Jack was. While he managed to maintain a steady stride, his glazed eyes gave away his inebriated state. When they reached the hostel where she was sharing a room with Debs, Cath finally listened to The Bliss Expert's warnings. 'Thanks for walking me home, Jack.' She kissed him on the cheek and turned towards the door.

Jack didn't release her from his grip and pulled her towards him forcibly. 'Hey, aren't I coming in with you?'

For the first time that night, Cath felt in control and it felt good. 'Sorry, Debs is in there, asleep. Goodnight, Jack.' She pressed him away, shut the door and fell into bed fully clothed. The empowered feelings soon dissolved as the extent of her betrayal hit her. *I'm sorry, Riley, I truly am.* With that, she passed out.

Chapter Eleven

Eyes half open, Cath peeled herself off her pillow and fumbled on the floor for a bottle of water. She found one and gulped down the entire contents.

From the other side of the room she heard Deb's voice, who had stopped mid-way while cleaning her teeth. 'What 'appened to you last night?' Toothpaste dribbled down her chin.

It took a few moments for the previous night's events to play out in her mind. 'I went off with Jack.'

Debs spat white residue into the sink. 'I know that, babe. What I mean is, what 'appened to *you*? You was proper 'orrible to me, like. Not seen ya like that before.'

It was as if a sledgehammer had been slammed into the side of Cath's head. Not only was she hungover and feeling guilty about cheating on Riley, now Debs was making her feel bad. It was like living with Rosie all over again. 'Sorry,' was all she could manage. 'Got any more water?'

Debs handed her a bottle. After glugging it in one go, Cath felt more awake and noticed Debs' face was clean of any make-up. It suddenly struck her how stunning she was. 'You're beautiful. You don't need to wear make-up. Why do you?'

Debs buried her face into a towel and shook her head several times before answering. 'Don't take the mick, babe. It's not kind.'

'I'm not! I'm serious. You're gorgeous. Let me see again.'

Debs turned her back on Cath and walked to the mirror and started applying foundation. 'I need it.'

'Why?'

'Makes me feel confident. Let's leave it, yeah?' Why were you so 'orrible last night?'

Now it was Cath's turn to be embarrassed. She flopped back onto the mattress. 'My best friend says I change when I've had a drink and there's a good-looking man around. She says I become super confident and, sometimes, super aggressive. That Cath hasn't appeared since I left England. Well, until last night. I'm sorry.'

Debs moved onto applying mascara. 'You left me, babe. In a bar full of leering men. I had to get home on me own. I was scared.'

Cath placed her hands over her face. 'I'm so sorry, Debs. If I could change things I would.' Cath noticed Debs had finished with the mirror and was stuffing clothes into her backpack. 'What you doing?'

'Gettin' the ten o'clock bus to Belize, babe.'

'What?' There was another blast from the sledgehammer. 'When did you decide this?' Cath sat up.

'Last night. Way I deal wiv fings, innit.'

Cath was numb. She lay on her bed, depressed. She was on her own again. *Maybe that's what The Bliss Expert was warning me about? Falling for a Riley lookalike meant I'd lose Debs?* While Debs hadn't been the brightest button in the box, she had been great fun and was an easy travelling companion.

And Cath had cast her aside like an old shoe as soon as a good-looking bloke arrived on the scene. Not wanting to think about what a horrible person she was any more, she put on her headphones and pressed the play button on her iPod. *Set Fire to the Rain* by Adele exploded into her ears.

By the time Cath got up, it was lunchtime. She went to Bananas where she and Debs had gone every day since they had arrived in Isla Mujeres. Another pang of hurt struck as she realised how much she missed Debs and that she'd still be with her now if Cath had listened to The Bliss Expert and not been so selfish and stupid.

As she tucked into her burrito and cola lite, Jack strolled in. Her cheeks flushed crimson. He headed towards her and loitered by her table as if he was unsure whether to stay or not.

Cath stopped eating. 'How you feeling?'

He placed his book on the table but didn't move. 'Crap.'

A few seconds of quiet agony followed. The previous night, the conversation had flowed as easily as the beer, yet now they were like two strangers on a train.

'You can sit down.' She gestured to the empty wooden chair opposite. Jack hesitated and surveyed the rest of the café before committing himself to the chair.

To break the silence, Cath resorted to asking questions.

Cath: 'How long are you travelling for?'

Jack: 'Not long enough.'

Cath: 'How long have you been away so far?'

Jack: 'Two months.'

Cath: 'Where have you been so far?'

Jack: 'A few places.'

Cath: 'Like where?'

Jack: 'Mexico.'

Cath: 'What have you enjoyed the most?'

Jack: 'Meeting lots of different girls.'

Cath: 'When do you go home?'

Jack: 'When I feel like it.'

Are you an arrogant, rude, lacking-in-personality and woman-ising twat?

Cath: 'Do you have any brothers or sisters?'

Jack: 'No.'

Cath ran out of things to ask. Jack was fidgeting with his book as though he wanted to read it and she knew she'd made a big mistake in getting together with him. Not only was he arrogant, she had lost Debs.

Jack shifted forward with his hands on the table. 'Need a drink.' He got up and headed to the bar.

Cath watched him walk away with her mouth agape. The Bliss Expert had been right to caution her about Jack. If only she'd heeded his warning.

Rosie's voice in her head told her to let him walk away and get the next available bus to Belize and grovel to Debs. But there was something inside her that needed to understand how someone could be so cold after what they had done together last night, so she followed him to the bar.

Six beers and three tequila shots later, Cath and Jack were back to normal, or as normal as things could be after knowing each other for just twenty-four hours.

In the crowded bar, Jack drew Cath close to him until there was barely a breath of air between them. 'You're so pretty...'

She grimaced at his cheesy come-on. 'Is that the only chat-up line you've got?'

He chuckled. 'Oooh, I love a feisty woman.'

'You ain't seen nothing yet!' She grabbed one of his buttock cheeks, impressed with its firmness.

Jack put his hands on either side of her waist. 'You've got amazing eyes. That's the first thing I noticed about you. And your curves.'

Cath grew red. 'It took a lot of hard work and money to get my body into this shape.'

Jack laughed. They continued with their banter until Jack looked at his watch. 'Can we go back to mine? If we go now, we shouldn't be interrupted by my roommate this time.'

'Nothing like a bit of foreplay, eh Jack?'

He held his hands up in defence. 'Aaron will be out until late so we've got a good couple of hours to have some fun.'

Unbelievable. He has it all worked out. 'I'd like to, Jack, but I can't. Not yet.'

'Why not? It's not like I'm asking for a long-term commitment, I just wanna have sex.' Then, as an afterthought, 'With you.'

Cath folded her arms and shook her head. 'You certainly know how to make a girl feel special!'

He slammed his bottle of beer onto the bar, a little too violently. 'When did Mrs. Bore come out to play?'

'Forget it. How could an egotistical twat like you understand?'

He stormed off.

Cath chased after him. 'Jack! I'm sorry. I want to have sex with you but I'm scared you won't want me once we've done it.'

He wrapped his arms around her and kissed her forehead. 'Don't be so stupid. Of course I will.'

They went to his room, where Jack led Cath to his bed, sat on the edge and manoeuvred her onto him so she was straddling him. As they kissed, Cath writhed up and down, knowing that her rhythmic hip movements were causing a stirring inside his shorts. Jack grabbed Cath's bottom firmly with both hands and used them to force her to move harder and faster. Then, he used his upper body strength to heave Cath off him and onto the bed where he yanked her knickers down from underneath her tent-like skirt. He spread her legs wide open and waggled his tongue at her before plunging it deep between her legs with a combination of licking, sucking and flicking. The hard metal on soft flesh was almost too much and Cath thought she could never enjoy a non-pierced tongue going down on her again. He then introduced his fingers, sinking them into the moist hollow, which tipped her over the edge. In seconds pleasure erupted from her sweet spot and spread throughout her body, making her lose all sense of time and space. She shuddered when the waves of ecstasy stopped. 'That was… amazing, Jack.'

'I know, all the girls love it.'

How many girls have you done that to, exactly? But before she could ask, he'd taken off his shorts, dressed himself in a condom, and was ready to dive in. She was so wet from her orgasm that he slipped in easily, groaning. He drove himself in and out, fast and hard, concentrating fully on his own gratification until, seconds later, a loud grunt exploded from his mouth. Then he withdrew and flopped onto the bed next to Cath, pulling a sheet over his lower half. *He's definitely better with his tongue.* But Cath decided she should give him the benefit of the doubt; maybe he'd been so quick because it was their first time. She hoped so.

Chapter Twelve

Cath grinned to herself as she smelt Jack's aroma on her from their early morning antics, which had been getting better and better each time. She giggled thinking about the three-times-a-day habit they had developed over the past week of sharing a room together.

'Hi stud,' she said as Jack swaggered into their room from the shower. He stood before Cath with a murky grey coloured towel around his waist, which she assumed had been white once upon a time. As she used her finger to mark where she'd got up to in her latest book – Bill Bryson's *Notes from a Small Island* – she asked what he fancied doing after another round of rampant fun.

'I've hired a motorbike. I'm exploring the island today.'

Cath closed her book, making a mental note that she'd got to page fifty-eight. 'You didn't ask me if it was okay to go!'

He dried himself off and threw the wet towel onto the bed, for which she had reprimanded him every single morning since they'd started sharing a room. 'That's because I don't need your permission. This is my trip and I'll do what I want. It's not as if you're my girlfriend.'

They had been acting like a couple so she didn't understand his frostiness. She sulked for a few seconds before asking if she could go with him.

Jack pulled a crumpled t-shirt from his backpack. 'I've been meaning to talk to you. You're too needy. I'm travelling. I don't need relationship crap while I'm away. I get enough of that at home! Best if we call it a day.' He continued ferreting in his bag looking for something as if they were discussing the weather.

Cath felt like someone had punched her in the stomach, broken through the skin and wrenched out all her innards. 'But you said you wouldn't hurt me.'

'Yeah well, I wanted to get you into bed, didn't I? It's what blokes do.'

'Oh,' was all that escaped her mouth.

Jack shrugged his shoulders, put on some shorts and left. 'See you when I get back. Not sure when that'll be.'

As he slammed the door, anger rose from the pit of her stomach. She was mad. No, furious. This hurt seemed to cut deeper than what she'd felt when all her other boyfriends had rejected her. She wanted to let him know how outraged she felt but something prevented her from expressing how she was really feeling. She wondered if all the pent up anguish she had bottled up after each rejection would, one day, explode like steam from a pressure cooker but, for now, she could keep it contained. She settled for bashing the living daylights out of a pillow.

Once Cath's exertions had sapped the anger of its ferocity, she didn't know what to do with herself. She'd been so used to being with the Italians, then Debs and now Jack, she didn't know how to be by herself. She contemplated going on a trip around the island so she could prove to Jack that she didn't need him but she worried that she might bump into him. But she knew the real reason was that she wanted to be around when he got back so she could persuade him she wasn't needy and that he'd made a big mistake.

Cath headed to a nearby internet café where she ordered a cola lite while waiting for her email account to open. There was still no reply from Riley. *What's going on? Has he forgotten about me too? Does he think I'm disposable like Jack does?* Despite The Bliss Expert telling her not to use Riley to make herself feel better, she couldn't help herself. She needed reassurance that he, at least, still wanted her.

> *Why the lack of contact? Please email me soon as I miss you so much.*
>
> *Please come over and visit me NOW. I can't bear to be without you for a second longer.*

Next, Cath felt the need to tell someone what had happened that morning, so she emailed Rosie.

> *Please don't judge me but I've been with a guy called Jack. He's just told me I'm too needy. How dare he?! I'm one of the most independent girls I know! How many people – let alone girls – go travelling by themselves? I hate him for hurting me so much and I'm annoyed at myself because he was an arrogant twat from the moment I met him but I went after him anyway.*
>
> *But, it leaves me in a dilemma. I've spent all my time with him and we're sharing a room together. If I tell him where to stick it, I'll be on my own and I'm not ready for that yet. Maybe it's best to travel with him for a little longer. Better the devil you know and all that.*

Anyway, I just needed to tell someone how angry I am. But please don't mention anything to anyone just in case it gets back to Riley.

Then she wrote to Debs apologising for her behaviour and asking her what she thought of Belize. She was about to open an email from *Los Cuadrados* when an email pinged in from The Bliss Expert. She had been right! She'd needed to meet Jack before he'd contact her again. She had to open it immediately, desperate to see what further advice he had for her, and what answers he had to her questions.

I knew my last email wouldn't stop you from eating the spaghetti or getting together with Jack; but I wanted you to know that I can predict your future and I have your best interests at heart. If you follow my advice, it will make the next few months a lot easier for you. For now, I want to reassure you that I know you're deeply sad, but sometimes things have to hit rock bottom before you're prepared to do something about it. Not until you heed my advice will I send you The Ten Steps to Bliss, which will help you find true love, happiness, and fulfillment.

I know you're desperate to know who I am and how I know so much about you but please be patient. I will reveal my identity when you're ready. Meanwhile, here's some more advice:

- *Contact your parents, they worry about you*

- *Have a good cry tonight, it will do you the world of good*

- *Know you'll be safe when you feel brave enough (or pissed off enough) to travel by yourself*

- *You're doing the right thing by going to Los Cuadrados but you may have to wait for the right time*

- *Take Spanish lessons but don't let your old patterns throw you off course*

The question is: will you listen to any of my advice? I strongly suggest you do but, whether you do or don't, you'll learn something about yourself.

What?! Cath reread the email from The Bliss Expert three times and she still couldn't believe it. It was akin to something in *Insurgent* but it was real and happening to her, right now. She wished she could have a face-to-face conversation with the mystery emailer so she could have answers to her mounting questions. Cath printed off his email, determined to heed his advice - this time - because so far everything he'd predicted had come true.

Given that The Bliss Expert had said that it was the right thing to go to *Los Cuadrados,* she wanted to open their message next. It said there was availability on twenty-first November, just under two months away. *The Bliss Expert is right! I do have to wait.* Cath felt determined to follow his advice, no matter what, so she replied to secure her place on the retreat then decided to adhere to more of his guidance and call her parents, rather than just send them an email. She dialled their number and waited for her mum to pick up the phone. 'Mum, can you hear me?'

'Yes, love. How are you?'

'Really good. It's great here. Sorry I haven't had a chance to phone you before now but it's expensive to call abroad. How are you?

'Not too bad.'

'Good. How's Dad?'

'He's doing okay.'

'Good, good.' After a few seconds of silence, Cath chewed

on her lip and continued. 'I can give you my number and you can call me back if you'd like.'

Cath told her the number. 'I'll wait...' But before she could finish her sentence, the phone cut off. 'I'll wait for you to call me.'

Cath waited for a few minutes and chuckled to herself. Her mum wasn't the quickest with technology. Perhaps she was gathering her dad so that they could call her back together. She waited for a little longer before it dawned on her that the phone wasn't going to ring. She waited another ten minutes, just in case, and then gave up. *The Bliss Expert is wrong about my parents, they're not worried about me!*

Cath wandered to her room, breathing deeply all the way in an attempt to keep her feelings in check. Something was clawing at her insides, anxious to get out, but she couldn't release it, not yet. By the time she reached the room, it was three o'clock and Jack still hadn't returned, so Cath whiled away the afternoon reading *Notes from a Small Island*, intermittently checking her watch.

By the time Cath had finished reading her book, it was dark and she was starving. She fancied something simple yet filling so meandered to *Bananas*, got a take-away burrito and headed back to her room, noticing that everyone else was enjoying themselves with their friends. As she approached the hostel, she peeked into *Brit's Abroad* and gasped. Jack was in there with the beautiful Polish girl who had left the *Travels* book in San Cristobel. His full body was pressed up against the girl's groin as she sat on a stool with her legs wrapped around him. Cath felt nauseous as she stood motionless, like in a movie where the main character is stationary but the world hurries past. The last thing Cath saw was them kissing passionately before she ran to her room and slammed the door shut while hurling her dinner across the floor. The tears burst out in a torrent. *How dare he? How can he be so cruel and heartless? Is it because I'm so ugly, fat and boring? Is that why he's rejected me, why Debs left me, why Riley's not been in contact and why my mum didn't phone me back? No-one gives a crap about me.* This last thought caused another assault of emotion until she was almost sick from over-exertion.

Cath had no idea if it were seconds, minutes or hours that had passed, but the dryness in her mouth and the throbbing in her head suggested she should stop crying before the physical pain took over from the emotional pain. The Bliss Expert's words echoed in her mind as she remembered that he'd said it would be good for her to cry. *How can he be right about this but not about my parents?* It didn't make logical sense and this only added to her list of frustrations.

Suddenly needing fresh air, Cath ran up the central staircase two at a time in a rush to reach the roof terrace. When she got there, she was met with the vast expanse of darkness glittering with twinkling stars and the moonlight dancing on the sea. While it was breathtaking, it made her feel even smaller and more insignificant than she already did.

A cool breeze washed over her while she witnessed the rising of a new day. With it, realisation dawned on her that she needed to get away from Jack and be on her own. She wished she'd listened to The Bliss Expert and Debs and had never got involved with him in the first place. *Maybe now is the right time for me to travel by myself?* The Bliss Expert said she'd be safe and she was definitely pissed off enough to do it. With renewed resolve, Cath climbed back down the stairs and opened the door to the room, expecting to see Jack asleep, but he wasn't there. Cath gathered her stuff and packed everything into her backpack. She was tempted to do something vindictive to Jack's belongings like urinate on his toothbrush or cut off the sleeves of his favourite blue and white checkered shirt but she chose instead to imagine him coming back to the room and wondering where she had gone.

After hurrying out of the room, Cath paid the receptionist her share of the bill and caught the next boat to the mainland. She fantasised about Jack going back to their room to find it devoid of Cath and her stuff. While she wanted to believe that he would be upset, or at the very least surprised, she was a realist and knew he'd be glad that he now had somewhere to take the Polish girl.

Once the boat had docked, Cath went to the first café she came across, ordered jam and toast, and reread the print out of The Bliss Expert's email to see if there were any clues as to where she should go next. *Ah ha, of course!* He'd mentioned learning Spanish so she could do that. Searching her *Lonely Planet,* she discovered that Antigua was *the* place to learn Spanish and it was *the most popular tourist destination in Guatemala. Result*! Happy that she had a plan, she had an hour to kill before the bus went to Tulum so she paid for an hour's internet time and logged on. First, she updated The Bliss Expert on what had happened over the last twenty-four hours, then she clicked on an email from Riley, happy he had finally deemed her important enough to send her a message.

Just been busy in work, nothing to do with you. Don't want to keep moaning about my boss being a proper dick.

Been staying in London for a couple of weekends in a row. Chocka both weekends.

This footy thing doesn't get any easier. We drew (again!) with the blue shite at the weekend, and I got a good punch in the back of my head for my troubles (I suppose it serves me right for sitting in the Everton stand, ha ha!). You probably heard Brendan Rodgers got sacked after the game? Bit unfair like, but hopefully Herr Klopp will do the business!

I want to visit you. I've just got to sort out when I can have two weeks (or more!) off work.

Cath reminded herself never to go to a football match with him. She didn't know who Brendan Rodgers was, let alone that he'd been sacked. Still, it was good news that at least Riley still wanted her and was still thinking about coming out to see her. Next, she clicked on an email from her mum.

I hope you're well. Your dad and I are worried about you. You sounded so low on the phone the other day, I hope you're okay? We tried to phone you back several times on the number you gave me but it didn't work. We were both so disappointed not to speak to you properly. Please let us know you're okay.

Cath swallowed back the tears. They did try to phone her back and The Bliss Expert was right, they were worried about her. She vowed not to doubt him ever again.

There was one final message was from Rosie.

Poor you. I'm so sorry to hear you've been hurt again by a man. But if you insist on playing with Jack the lad (!), I'm afraid you are going to get hurt. Why don't you leave boys

alone for a while and concentrate on you? You've got Riley,
can't he be enough for you?

Rosie was right, as usual, but it was easy for her. She'd met the love of her life when she was just twenty-one; she'd never gone through the continual rejection Cath had faced. While she wanted to write something to this effect, for the sake of their relationship, she didn't.

Her time was nearly up, but just as she was about to log off, a message pinged in from The Bliss Expert. She had to read it!

I'm glad you allowed yourself to cry, you needed it. I know Jack hurt you but it's good that you experienced the pain because you might be a little more aware of what's really going on now. Before you get to the retreat, here's something for you to reflect on:

Who and what are you really upset about?

Once you've figured this out, you'll understand why you are attracted to men like Jack. To give you a hint, the pain you are feeling is not about Jack; he has merely triggered old hurt that's been inside you for a long time.

Cath had to reread his email several times. *Good that I experienced the pain? How dare he?! How could it possibly be good to feel that bad?* What did he mean by *old hurt and why was she attracted to men like Jack?* Cath was desperate to know what he was talking about and wished he wouldn't be so cryptic, but the screen went blank; she was out of time and she needed to get to the bus stop.

Chapter Thirteen

Brown on Tour
Day 59: Guatemala City, Guatemala

Boy have I been busy travelling from one beautiful place to another! Here's a quick synopsis: I left Isla Mujeres and stopped off at Playa del Carmen, went to Tulum and then to Chetumal. Suffice to say, when I thought I couldn't possibly see a more striking stretch of powder-white sand, azure sea and magnificent Mayan ruins, I moved onto the next place and it blew this thought out of the water with lush tropical jungle and archeological sites perched on cliff edges overlooking crystal clear, turquoise waters!

Next, I crossed the border into Belize. Not knowing much about this country before I got there, I was surprised at how different it was from Mexico. Firstly, Belize has more in common with its nearby Caribbean islands than its bordering Spanish speaking countries and secondly, they speak English, albeit with heavily accented Kriol (Creole). Their main motto is 'Go Slow,' which sums up Belize. Think wooden shacks, swinging hammocks, impenetrable jungle, beautiful coral reefs, translucent sea, and white sand.

The food was different too. I could have anything from spicy Creole creations to English corned beef and Mayan delicacies (such as fried paca, which is a small rodent). Being a vegetarian who doesn't like spicy food, I stuck to fried rice and vegetables, which made a pleasant change from burritos.

If it makes you feel better, the bus journeys have been boring. In addition to being squashed, I've had to sit next to smelly guys reading dirty comics and listen to music pumped up to ear-splitting volumes.

I've just arrived in Guatemala City and will be heading to Antigua shortly to begin three weeks of Spanish lessons.

Then, it was time to be honest, with Rosie.

Thanks for your last email. I know you're right but I never seem to meet the right sort of man. I wish I could meet someone like Terence and settle down like you have. You are very lucky, you know.

I know my blog makes it sound like I'm having a blast but I've been travelling for over two weeks on my own and I hate it. While the places I've visited have been stunning, I've not been able to appreciate their beauty because I've felt so sad and lonely. I haven't clicked with any nice people since I left Jack so I've had to eat breakfast, lunch and dinner by myself, I've had to sunbathe on my own, sleep on my own and explore ruins by myself. I've cried myself to sleep most nights.

To add to my misery, I've had to get up ridiculously early to catch buses (i.e. 4.15 a.m.) and for pretty much the whole time, I've felt scared and on edge. For example, I got dropped off in Tierra Linda where I was supposed to get a connecting bus to Coban. But Tierra Linda wasn't really a place, it was more of a crossroads for buses to drop off and pick up passengers. I had to wait on my own - literally in the middle of nowhere - wondering whether the bus was going to turn up. When it did arrive (thankfully) an hour later, it wasn't a bus at all but a pick-up truck! And the journey that was supposed to take three hours, took ten!

So that's the truth behind all the beauty I'm surrounded by. I'm feeling thoroughly lonely, overweight and miserable. I hope all's good with you.

Cath signed off and ambled to the bus station. She climbed onboard the brightly coloured, ex-American school bus and sat on her own, again, waiting for it to take her to Antigua, which was only about an hour away. She hoped that following The Bliss Expert's advice to learn Spanish was the best thing for her. Things surely couldn't get much worse.

Chapter Fourteen

The bus screeched to a halt at the terminal in Antigua. Cath grabbed her belongings and marveled at the thirty or so *chicken buses* coming, going or standing stationary. There were no-one-shade-of-yellow buses in sight here. These were pimped-up carnival machines covered in a rainbow of vibrant swirls and shapes that would have looked more at home at a Mardi Gras than in this dusty, potholed, over-sized car park.

Cath consulted her guide book and headed towards the school she had chosen. The cobblestone sidewalks were so narrow she found it easier to walk on the street, even with the traffic whizzing by. She was so captivated by the historic buildings, monuments, fountains, and ruins that she nearly twisted her ankle a couple of times in the numerous potholes along the way.

Cath found the Spanish school she was looking for and booked lessons for the following three weeks. She hadn't realised that the reasonable price included board and food with a local family and she wasn't sure how she felt about this. While it would be wonderful to have some company at meal times and eat home-cooked food, she wondered if it would also be awkward.

The walk to her host family's house took roughly ten minutes and she was welcomed by a middle-aged couple called Carlos and Clara and their ten-year-old twins, Camila and Carla. It seemed only people with a name beginning with the letter C were allowed into the Méndez family's home. They seemed friendly but Cath hadn't appreciated that they would speak only Spanish to her, which caused more than a few uncomfortable silences and uneasy giggles. Cath had no idea what they were saying and felt thankful that the international sign language for I don't understand was also recognisable in Guatemala. Unsure how many more fake smiles and thumbs-ups they could manage, the family resorted to showing Cath to her bedroom, which had its own wardrobe-sized bathroom adjoining it. Both were next to the dining room and gave her a semblance of privacy as they were separate from the family's sleeping quarters upstairs. Carla gave her a key, another thumbs-up, and that was that. She was alone. Again.

Brown on Tour

Day 76: Antigua, Guatemala

I've been in Antigua for over two weeks now and it is absolutely beautiful. In fact, it's my favourite non-beach place so far. It has a wonderful, open feel about it, and the colonial buildings are stunning and add to its old-world charm. If it weren't for the indigenous people kitted out in their vivid traditional garments, sitting along the roadside selling their wares, I could be transported back in time to mainland Spain in the 1800s. While the town is lovely, the view is even more stunning with volcanoes bordering it in every direction.

Despite the vibrancy of the town, I've been anything but vibrant. Every day I follow the same routine: I get up early, spend the morning learning Spanish, eat lunch, check my emails, wander around the town, study and then have dinner. I'm in bed by 8:00 p.m.!

I'm living with a local family who are great, but because I eat every meal with them, I have to converse in basic Spanish. Unfortunately it takes a lot of effort, and I find myself wolfing down my food so I can leave the table as quickly as possible!

Cath then wanted to be honest with Rosie.

I'm not sure I'm cut out for studying. Ever since I started my Spanish lessons I've had a bad headache, haven't slept properly and have had a recurring dream in which I'm about to sit an important exam, but because I haven't been to any lessons, I can't answer any of the questions. I sit there feeling stupid and out of place. The dream is obviously connected to my Spanish lessons but I can't work out why I am taking them so seriously? It's like being back at school; remember how stressed I used to get?!

I don't know who I am anymore. For almost two months I was a party girl – and I got fed up with that - but now I feel like a recluse – and I don't like that either!

Last night, I looked in the mirror and was depressed to see that I looked as bad as I feel. It is as if my internal depression is being reflected on the outside. I am spotty, my hair is greasy and in desperate need of a cut, my eyes look like they're drained of all life, and my skin looks dull. And I've put on more weight and need to buy new, larger clothes.

Sorry but I needed to tell someone before I scream.
Maybe a night out might cheer me up and relax me a little.

Cath logged off, grabbed a cola lite for some much needed caffeine, and dragged herself to school. When she arrived, her teacher Maria greeted her with a barrage of Spanish that sounded vaguely familiar but contained too many words for Cath to translate all at once. Instead, she concentrated on the battle raging inside her mind. Part of her wanted to be a dedicated student but that required an immense amount of effort, which she wasn't prepared to give at that moment. The other part wanted to relax and have fun, but that meant giving up, which wasn't in her nature. Her thoughts were at loggerheads with each other and, with them, came an angry knot of frustration, which seemed fuzzily familiar.

That evening, after quickly finishing dinner, Cath excused herself and went back to her room. She studied for a while but gave up and stared at herself in the mirror instead. *How have I allowed myself to get this fat?* She prodded her bulging thighs. *Look how ugly I am.* She stretched back the lines above her cheekbones and then her eyelids. She thumped her thighs a few times in anger, stuck her two fingers up at her reflection, and went to bed feeling angry and upset.

After two hours of tossing and turning, Cath decided the cure would be to go out and have some fun. Being a boring student was – well – boring, and stressing her out. She'd heard *The Casbar* was *the* place to go so she rummaged in her backpack to find the best outfit that still fitted her, applied a little too much make-up, and headed to the bar before she chickened out.

It took every ounce of strength to walk into *The Casbar* on her own. No sooner had she got through the door than she noticed an extremely good-looking, dark-haired guy to the right of her. She assumed that, because he was gorgeous, he wouldn't be interested in her, so she continued walking until she reached the bar. She stood next to a couple of girls who had just finished doing a shot each. 'What can I drink to get drunk? Fast.' She hoped they wouldn't think she was weird.

'Here.' One of the girls handed her a shot of murky yellow-brown liquid. There was a row of identical looking shots neatly lined up along the bar in front of them.

'Thanks!' Cath raised the glass up to the two girls who were now also holding up a glass each, took a deep breath, and threw the liquid down her throat. 'Tequila?' she asked screwing up her face.

'Ja!' And she handed Cath another one. The three girls continued the same process until the row of shot glasses were empty and turned upside down.

'I'm Cath by the way. How much do I owe you?' she asked as she pulled her purse from her bag.

It was the girl with the long hair who replied, 'Eish! Don't worry about it.'

Cath detected an accent and had become quite adept at identifying them. 'South African?'

The girl with the bobbed brown hair nodded. 'Ja. That's right!'

'Let me get you both a drink. More shots or beer?'

'I think beer, hey?' the same girl answered.

Cath got served in a matter of seconds, handed the girls each a cold bottle of beer, and asked them their names.

The bobbed brown-haired girl answered again while the other girl looked at her friend. 'I'm Anna. This is Fran.' Cath wondered if Fran was okay. She hadn't said much, nor looked at Cath for more than a fraction of a second.

The girls chinked their bottles together and Anna shouted to be heard above the thumping music. 'Where you from, hey?'

'London.' Cath was momentarily distracted as she spied the same handsome guy in the middle of a throng of people. She noted he was chatting to a group of male friends when Anna interrupted her ogling.

'Izit! Where exactly? I lived in London, couple of years, hey.'

'Sorry, I never like to assume... West Hampstead. Do you know it?' Still shouting.

Anna nodded. 'Ja. Lived in Kilburn. Not posh like West Hampstead, hey.'

Cath's cheeks burned. To change the subject, she turned to Fran. 'You been to England?'

Fran seemed surprised to be involved in the conversation. 'Ja.'

Cath wondered if she'd made a mistake in trying to engage Fran in conversation. It was going to be as hard as algebra to get her to talk. 'Where did you live?'

'With Anna.' Then she promptly looked at the floor again as if there was something really interesting there. Cath followed her eyes to see what she was looking at but her suspicions were right, there was nothing more than cigarette butts, empty bottles and screwed up flyers. Cath surmised that Fran was painfully shy. As Cath was wondering what to ask her next, she was distracted by how pretty she was. Fran had delicate freckles that covered her face and red-tinged auburn hair that framed her angled features perfectly. She didn't have a smidge on of make-up and she was slim too. *If I were that attractive I'd be the most confident girl in the room. How come Fran is so introverted? It doesn't make sense!* Cath was about to ask another inane question when the strikingly good-looking guy she had seen earlier came over. Cath shifted uncomfortably, assuming he would continue past her to Fran, but to her surprise, he stopped at Cath and said, 'Shalom.'

'Hi.' She was still in shock and wasn't sure what to say next.

'I see you and I want to talk to you. You're pretty. I like, how you say, shape. Very sexy.' He craned his neck to look at her behind, obviously checking her out.

'Err, thanks. You're Israeli then?'

He smiled. 'How you guess?'

'You're bold and your English is good. Both dead give-aways! I'm Cath.' She proffered her hand, but instead of shaking it, he kissed it. Cath was glad the bar was so dark or he would have seen her cheeks glow traffic light red.

'Erez.'

Cath turned her head to look at the South Africans. Anna smiled while Fran looked expressionless. Cath semi-smiled in return.

'Your grey eyes are beautiful. You have boyfriend?' He sipped on his straw, drawing up a dark brown liquid. Cath couldn't smell any alcohol on his breath so she guessed his drink was neat cola.

With the tequilas providing her with some courage, Cath looked at him directly. Upon closer inspection, Erez had tight curly hair that was a bit unruly, and thick stubble covering most the lower half of his face. His eyes were large and hazel brown. He looked like a petite and tanned version of Ewen McGregor. 'Are you always this forward?'

'Why, you don't like?' he raised his eyebrows up and down in quick succession.

Yes but I'm not going to admit it! She chose to smile instead.

After a few moments of silence, Erez chinked her bottle with his glass. 'Do you like what *you're* seeing?'

Cath had known confident men before but never this self-assured. She felt unnerved.

Erez continued, 'I'm from Israel. Everyone is beautiful.'

Cath hoped for a hint of a smile to show he was kidding but all she could focus on was the white spittle forming in the corners of his mouth. 'Well, I must put Israel on my to-do list then.'

'Why not?' There was no hint of his mouth turning up at the sides. While he may have been struck by the handsome stick, he had obviously bypassed the sense of humour one.

Just as Cath was about to turn to the South Africans for support, Erez's face exploded into a grin and he elbowed her jovially. 'English humour. Very funny. I like very much.'

Thank goodness; he does have a sense of humour.

Their conversation continued for another few minutes. His incessant compliments encouraged her confidence to grow in equal measures to the amount of tequila consumed.

'I go now,' Erez announced before marching towards a blonde babe, slipping his arm around her waist and walking out of the bar.

Cath stood there with her mouth agape, trying to work out what had just happened. No longer in the mood for partying, she said goodbye to Anna and Fran and left feeling fat, ugly and boring.

Chapter Fifteen

It was Saturday, which meant no school. Cath didn't have any plans but she was adamant about not studying. She wandered into town and went to an internet café. There was an email from her best friend, Rosie.

So sorry to hear you've been feeling so alone and that you're not enjoying yourself. I remember how you were at school so I'm glad I'm not there with you now! You always put an immense amount of pressure on yourself to succeed, which I never understood. Can't you find a happy medium between party girl and bore/stress-head? That sounds like a sensible option to me.

As usual, Rosie was right and it irritated Cath. *It's alright for her. She always does the right thing. She doesn't mess everything up like me!* Just as she finished typing, an email pinged in from The Bliss Expert.

I would advise you to leave Erez alone but I know you'll ignore me and chase him anyway. One day, you'll understand why you're attracted to such men and what's driving you to feel so frustrated. When you get to the retreat, use what you learn from Erez to be curious about whether similar patterns have played out in your past relationships.

You will soon receive the first Step to Bliss which will help you understand yourself better but you've got a bit more to experience yet. Only when the student is ready, will the master appear. Have patience and you will find out what you need to know at the exact moment you are ready to hear it.

How can he advise her to leave him alone when nothing happened? *He went off with another girl for goodness sake! And more to experience? When the student is ready, the master will appear? What's he talking about?* If The Bliss Expert was standing in front of her and was a real human being, she would have hit him.

When Cath emerged from the café, the sun was so bright it blinded her for a few seconds. When she could see again, she noticed Erez standing outside Mickey's café looking like he was waiting for someone. He looked even more dashingly handsome than he had last night and it took her brain a few moments to get into gear and decide what to do. She could listen to The Bliss Expert as well as her pride and do an about-turn and hope he didn't see her, or she could casually walk past, pretending she hadn't seen him. Before she had time to choose, he spotted her and strode towards her. He greeted her with a kiss on the cheek as if they knew each other well. 'You come in for drink?'

While she was still assessing her options, she was surprised to hear, 'Sure,' slip out of her mouth, as if his attractiveness had disarmed her.

'Okay, come with me,' he ordered, and Cath followed dutifully.

Mickey's was a well-known Israeli hangout so it didn't surprise her that Erez knew most of the people there. He grabbed two empty chairs and placed them at a table where five of his friends were already sitting. After being introduced to them, Cath couldn't remember a single name but beamed a smile at them anyway. She ordered a cola lite while Erez pulled his chair as close as possible to hers and placed his hand on her knee. She shifted so his hand slipped off her leg. 'Where is your girlfriend?' she asked.

'Eh?' Erez looked at his friends and smirked.

Cath noticed the spittle clinging to the corners of his mouth and was tempted to hand him a napkin to subtly suggest he wipe it off, but she knew that would be unkind, so she kept quiet. 'The girl you went off with last night,' she clarified.

'You know, she not my girlfriend. She go now. You next.' Sniggering, his friends found their conversation amusing.

Cath didn't. 'How long were you together?'

'Not long. Shall we go back to mine?' More laughter exploding amongst his friends.

Talk about uncomfortable. Cath wanted to run out of Mickey's and never look back, but something stopped her and she was glued to her seat. She liked self-confident men but he was arrogant. 'Erez, you're a nice guy but... but I've... I've just met you.' She was retreating more and more into her shell and wanted the ground to eat her up.

'I mean to play Backgammon.' More sniggering.

Cath withdrew more into herself. This didn't happen to her, ever, especially around good-looking men. She usually thrived on chasing them but it was different with Erez; he was chasing her. She was the gazelle rather than the lioness and she didn't like it; it felt alien and uncomfortable. The choice was simple: stay with Erez and his friends, or leave on her own – there was no way she was going back to his "to play Backgammon". While she was still deciding what to do, she spied a Backgammon box in a pile of other moth-eaten games in a corner of the café, which gave her an idea. She appraised Erez one last time, and as much as she knew she should leave she couldn't help but admire his good looks, which were so sculpted he was almost beautiful. 'Okay, let's play Backgammon. But here. First to eleven?'

As Cath got up to order a beer and grab the game, Erez's smile disappeared as he nodded his agreement. On her way back to the table the waitress handed Cath her beer just as it occurred to her that she needed to sit opposite Erez, not next to him, to play the game properly. Moving her flimsy plastic chair so that she was facing him, she made herself comfortable, and took her first sip of the fizzy, cool, and malty drink. It went down a little too well. Before they had finished their first match Cath was already on her second beer. By the third game, she had downed five bottles, and as she finished her fifth drink Erez shook his head. 'You drink a lot.'

'Thanks.' Cath threw the dice, and grimaced when she realised the two and one she'd cast would lose her the third game in a row. 'You were just lucky. Let's play again, only this time I'll concentrate.'

Cath felt like she was falling into Erez's cavernous hazel brown eyes as he answered, 'Don't you think you lose enough?'

Cath's confidence was sky-high. 'No way! I was just warming up.' Then she ordered another beer from the passing waitress.

After she'd won the next four games in a row, Cath secretly thanked the gaming gods for her fortune. It would not have been an acceptable outcome for a man to have beaten her.

By the time it got to ten games all, Cath was glad she had chosen to stay at *Mickey's*. She was feeling confident, the competition was exhilarating, and Erez seemed calmer, and less brash. Almost funny. So much so that she could almost overlook the spittle on the sides of his mouth.

They must have been sitting for over an hour so Cath's legs were aching. She kicked off her flip-flops and stretched her legs out under the table, accidently touching Erez's groin with her right foot. Giggling to herself when she realised what she'd done, she decided to turn the unintentional encounter into deliberate titillation. Cath rubbed her bare foot with greater force, and grinned when she felt a solid bulk develop beneath her touch.

Erez stopped setting up the counters for the next game and grabbed Cath's right hand, squeezing it tightly. 'Let's go back to mine.'

Choosing to laugh off his suggestion as a joke, Cath released her hand from his grip, and took over the job of getting the board ready for the decider.

But Erez stopped her as he squeezed her arm with double the amount of force than last time. 'No. I mean it.'

'I'm enjoying myself, Erez. Let's stay.'

Cath was half pleased that he'd wanted to take their relationship further, but she was also half offended. As much as she had enjoyed teasing him with her foot, she hadn't meant it to develop into any more. *Does he really think I'd go home with him after knowing him for such a short while?* Erez let go of her arm, so she was able to start the deciding game.

After Cath won by a comfortable margin, Erez seemed more interested in persuading her to go back to his bedroom than on congratulating her. While Cath was secretly pleased he wanted her – it was making her feel like a lioness again – she didn't want to kiss him, let alone anything else, and she wanted to head home before things became awkward. The room was also spinning slightly.

'I'm going home Erez. Alone. But I'll see you tomorrow!' With that, Cath got up and clumsily marched outside into the chilly night air.

As she swaggered home in the dark, she was smiling from ear-to-ear. Confident Cath was back and things were looking up! There was a budding romance with a handsome man, a potential friendship with Anna and maybe Fran if she'd lighten up, and exciting nightlife on offer as well. I should never have listened to The Bliss Expert's advice. Stupid Spanish lessons! At that moment, Cath tripped up on one of the uneven cobblestones and fell flat on her face. Landing with a smack, she was so badly winded that she couldn't breathe. When the worst of the pain had passed, she crawled to a wall and slumped next to it. The tears poured out as she wondered who she was trying to kid; The Bliss Expert was right to warn her about Erez and she knew that she was only feeling positive because of the alcohol. It didn't take a genius to know that men and partying weren't the answer to stop the hurt she felt deep inside. *But who or what is the cause and how do I stop it?* Cath looked up to star-sprinkled sky and pleaded, 'If anyone's listening, please help me. I can't take this much more.'

Chapter Sixteen

Cath was sitting on her bed, downing five cans of lager in quick succession. The four walls of her room felt more like a prison than a bedroom and seemed to close in on her with every gulp of alcohol. It dawned on her that she had a choice: she could change her mind and stay in, but what would that achieve, apart from making her feel more miserable? Or she could go to meet Erez as planned. Generating conversation might be a struggle but it would give her something to do and Erez would make her feel better, even if it was only temporary. However, the thought of getting physical with him was putting her off; his brashness, petite frame, and the sputum that clung to the sides of his mouth made her feel sick. Even so, she didn't want to be alone, so she guzzled her last can of beer before heading out.

Erez greeted Cath warmly, along with his friends. She ordered a beer and leant over to whisper in his ear. 'Fancy watching *Mission: Impossible – Rogue Nation*? It's about to start.' She tried to make it sound like a casual suggestion but it was her cunning plan. Watching a film was the perfect solution to avoid having to converse with Erez, which was as painful as speaking Spanish.

'Why not?' He put his arm around her shoulder and squeezed it.

Throughout the film, Erez stroked her hand gently and brushed her knee affectionately. As soon as the credits flashed up, Cath felt mildly confident. Pointing to the Backgammon box in the corner, she said, 'Fancy a rematch?' It was all she could think of to ensure they stayed in the café.

'Sure?' He got up to fetch the game.

After winning ten games in a row, Erez stretched out and gave a fake yawn. 'I'm tiring.'

'Me too,' said Cath. And she was fed up with losing.

'I come with you.' Before she had a chance to respond, he had grabbed her hand and was leading her through the maze of chairs towards the exit.

Cath panicked. As she imagined globules of spittle oozing into her mouth, even the idea of kissing him revolted her. And sleeping with him? He had to be joking!

The cool night air was refreshing after the stuffiness in Mickey's but it didn't stop Cath's heart from pounding. 'I'm in a house with a young family; I can't take anyone home.'

He drew her close and gently swept a strand of hair back to where it belonged. 'You come back with me.'

'I need my beauty sleep. I have school in the morning.'

'I think you play with me.' Erez leaned in for the kiss, which was in slow motion while Cath considered how to get out of it. She felt sick as his lips moved in for the kill and she saw spittle leaking from both cracks in his mouth. It was as appealing as kissing a toothless, slimy fish. She managed to extricate herself from him with a gentle push. 'Goodnight, Erez. I'm tired and need to sleep. But I'll see you tomorrow.' She left him standing outside Mickey's and he didn't look happy.

Chapter Seventeen

After another frustrating morning learning Spanish, Cath felt miserable and argued with herself until she caved in and walked to Mickey's. Her need for companionship overruled her revulsion at the idea of having to kiss Erez. He was already there when she arrived. He half-greeted her with a mouthful of falafel and continued his conversation with his friends as if she was invisible.

When there was a gap in their conversation, Cath interrupted and spoke to Erez directly. 'Backgammon rematch?'

Cath could have sworn he rolled his eyes to his friends, but before he answered, the two South African girls Anna and Fran walked in. Cath almost jumped up in jubilation but settled for waving at them instead. Pointing to two free chairs next to her, she prayed they would join her. To her relief, they did. 'How you doing?'

The girls looked a little overwhelmed at the gang of boys huddled around the table staring at them, or at Fran, to be precise. Anna broke the silence, directing her conversation to Cath. 'Hey, Biscuit. Howzit?'

'Good, good.' Cath had an urge to drink something stronger than cola lite. 'Haven't seen you in a while.'

'We've been around, hey. Just not here.'

'Fancy an alcoholic drink?'

Anna smiled and Fran nodded. Cath caught the waitress's eye who was clearing the table of the Israelis' empty lunch plates, held up three fingers and mouthed, 'Beer.' She didn't bother to ask Erez, knowing he'd stick to his soft drink. 'How are you both?'

'Good, hey.' No surprises that it was Anna who answered, but she seemed distracted. Cath followed her line of vision and saw she was glancing towards Erez's friend, who had bright blonde hair and black roots.

Cath cupped her hand into a semi-circle and whispered behind it so only Anna could hear what she was saying. 'His name's Yaniv. He's nice.'

Her face broke into a smile. 'Izit.'

Cath giggled and looked at Fran who was staring intently at the television on the wall. 'How are you?'

She didn't move her eyes from the screen. 'Good, hey.' She didn't elaborate so Cath turned to Anna again. 'What you up to today?' Before Anna could answer, the waitress handed them their cold beers.

The three girls chinked bottles while from the corner of her eye Cath observed the Israelis staring at Fran. Erez included.

Anna guzzled half her drink down in one. 'We're fixed up to climb Pacaya later. Want to come with us?'

She turned to Erez and nudged him with her elbow to get his attention from gawking at Fran. A pang of jealousy hit Cath unexpectedly. 'Do you mind?'

He turned to face her, furrowed his eyebrows, and ignored her question as if it wasn't worthy of an answer.

Cath made a snap decision. 'I'd love to!'

The girls ordered lunch and had a couple more beers before it was time to leave. Having not received any attention from Erez since the South Africans had arrived, Cath wanted him to want her, not Fran. So she prodded Erez. 'See you here at seven tonight?'

Erez answered a little too loudly, 'Yes. You and your friends.'

On the bus on the way to the volcano, Cath was deep in contemplation. *Has Erez lost interest in me? Does he want Fran instead?* He suddenly seemed attractive and even his spittle didn't revolt her anymore. Now she wanted him.

When they arrived, their guide pointed towards the towering black mound of an imposing volcano. Cath shuddered. 'I'm not sure it was wise to drink.'

Anna pushed Cath forward playfully. 'Chill, bru, it'll be fine.'

Cath followed the guide with a heavy heart. *Perhaps I should have had sex with Erez last night? Maybe he wouldn't have given Fran a second glance if I had?* But before she could answer her own question, Anna distracted her with stories from their travels, which included being caught up in the middle of rival football supporters, robbed at knifepoint, flashed at, and narrowly missing being blown up in a bomb attack.

Assuming she was talking about Colombia or El Salvador, Cath wanted to know where to avoid. 'Where was this?'

'London.'

Cath made a mental note to find somewhere else to live when she returned to England.

The climb was so effortless that Cath almost skipped through the first part of the trek. Then they reached large black lava rocks which they had to clamber over, and which was slightly more challenging but manageable, until – just as they could see the summit – the rocks turned into fine, black ash, so soft it was like walking on quicksand. For every one step up, she slipped down three. Suddenly, the altitude made breathing difficult and the temperature dropped dramatically. Her muscles began screaming, bitter cold sliced through every pore in her body, and fierce wind threatened to topple her over. And this went on for thirty minutes. Cath swore, stamped her foot, and was close to tears.

When she finally reached the summit and saw the magnificent view, words failed her. There was a fusion of intense oranges, pinks, and yellows streaking across the sky, intertwined with frothy clouds and patches of bright blue. For miles around, there was a vast expanse of land dotted with large cities, tiny villages, forebidding volcanoes, grass, fields and forests.

'Wow!' was all she could manage to say through the fierce wind.

The heat of the lava seeped through the thick soles of her hiking shoes and warmed her feet. Cath was instructed by the guide to lie on her stomach to get out of the full force of the wind and look into the centre of the crater. Much to her disappointment, there wasn't any bubbling lava and she could only bear to stay in that position for a few seconds because great wafts of thick smoke gushed into her mouth, filling it with sulphur and toxic gases and threatening to suffocate her. The heat coming through her clothes was comforting and warming for short bursts but unbearable for any longer than a few seconds. So she alternated between standing up and lying on her stomach, as if she were practising getting on and off a surf board. A few minutes later, the sun disappeared behind a thick blanket of cloud and, with it, the temperature plummeted. It was time to leave. Cath laughed as she glided down the soft ash as effortlessly as if she were skiing. It was the first time in a long while that she had felt so exhilarated and alive.

After returning from the trip, she had twenty minutes to shower and get ready before she was due to meet Erez in *Mickey's*. She arrived fifteen minutes late but she couldn't see Erez anywhere. Cath ordered a shot of tequila with her beer.

By the time Erez turned up two hours later, Cath was furious. Her plan was to ignore him as he would then chase after her to win back her affections. Instead, he ignored her and flirted with Fran. *How dared he!* Luckily, Fran wasn't interested, but as the night wore on and Cath hit the tequilas hard, anger began bubbling up from the depths. Stumbling to *The Casbar*, it didn't take long for Cath to approach Erez but, when she got close enough to say, 'Hi,' he turned his back on her. She wanted to understand why he had gone from being attentive to being so cold. To regain his attention, Cath grabbed his shoulder a little more roughly than she had intended and managed to pull him round so he was facing her.

The anger in his eyes said what his words couldn't express. 'Leave. Me.' He slammed his barely touched drink on the bar and walked away. She followed him and stood, swaying, in front of him trying to block his exit.

'I,' (hiccup) 'just wanna talk. Why won't you talk… to me?'

'Leave me.' He pushed past her and out of the club with Cath stumbling behind him. He got into a taxi and she climbed into the taxi with him. He glared at her incredulously, shook his head, and got out the other side. She clambered out of her side of the cab and followed him. It was as if a demon had possessed her and would not give up until she had answers.

Erez climbed into another taxi and slammed the car door. Cath opened the door he'd just shut when she felt someone grab her other arm with force. Cath turned her head and nearly lost her balance when she saw it was Fran. 'Not worth losing your self-respect for, hey.' Even in her drunken state, it stopped Cath in her tracks. Fran had been like a wilting flower for the whole time she'd known her so Cath had no idea she could be so forthright. Cath bent down to look at Erez with pleading eyes for one last chance to talk. He looked straight ahead as if she were invisible, shook his head, and slammed the taxi door shut.

Cath followed Fran back into the club and ordered another drink. She then went onto the dance floor holding her drink when a girl approached her. 'Put your drink on the side while dancing.'

Cath stared at her through glazed eyes. *Ha ha, funny!* They were in a country not exactly known for its stringent health and safety regulations. Cath carried on dancing whilst firmly holding onto her bottle of beer until the girl again pleaded that she put her drink on the side.

'Pish off.' Cath continued to sway with the music.

'What did you just say to me?' asked the girl, who was a few inches shorter than Cath but equally as wide.

'I shed pish off.' Cath stopped dancing.

The girl attempted to grab Cath's drink from her hand. 'Who do you think you are?'

Cath tightened her grip on the bottle and yanked it away. 'I'm very drunk. I want to dance. Get outta my face? Or I'll...'

'Or you'll what?' She squared up to Cath, trying to make herself look as tall as possible.

'Do this.' Cath grabbed hold of the other girl's hair and wrenched her head to one side. 'Leave. Me. Alone. Or.' Cath saw fear in the girl's eyes and stopped. *What am I doing?* It was as if the demon that had wanted answers earlier now wanted to unleash its anger and Cath couldn't stop it. Feeling a little more sober, she added, 'I'm going to let go of your hair in a minute and, as soon as I do, I want you to leave.' Cath let go of the girl's hair and hurried out of the club.

The next day Cath felt terrible. Not so much from a hangover but more because of what she remembered of the night before. She recoiled in embarrassment over the taxi episode with Erez and felt physically sick at her aggressive behaviour towards the girl who had asked her to put her bottle to the side. She knew she had pent up feelings inside but she hadn't acted upon them before. It scared her. Rosie had told her that she got aggressive sometimes when she was drunk — and she was certainly drunk last night — but, until now, Cath had never believed her.

Cath had her last day of Spanish lessons to go to but she couldn't face anyone and just wanted to disappear, so that's what she decided to do. *Sod it! I'll go to San Marcos and hope they've got somewhere for me to stay. I'll only be three days early.* So she packed her belongings, closed the front door as quietly as she could on her way out, and posted the key through the letter box. Then she walked quickly to the bus station, keeping her head down the entire time, hoping she wouldn't see anyone she knew. Cath climbed on board a minibus heading for Panajachel and braced herself for she knew that it was self-excavation time. She didn't know if she was more scared about what she might find or that she wouldn't find anything, and would just stay miserable for the rest of her life.

Chapter Eighteen

Brown on Tour
Day 85: Panajachel, Guatemala

Having finished Spanish lessons in Antigua, I travelled to Lake Atitlán where the steep, winding road leading down to the lake was dramatic and spectacular. Think huge, mesmerizing body of water so calm and lucid-blue that it blends into the sky so perfectly that it's impossible to tell where one ends and the other begins. The picture-postcard look is finished off with a backdrop of three cone-shaped volcanoes. Simply stunning.

I'm writing this from the main town called Panajachel, or Pana as it's known to the locals. It's a bustling metropolis of brightly coloured wooden shacks, art galleries, restaurants, cafés and vendors selling anything from handmade pottery, wood carvings and jewellery to leather goods, souvenirs and artwork.

Right now a child of about five is offering to polish my flip flops! His face is mottled with dirt, there's thick green snot dripping from his nose and his ragged clothes look two sizes too small for him, but his smile and big brown eyes are so gorgeous, I can't help but give him a few quetzals.

I'm staying in a small village called San Marcos, which is an hour's boat ride across the lake. It's like a ghost town compared to here as there's not much of anything there so I have come to Pana to use the internet. I'm staying in a wooden hut at a centre called Los Cuadrados where I'm due to start a month-long retreat in three days' time. I know you're all going to be shocked but it's true, honest! The accommodation is what I'd call rustic (the shared toilets and showers are outside!) but it has everything I need and I was lucky to get a room before my retreat officially starts.

Wish me luck!

Cath logged off, ate her newest favourite treat - pancakes, cream and maple syrup - and headed to the pier at the bottom of the main street, *Calle Santander.* She was getting the hang of marching forward with purpose whilst saying, 'No, thank you,' firmly to persistent children and vendors selling their wares. The boat journey back to the retreat enabled her to enjoy the passing scenery of make-shift jetties, multi-coloured boats floating in the middle of nowhere, and wooden shacks held together with tin roofs, built into the side of steep slopes. What shocked her the most was young girls in traditional dress climbing out of boats with piles of breeze blocks tied to their backs. These extraordinary sights were everywhere and Cath was able to see them all with the wind in her hair and a backdrop of imposing volcanoes.

Cath had agreed to join the current group's activities more for something to do than a desire to do them. The first session — meditation — was due to start in an hour so she relaxed on the jetty with her latest book: *The Alchemist* by Paolo Coelho. She struggled to keep her eyes open because the gentle rocking motion caused by the soft ripples of water brushing against the jetty's wooden stilts was incredibly soothing. Giving up on her book, she absorbed the stunning scenery, the quiet from no cars whizzing by or people chattering, and the hypnotic motion of the waves. Despite such beauty, Cath could not quell her unpleasant internal thoughts. She felt ugly, frustrated, and annoyed at herself. It was hot enough to put her bikini on but she felt so unsightly that, even though there was no-one else around, she didn't want to expose her flabbiness to the outside world. After a while she got up, followed the muddy makeshift path to the small shop next to the fruit and vegetable stall, bought a warm cola lite, and then headed back to the jetty. Time seemed to be standing still.

When she arrived back at the jetty, there were two Western girls in her spot. Cath grinned at them and, while they smiled back, one of them put her finger to her mouth to indicate for Cath to be quiet. *How rude!* She dug out her iPod, put on her earphones and floated into one of her favourite tunes from the summer, Calvin Harris and Disciple's *How Deep Is Your Love*, in the hope that the thumping beats might distract her from her negative thoughts.

At five o'clock she joined the others who she assumed were also going to meditation. They all seemed jubilant, hugging each other and jumping up and down, but they weren't talking; it was very odd. Cath felt left out and alone.

The meditation building was square and smelled of brand new wood as if it had been crafted hours before. Every building in the complex was square-shaped and it dawned on Cath this was why the retreat was called *Los*

Cuadrados: squares. The door to the meditation square opened and everyone nudged each other with anticipation. Cath looked around. The others took off their shoes as they entered so Cath did the same. They had to crouch down and crawl through a dark tunnel, which was like a rabbit hole, before reaching a set of wooden steps that led to a large empty room. The sweet smell of incense hit her nostrils as her eyes adjusted to the candlelit room. The room was sparse apart from colourful cushions, which were arranged like the numbers on a clock, and encircled a serene-looking woman sitting cross-legged on the floor in the centre. Her hands were resting gently on her knees while the candles bobbed about as merrily as the attendees had been doing shortly before. Even though the serene woman's eyes were open, she seemed lost in her thoughts and Cath wondered if she was aware that the room had filled with fifteen excited people, and one disheartened one.

Everyone, apart from Cath, took a seat on the cushions and sat in the same crossed-legged position as the woman in the centre. Cath lingered outside the circle until she took her place on the one spare cushion remaining. The woman's gaze shifted as she become more aware of her surroundings. She smiled and said, 'Welcome.' After a few slow deep breaths, she began to speak in heavily accented yet fluent English.

'Well done to those of you about to break their fast and vow of silence. We will be doing some meditation to help you focus on your insights.'

Cath's mind started to race. *Fast? Vow of silence? What have I got myself into? Have I joined a cult?* At least it made sense why no-one was talking outside the building and why the girls earlier had indicated for her not to speak to them at the jetty.

'For those of you who have joined us for the first time tonight,' looking directly at Cath, 'my name is Za Za. Don't be afraid, as you will learn a great deal and will be able to teach others from your experiences here. After all, Los Cuadrados has two meanings: squares and beginning of a new direction to help guide seekers out of their confusion.'

Cath stared at her in awe. *How does Za Za know why I'm here?* As quickly as she made Cath feel like she was the only person in the room, she turned to address everyone else.

'Let us begin. We will meditate to get you into an open state and then you will break your silence by sharing with the rest of the group how you are feeling right now in the present moment.'

Cath closed her eyes and attempted to meditate but every time she tried, thoughts of Erez and the girl she had nearly bottled paraded in. The more she tried to brush them aside, the more they persisted. They were like zombies creeping out of the dark nooks and crannies of her mind. No matter how hard she tried, she could not stop them.

When it came to the group sharing what they had experienced during the session, Cath had to do everything in her power to not laugh: 'I am the light, I am the earth, I vibrate in all that is around me, I am the energy of the world, I am the essence that is.'

Cath wanted to shout, 'You stupid, arrogant, self-opinionated idiots!' but instead she simply smiled.

After class, Cath put her head down and went straight back to her room without saying a word to another human being. It took every ounce of willpower to stay and, if it wasn't for The Bliss Expert, she would have packed up her bag and left. Because he'd been spot-on about everything else he'd said, she had to believe that he was correct about Los Cuadrados too. Maybe his comment about waiting for the right time meant waiting for the new group to arrive, which was when she would have started if she hadn't made a mess of things in Antigua and arrived early. *Does that mean he knew I'd mess things up with Erez?* A shiver ran down her spine that her behaviour with men was so predictable. *What was it he'd said about not letting old patterns throw me off course? Maybe this is connected to who and what I'm really upset about?* Cath remembered that The Bliss Expert had said to be curious about whether similar patterns had played out in her past relationships, so she pulled out a piece of paper and began writing a list of what she had learnt from Erez.

1. *I was attracted to his good looks but I didn't fancy him and he turned out to be arrogant. Yes, this is the same as Jack and Brian and every other boyfriend before him!*

2. *His attention made me feel good about myself. Temporarily. Yes, Jack and Brian (and my previous boyfriends: Jess, Mark, Seb and Rich) all boosted my ego and made me feel good about myself because they were good-looking and they wanted me.*

3. *I was angry when he didn't want me anymore. Yes, I was furious when all my boyfriends finished with me. How dare they!*

4. *I felt frustrated because I didn't know why he stopped liking me. So much so that I nearly glassed someone. Yes, all my other boyfriends finished with me out of the blue and with no explanation, which made me feel incredibly frustrated.*

Cath finished and reread what she'd written. She couldn't believe that she'd never noticed a pattern before but there it was in front of her. However, it made no sense who or what she was really upset about – it was the bastard men who made her feel bad – so she vowed to go into Pana the next day to update The Bliss Expert on her findings. Perhaps her insights would be rewarded with suggestions on how she could stop being such an idiot where men are concerned. *Maybe I will finally find a boyfriend I really like and who really likes me?* Cath made a decision to keep a low profile until the new group started in a couple of days. In the meantime, she could sunbathe, read, explore some of the other villages around the lake, and maybe even learn some Spanish verbs. It was exhausting thinking so deeply that she climbed into bed and was asleep before her head hit the pillow, dreaming of being in love. And feeling happy. It was the first time she'd had a glimpse of what it could be like, even if it was just in her dreams.

Chapter Nineteen

Brown on Tour Blog
Day 95: San Marcos

I've been doing my retreat for a week now and I'm loving it. Every day, we do yoga, metaphysics classes and meditation. I'm not fully convinced about much of it yet but I'm finding it interesting.

There are eleven other people doing the retreat with me and they're from countries all over the world, although mostly English speaking countries (Ireland, America, Canada, Australia, New Zealand and the UK). I've particularly bonded with a girl from Dublin called Sophie who is fantastic. Her only downfall is that she is naturally beautiful (long glossy blonde hair, stunning green eyes, tall and slim. Grrrr!). And young (21!). Apart from having to put up with her good looks and youth, I'm enjoying myself and I'm glad I came.

Next, she wanted to update Rosie and give her the whole truth.

I've got so much to tell!

Coming to Los Cuadrados was definitely the right thing for me. I hated it when I first got here, but after a few days I've started to enjoy it. It's so peaceful, the people are great and I'm learning loads. It's like a spiritual boot camp for the soul. I've also had some weird experiences. The other day I treated myself to a massage. When it was finished, I felt a strong, bright heat on the left side of my body as if the sun's intensity was magnifying through the glass window. I lay there for five minutes basking in its glorious warmth until it seemed the clouds must have covered the sun and it got chilly. When I opened my eyes, there was no window! Afterwards, the masseuse told me that I had a huge blockage in my back and stomach where the emotional chakra is located.

I meditated on it and realised that my biggest issue is an emotional blockage that is causing me to feel deeply sad and angry. The next step in my journey is to discover what the blockage is and how to heal it.

Tell me your news, I haven't heard from you in ages...

Just as she was about to open up an email from Riley, a message from The Bliss Expert pinged in so she clicked on that instead.

Well done on identifying some of the patterns you keep repeating in your life. Learn from what you've noticed and avoid intimate relations with men for now, especially of the Australian kind.

You're nearly ready to receive your first Step to Bliss that will help you find love, happiness and fulfilment. I'm glad you stayed at the retreat, you would have taken much longer to learn what you need to if you'd left.

There's one thing I want you to do before I send you the first Step to Bliss: be honest with more people than just Rosie. Perhaps you could start with Sophie? Let me know how you get on and good luck!

Cath felt like she'd been given a gold star by her teacher. She felt confident that she wouldn't be tempted to fall into the same trap with a guy from Australia because there weren't any at the retreat; the only Australian was a girl from Perth. She vowed to be aware of any opportunities to be honest that might present themselves because she was desperate to receive the first Step to Bliss. Before time ran out, she clicked on Riley's message.

I'VE PASSED!!! You can now call me Dr Bradbury!

Wha-hey - I'm made up!

I only found out in the post about an hour ago, and I've spent most of the morning telling everyone. Going out for a few bevvies with work mates, then out for one or two more after work. Can't remember being so happy since I met you.

And with the footie, at last, a win! It's only been five games, like! It was only Bournemouth, but it's still three points. The Chelsea and Man City games were amazing – proper good atmosphere at Anfield now (we won't mention the Palace defeat!). Going home for a week – will be full on seeing my mates. And the Reds are playing twice – proper crunch match against Bordeaux - and league match against Swansea (we should win).

I still haven't sorted out a date to come out to see you but you'll be the first to know when I have!

Cath pressed the reply button and sent him a huge kiss as her way of congratulating him.

After she'd finished emailing, Cath met Sophie in a bar next door. Five beers and lots of gossiping about the other people on the retreat later, Cath turned serious. 'Why are you here, Sophie?' When she got a blank look in response and no answer, she clarified: 'What I mean is, why are you travelling? Why are you at the retreat?'

'Ah, yer know, I'm after finding what to do with me life. Me sister married an eejit and has three wee ones. She cooks, cleans and looks after the babbies while he messes about. Jayzuz, that's not fer me,' she paused. 'So I left.' With this, she flicked out her long blonde hair as if she were in a shampoo advert. It should have been in slow motion. 'How about you?'

'Similar,' Cath was about to give her usual spiel about wanting to experience different cultures but stopped. The Bliss Expert had just asked her to be honest and she was about to lie. At least this was giving her an opportunity to be truthful and get nearer to receiving the Steps. 'It's because I don't like myself. I'm hoping the retreat will help me to understand why I'm so unhappy. And aggressive.'

'Aggressive?' Sophie leaned forward and attempted to put her chin on her fist but she missed and her chin nearly slammed into the table instead. With a second attempt and with more concentration, she managed it. 'Yer not aggressive. What eejit told you that?'

Cath shivered as she remembered the night in *The Casbar*, which seemed like a lifetime ago but was, in fact, only ten days earlier. She gulped hard. 'I nearly bottled a girl recently. I was very drunk and angry.' She stopped as her cheeks grew redder and redder.

Sophie sat back in surprise and nearly fell off her chair. 'Ah, would ya get outta here!'

'Luckily, I only pulled her hair but I dread to think what could have happened if she'd been more feisty.' Cath took a swig of beer and placed the cold bottle against a cheek in the hope it might calm the heat down. It didn't.

'Not only that, a few months before I flew to Mexico, one of my staff,' Cath swallowed hard, 'reported me for bullying. Fortunately, my boss sided with me so it never came to anything.' She sighed and took another swig of beer.

'Feck. I would never have believed it!' Sophie burped into her hand. 'Sorry, go on.'

Cath smiled at how uncouth someone so beautiful could be. 'The girl, Hayley, said I was aggressive, belittled her and intimidated her. I had no idea I was like that. Then,' Cath stopped for dramatic effect, 'it was something else that actually made me quit my job and book my plane ticket!'

'Feck off! There's more?' Sophie slurred as she downed the rest of her beer. 'Sounds like you need some luck of the Irish.'

'At about the same time that she reported me, a guy I was seeing, who I thought was The One, dumped me. On my birthday.'

'What a gobshite! Yer better off without him.'

'I know! But he was one of many. I never seem to be able to keep a bloke for more than a few weeks. Of course, it's always them who dump me. And the same has been happening out here as well. It's left me wondering what's wrong with me. Am I really that fat, ugly and boring? You don't need to answer that, by the way!'

Sophie shook her head and played with her perfect locks again, 'Don't be daft! Any fella would be lucky to have yer.'

'Thanks. But I need to leave men well alone for a while and focus on myself for a change.' As Cath looked down in self-reflection, she noticed the time. 'Oh no, if we don't hurry, we'll miss the last boat back.'

With this the two girls staggered to the port, giggling. They made it just in time.

After Cath said goodnight to Sophie, she swayed to the outside toilet for what she hoped would be the last visit of the night. On her way back, a guy she hadn't noticed at the retreat before said goodnight to her. She had no idea who he was but he had dark curly hair, which was just long enough to tuck behind his ears, bushy eyebrows and full lips. His t-shirt clung to his body, revealing a muscular yet slender frame. In the semi-darkness, she couldn't make out the colour of his eyes but, all in all, he could have just stepped out of the pages of a catalogue. He beamed a smile at Cath and she almost fainted. *Wow! He's hot.* She stumbled back to bed with a big grin on her face.

Chapter Twenty

At yoga, Cath spotted the handsome new man and tried not to stare too much, but it was difficult because her eyes were magnetically drawn to him.

Straight afterwards was breakfast, where Cath joined Sophie. 'Thanks once again for yesterday. I really appreciate your listening to me drone on.'

Sophie had a mouthful of porridge. 'All part of the service.' Specks of food landed on the table.

Cath giggled at her friend's uncouthness. 'There is someone I'd like to service!' She strained her head round to glance over to the kitchen where the new guy was deep in conversation with another of the retreat guests, Doug.

Sophie followed her gaze. 'Ah grand, yer've noticed Doug, finally.'

'Eh? What? No! I was looking at the new guy!' she said, snapping her head back before the boys could notice her staring.

Sophie leaned forward and whispered, 'Oh him. Yer know Doug's into you, don't yer?'

No! She turned around again and eyed Doug up and down. He had a ginger-tinged beard, blue eyes and a mop of thick sandy hair that looked like it needed a good wash. Cath had never been keen on facial hair on a man and he had sloping shoulders and needed to gain a few pounds to fill out his lean frame. She was about to check out the new guy when Doug glanced over. His smile was wide and warm. She spun round quickly. *Yikes! Maybe Sophie's right, he does like me.*

Bright red, Cath changed the subject from Doug. 'Who's the new guy? He's gorgeous!'

'Feck if I know! Not sure what yer see in him anyway. Doug's far hotter.' Sophie scooped more porridge into her mouth and used her sleeve to wipe droplets of cream slime from her chin, then rolled her eyes and shook her head. 'Thought yer were giving up men for a while?'

But before Cath had a chance to answer, Doug walked over to them.

'Hi, can I join you?'

'To be sure.' Sophie's face lit up as she gestured for him to sit next to her. Cath smiled but didn't say anything. She left Sophie to chat to Doug as she was clearly into him. Instead, she looked around the breakfast area and noticed the other girls on the retreat were slim, young and pretty. She felt a bundle of anger, jealousy and resentment.

Cath's self-confidence was still low by the time the spiritual awakening class started, so, in an attempt to make herself feel better, she positioned herself in the room to ensure she was sitting next to the new guy. Before long she found out his name was Gus and he was Australian. She nearly fell backwards! *How could The Bliss Expert know about Gus?* Whatever the answer, he was right to warn her off him because she would struggle to concentrate with him next to her.

After dividing into pairs, they were instructed to take it in turns to lie down while the other person noticed the sensations they felt at each chakra. Cath lay down first. At her heart chakra, even though his hands were at least a foot away from her body, Cath felt like Gus was caressing her left breast. *I wish!* She giggled. The more she knew she had to be serious, the more she had to stifle her laughter. Gus didn't seem to notice. 'Right, your heart chakra is hot but your throat chakra is cold. It's like a mad woman's breakfast down there.'

Cath laughed, assuming he was being funny and not rude.

Then they swapped places but all Cath could think about was Gus's dimpled chin, which reminded her of a young Kirk Douglas in Spartacus, a film she remembered watching with her family at Christmas time. Cath took a few deep breaths in an attempt to ignore her attraction to him and to concentrate on the task at hand. It seemed to work because, around his sacral chakra, she sensed an odd buzzing sensation, while around his solar plexus, it was so cold her hand almost froze. She told him what she'd felt.

After class, Cath agonised over asking Gus to go with her to the jetty. The voices inside her head were battling it out and driving her mad: *Don't ask him, stay away from him, he's too young and I must listen to The Bliss Expert. I promised to give up men for a while, remember?! But he's so gorgeous, what harm could it do asking him to join me? What have I got to lose?* She wished The Bliss Expert would hurry up and send her the First Step so she could start to understand herself more. Before her mind could stop her, her mouth opened. 'Fancy coming to the jetty?'

Gus looked at the ground and shook his head. 'Nah, got stuff to do.'

'Ok, no problem.' Cath wanted the ground to swallow her up. *Idiot! How could I be so stupid to think that someone as gorgeous as Gus would want to spend time with me?*

At the jetty, Cath had the wooden platform to herself so she took out her new book, *The Beach* by Alex Garland, and lost herself in a world of crazy adventures on a remote island in Thailand. It wasn't long before Cath's eyes felt heavy and she fell asleep.

As she came round she heard footsteps creaking on the wooden planks so she blinked in quick succession to get her eyes adjusted to the bright daylight to see who was there. It was Doug and he was squatting in front of her, which was disquieting, to say the least. He was just inches away from her face and staring at her with his baby blue eyes.

'Sorry, I didn't mean to startle you.' He sat down and crossed his legs.

She sat up and shifted back a little to create extra space between them. Then there was awkward silence before Cath broke it with a question. 'How did you find this morning's class?'

'Good, but I need more practise. What about you?' Doug stretched out his legs to the side of Cath.

'Yeah, the same.'

'Anyway,' Cath put her book into her bag, 'I should get going. I want to shower before meditation. See you later.' As she stood to gather her towel, she registered the disappointment on Doug's face. Even though she felt bad, she couldn't stay because there was a sick feeling rising up in her stomach for which she had no logical explanation.

'Okay.' He looked like he was going to get up but then he must have thought better of it and stayed put.

During meditation, after several attempts at clearing her conscious thoughts, Cath saw in her mind's eye two versions of herself. One was called Cath and she was a party girl who liked to pursue men and was over-confident, determined and independent. She became aggressive and cocksure when she drank alcohol. But there was another version called Catherine who was quiet, shy and preferred solitary pastimes like reading and meditating. She felt insecure around men and compared herself negatively to other girls.

That evening over dinner she announced to everyone that they were to call now her Catherine, not Cath, and she explained her vision. She told them how she wanted to explore being the nicer version of herself while she was on the retreat. Everyone laughed and cheered with pleasure that Cath – sorry Catherine – had gained so much from the meditation session. Gus, in particular, she noted, seemed amused.

Chapter Twenty-one

Cath rubbed her eyes and saw it was only six o'clock. *Damn it!* It was her one and only day of the week to have a lie in. By the time she'd remembered her decision to be Catherine, she reproached herself for the brash language and negativity. Catherine would be more polite and positive so she re-thought what Catherine would say: *Oh good, it's six o'clock; more time to make the most of the day.* She wasn't sure who she was trying to kid, so she turned over and fell back to sleep.

Coming around into consciousness later, Catherine saw it was now a respectable nine o'clock. *That's more like it!* She got dressed and knocked for Sophie. 'Ah Cath, I mean Catherine, I'm after finding meself some more sleep. But the boys are going to Panajachel. Hurry to the jetty and yer might catch them.'

'Are you okay, Soph?'

'I'm grand. Now, stop blathering and get outta here!'

'Well if you're going to be boring, I will.' Catherine laughed, ran back to her room, grabbed her purse and made it to the jetty as the boat was arriving. When she climbed on board, to her surprise, Gus sat next to her, 'How's Catherine this beaut of a morning?'

'Catherine is feeling very positive and upbeat, thank you, and she's looking forward to having granola and yoghurt for breakfast. Cath, on the other hand, is tired, wants some stodge and is looking forward to pancakes, whipped cream and maple syrup.'

'Awesome. So what are ya going to have?'

'Eh?' The boat's engine roared into life.

Gus had to shout as he was now in competition with the rhythmic growl of the boat's engine. 'Healthy or stodge?'

Catherine budged up as close as she could to Gus, cupped her hands around his ear and shouted into it, 'I should have the granola but I know I'll have the pancakes. I need to lose weight but not eating for a week on the fast should shift some of the excess pounds.'

Gus shook his head, 'Rack off! Ya don't need to lose weight. Fellas like a bit of meat on their women!'

'Only a six-foot gorgeous Adonis with a six-pack can say that!' The engine spluttered as it went down a gear and, with it, the growl softened to a low hum. Everyone within a three foot radius heard what she had said, including Doug.

After the pair's laughter had subsided, Gus cupped his hands around her ear again, 'Ta, but howd'ya know I've got a six pack?'

Prodding her index finger into his stomach, she said, 'I was feeling that instead of your chakras yesterday.'

'Ya ripper, that's what ya were doing? I reckoned ya stayed on the solar plexus for a bit too long.'

Catherine noticed that Doug was watching her and Gus banter with each other during the whole journey.

As the boat was pulling up to the jetty, Gus placed his arm around Catherine's waist, making her flinch momentarily. 'I reckon I gotta go to breakfast with ya, check ya eat heaps of pancakes.'

Catherine nodded. They were nearly off the jetty when Doug caught up with them, out of breath. 'Can I join you?'

No! But Gus answered before Catherine could think of a reason why he couldn't. 'No worries, mate.'

At the café, Catherine made sure she directed her eye contact and conversation to Gus. She wanted Doug to know he had gate-crashed their fun and ruined it. Her pancakes barely touched the sides as she wolfed them down quickly before disappearing to the internet café next door.

Catherine read through her emails, finding out about the latest news from her friends. There wasn't anything from Riley or her family but there was one from Rosie. Before she read it, she emailed The Bliss Expert about her decision to be called Catherine and her reasons for doing so. She also told him about being honest with Sophie but failed to mention how irresistible she was finding Gus. Then she opened the email from Rosie.

> *I'm glad to hear you're finally on the right path and you are doing what you set out to do on your travels. Just steer clear of men for now. Hopefully, the retreat will throw some light on everything for you. (Your experiences sound quite crazy!)*
>
> *Sorry for holding out on you but I didn't know how to break the news to you so I kept putting off replying to you. Terence and I got engaged. After eight years of being together, we felt it was time! Sorry you're going to miss out on the engagement party, it won't be the same without you. x*

The news hit Catherine hard. She couldn't be happier for them; Terence was a great guy and made Rosie happy, but it was a stark reminder that *she* was single and running around Central America chasing young Australian men. No sooner had she replied to Rosie to congratulate her on her news than an email from The Bliss Expert whizzed in.

Congratulations on being truthful with Sophie and on your awareness that there are both Cath and Catherine living inside of you. They are both signs that you are now ready for your First Step! This is the beginning of your real journey to help you discover who you truly are, why you keep repeating patterns that are not working for you, and how you can turn them around to find bliss. Remember my first email where I asked you if you wanted it all, including:

- *Being happy?*

- *Being in a long-term relationship with someone who loves and respects you as much as you do him?*

- *Having a close relationship with your family?*

- *Being fit, slim and healthy?*

- *Having a job you feel passionate about, and a career that fulfils you and earns you a lot of money?*

If you still want all these things, you must follow The Ten Steps to Bliss that I will send you as and when you are ready to receive them. Here is Step One.

STEP ONE TASK:

1. *From your perspective, what positive and negative characteristics would you attribute to your mum and dad?*

2. Write down a list of positive and negative characteristics you would attribute to Cath and Catherine.

3. Compare and contrast the lists from 1 and 2. What do you notice?

Good luck!

At last, the First Step! Catherine had been waiting for it for so long, she felt relieved to have received it, finally. She was puzzled by The Bliss Expert's questions yet intrigued too, so she printed them out in the hope that she would have time to work on them later. She put the print-out in her bag before heading to catch the next boat back to the retreat. As she was turning the corner, she nearly crashed into Doug. 'I'm hoping to get the next boat back, so I'm in a hurry.' She sped up as if to emphasise that she didn't want to wait for him.

Either Doug didn't notice or he didn't care and he matched her pace. 'I'm heading that way too!'

Catherine flashed him a false smile and carried on walking as fast as her short legs could take her. Doug tried to engage her in conversation but she wasn't in the mood for chatting, at least not with him, so there was silence all the way to the jetty. The boat journey back to San Marcos was a long and uncomfortable hour of more silence.

When they arrived back at San Marcos, Catherine dashed off, telling Doug she had something to get on with. He looked like a woeful puppy whose master had left him outside for the night. Catherine had to get away from him as she felt unnerved in his presence. And she wanted to get on with answering the questions from The Bliss Expert.

She reread the print-out several times. She couldn't understand why The Bliss Expert was asking her about her parents and their characteristics. However, she was so desperate for positive change in her life that she took a deep breath and began writing.

Dad +	Dad -	Mum +	Mum -
Determined	Stubborn	Caring	Passive
Sense of humour	Short fuse	Warm	Quiet
Independent	Selfish	Loving	Selfless
Intelligent	Detached	Kind	Self-critical

Cath +	Cath -	Catherine +	Catherine -
Independent	Aggressive	Thoughtful	Recluse
Strong-willed	Cold	Feminine	Needy
Intelligent	Selfish	Kind	Lacks confidence
Sense of humour	Arrogant	Warm	Self-critical

Catherine got a strange tingling feeling all the way down her spine. She stared at the lists and couldn't believe what she was seeing. There was no need to compare and contrast them; the similarities were obvious. She was her parents' traits. She felt exasperated that she couldn't dash back into town straight away to find out more from The Bliss Expert but it was too late to get into town and back before the last boat made its final journey of the night. She would have to wait.

At dinner, Catherine asked Sophie whether she thought she was anything like her parents.

'Ah Jayzuz, I hope not! I love me ma and da but I don't want to be like them!' She sucked up knotted strands of spaghetti, spraying tomato sauce onto her arm, the table and Catherine's plate.

'What about you, Gus? What do you think?'

'Soph's right. My old man's as mad as a meat axe.' He then stood up. 'I'm bushed, goodnight.'

Eh? What's going on? Why's he being like this? He didn't even glance in Catherine's direction, which was an about turn from his flirtatious behaviour on the boat earlier. Catherine fixated on the overly familiar term, 'Soph', he'd used, and her mind was overflowing with wild hypotheses: *Had Gus tried it on with Sophie last night but she'd rejected him? Was that why Sophie hadn't gone to Panajachel with them earlier? Had Gus only been friendly to me because he wanted it to get back to Sophie?* As she was about to ask Sophie for a private chat, Doug interrupted. 'You'd be surprised but parents have a big role to play in how we turn out.'

'Mmmm, well, I agree with Sophie and Gus.' She paused, 'I'm knackered so I'm off to bed too.'

With this, Catherine stormed back to her room. She was irritated with Gus's behaviour and curious to know what had happened between him and Sophie.

Chapter Twenty-two

In class, Gus and Catherine were paired together. The exercise required them to share something intimate about themselves. This time, Catherine wished she had been sitting next to anyone but Gus. Neither of them volunteered to go first.

Catherine sighed. 'Okay, I'll go.' She paused. 'I've got two sisters and when they turned eighteen, my dad took them to the pub. But when I turned eighteen, he didn't ask me to go. And he never has. I felt left out and that he didn't care about me.' Catherine's cheeks were on fire.

As part of the exercise, they were told not to comment on or give any advice on whatever the other person said. The listener's job was to simply listen. So Gus did exactly that.

Catherine took a deep breath. 'Now it's your turn.'

Gus didn't speak for a few seconds but then he started, 'Okay, I'll give it a burl. I reckon I like to get my own way and sook when I don't.'

'What's that mean?'

His eyes were fixed to the floor. 'Sulk.'

'Oh, like last night you mean?' Catherine shifted towards him. When his eyes still didn't engage with her, she knew she would have to probe him some more if she was going to get anything else from him. 'Why was that?'

'You left me like a shag on a rock in Pana. Then I saw you get the boat back with Doug. I felt like a right drongo.' He still didn't look at her.

Catherine's mind was doing somersaults. *How had I read the situation so wrongly?* She giggled.

'Rack off.'

Catherine stopped chuckling. 'I'm laughing because I thought *you* were ignoring *me*. And I thought you'd tried it on with Sophie!'

'Well, she *is* kinda hot.' A grin spread across his face and he gave Catherine eye contact at last.

She play-hit him. 'I know we're only supposed to share one secret but you know I like you, don't you? Not Doug. Definitely not Doug.' *Maybe this is what The Bliss Expert meant by being honest?* But deep down Catherine knew it wasn't because he'd tried to warn her off Gus.

'I do now!' He squeezed her shoulder and Catherine noted the power of his huge hands. 'Let's go for lunch after, just us.'

She hadn't expected this turn of events. She wanted to say yes but she also wanted to get to the internet to tell The Bliss Expert what she'd learnt and ask the questions in her head. If she didn't go after class, she wouldn't be able to go until the following day.

'Okay, where shall we go?' As the words flew out, she berated herself for being so easily swayed by male attention.

'How about San Pedro?'

Lunch was highly charged. Gus touched her knee at every opportunity and she stroked his leg in return. However, they had to remember they were in the middle of a busy café. 'I don't think taking things further here is appropriate!' Catherine declared.

'What are we still doing here then?' said Gus. With that, he grabbed her hand and led her to the jetty.

During the boat trip back, Catherine cuddled up to Gus and he held her protectively, which felt warm, loving and tender. On the walk back to Gus' room, they bumped into Sophie and Doug.

It was Sophie who spoke. 'Jayzuz, where have yer been? We're after finding yer for ages.'

Gus piped up. 'We had a bite to eat in San Pedro. The tucker was right but I had to put up with this dag.' He elbowed Catherine playfully.

'Oi!' Catherine pinched his arm back.

'Yer floozies. Now that we've found yer, come to the jetty with us, won't yer?' Sophie stared at Catherine, nodding to signal that she should go with them.

Catherine shook her head. 'Thanks, but we'll give it a miss. Have fun and see you at meditation.'

'Are yer sure now?' Sophie glared, her striking green eyes boring into Catherine like a power drill.

'Absolutely.'

Sophie shrugged her shoulders and put her arm through Doug's as they walked off together. After a few paces, Sophie turned her head to look back at Catherine. Sophie shook her head. Catherine felt like she'd been told off by the headmistress. Or Rosie.

The door had barely closed before Gus thrust his tongue onto Catherine's. Despite his over-eagerness, his action created a surge of desire so she positioned her hands underneath his t-shirt and explored his torso. Gus's skin was soft and smooth and he didn't have an ounce of fat on his body. His taut muscles felt hard beneath her tender touch. Catherine envied him his youthful skin and reminded herself to find out his age at some point. This question didn't linger for long before his tongue moved from her mouth and delved into the sensitive depths of her neck. She moaned with pleasure and ripped off his t-shirt while kissing and licking his neck and chest until she reached the waistband of his shorts. Hesitating momentarily, she knelt down and stared up at him with a mischievous smile, then unfastened his belt. Gus tugged down his own shorts and pants and a very large penis, standing to attention, almost smacked Catherine in the face as it sprang out. She tried not to giggle and instead focused on stroking his stiffness softly, toying with him until she sped up her rhythm with greater insistence. Using spit, she moistened her hand and the movement flowed even quicker. Gus placed his hands on Catherine's head and gently tried to move her face closer to the action. She shook her head, stopped moving her hand and tried to convey reprimand with her eyes. He looked so disappointed she almost felt sorry for him. 'I think that's enough for now.'

'Don't be a drongo,' he said and he placed his hands on her head again.

She stood up and stepped back leaving a perceptible gap between them. 'No, really.'

'What? Why?' Gus threw his hands up in frustration.

'If we go any further, we'll end up having sex and I'm not ready. Maybe we should join the others at the jetty.' She smiled, hoping it would cause him to smile too. It didn't.

'Nah, I reckon I'll stay here. Got stuff to finish up. Unless I can change your mind...' He sauntered up to her and grabbed her by her waist.

Catherine caressed his face. 'No, you do what you need

to do to and I'll see you later.'

On the walk back to her hut, Catherine felt uneasy. On the one hand, she knew she'd done the right thing by halting things with Gus, remembering The Bliss Expert's warnings about avoiding intimate relations with an Australian man. On the other hand, she felt guilty for leading him on and wondered if he'd still be interested in her. She wasn't sure which made her feel worse: not listening to The Bliss Expert and her intuition, or losing Gus's interest.

Chapter Twenty-three

The following morning Gus wasn't at breakfast so Catherine headed straight to Pana at the expense of going to the morning's class.

It seemed to take an eternity to arrive at the internet café and log on, but when she did, she quickly typed her answers to Step One, apologising for the delay due to lunch with Gus, and emailed them to The Bliss Expert. She read a few emails from friends and sent several replies before she saw a reply from The Bliss Expert. She promptly opened his message.

Well done on your insights with regards to your parents. It's a shame you allowed yourself to be distracted by Gus but continue with the Steps to Bliss and you'll understand why you focus your energy on men, why you can't stop yourself and fall into the same trap time and time again, and what you can do to stop it. Again.

Forgive yourself for this glitch and, instead, focus on the realisation that you are your parents' traits and know this is the first Step towards bliss.

STEP ONE EXPLAINED: MODEL PARENTS

The answer to your question, How is it possible that you are your parents' traits? is simple. Partly, your parents passed on their genes to you, but also your parents were the people who you were exposed to the most, certainly until you were four years old when you went to school, so they were your role models on how to behave. The good news is that, because many of the traits and behaviours you developed were created by observing your parents, not inherited from them, you can change them. In fact, you'll soon find out that Cath was an illusion you created to fit in and survive.

Catherine was bewildered and overflowing with questions. *How did observing my parents teach me how to behave? What does he mean about Cath being an illusion? How does he know so much about me?* Part of her wanted to stop this now before she got in too deep, but the other part was too intrigued to stop. Somehow he knew her inside out and could, potentially, help her beyond her wildest dreams. She had to read on.

STEP TWO TASK:

1. Who are you when you're totally alone?

2.

    a. How do you like others to see you?

    b. If you were trying to prove something to other people, what would it be?

3. How do you think these traits connect with your parents, Cath and Catherine?

Catherine wanted to reflect on the questions before she headed back to San Marcos so she printed off the task, sat at one of the tables, ordered a cola lite and began writing as the answers came to her.

1. *Who are you when you're totally alone?*

   Sensitive, serious, studious, silly, clumsy, soft, reflective, warm, kind, caring, thoughtful and inquisitive

2.

   a. *How do you like others to see you?*

   Confident, strong, outgoing, fun, sociable, determined, independent, quick-witted, energetic, carefree, competent, assertive and attractive

   b. *If you were trying to prove something, what would it be?*

   I'm the best, highly successful and intelligent

3. *How do you think these connect with your parents, Cath and Catherine?*

Catherine was not sure how to answer the last question. In Step One, the connection between Cath, Catherine and her parents was clear but Step Two was not as straightforward. She logged back onto the internet and sent her answers to The Bliss Expert hoping he would reply as quickly as he had earlier. She was delighted to see a message ping into her inbox a few seconds later.

Well done for completing Step Two so quickly. You are a keen student. It's amazing how much you can achieve when you're not allowing yourself to be distracted by a man! Here's what Step Two means.

STEP TWO EXPLAINED: BURIED BEAUTY

Step Two is about understanding that there are two parts that make up 'you':

1. Your Real Self.

This is who you were born to be before you were influenced by anyone and anything. Your real self is perfect, like a flawless diamond.

2. Your Ideal Self.

This is who you decided you wanted to be. From a very early age, you received explicit and implicit expectations from others who put unrealistic demands on you. You also got your first messages of non-acceptance and criticism. Of course, much of this was unintentional from your well-meaning parents, but it happened nonetheless. Even the word No, which your parents said to you to keep you safe, led to you receiving the message that you were wrong or not good enough. As a result, you learnt how to fit into your family environment and how to protect yourself by covering up your Real Self. Often, the only choice you think you have is to be like your mum or dad.

Your Ideal Self takes up a lot of time and energy to maintain and it can be exhausting. And it means that the core of the Real Self is so far hidden beneath the Ideal Self that the Real Self is lost. It is as if layers of dirt are covering a flawless diamond within and, eventually, only the dirt and not the brightness of the diamond can be seen because it is buried so deeply beneath.

This should help you answer the third question. In the meantime, I know you want to know who I am but you must trust that I am here to help you and that I only have your best interests at heart. What is important is that you listen to and learn from me. When you are ready, I will reveal who I am.

Catherine's mind was whirring with ideas so she hit the reply button and wrote down her thoughts as they came to her.

Okay, I won't dwell on who you are for the time being.

I think what you are saying is that I decided I couldn't be my Real Self in my family because I would not have survived. My dad was strict and had high expectations of me and I was the youngest of three sisters. If I had have been sensitive, warm, kind, caring, soft, thoughtful, reflective, et cetera, I would have been bullied. So I needed to adopt traits that helped me to fit in, survive and be accepted. As my mum's traits were too similar to my Real Self's, I needed to develop my dad's traits, which became my Ideal Self.

I'm guessing Cath is my Ideal Self while Catherine is my Real Self? And I need to get back to being Catherine?

Are you also saying the message I received as a child was that I had to be the best, and be successful and intelligent?

She pressed the 'send' button. If she had understood Step Two correctly, she felt sad that she had lost herself underneath a heap of stuff she'd picked up from her parents. What's more, it had taken twenty-eight years to discover it. However, before she had time to think about it in any depth, another email pinged through from The Bliss Expert.

In answer to your first question, Cath is your Ideal Self while Catherine is an interesting one. She is your Real Self but she is covered with many layers of 'dirt' that need dusting off. She has too many negative beliefs and judgements about herself - as well as unrealistic expectations - that are holding her back from being her Real Self. More on this later.

Yes, you did want to be the best, successful and most intelligent to prove yourself to your dad because this was the only way you thought you could fulfil his expectations of you. Your last question is indeed an excellent one. Follow the Steps I send you and you will find out how to find the real Catherine: your diamond within.

As Catherine pulled her eyes from the screen, she realised she was more like her mum than she had imagined, while Cath was like her dad. But it seemed The Bliss Expert was saying that both were illusions. It made sense why, most of the time and especially when men and alcohol were involved, she was Cath, yet when she was alone, she was Catherine. She guessed that neither personality made her happy because neither was her Real Self.

Catherine had never questioned why she had worked so hard at school and put so much pressure on herself to be the best and to succeed but now it made sense. It was to impress her dad. This sparked off a memory of when she'd got her GCSE results: three A's, three B's and three C's. Catherine had been so pleased when she'd seen her results and had phoned Rosie immediately to find out her grades. Rosie had passed all her exams and her parents were so proud of her they had given her a bottle of expensive perfume and taken her out for a celebratory lunch. But when Catherine had shown her results to her dad, he'd said, 'Make sure they're all A's next time.' His attitude towards her success had driven her to work tirelessly in order to live up to his high standards and to gain his attention. A flood of anger arose within as she finally understood what drove her to work so hard.

She had only fifteen minutes of time left on the internet so she swallowed back her tears and refocused on the email in front of her.

> *You need to take your time to get back to your Real Self because you've got twenty-eight years of 'dirt' to clean off first. Step Three will help you to understand your choice of partner and why this dominates your life so much. Eventually you will understand that your energies could be more usefully employed in other areas of your life, such as being happy. Good luck.*

STEP THREE TASK:

1. *List the last five men you've dated, and describe their characteristics in terms of how you perceived them in the relationship with you?*

2. *What happened in each of the relationships? What pattern do you notice?*

3. *How did each relationship make you feel when it ended?*

4. *How did your father make you feel when you were a child?*

5. *What conclusions can you draw from this?*

Catherine knew that answering these questions would take a while so she printed them out and logged off the internet. She rushed back to the port to catch the next boat back in time for meditation.

Catherine made it back with minutes to spare, and enjoyed the class. As usual, most people went to the restaurant next door for dinner afterwards. Gus sat next to Catherine but didn't say much, while Doug kept a watchful eye over them. She also noticed Sophie watching Doug. When she went to the toilet after supper, Sophie followed her.

When she caught up with her, Sophie threaded her arm through Catherine's as they walked to the outside toilet behind the restaurant. 'I'm after finding out what's going on with the two of yer?'

'We went to San Pedro, flirted over lunch and had a bit of a kiss after but that's it.'

They arrived at the wooden hut that housed a hole-in-the-ground toilet. Catherine went in first while Sophie guarded the door from the outside. Sophie continued with their conversation but raised her voice to be heard. 'What the feck are yer doing? Yer told me that yer were leaving men alone for a time. That's why I tried to get yer away from messing with Gus yesterday. Yer hurting Doug too.'

Catherine didn't answer while she used an old saucepan to gather water from the drum and pour it down the toilet. She tapped on the door to indicate she had finished and wanted to exit. 'Why does it bother you that I'm hurting Doug?'

Sophie shut the door behind her as she took her turn in the toilet. 'No reason.'

When Sophie re-emerged, Catherine handed her an antibacterial wipe from her bag and the girls cleansed their hands. 'I'm not intentionally hurting Doug; I can't help it if he fancies me.'

Sophie put her arm through Catherine's again and the girls walked slowly back to the main restaurant. 'I know but yer are cold to him, yer know.'

Catherine stopped. 'I can't help it! I feel so uncomfortable around him that I, I...' She couldn't put it into words. 'I just don't want to be around him or encourage him in any way. Oh, I can't explain it!'

Sophie pulled a face to imply she was confused. 'Jayzuz, yer weird.' Then, a change of subject. 'Tell me the crack between yer and Gus.'

'Not much to tell. I'm distracted with my personal journey at the moment so I'm not sure I want to take it any further now.' Catherine was not sure who was more surprised by what came out of her mouth, her or Sophie.

Sophie added, 'That's grand,' as they reached the table.

Catherine was tired so she said goodnight to everyone and walked back to her room. On her way, she heard someone run up behind her – it was Gus.

'Thought ya might like some company. And to finish what we started yesterday.'

'Gus, I've got some personal stuff I want to get on with. Maybe we could have some fun at the Toy Fiesta?'

He looked disappointed. 'No worries.'

She gave him a peck on the cheek and briskly walked back to her room feeling proud of herself. She needed to focus on herself for a change. She had let men dominate her life for too long.

Chapter Twenty-four

After a good night's sleep, Catherine sacrificed yoga so she could begin to understand her behaviour with men. She pulled the print-out from her bag and lay on her bed, ready to answer the questions.

1. List the last five men you've dated and describe their characteristics in terms of how you perceived them in the relationship with you?

   Brian was arrogant, selfish, detached and independent

   Riley is considerate, loving, strong-willed and passionate

   Jack was strong-willed, independent, self-centred and arrogant

   Erez was strong-willed, independent, unemotional, stubborn, and arrogant

   Gus is confident with glimpses of aloofness

Catherine's mouth was agape. She couldn't believe the emerging pattern. What she found the most disturbing was that she had never noticed that the men she went for all had similar characteristics. She wondered why she had not seen the similarities before and, more importantly, what it all meant.

2. What happened in each of the relationships? What pattern do you notice?

Brian finished out of the blue with me on my birthday. I wanted to know why he suddenly changed his mind about me and why he didn't want me.

Riley – who knows what will happen...

Jack rejected me. I wanted to know why he didn't want me.

Erez ignored me. I needed to know why he didn't want me.

Gus – who knows what will happen...

In all my relationships, I've chosen men who have finished with me out of the blue with no real explanation as to why. They left me wondering what was wrong with me.

Tears flowed down Catherine's face. It was nearly time for class but she was in too deep now, so she had to finish. She could catch up on what she'd missed from Sophie or Gus. As she was thinking this, there was a knock at the door. She opened it, surprised to see Doug.

'Hi,' she said, trying to avoid eye contact in the hope he wouldn't notice that she'd been crying.

'Hi, are you okay? We're worried about you. First, you left straight after dinner last night, then you missed yoga, and now class starts in five minutes and you're not there. Judging by your face, I'd say you're not okay.'

'I'm fine, honestly.' Instead of being irritated with him, she felt touched that he had gone out of his way to check on her. She pointed to the numerous sheets of paper strewn across her bed. 'I've got a lot on my mind at the moment. But now I've stopped, I'll come to class with you. Give me a couple of minutes.' She ran to the mirror and dabbed concealer under her eyes to cover up the redness, then she joined him outside.

After class and lunch, she rushed back to her room to finish answering the questions. She tried to remember where she'd got to. Oh yes, all the men she'd been with who didn't want her. While she'd been able to observe a pattern, she didn't understand where all of this was going.

3. How did each relationship make you feel when it ended?

With Brian, I felt frustrated that I didn't know why he'd finished with me. I felt unloveable, unattractive and undesirable.

With Jack, I felt frustrated that I didn't know why he'd finished with me. I felt unloveable, unattractive and undesirable.

With Erez, I felt frustrated that I didn't know why it ended. I felt unloveable, unattractive and undesirable.

4. How did your father make you feel when you were a child?

I felt unloved because he didn't show any emotion, which I interpreted as his not caring about me. I felt frustrated because I didn't know why he didn't care about me. I thought there must be something wrong with me.

5. What conclusions can you draw from this?

With men, I am replaying childhood patterns. I want a boyfriend because I need a man to love me in order to make me feel loved and wanted. But somehow, I attract men who don't want me. I also feel frustrated because I don't understand why they don't want to be with me, which leads me to believe there's something wrong with me.

It fell into place like a jigsaw. But there were a few things puzzling her. *How is it possible for me to be able to sniff out a man across a crowded room and know that he will replicate how my dad made me feel as a child? How could I know that, within a few weeks they would finish with me? Most of my 'boyfriends' seemed nice – albeit arrogant - when I first met them. How could I guarantee that each relationship would end up the same way and leave me feeling frustrated, unattractive and unloved?* She slammed her fist on the bed in frustration and felt pain simmering in the depths of her being.

During meditation, Catherine was supposed to focus on astrally-projecting herself onto another plane but her mind was on what she'd learnt in the first three Steps with The Bliss Expert. She had never considered how one's parents could influence their children so much. But it made total sense.

She was attracted to emotionally unavailable men because, growing up, she'd thought her dad was emotionally unavailable to her. This realisation made her angry. Catherine had resented her dad for not showing her any love or affection and, as a result, she had emotionally withdrawn from him too, which had led to a strained, distant relationship. But she had never appreciated that it was his lack of love and affection that was causing her current predicament of being constantly single.

After meditation, they visited the local village's Toy Fiesta, which for the group meant a celebratory meal and a few beers. For Catherine, it meant getting drunk. Apart from beating up an innocent pillow, this was the best way she knew to deal with the anger, hurt, confusion, frustration and pain.

With each and every drink, the exuberant Cath began engulfing the meek Catherine. Even though she didn't like who was emerging, she couldn't stop herself. And she didn't want to. She was on a mission to get drunk.

Cath became increasingly overconfident as the night drew on. She saw Gus walk to the toilets so she followed him. 'Wanna finish off where we left off after San Pedro?'

Gus didn't need to be asked twice. Grabbing her hand, he led her back to his room, where they kissed so passionately Cath could barely breathe. Gus tugged her bra up and over her breasts, massaging the smooth flesh roughly before replacing his fingertips with his tongue. The softness of his mouth, mixed with the wetness of his saliva, catapulted Cath to another level of enjoyment while he alternated between licking, flicking and sucking, which teased Cath into a frenzy. He plunged his hand beneath her knickers and was greeted with a moist welcome. 'Ya like that then?'

Cath used her hand to nudge Gus's head forward to reposition his lips onto her breasts, triggering an abandoned moan to slip out as her head fell back in delight. The pleasure was building up like a pressure cooker and she was going to blow if he didn't stop. Cath grabbed his hand, shook her head and smiled. She pulled off his top and pushed him onto the bed with more force than she'd intended.

'Ya like it rough, huh?' With this, he flipped Cath so he was on top of her. She rubbed the outside of his jeans, grinning that he was as turned on as she was. After fumbling with his belt, she found what she was looking for and grabbed his stiffness. This time it was his turn to groan. Cath massaged him up and down, varying the pressure of her grip, and hoping her skillful strokes wouldn't cause a premature explosion.

Gus grinned and used the full length of his body to stretch one of his arms to the bedside table. Opening the wooden drawer he pulled out a condom and held it up as if it was a trophy. Cath froze and Gus's smile evaporated as quickly as ice in boiling water.

'What now?'

'We should stop before this goes any further.' Even though she was drunk, the condom – and what it represented – had sobered her up.

He rolled his eyes. 'Not again! Why not give it a burl? Ya were up for it seconds ago.'

'I'm sorry. Cath wants to but Catherine's butting in. She likes you and doesn't want to get hurt.'

'Pig's arse! We're young and having fun. It'll be alright.'

'Exactly how young are you?'

'Rack off. What's *that* got to do with anything?'

His about turn in behaviour had wound Cath up. 'I think you're a lot younger than me. It matters to me.'

'Eighteen.'

'Oh.' The word hung in the air like a snake about to strike. 'I'm twenty-eight.'

'And...? You're a Pom, I'm an Aussie, it's not like this is going to be long-term. I reckon we should enjoy the moment. Cath wants to.'

'I thought you were different, but now I know you're the same as every other man in the world. All you want me for is one thing.' With this, she readjusted her clothes, turning away so he couldn't see the tears rolling down her face, then opened the door and slammed it shut behind her. In a flash, she had gone from feeling special and attractive to feeling cheap and undesirable. Cath's confidence had slipped away as quickly as the alcohol had slipped down her throat.

She rushed back to her room and slammed the door behind her. She threw herself onto her bed and felt so confused she couldn't decide if she was crying about Gus, Brian, Jack, Erez or her dad. Whoever, they were causing her a great deal of pain and she didn't know how much longer she could take it.

Chapter Twenty-five

While everyone else was in class, Catherine scurried to catch a boat to Pana. Just her and her hangover. She wolfed down pancakes, cream and maple syrup and then went to the internet café. She emailed The Bliss Expert with an update of what had happened with Gus and the work she'd done on Step Three, and then sent a few messages to friends while she waited for him to reply. It didn't take long before she saw a message fly in from The Bliss Expert. She expected to be reprimanded for her behaviour the previous night.

> I'm sorry that you're feeling sad and angry. I promise you that everything will make sense by the time you've finished all Ten Steps. It probably doesn't feel possible at the moment, but you will come through the other side feeling very different about a lot of things.
>
> Well done for the insights you gained in Step Three. You now understand why you keep attracting the 'wrong' type of guy. I will reveal the how when you're ready.
>
> **STEP THREE EXPLAINED: AUTOPILOT**
>
> As you've already noticed, in terms of your relationships with men, you are replaying patterns from your childhood.

Your father was brought up to believe that his role was to provide for his family's practical needs while it was your mother's role to be the nurturer. Like all little girls, they think they should be the centre of their father's universe: loved and cherished by him.

Of course, this is where it can be confusing. Because your father focused on putting food on the table and a roof over your head, you perceived his detached behaviour as meaning he didn't love you or care about you. (Oh, how wrong you were!) As a result, you tried everything in your power to get your father to notice you and love you – like working tirelessly to succeed. However, the truth is he always noticed you, loved you and was proud of you, but you couldn't see it (more on why later).

You tried to get him to love you and give you some attention but, in your eyes, you failed and this left you thinking you had done something wrong and he didn't want you. This caused an inordinate amount of pain, hurt and frustration.

This was the pattern you carried into adulthood. You are so desperate for love that you go for men who act out how you perceived your father when you were little, i.e. men who don't want you. They're easy to spot because they're quite clearly men who are not ready to settle down yet. You may find that, men who are interested in you and who are ready to settle down make you feel uncomfortable. Doug for instance? This is because it is not in your current experience for a man to want you. It is so alien that it creates discomfort and you feel you have to run away from it. Of course, none of this is the truth but it's what is. Until you learn how to change things, which is what I will show you how to do.

This is your pattern with men, as is the case with many other women. And what happened with Gus last night is yet another example of your pattern playing out.

Often, many people – yourself included – use so much energy in recreating these patterns from childhood that it is exhausting. It can even dominate your life. The good news is it is possible to change these patterns. And you will find out how by following all Ten Steps. Sometimes the realisation of what you have already learnt is enough to make a shift in your old patterns.

Catherine swallowed and stared at the screen. It was too much to take on board. It was incredible and fantastic yet it resonated on so many levels. There was more, so Catherine continued reading.

Before we continue, you need to decide whether you want your life to change. How much do you really want it to? On a scale of 1 – 10, how much do you want it to change? (1 being not bothered - 10 being more than anything.)

Catherine reflected upon how unhappy she had been in her life. She thought about all the times she had felt low and helpless. She had hated her jobs where she worked long hours, she had felt directionless and that her life had no meaning, and she had distanced herself from her family and felt separate from them. To top it off, she felt fat and ugly. It was time for change. She emailed The Bliss Expert and wrote *10/10*. Almost immediately, a reply flew in.

Good, in that case, you're ready for the next Step. If you'd have answered anything less than a 10, then you wouldn't put in the necessary effort required for the change you desire.

STEP FOUR TASK:

When Jack finished with you, you felt…?

When you're with Sophie, you feel…?

When you're with Rosie, you feel…?

Catherine was wondering where The Bliss Expert was going with this but answered anyway. She started typing.

When Jack finished with me, I felt… angry and hurt

When I'm with Sophie, I feel… insecure

When I'm with Rosie, I feel… like a naughty schoolgirl

Catherine pressed the send button and waited for a reply. When nothing came through, she checked the rest of her inbox and opened a message from Riley.

Not much news my end. Reds are in the knockout stage of the Europa League and we beat Swansea, thanks to a penalty from Milner, and get this - we beat Southampton 1-6 after being 1-0 down in the first minute! The hat-trick from Origi was superb.

John is still a dick.

PS Think I've got a new job so, with a month's notice, I could come out in January.

Her heart sank when she read this. She was in the middle of discovering who she really was and now he wanted to come out to see her. She didn't know what to do so she pressed the reply button in the hope that the right words would flow.

Great news about the new job. January could work but can I finish this retreat and see where I am before you book any flights? I'm not sure of my plans so wouldn't be able to tell

you where to fly in to! But when I do have a better idea, I'll
let you know.

Happy that she'd been nice without committing to anything, she checked her inbox and grinned when she saw an email from The Bliss Expert.

STEP FOUR EXPLAINED: RESPONSE-ABLE

Did you know that no-one can 'make you feel' anything. Jack cannot make you feel angry and hurt, Sophie cannot make you feel insecure, and Rosie cannot make you feel like a naughty schoolgirl. Unfortunately, the English language would make it seem that they can. But it is liter-ally not possible for one human being or a situation to create an emotion in another human being. If I laughed at you for having purple feet, it wouldn't provoke a reaction in you. However, if I laughed at you for being overweight, I'd make you feel bad about yourself, but only because you already feel sensitive about your weight.

What's actually happening is that one person is assign-ing responsibility for their emotions to someone else who, or something else that, is outside of their control. Put another way, the person is taking no responsibility for the way they react and act.

As a controversial but powerful example, think of a piece of white paper with a black shape drawn on it: an equilat-eral cross with four legs bent at ninety degrees. Show this to a young child and they might say, 'That picture reminds me of helicopter blades.' Hence their interpretation will cause little or no reaction.

Show this picture to an Israeli and they might say, 'It makes me feel sick,' because it is a Swastika and reminds them of the atrocities that were forced upon their Jewish grandparents. It might cause them to retaliate or seek revenge.

Show the picture to a member of a neo-Nazi group and they might say, 'It makes me feel proud and superior,' because, for them, it represents the symbol of a great leader. It might cause them to attack someone who is different to them.

Show it to someone who practises the Hindu religion and they might say, 'It makes me feel lucky,' because it's a sacred and auspicious symbol. It might cause them to apply for a job they might otherwise have ignored.

Ultimately, the picture of the shape in itself means nothing but it's how the perceiver interprets it that causes them to feel something (or not). As you will also see in Step Seven, how someone feels then creates their reality.

So if you are interested in creating a happier and more fulfilled life, you must accept this one fundamental fact: once you leave childhood, there will never be anyone who can make you feel better. Apart from you. The only way is to let go of the past, take responsibility for yourself, and focus on the here and now. The past is in the past anyway, so why hold onto it and allow it to affect the here and now?

The next time you hear yourself blaming someone or something else for the way you are feeling, stop and ask yourself the following:

- What is happening to cause you to feel that way? (More in Step Six)

- How are you choosing to perceive a person or situation that is making you feel that way? (More in Step Seven)

- *How could you choose to react differently in order to create a different outcome? (More in Step Nine)*

All of these insights can be applied to any relationship that you have with another human being – people you work with, your siblings, friends, as well as your lovers. Gus, for example, could be a good person for you to test this stuff out on. He'll be receptive to it if you talk to him honestly about things from your perspective. One day, you'll also have an opportunity to help Riley understand the challenges he's facing with his boss. But he might not be as open to hearing it. Remember it's his choice whether he listens to what you tell him. Not everyone is as ready as Gus to hear that they're responsible for how they feel and act.

What the?! Catherine was over-awed by the heavy duty information. *Is he saying I've got to speak to Gus?* Just the thought caused her cheeks to explode with heat. *I'm not ready! Besides, I wouldn't know what to say!* Catherine signed and wished she had a real live, breathing human being with whom she could talk to face-to-face about this Step. But the time she had left on the internet was running out so she printed off everything The Bliss Expert had sent, knowing that she needed to read this Step at least five more times.

On the way back through town towards the make-shift port, she was surprised to see Doug ahead. She was about to slow down so she wouldn't catch up with him but she stopped in her tracks. The Bliss Expert had said that men who wanted her made her feel uncomfortable. But he had also said that she was playing out a pattern from her child-hood and no-one could make her feel anything; it was a choice. So, she now had a choice about how to react to him liking her. In the cold light of day, there was no reason why she couldn't be friendly towards him. Before she had time to think about what she was doing, she increased her pace until she was right behind him. 'Boo!' She tapped him on the shoulder and wondered if he was shocked because she scared him or because she'd been frosty up until now. 'Are you getting the boat back?'

'Errr… yes. You?'

'Yes. If we hurry, we should make the next one, which is in about ten minutes.'

'Let's go then!' With that, they frog-marched down *Calle Santander* to the jetty and managed to catch the next boat just in time. Luckily it was a calm, warm day and so they were able to chat on the journey back without having to shout. Catherine found out that Doug had needed to send an urgent email so he had skipped class too. They then talked about their thoughts on the retreat, how hard they found yoga, and what they'd learnt so far. Then they got onto the subject of the UK.

'But do you think that the Welfare State is a good thing?' Catherine's hair was fluttering into her mouth every time she spoke so she tied it into a ponytail.

Doug watched every movement carefully as if she were performing a surgical procedure. 'Yeah, it's great up to a point. I mean, where else would you feel secure that, if something happened to your job or health, you'd be okay? But I think it's got limitations.'

'How so?' Catherine's neck was aching so she shifted her bottom around so she was facing him.

'It gives people a get-out clause for not taking responsibility for their lives. I find it frustrating when people blame everything but themselves for their unhappiness. They don't look at themselves and wonder if there's something they could do to make changes to their lives.'

Catherine couldn't believe her ears. It was as if he knew what The Bliss Expert had been explaining. Her eyes were wide with interest and she smiled, which encouraged him to continue talking.

'My aunt's unemployed and blames the government for her situation. But in reality, she was offered jobs and training but she didn't take the opportunities because she said she'd be worse off.'

'Oh,' was all Catherine could manage. She was in awe that Doug was verbalising what The Bliss Expert had just told her.

'I'm frustrated with her because she's intelligent and capable yet she chooses to blame the government rather than take responsibility for herself. She has now been unemployed for twenty years so she has made herself unemployable. She's full of so much anger and hate that she's a bitter, miserable person. Yet think where she could have been now if she'd taken one of the jobs! That's one reason why I'm here at the retreat, because I want to take responsibility for my life and be happy that I've made good choices.'

Catherine regretted not getting to know Doug sooner. 'I'm sorry I've been so distant; I've had my mind on other things.'

'Gus. Yes, I'd noticed.' Doug looked down as if he was embarrassed at what had shot out of his mouth before he'd had a chance to censor it.

'Well yes, other stuff too,' but Catherine was keen to move the conversation away from Gus. 'I've been learning about taking responsibility for my life and now we're having this conversation.'

Doug looked back at her. 'That's called synchronicity.'

Catherine was puzzled. 'What's that?'

'It's when you think about what you want and the Universe responds by ensuring you come into contact with the people or things that can help you in whatever it is you want. For instance, you may think about buying some flowers to freshen up your lounge when a friend arrives for lunch holding a bunch of flowers for you.'

Catherine shook her head remembering how the Polish girl had left her the Michael Crichton book at the exact time she needed it. 'That's amazing. I wanted someone to explain it to me in layman's terms, which you've just done, so thank you very much. I'm glad we bumped into each other.'

'Me too.' His smile engulfed his cheeks.

Catherine understood she could continue to allow her feelings to dictate how she responded to certain people and situations or she could choose how she responded. She didn't want to be like Doug's aunt. She felt positive that her life could be different, but she had to choose it. It occurred to her that he might be able to help her with something now, so she asked him.

'In the first year of University, I would pop to my parent's house for a weekend visit, but when I got there, no-one was in! Often, my dad was in the pub, my mum was out shopping, while Lou - my sister - was out with a friend. I'd wait in the house for a couple of hours, wondering why I'd bothered, as no-one seemed to care whether I was home or not. I guess in a misguided attempt at protecting myself, I withdrew from my family and stopped visiting except for major holidays like Easter and Christmas.'

Doug looked sad. 'Go on.'

Catherine couldn't look at Doug, as she was embarrassed by her feelings. 'I've been angry with my family for making me feel unwanted, unloved and like there's something wrong with me. Otherwise, surely they'd want to spend time with me?'

Doug tapped her on her knee to get her attention away from the floor. 'Well, that's your perception. But what do you need my help with?'

Catherine managed to look at him this time but her cheeks were on fire. 'I want to know how I change it? I understand the principle of taking responsibility for myself but I don't get how to change in reality. With my family.'

Doug lowered his tone. 'I don't mean to pry but I'm guessing you have a pattern of feeling unwanted, unloved, and like there's something wrong with you?'

Catherine wanted to dive into the water to cool down. 'How do you know?'

'Because you told me! But you'd assigned those feelings to your family rather than taking responsibility for yourself.'

She didn't know it was possible, but the heat in her cheeks reached a new high. 'Oh.'

'How did you choose to react when they finally came home?'

Catherine thought for a few seconds. 'I acted as if nothing was wrong.'

Doug raised his eyebrows. 'So they had no idea that you were upset?'

She shook her head. 'No.'

'How could you have reacted instead?'

'I could have told them that I was upset.'

'How might that have changed things?'

'I guess they'd have been more mindful the next time. And I wouldn't have had to withdraw from them, plus I wouldn't have felt bad about myself.'

Catherine paused while she absorbed the information. 'Wow, thank you Doug. You're good at this stuff.'

He looked like he'd just been crowned King. 'It's my pleasure. Glad I could help.'

By the time they reached San Marcos, Catherine had made up her mind to be honest with Gus. Just thinking about it caused her heart to pound so hard she could hear it. She had never opened up to a man before so she felt as nervous as if she were about to face a firing squad. She couldn't disregard everything she'd learnt from The Bliss Expert and Doug and continue to blame Gus for hurting her. That would end up with her either ignoring him or pretending everything was fine. Just as she had done with her family. And look where that had got her! The Bliss Expert was right; she had an opportunity to choose to react differently.

No sooner had she climbed out of the boat and onto the jetty than she saw Gus waiting for the boat. *Talk about synchronicity.* It was crunch time; she had to talk to him. Nerves sucked all the liquid from her mouth and transfered it to her palms.

Chapter Twenty-six

By the time she was standing face-to-face with Gus, Catherine was the colour of Santa Clause's jacket. 'Hi.'

Gus looked at the ground. 'Hey.'

Doug climbed out of the boat and must have sensed the tense atmosphere between Catherine and Gus. 'I've got stuff to do. See you later.'

Catherine took a deep breath and promised herself that she would speak the truth, no matter what. 'Can we talk? Or are you taking the boat?'

He continued concentrating on the area around his shoes. 'I was, but no worries, I can get the next one.'

'How about walking up the hill behind the retreat?' She tried to sound upbeat while her hand shook as she pointed in the general direction of her favourite walk. She subtly brushed her sweaty palms on the side of her shorts.

'Right.' He looked up and their eyes met. Catherine thought he looked sad.

She focussed on keeping her nerves in check. 'I'm sorry about last night.'

'Me too. I reckon there might be a Gus and Augustus inside of me too!'

Catherine was too fired up to banter. She needed to continue before she bottled out. 'I over-reacted.' She saw a clearing in the sun and sat down. Gus sat next to her. 'You know I've been pre-occupied over the last few days.' She paused. 'I've been reading up on some stuff and, in addition to realising that there are two me's, I've also found out I have a pattern of chasing men who don't want me.'

'But I wanted ya...'

'Please. Gus. Let me finish. You only wanted me for sex.'

'I reckoned ya were up for it too?'

'I was but...,' Catherine wasn't sure where this was going. 'I was scared that, once we'd gone all the way, you wouldn't want me anymore. And that would have really hurt. Whereas leaving off where we did at least allowed me to retain some dignity.'

Gus shook his head. 'You women are complicated!'

'I know! Now I'm saying it out loud, it doesn't make a lot of sense and it seems that no matter what I'd done last night, I would have proved myself right: men don't want me.' Catherine stopped and wondered if this had been the case with every man she'd met. Then she realised this hadn't been the point of their conversation. 'Usually, I'd have blamed you entirely for what happened last night yet I would have acted as if nothing was wrong. But I know I led you on and then backed off before we went too far. I'm sorry for the part I played in what happened.'

'Nah, pig's arse, it was *all* ya fault.' Silence hung between them until Gus broke it with laughter. 'Ripper, that was intense! Sorry for my part in it too. But where're you getting this stuff from? We've not covered it on the retreat.'

'You wouldn't believe me even if I told you. Come on,' she slapped his thigh, 'let's head back so you can get the next boat.'

'Right.' He started to follow Catherine but then stopped.

'Einstein's definition of insanity is doing the same thing and expecting a different outcome.' Then he continued walking.

Catherine turned round to face him. 'For an eighteen-year-old you're more mature than many of my friends!'

'Too right, grandma!'

They sauntered arm-in-arm back to the retreat and Catherine almost skipped; opening up to Gus had felt really good. It was the first time that she allowed herself to believe that The Bliss Expert could help her change her life. She wondered what he had in store for her next.

Chapter Twenty-seven

Brown on Tour

San Marcos: Day 105

I'm about halfway through the retreat and I'm blown away by what I'm learning on a physical, emotional, mental and spiritual level. We're studying some really cool (and whacky) stuff like lucid dreaming, astrology, numerology, systems from the Tree of Life, mantras, and the Tarot.

I've got one more week left before we start our seven-day fast and vow of silence, which I am a little intrigued about and a whole lot scared. Eek! I'm more concerned about the lack of talking than the lack of food!

Other than that, my days are filled with much the same routine of yoga, class and meditation. It's Saturday today, which means our 'day off' so a couple of friends from the retreat and I have come into Pana to use the internet. While I'm loving the retreat, I look forward to my weekly visits here as it means I can eat any food I desire and stock up on supplies.

Next, Catherine updated The Bliss Expert on her conversations with Doug and Gus and, while she was waiting for a response, she read and replied to various friends' emails. When a message pinged in from The Bliss Expert, she clicked on it immediately.

I am really pleased that you chose to react differently to Doug and as a result saw the beauty that resides in him.

Also, well done for having your first adult, honest conversation with a man, and for taking responsibility for yourself. I'm proud of you. Doesn't it feel good?!

Now let's move onto the next Step where you will start to look at the world very differently and see the beauty that lies within everyone, including Brian, Jack, Erez, Gus, Doug, your mum, dad and yourself.

STEP FIVE TASK:

What were your general perceptions of Mexico?

Catherine typed her reply:

It was loud, the locals were liars, unfriendly and wanted to rip me off all the time, and the weather was unpredictable. All in all, I didn't have a pleasant experience.

She pressed the send button. She only had to wait two minutes before another email from The Bliss Expert popped into her inbox, so she opened it.

STEP FIVE EXPLAINED: TUNNEL VISION

Did you know that there is no such thing as reality? There is only what your brain chooses to let you see and experience?

Every day your senses are exposed to millions of bits of information, yet only a fraction of these get through to your conscious mind. So there is a lot of information that goes missing between what goes in and what gets through for you to experience as reality. How this works is that the brain has a highly sophisticated filtering system that automatically sifts through the information and decides which data does and doesn't get through. Think about what an anorexic person 'sees' in the mirror. When they 'see' their grotesquely fat body staring back at them, is this the 'truth' when they weigh barely five stone?

Did you wonder why, as soon as you decided you wanted to buy your Mazda MX-5, you saw this model of car everywhere? Or, when you decided to give up smoking, why everyone seemed to smoke?

This is an example of your brain's filtering system at work. Once you consciously set your mind to something – rather like an internet search engine – your filtering system hunts those millions of bits of information for anything that matches and brings only those items into your conscious awareness. This filtering processing of information is what creates your reality. The Mazda MX-5s and smokers were always there, but your brain chose not to bring them to your attention because it deemed them unimportant. Then, when you identified them as being important, they were allowed through into your conscious awareness and you saw them everywhere.

In essence, we don't see the world as it is, we see it the way we think it is. Like with knowing you have a choice about how you react to certain people and situations (in Step Four), you also have a choice about how you perceive situations and how you interpret experiences. How you perceive and interpret an experience will cause you to feel a certain way and, as you will see in Step Seven, this will create your reality.

When you arrived in Mexico, your over-riding thought was that you'd made a huge mistake in going there. You felt scared and negative. You also had certain assumptions about Mexicans. Films like Once Upon a Time in Mexico led you to think that the locals would be dangerous and untrustworthy drug lords. It was not surprising that you experienced negativity in Mexico and with its people. The constant noise, the lying, the poor weather conditions and unfriendliness were because you were tuned into these experiences.

Essentially, your experiences in the outer world match your expectations, beliefs and assumptions in your inner world (more in Step Eight).

This blew Catherine's mind and she sat there for ages staring into space. As the screen went blank, it jolted her back to reality. She wanted to print off this Step so she could reread it until it made sense, which meant paying for another fifteen minutes of internet time. She logged on again and only just managed to print off the page before her time was up. Doug, Gus and Sophie were in the adjacent café so she wandered around there and joined in their conversation. 'What are you three conspiring about?'

Sophie swallowed her mouthful of sandwich before speaking and Catherine wondered who she was trying to impress. 'We're after finding out where everyone's off ta next.' She took another bite and chewed as she spoke. All is good in the world. Catherine giggled internally. Sophie continued, 'What're yer plans?'

'No idea. I'm flying home from Rio, but I don't know where I'm going next.' What about you guys?' She looked at Gus first.

'I'm going home as soon as the retreat's finished. I'm starting Uni in January.'

Catherine's face grew red. University was a long time

ago for her. Everyone turned their attention to Doug so Catherine realised that no-one had noticed, or cared.

'I'm flying to Colombia straight after the retreat finishes.' He turned to Gus. 'We could get the bus to Guatemala City together if you like?' Gus smiled as if silently agreeing while Catherine felt gloomy. Everyone else seemed to know their next steps except for her.

Catherine could see the remnants of Sophie's lunch clinging to her teeth as she spoke. 'Tanks for asking me, yer Eejits! If anyone's interested, I'm off te Mexico and maybe Cuba. What d'yer think of Mexico, Doug?' She focused her eyes firmly on him.

'It was great! Beautiful white sandy beaches, bustling cities, ancient ruins and everything in-between. The people are really friendly too. Shall I write a list for you?' Sophie seemed pleased and nodded excitedly while Doug turned his attention to Catherine. 'What did you think of Mexico?'

What?! How could Doug be asking the exact same question The Bliss Expert had just asked her. *Is it synchronicity again?* Catherine realised so much had been going through her mind that she hadn't answered. She wanted to be positive but didn't want to lie either. 'I loved Isla Murejes and would definitely recommend going there.' Doug frowned but didn't pursue his line of thought.

It was time to get the boat back to the retreat so the four friends headed to the jetty. Sophie and Gus paired off so Catherine approached Doug and threaded her arm though his. They strode down the cobbled street like they'd known each other for years. 'Did you really like Mexico *that* much?'

Catherine sensed Doug flex his muscles and hoped it wasn't for her benefit. 'Yeah. Why? Didn't you?'

'My experience was somewhat different to yours. I found it loud, the weather was erratic and the people either lied to me or ripped me off.'

All the way to the jetty, Doug told her a story about a wise old man who had been sitting outside the walls of a grand town when he was approached by a stranger: 'The stranger asked him what the people in the town were like. The old man asked the stranger how he had found the people in the town he had come from. The stranger said that they were mean-spirited, cruel, unfriendly and aggressive. The wise old man replied that the people in the grand town would also be like that. Not long after, the old man was disturbed by another stranger who also asked him what the people in the town were like. The wise old man asked the stranger the same question of how he had experienced people in the town he had come from and the stranger replied that they were compassionate, giving, friendly and warm. The wise old man told this stranger that the people in the grand town would also be like that.'

They arrived at the jetty and found an empty wooden bench while they waited for the next boat to San Marcos. Catherine remained silent while she thought about what Doug had told her. As she was processing it, she noticed Sophie watching them from an opposite bench with the same intensity with which Doug used to watch her and Gus.

'Earth to Catherine,' interrupted Doug.

'Sorry! But I'm not sure I understand.'

'What people think is directly reflected in their experience in the outer world. If you think something is going to go wrong, you'll be aware of the negative stuff around you. But if you think something is going to go well, you'll focus on the positive stuff.' He stopped for a moment to give Catherine time to absorb his words.

Catherine rubbed her chin to indicate she didn't understand it.

'Essentially, it's only possible to focus consciously on a small amount of what's going on around you at any one time. If you decide that everyone is mean and nasty, you will focus your attention on all the mean and nasty traits that exist in the people around you. But, if you decide that everyone is polite, kind and generous, you will focus on all the polite, kind and generous things that happen around you.

Doug continued, 'Remember what you told me about visiting home? You interpreted your family's absence as meaning they didn't care about you because it was in your mind to think that. But there could have been many other explanations, such as they wanted to get everything done so they could spend quality time with you. Perhaps they thought you'd get in later than you did. Perhaps they had stuff to do but it had nothing to do with how they felt about you.'

Catherine sat there in awe. *Not only does Doug have an amazing ability to explain difficult concepts in a clear and concise way but he's explaining something I'd been keen to know more about just an hour before. How might my experiences in Mexico have been different if I'd been thinking differently when I'd first arrived? I must have been really negative when I first arrived in Central America to have encountered so many negative experiences. And he's right about my family; there could have been other reasons for their absence.*

'Wow! How do you know all this stuff?'

The boat arrived so everyone pushed their way on board. There was no such thing as queuing in Central America.

Once they found themselves a seat, Doug continued. 'I did psychology at university and studied NLP too.'

'What's NLP?'

There was a pause while the engine roared into life. Once it had settled into a gentle growl, the boat bumped up and down in time with the waves, which were larger than usual. Doug had to shout to be heard. 'It stands for Neuro-Linguistic Programming. It began as a methodology which studies or 'models' the behaviours, attitudes, beliefs and skills of successful people so that the modellers can replicate the results and teach them to other people. It means that it's possible to be success in a fraction of the time it took the experts to learn how to. Now it has developed into being described as a 'user's manual' for the brain. One of its main principles is that human beings do not experience an absolute reality but only their perception of reality.'

Shivers ran up and down her spine. If she didn't know better, Doug was The Bliss Expert. He was explaining the exact same thing that she'd read just an hour ago. Doug interrupted her thoughts.

'It's a bit like what we were talking about earlier with Mexico and your parents. You weren't experiencing reality in Mexico or when you visited your parents but you were experiencing your version of reality based on the internal map you'd created.'

Catherine screwed up her nose. 'Internal map?'

'Essentially, as humans, we create an internal map of the world as a result of the way we filter and perceive information absorbed through our five senses from the world around us. Those filters are influenced by past experiences, beliefs, values, and attitudes, et cetera. It's the internal map that drives how we interpret and respond to situations and people in our lives.'

Doug was about to continue but swallowed hard as the boat flew over a huge wave. 'I might throw up.'

Catherine noticed that he was looking a pale shade of green but her head was bursting with so many questions that she forgot to ask if he was okay. *User manual for the brain? Internal maps? Not experiencing reality but our perception of it? It sounds like the film The Matrix!* Before she could question Doug further, she held onto the seat tightly as the boat smashed against another wave. It was going to be difficult to ensure that her delicious pancakes wouldn't see the light of day again

Chapter Twenty-eight

It was the final day of the week-long fast and silence. Catherine could not remember the last time she'd felt so alive, exhilarated and refreshed. It was as if someone had pressed her reset button. As she sashayed to the meeting point, she wondered what insights she might gain from the blindfolding experience. It wasn't until Sophie secured the blindfold around Catherine's head that she started to feel a little anxious. She checked that Sophie had secured the piece of cloth tightly enough that she couldn't cheat but not so tightly that the blood supply to her eyes would be cut off. While she was keen to learn from the experience of not seeing, she did not want it to be permanent. As Catherine struggled to put Sophie's blindfold on for her while she was blindfolded herself, she heard the sound of Za Za's chiming bells. It was the start of their 'blind' experience. Catherine decided to attempt to walk to the pier to sunbathe, partly because it was a beautiful day but also because she couldn't think what else to do. Her first few steps in complete darkness caused her to giggle when she remembered one of the items she had packed in her bag for the morning: a book.

Catherine visualised the route she'd taken many times over the past three weeks and took a few tentative steps, holding her hands out in front of her like an Egyptian mummy in a black and white horror movie. Then she felt her left foot jam up against a rock, and when she took another step forward, her right foot was elevated above her left. But the ground became soft, which wasn't what she had been expecting. She took another step forward and felt something prickly brush past her nose. Within two more moves, she was rammed up against the rough texture of what she assumed was a tree. She stopped and pondered her options. She could sense someone to her left and considered asking them to point her in the direction of the jetty when she stopped herself. *I'm not allowed to speak!* She stood there for a few moments, unsure of how to proceed. It had only taken her a few steps to become lost. Carefully taking a few paces back, she turned around and found solid, even ground again. She passed a post which she thought was the sign to the jetty, so she continued walking until she felt the creaking planks of wood beneath her feet. She had made it to the jetty. And she was still alive.

Not wanting drowning to be part of her experience, she was careful not to walk too far. She stripped off her dress to reveal her bikini underneath and fumbled about in her bag until she found her towel and shook it out onto the wooden slats. She lay down on it, pointed her face in the direction of the burning rays of the sun, and relaxed. It dawned on her that she didn't care what she looked like. Usually, she would be fretting about what people thought of her nearly-naked body. She would assume they were judging her for the odd proportions of her body. They might admire her upper half with her relatively slim stomach and semi-muscular arms but, as soon as they looked down, they'd see large, flabby thighs covered in cellulite. But right now, Catherine didn't care. Knowing that she couldn't see what she looked like somehow made her accept her body. For the first time in her life.

She also thought about how lucky she was to be able to see and how scary the world must be for those who cannot. She thanked her lucky stars that her 'blindness' was only temporary as she drifted into a peaceful slumber.

The loud sound of a horn awakened Catherine with a jolt. When she came round, she remembered the noise was a sign that the three hours were up and that she could take off her blindfold. She ripped it off and blinked in the bright sunshine whilst refocussing her eyes. She expected to be alone on the jetty but there were two western girls there. She didn't recognise them. They stared at her so Catherine smiled, shrugged her shoulders, put on her dress and sauntered back to the retreat. She floated back to her room in a cloud of euphoria. While she wanted to attribute her elation to the amazing things she'd learnt over the last few hours, she wondered whether it was because the fast was almost over.

At five o'clock she joined the others outside the main building. They smiled at each other, hugging whoever happened to be closest, and jumping up and down like goofy teenagers on the last day of school. The door to the meditation building opened and they nudged each other with anticipation because they knew that shortly they would be able to exercise their vocal cords for the first time in a week and, more importantly, they would be able to eat. The jubilant group sat down on the cushions that were placed in a circle surrounding Za Za. The excitement in the room was palpable as Za Za began to speak.

'Welcome all and everyone. And a special well done to those of you who are about to break your fast and vow of silence. We will shortly do some meditation to help you focus on your insights.'

Catherine looked around and noticed the two girls from the jetty earlier. She grinned at them in the hope of transmitting a careful mixture of sympathy and encouragement for what they were about to experience, if they chose to stay. She remembered how she had felt in their shoes a month before and wanted her eyes to be kind and her smile to be generous in order to communicate, 'Stay, you are about to embark on an incredible journey.' They both shifted nervously and looked towards the exit.

'For those of you who have joined us for the first time tonight,' she looked directly at the two new girls, 'my name is Za Za.'

Catherine peeked a sneaky look at the two girls and they looked like they were about to cry.

'Don't be afraid. You will learn a great deal and you will be able to teach others from your experiences here. After all, Los Cuadrados has two meanings: squares and beginning of a new direction to help guide seekers out of their confusion. Let us begin. We will meditate to get you into an open state and then you will share with the rest of the group how you are feeling right now in the present moment.' She closed her eyes and the group followed her lead.

Catherine drifted into nothingness. Every time a thought entered her head, she thanked it for being there and allowed it to float back to where it had come from. Unsure of how much time had passed, she stirred sometime later as Za Za tinged her tiny bells to signal the end of the meditation.

'Now it's time to share what you experienced during the session.'

Catherine reflected on how, a month earlier, she had tried not to laugh at what she had, back then, deemed to be ridiculous responses from people with over-inflated egos. This time, it was different. Catherine's interpretation of the responses and how she felt about them had done a one-hundred-and-eighty-degree turn. The Bliss Expert was right: the way we experience the world is based on the way we think.

Gus: 'I dig the free-flowing energy all around us.'

At this, one of the new girls' faces broke out into a smirk but she quickly covered it up by putting one of her hands in front of her mouth.

Sophie: 'I vibrate to the frequency of the world and I choose to join in the field of possibility.'

Doug: 'I am at one with the world and the world is at one with me.'

The other girl was now smiling. Catherine ignored her and spoke up. 'I feel serene in the knowledge that we're not alone.'

At this, the other girl elbowed her friend and the friend rolled her eyes in response. A month ago, Catherine would have been infuriated at someone doing this and would have been absorbed by negative emotions such as thinking about what she was going to do or say to get even. She felt proud of herself. She observed their behaviour and allowed it to wash over her like a shallow wave in the ocean. Instead of allowing them to affect her, she transmitted forgiveness and hoped they stayed to get as much out of the retreat as she had.

No sooner had the session finished than the euphoric group was outside in the fresh air, chattering like old ladies at a coffee morning. Sophie looped her arm in Catherine's and they merrily skipped to the restaurant next door, discussing their experiences from the previous week. To avoid the potential adverse effects of eating again, they had been advised to nibble on something light as their first meal to break the fast.

Sophie licked her lips. 'Feck, don't know about yer but I want pancakes and cream.'

Catherine joined her with the pretend lip-licking. 'You read my mind, but it's the chocolate cake I've been lusting after. And a cola lite.'

They ordered their food. Catherine leaned forward to engage Sophie in conversation. 'So, come on, how did you find it?'

Sophie sat back in her chair, chewing her nails. 'Jayzuz, the first few days were murder. I didn't mind the not talking but the not eating nearly finished me off! How about yer?'

'I felt really ill for the first few days but then I felt amazing. Like I could walk on water.'

The waiter brought over their order and Sophie placed her fingers to her lips. 'Shhh, be quiet, will yer? I want to savour this.'

Catherine bit into the cheese empanada. The soft and stringy tanginess of the cheese mixed with the hard yet flaky saltiness of the pastry set sirens off in her taste buds. A deliciously mouthwatering, savoury, lip-smacking sensory delight rippled throughout her body. Nothing had ever tasted this good. Then she took a sip of cola lite. The hit of cold, sugary bubbles sent her senses into sweet overload and she was transported to heaven. 'Oh my goodness!'

'Shhhhh,' was all Sophie could manage. Catherine understood the pleasure she was feeling and let her enjoy it in silence.

Catherine was about to attack the chocolate cake but realised she felt full to the brim and would most likely be sick if she continued. 'Damn, I'm going to have to stop.'

With a mouthful of food, Sophie rubbed her stomach. 'Know what yer mean. I'm stuffed.'

Catherine wrapped the cake in a napkin and asked for the bill. 'There's supposed to be a meteor shower tonight. Fancy going?'

'Fer sure!'

They paid, and headed to the jetty. When they got there, Doug and Gus were already there, lying on their sleeping bags and staring up at the stars.

'Alright boys, mind if we join you?'

'Of course not.' Doug shifted over to make room for one person. Catherine was about to sit down when Sophie beat her to it so she squeezed next to Gus instead and stared up into the black abyss, thinking about how sick she felt from overeating, when she saw a flash of light streak across the sky. 'I just saw one!'

'Good onya. I've seen ten already,' said Gus.

Catherine continued to scan the heavens and it was a matter of minutes before she saw another meteor streak across the sky, and then another, and another. Catherine's heart raced as lights blazed across the sky in quick succession. 'I've never seen anything like it!'

'It's awesome, isn't it?' Gus offered his arm to Catherine as a pillow, so she rested her head on his biceps. His aftershave smelt alluring and she was tempted to snuggle into him and fall into her old trap. But she had promised herself she wouldn't be tempted to go back to her old ways. So she stopped herself; she wanted to be Catherine, not Cath.

Eighty-seven shooting stars later, Catherine didn't feel sick anymore but she did feel exhausted, so she called it a night and went back to her room, alone. The following morning she was going to need all the strength and determination she had to jump off a ten-foot cliff with Doug.

Chapter Twenty-nine

Catherine was standing on the edge of a cliff wondering why she had agreed to jump ten-feet into freezing cold water.

It was as if Doug could read her mind. 'Apparently, it's legendary; locals do it as a display of bravery.'

Looking down into the deep green water below, Catherine's entire body was shaking. Then Doug began counting, 'One, two...'

Crap, crap, crap! 'I can't do it!' Catherine shouted as she took a step back.

'Yes you can. Remember, it's all in the mind. Don't let the fear overcome you. In the words of Susan Jefferson, "Feel the Fear and Do It Anyway."'

Catherine had no idea what he was talking about but she liked the saying and made a mental note to ask him about it when she was not frozen with fear. But she couldn't do the jump and took another step back to the safety of solid ground.

'I didn't think I was afraid of heights, but as soon as I took a step too close to the edge, I froze.' Catherine showed him her shaking hands.

'You wouldn't be human if you didn't. From your mind's perspective, you're about to hurt yourself if you jump. No amount of reassurance can tell your mind it's safe to step off the edge. That's why jumping is a rite of passage for the locals. It shows they've got balls! It's a great analogy for life. Most people get so scared by stuff they don't do it. It's easier not to. But if they want to change, they need to go beyond their comfort zone and "feel the fear and do it anyway." Great book, by the way.'

When he'd finished his rant, they noticed an officious-looking policeman walking up beside them. He said something to them in local dialect Spanish, which neither of them understood. Then he started pointing rather aggressively at the cliff edge. As she didn't need much of an excuse not to jump, Catherine started to put her clothes back on. Then, the policeman smiled, stripped off every item of clothing, including his pants, took a running jump and hurled himself into the abyss.

'Did that really just happen?' Catherine asked with her hand over her mouth, peering over the cliff edge.

'If it wasn't for the pile of clothes, I wouldn't believe it!' Doug also peered over the edge, waiting for the policeman to bob to the surface.

He finally came up for air and waved furiously at Catherine, beckoning her to join him.

'You have to jump now!' Doug grabbed Catherine's hand and, before she had time to think, they ran up to and over the edge. She screamed wildly as the next few seconds disappeared from her memory, and her body, followed by her mind, plunged into the depths of the bitterly cold water. As she floated to the surface, Catherine didn't think it was possible to feel any higher than she had over the last week, but accomplishing something she was so afraid of doing made her feel really proud of herself. Gasping for air, she shouted, 'I don't think I need to read that book, I think I get the message already!' while she furiously trod water to keep afloat.

After they climbed back to the top of the cliff to find their clothes, the policeman was waiting for them. Still naked, he proffered his hand to Catherine. She looked at Doug, unsure of what to do, then gave the policeman her hand – all while keeping her eyes firmly on his and not daring to let them wander downwards. When she and Doug were out of earshot, they burst out laughing.

On the walk back to the retreat, and after a long silence, Doug became serious. 'Please don't freak out on me, but why don't you come with me to Colombia?'

Catherine hesitated before answering. 'I would, but I've got three more countries to visit in Central America. If I came with you now it'd be because I'm scared to be on my own rather than because I want to go to Colombia. No offence! Besides, I've got to 'feel the fear and do it anyway,' right?'

'Okay. But I have a feeling we're going to travel together at some point so we must keep in touch.'

With that, they walked in a comfortable, happy silence back to the retreat in time to witness the solar eclipse. They joined everyone from the retreat, minus the two new girls, and huddled onto the jetty. Catherine sat next to Sophie and squeezed her hand in anticipation of the solar eclipse. Ever so slowly, the moon began sliding over the sun and, with it, the light gradually faded around them until they were in virtual darkness. Catherine wanted to remember this moment for the rest of her life: a group of like-minded people all high from the drug-like euphoric effects of the retreat mixed with love and appreciation for each other.

She stared into the darkness and asked the Universe silently where she should travel to next that would enable her to continue her journey of self-discovery.

Chapter Thirty

Catherine dashed around packing up her belong-ings. She wrote Za Za a thank you note, and then met the gang for their last breakfast together. She could barely eat because she felt so sad. She had felt connected in a way she'd never experienced before and she knew it was about to end. Plus, she still didn't know where she was going to next.

Departure time arrived and they boarded the boat for the last time together. Everyone was quiet. When they reached Pana, Catherine hugged Gus, Doug and Sophie goodbye and then she was alone. Although they had promised to email each other, she knew things would never be the same again. She held back the tears because it was fruit-less to cry about something over which she had no control. She didn't want to leave the cocoon of the retreat and be confronted with reality once again. The retreat had felt a safe place for her to be Catherine, while the outside world was scary.

To stall making a decision about where to go to next, Catherine went to her usual internet café, ordered a cola lite, and updated her blog.

Brown on Tour

Day 114: Panajachel, Guatemala

Well I survived the week-long fast and vow of silence. Actually, I more than survived it, I loved it but I'll get to that in a bit because it didn't start off this way.

The first day was hell and I didn't think I'd be able to do it. I stupidly ignored the retreat's advice to have something light and simple the night before we started and stuffed my face instead. I thought it might satisfy my soon-to-be-screaming hunger pangs. It didn't, and, in fact, it made things worse because after twelve hours of not eating, I was starving, irritable and moody. I wanted to eat something but I couldn't; I wanted to complain to someone that I wanted to eat but I couldn't do that either.

By the first night, my head was pounding so hard that I couldn't sleep and my body was aching so much it felt like I was coming down with flu. I reprimanded myself for not phasing out my daily caffeine hit and I wondered where I could get hold of a cola lite at four in the morning.

After three days, however, I no longer felt hungry, nor did I have a headache. Instead of feeling exhausted, sick and hungry, I felt strangely light and calm. I struggled with not being able to talk but I did it!

When I first started the retreat, I wasn't sure why we had to fast or be silent, but by the end of the seven days, I knew why. Firstly, I really appreciate how fortunate we are to live in a place where food and drink is readily available. Secondly, I understand how many times a day I obsess about food and how much time and energy it wastes. And thirdly, how much further time I waste on mindless gossip. I am hoping that I'll be able to remember these things and continue to be mindful of them.

I've now finished the retreat and am ready for the next instalment in my trip. I'm not actually sure where that is but I'll let you know when I do!

Catherine worried that she had been too truthful and that her friends might think she'd turned into a hippy, but The Bliss Expert had wanted her to be more honest with people other than just Rosie and Sophie and so she figured it was time she was.

Scanning her inbox, she saw she had lots of emails to wade through, but she wanted to read the one from The Bliss Expert first to find out if he had any guidance for the next part of her journey.

Well done for everything you've learnt so far. There is so much more you need to learn but, until that point, here are some further comments:

- *Well done for being more honest in your blog.*

- *There's a surprise coming your way, which is a consequence of your past actions (that I warned you about).*

- *Don't let your judgements get in the way of giving people a chance. They might surprise you and even help you.*

- *Christmas provides an opportunity to learn something huge about yourself.*

- *Travel with Doug when it feels right (but not yet).*

Good luck on the next part of your journey!

Eh? Catherine felt a knot of frustration. *Why can't he just tell me this stuff straight?* She printed the page out and continued with the rest of her messages. There was one each from Rosie, her mum, and Lou, and four from Riley, as well as a dozen or so from other friends. She read them all before clicking on Riley's emails in chronological order.

I've given my notice in and I'm made up! John is grovelling!

I start my new job on 18 January so I can come over for New Year and stay for just over two weeks. So... tell me where to fly into and I'll book a flight as soon as.

...

I assume you've not checked your emails!

I've had a look at a map and it looks like Honduras is the next country after Guatemala so I'll book a flight to there. I'll email you as soon as I've booked it to give you dates and times etc.

...

I've not heard back from you so I've booked a flight to San Pedro Sula, arriving on Monday 28 December at 3 p.m. local time and flying out of San José on Friday 15 January. Let me know.

...

You there?

Not sure what's going on. You have my flight details so, hopefully, I'll see you at the airport. If not, I'll travel on my own. No drama.

Only 5 days to go until I see you. Hopefully!

Catherine gulped. *What the...?! That's what The Bliss Expert was referring to.* He'd warned her not to use Riley to make her feel better about herself. His coming over was the consequence. Catherine visually ticked off one of The Bliss Expert's pieces of advice now that she knew what he had meant by it. Part of her was excited about Riley coming to see her but it was more because it gave her an objective for the next few weeks, rather than wanting to see him. The other part was concerned that she'd ruin all the work she had done on herself.

So so so sorry for not replying sooner. This is the first time I've checked my emails since last time I wrote to you. I can't believe you're actually coming out to see me! I guess I'll see you on December 28 at 3 p.m. then! I'll have a look at where we can go from there – probably a party place for New Year's Eve. See you soon!

After logging off, Catherine got out her guidebook to find a place she could go to until 28 December. After half an hour, she found it: a beach resort called Monterrico which was only a few hours away by bus, and was said to be the best of the Guatemala beaches. As she headed off to find the next shuttle bus, she wondered how long she could continue to be Catherine outside of the retreat, especially with Riley coming over. *Only one way to find out.* With that, she stepped onto the bus, and said a silent thank you and goodbye to Lake Atitlan while crossing her fingers tight that she'd be strong enough to stay focused on her journey.

Chapter Thirty-one

Catherine was sweating profusely and had an ache in her right ear. She scanned the bare wooden shack that was to be home for the next few days and her heart sank. *No way I want to spend Christmas here!* As she took a deep breath, a musty dampness invaded her nostrils and she felt sick. It smelled of dead bodies.

She gave up any hope of falling back to sleep so she succumbed to her body's early-rise rhythm, got up and took a painkiller, hoping it would pacify her earache. She walked to a deserted beach a few hundred yards from her wooden shack and stood there hoping the beauty would quash her negative thoughts. The glistening black sand stretched as far as the eye could see and footsteps imprinted into the volcanic granules zigzagged their way into the distance like train tracks. Motionless palm trees fringed one side of the beach while crashing waves pounded the other. A lone horse rider galloped across the beach kicking up grains of sand.

The sun beat down and was already burning the back of her neck; it was only six o'clock. As she attempted to do some yoga, the pain in her ear made it difficult to do many of the moves without aggravating it further. She also developed an equally painful ache in the pit of her stomach. Just the thought of the retreat made her want to cry. Only a couple of days before, she'd been surrounded by people who cared about her and who made her feel warm and loved, merely by their presence. Now, she felt empty and alone despite being in a picture-postcard location with gorgeous sunshine. She allowed the tears to flow, knowing the beach was still deserted.

Catherine wasn't sure how long she'd been on the beach but she was feeling hungry so she went back to the same rustic café she'd frequented the day before and had a slice of toast and jam. Next, she headed next door to an internet place as something to do. She wrote long emails to her mum and Rosie, trying to sound upbeat yet honest, then she read a message from Riley, which basically said he was relieved to have finally heard from her and that he was looking forward to seeing her. She was about to log off when an email pinged in from The Bliss Expert.

After a couple of days since leaving the retreat, I suspect you're feeling low by now. Sorry about that but it's an unfortunate side-effect of relying on getting love from external sources. What I want is to share with you how you can feel the way you did on the retreat all the time.

Perhaps working on the next Step will help. From now on, I will provide the explanation with questions to follow.

STEP SIX EXPLAINED: MIND INTO MATTER

As you saw in Step Five, the brain filters what information it lets through to the conscious mind, and influences what an individual experiences as 'reality.' But how does the brain know what to filter in and what to filter out? One answer is beliefs. But what are beliefs, and why are they important?

Beliefs are often said as statements of fact – 'I am fat,' 'I am intellectual,' 'I am good at drawing,' but they are actually just personal viewpoints which provide a set of rules by which we live our lives. They are created out of a need to organise and store experiences in a way that helps us to make sense of the world.

Most beliefs are formed between the ages of zero to seven, which means the beliefs will have been shaped by parents, siblings, teachers and peers, who have all inadvertently passed their beliefs and their versions of the truth onto the innocent child: you. These beliefs become hardwired into your own brain and become your 'truths.'

As it is bombarded with new information all the time, the brain needs to be able to process this data efficiently, so the brain compares new information to what it already knows. A belief is nothing more than a thought we keep on thinking.

What is particularly important for you to understand is that your beliefs are a self-fulfilling prophecy:

*Your **beliefs** cause you to **think** a certain way.*

*What you **think** determines how you **feel**.*

*How you **feel** determines what you **do** in terms of your behaviour.*

*What you **do** has a direct impact on what you **get** (your outcome).*

*What you **get** reinforces your **beliefs**.*

*Your **beliefs** impact what you **think**.*

*What you **think** impacts how you **feel,** and so on.*

*For example, if you **think** that men don't want you, that they'll leave you after a short period of time, you'll **feel*** *insecure. If you feel insecure, you'll be needy (**do**). If you are needy, many men will find that off-putting, so they will finish with you (**get**). And that reinforces your belief that men don't want you and that they'll leave you after a short while. And so it goes on.*

Does this sound familiar?

Oh yes! It certainly explained what happened between her and Brian, her and Jack and, most probably, between her and Erez.

While you will have many beliefs which are positive and will create conditions of success, you will also have beliefs that are limiting and will hold you back from success. And as beliefs are just thoughts you keep on thinking, you can change them. But more on that in the next Step.

STEP SIX TASK:

1. What beliefs do you have about:

- *Family?*

- *Men?*

- *Friends?*

- *Work?*

- *Body image?*

2. How do these beliefs play out in the belief cycle?

3. Which beliefs are positive (empowering), and which are holding you back (limiting)?

Wow! Catherine felt exhausted after simply reading them, let alone answering the questions. While she grasped the Sixth Step in principle, she wished that Doug were with her to help her understand what her beliefs were. Just as she was thinking this, and while she was waiting for the printer to finish off churning out Step Six, an email pinged through from Doug. She couldn't believe it. *Talk about coincidence.* She clicked on it to find that it was a short message.

I hope you managed to find somewhere fun and exotic to travel to. I also hope you're continuing to be Catherine as I know this was one of your concerns. As promised, here's my email address so we can keep in touch. I hope we do as I feel strongly that our paths will cross again.

By the way, Bogota is amazing so I would highly recommend you come here, even if it's not with me. I'm heading off to the coast in the next couple of days so let me know if you want to join me and I'll tell you where I am.

Catherine sent an equally short message back saying she would love to join him but, if she did, it would be mid to late January at the earliest. She then wandered to the beach and spent the rest of the day sunbathing, feeling slightly more upbeat.

In the evening, Catherine went to the café nearest to where she was staying. There was one other Westerner there but one glance at her told Catherine they wouldn't get on. She had mauve dreadlocks that were threaded through with brightly coloured beads, and she was wearing a floral tent skirt with a draw-string cotton blouse ensemble, which made her look like a middle-class hippy. Before Catherine had time to assess her further, the girl approached her.

'Hi, man. Fancy a bit of light-and-love company?'

Oh no, you have to be joking.

'Sure.' *What else can I say?* Before Catherine could utter another syllable, she had found out that the girl's name was Willow, she was from Brighton and she'd been travelling for six months in Central America. She had a boyfriend in Nicaragua but they were having a break.

Munching on her chips and trying to keep focused, Catherine asked Willow why she was having a break from her boyfriend. She then continued eating. By the time she'd stabbed the last chip, Willow had still not replied. Instead, she was staring penetratingly at Catherine.

'I'm pregnant, man.'

Catherine's jaw dropped open. 'Should I be congratulating you or commiserating with you?'

'It's light-fantastic in a spiritual fest way, man, but it's also, like, wow, this is heavy stuff, man. I'm freakin', deakin' out.' She propped her head up with both hands and sighed as her purple dreadlocks soaked up the vinaigrette on her plate. Catherine was going to tell her about her hair but Willow was staring so intently into Catherine's eyes that she was distracted by thoughts that were racing through her mind like a ticker-tape display.

For something to do, other than look at Willow, Catherine used her fork to play with the non-existent food on her plate. Then she had a better idea and ordered a beer. She was so used to ordering one for Sophie too that she was about to order one for Willow when she stopped, 'Sorry.'

'Hey man, no big deal, I only drink the natural, pure liquid provided by Mother Nature anyway.'

Catherine's beer arrived and she sipped on it, savouring every taste. 'Could you raise the baby with your boyfriend?'

'Hey man, he's a beautiful soul and I'll always love him on a transcendental level but living the rest of my physical existence with him, over here? Not possible, man. I'd have to go home. But living on pure love and light on the physical plane is a challenge and that's without a new soul to nurture too. I don't know, man. What do you think?' She buried her face in her hands and shook her head.

Catherine tried to buy herself some time while she figured out what Willow had just said but all she could focus on were Willow's dreadlocks still dowsing themselves in vinaigrette. 'I really don't know what to say. Could your parents help out?'

Willow looked up. 'The woman who bore me is a cog in the establishment wheel that I can no longer engage with.'

Catherine was getting frustrated with Willow's roundabout way of saying stuff. 'What do you mean?'

Willow smiled and looked directly at Catherine again. 'She'll disown me when she finds out her twenty-four year old daughter is pregnant by a guy from Nicaragua.'

Catherine noticed that she only spoke about her mum, so assumed her dad wasn't in the picture. She didn't want to probe too much for fear she wouldn't understand the answer anyway, so she drank the last sip of beer and held the bottle up to the waitress, giving a thumbs-up with her free hand. The message was understood and Catherine's empty beer bottle was promptly replaced by a full one.

Willow's mood etched up a notch. 'Let's dialogue about something else, man. Divulge something about yourself that no-one else knows.'

Catherine debated in her mind whether she should tell Willow about The Bliss Expert, and decided that she had nothing to lose. 'I have a mysterious stranger who sends me emails to help me on my journey. He gives me advice and encouragement as well as some Steps which promise to help me achieve happiness.'

Willow raised one eyebrow.

'Cool pyjamas! What are the Steps?'

Catherine rummaged in her bag and pulled out the piece of paper she'd printed off earlier and handed it to Willow. Catherine was relieved that there was a break in eye contact, but it didn't last long, Catherine wasn't the only fast reader in the café.

Willow was staring again. 'What are your thoughts on these words of wisdom?'

Catherine took another swig of her beer, averted eye contact and shrugged her shoulders.

'Want me to explain, man?'

This time it was Catherine's turn to stare. And almost choke on her drink. She wondered how it was possible that she'd managed to meet the only Westerner in the town who turns out to be a female version of Doug, after having wished Doug was here to help her earlier. *This must be synchronicity. Again!* She gulped down the rest of her drink to give herself time to process the confused thoughts whirring around her head. She smiled, concluding that it was time to celebrate because good things were still happening to her. She ordered another beer and hoped Willow would speak in less convoluted language. 'How do you know about this stuff?'

'The woman who bore me is a psychologist and practices CBT – Cognitive Behavioural Therapy. I've been exposed to it for years, man.'

Silence. For once, Willow wasn't looking at Catherine but was concentrating on reading the print-out again. She looked up and gazed intently into Catherine's eyes again. 'In essence, those who bring life into this world inflict their

beliefs onto their seed until said seed is old enough to realise they are establishment-led shackles.'

'If your mum's into all this stuff, won't she be supportive
of you?'

'No way, man. I've already disappointed her by turning
out the way I have.' She smiled. 'Good deflection, man.
Back to beliefs.' She prodded the piece of paper she was
holding in her other hand. 'While many beliefs can work
for us, there are many which restrict us like a cage.'

Willow told her a story about a bear who was set free
after years of captivity. He was transported to the wilder-
ness, where he could roam free for the rest of his life. But
when the cage door was opened, the bear stayed inside.

'He was so habituated to the restrictions he'd endured all
his life that when he was offered freedom, he chose to stay
behind bars. It was where he felt comfortable. Some beliefs
are like a cage for many people because they don't know
they exist. Or how to change them. But not me, man. That's
why I escaped the chains of convention.'

Catherine remembered the tiger she'd seen in Isla
Mujeres. She wondered if she'd been witness to mysterious
signs from the beginning of her journey, and she marveled at what else she might have missed along the way. She
didn't want to be like the bear, so she asked, 'But how do I
change my beliefs?'

'Step Six isn't about that, man. It's about finding out
your beliefs and understanding how they play out in your
luscious life.'

Catherine ran her fingers through her hair, located a
knot and tugged on it until it broke free. 'How do I find out
what they are?'

Willow picked up the print-out and scanned it. 'What beliefs did you develop as a child with your family?'

Catherine's positive mood vanished as her mind shut down, not wanting to reflect on her childhood. Thankfully, Willow must have sensed her uneasiness and interjected before her thoughts had time to develop.

'Okay, think of it this way, man. Describe your family. Think of something that stands out. Or the messages you received about how you should behave?'

The last sentence struck a chord and a lump formed in her throat. She watched the waitress walk elegantly towards their table from the bar, giving her time to process her feelings. And it helped her to avoid speaking, because doing so would have exposed her upset. After swallowing hard, the lump disappeared and she could talk. 'My family doesn't show emotion.'

'I sense that it's rubbed off on you too, man. No offence.'

Catherine's eyes welled up and she looked away, knowing she'd been caught.

Willow brushed Catherine's arm for an awkward, brief moment. 'What do you do with emotion, man?'

Catherine faced Willow again. 'I bury it as deep as it'll go. I don't do crying. As much as possible, at any rate. But...'

Willow interjected, 'Why not?'

Catherine felt her teeth grind together. 'Because it reveals vulnerability, weakness. It's safer to keep these feelings to yourself.' Catherine couldn't believe what had just come out of her mouth. It was like someone else was speaking for her.

Willow fired her next question. 'How does this play out for you as an adult?

'I keep everything bottled up until it leaks out as either aggression or tears.'

'Okay. There's your first belief. It's weak to show emotion. This makes you **think** that showing emotion exposes your vulnerability so you **feel** you have to hide your feelings. When you're upset or hurt, you **act** as if nothing's wrong. This means the other person assumes you're okay but what it means is that you **get** the impression they don't care about you. Because of that, you know you were right to keep your feelings to yourself.

Wow, Willow's good at this! This is exactly what Doug had said happened when I was at university and used to visit my family. And thank goodness she's speaking in normal sentences.

'Next,' Willow's upbeat voice made her sound like she was enjoying herself. She glanced at the sheet of paper again. 'Men? What themes do you notice with men?'

'That's easy.' Catherine was about to order another beer when she stopped. She wanted to stay sober; she might not see Willow again so she wanted her help while she had it. 'Men don't want me. They dump me after a short while.' She fumbled in her bag and found what she was looking for. 'Here, The Bliss Expert has already done this one for me.' She handed the piece of paper to Willow for her to read.

> *If you **think** that men don't want you, that they'll leave you after a short period of time, you **feel** insecure. If you feel insecure, you **act** needy. If you act needy, many men will find that off-putting, so will finish with you (**get**). And that reinforces your belief that men don't want you and that they'll leave you after a short while. And so it goes on.*

'Okay,' Willow frowned, picked up the print-out and scanned it for the next item on The Bliss Expert's list. 'Friends? How do friendships play out for you?'

'Rosie is my best friend. I tell her everything.'

'Even your feelings?'

Catherine nodded.

'So despite your 'it's weak to express emotion' belief, you have a clause which says that it's okay if you…?'

Catherine held up her hand to give herself space to think. She thought about the times she'd opened up to Rosie, and even to Sophie, and wondered why it was okay to do so. 'The belief stands but I can be open with friends. With girls I trust.'

'So you **think** it's safe to be open and honest about your feelings with female friends and so you **feel** safe to **act** and be yourself. Being yourself means you **get** others responding sensitively to your feelings and you get the impression that they care. You end up knowing you were right to be open, honest and yourself with friends.'

'You're really good at this, Willow.'

'Thanks, man. I'm quite enjoying it. It's taking my mind off my worries!' She scanned the print-out again. 'Next one: work. What themes do you notice with work?'

Catherine's mouth involuntarily turned up at the corners. 'Without meaning to sound big headed, I succeed at whatever I focus on.' She ignored the bullying incident at work because that was about venting aggression, not about her capacity for smashing every sales target given to her.

'What drives you, man?'

'To do my best. And I never give up until I succeed.' Catherine reflected back to what she'd learnt as a result of Step Two, about how she had worked tirelessly in order to get her dad's attention. To prove that she was good enough. 'Another belief is something like, "I must do my best to succeed and never give up."'

Willow cleared her hair away from her face and, as she did so, noticed that the ends of her dreadlocks were damp, so dabbed them furiously with a paper napkin. 'And what's the result?'

'I achieve success in what I put my energy into.' Catherine paused. 'But I also get stressed so I eat junk food and drink a lot to cope.'

Willow yawned and stretched her arms over her head. 'Sorry, man. Let's do the last one, then I need to rest my head on my pillow.'

'As long as you're sure? This is really useful.'

Willow nodded while she checked the last item on the list. 'Body image. Tell me about that.'

Catherine fidgeted in her chair and stroked her empty beer bottle. 'I get angry that I'm not a straight-up-and-down, size eight, six foot tall model.' Before Willow could ask her what her belief is, she continued. 'So my belief is, I must be stick thin.'

'In order to...?' Still dabbing away at her hair.

'Be good enough.' Catherine was stunned by what had shot out of her mouth. Her words were like a jack-in-a-box, surprising her when they popped out. 'I'd never thought of it that way.'

'And the result?'

'I beat myself up because, no matter how much I diet, I'm never going to be a Kate Moss. So I eat junk food to make myself feel better. And I put on weight.'

Catherine sighed, sank in her chair and let her arms hang. 'Wow!' She was relieved to have finished what felt like a mammoth task. 'Now *I'm* tired!' Willow nodded in agreement and signalled to the waitress for the bill. While they were waiting, Willow told Catherine she was heading to Antigua after a couple of days of chilling on the beach in Monterrico, and asked whether she would like to join her.

After having left Antigua under a dark cloud of shame, Catherine didn't want to go back but it would be better than staying in Monterrico by herself. 'Why not? Meet you here for breakfast?'

Catherine went to bed feeling happier than when she'd woken up that morning. She mentally ticked off another piece of advice from The Bliss Expert's list, feeling proud that she hadn't allowed her judgements to stop her talking to Willow. However, there was a sense of trepidation lurking in the darkness as she wondered if Step Six had poked a hibernating bear somewhere deep inside.

Chapter Thirty-two

Catherine felt a mixture of happiness and sadness when the bus pulled into the depot. The familiarity, the smell and the vibrant bustle of Antigua put a smile on her face, while the memories of what had happened between her and Erez created an ache in the pit of her stomach. As they walked through town, she hoped she wouldn't bump into the Méndez family, whose house she had left without so much as a goodbye.

'Come on, I know a hostel.' With that, Catherine led Willow to the hostel Anna and Fran had stayed in, assuming that, nearly five weeks later, there wouldn't be anyone there she knew.

She was right, as she didn't recognise a single person. Although she would have loved to have seen Anna and Fran again, especially to apologise for her disappearing act, it was good to start afresh with no-one knowing her baggage. Once they'd dumped their bags, the two girls went to the nearest internet café. Willow went to phone her boyfriend while Catherine checked her emails. After reading several from friends and sending a group email, she sent one to The Bliss Expert updating him on her friendship with Willow. Almost immediately, The Bliss Expert replied.

I'm glad you didn't allow Willow's 'hippy' appearance to put you off befriending her. I hope you're starting to understand that appearances, or rather your perception of appearances, can be deceptive. She has been a real help to you and you are fortunate to have met her. You may find that you will be of help to her too. Just don't allow her staring or long-winded waffle put your off; they're just two of her foibles. Everyone has them. Even you!

Catherine pulled her eyes from the screen and vowed to help Willow if she got the opportunity, even if it was only to listen and be there for her. She was surprised there wasn't more to the email but then she realised that she hadn't let him know about her beliefs so she emailed him a summary from the night before.

Thank you for your kind words. I will try to support Willow as and when I can. In the meantime, here are the beliefs she helped me to discover last night. She also helped me to put them into the context of the belief cycle.

Family: It's weak to cry and show emotion (limiting)

Men: Men don't want me (limiting)

Friends: I can be open with female friends (empowering)

Work: Do my best and never give up until I succeed (empowering and a little limiting when it causes me to be exhausted and stressed)

Body Image: I must be slim in order to be good enough (limiting).

Catherine pressed 'send' and tapped her fingers while she waited for a reply from The Bliss Expert. She didn't have to wait long.

Well done, you have correctly identified some of your beliefs and whether they are helping or hindering you.

Remember that because many beliefs are formed during childhood, they work perfectly for the person as a child. But as an adult, some beliefs are no longer fit-for-purpose and so they don't work. In fact, they cause us problems instead.

More often than not, when you are not getting what you want in certain areas of your life, there is likely to be a limiting belief causing it, which is lurking in the unconscious mind.

What you really want to know, of course, is how to change limiting beliefs. Here's how in the next Step:

STEP SEVEN EXPLAINED: CHANGING FORTUNES

The key to changing limiting beliefs is to become conscious of them. Once a belief is drawn out from the unconscious mind and into the conscious mind, you have the power to change it so the process of detecting your limiting beliefs can be very powerful.

The next step is to challenge them. Are they really true or did they just become so because of the self-fulfilling cycle? (The answer will be Yes because, in the words of Henry Ford, "Whether you think you can or you think you can't, you're right.")

The final step is to think of a new positive belief that will reverse the limiting belief. Then you need to act 'as if' you believe in this new belief, because changing the way you think will reverse the self-fulfilling cycle from vicious to virtuous. It works because it creates new neural pathways in your brain, which will replace the old ones when you've done it enough times.

The good news is that by being conscious of your limiting beliefs, you can change them. The not-so-good-news is that it takes a lot of consistent effort until the new positive belief becomes so habitual that it goes to the unconscious mind where it can be left on automatic pilot.

In Step Three, the reason I needed to hear you say that you wanted to change 10/10 was because it is going to take effort – consistent effort – to create the change you want. But if you are willing to put in the effort, you will reap huge rewards. (Although there is a short-cut to this process, which I'll share with you in the final Step). Here's a summary of how to change limiting beliefs:

- *Be aware of your beliefs and the effects they're having on your life. (You've already done this for five areas in your life.)*

- *For beliefs that are having a negative impact in your life or are preventing you from getting what you want, challenge them. Are they really the truth?*

- *Assuming they are not the truth, think of a new positive belief and act 'as if' it is true and it will become so.*

STEP SEVEN TASK:

1. Challenge the beliefs you no longer want. Look at them from an objective viewpoint: are they really the Truth? Or did you choose to believe them? (More on why you would have chosen to believe them in Step Eight).

2. What new positive and empowering beliefs could you have with:

- *Family?*

- *Men?*

- *Friends?*

- *Work?*

- *Body image?*

3. Act 'as if' it is true and it will become so.

As usual, Catherine needed time to absorb The Bliss Expert's information so she printed out the Steps, logged off, and bought a cola lite to take away. She walked to the park where she had arranged to meet Willow around the corner from the café. Willow wasn't there yet so she lay down on the grass, basking in the warmth of the sun, reread the print-out three times, then closed her eyes while she reflected on The Bliss Expert's questions.

First off, **it's weak to cry and show emotion**. *Is this true? No, it's just what I assumed from having observed my parents, who didn't show emotion. Or did I also make that up? Or was it what I chose to believe?* Catherine wasn't sure what was real and what wasn't anymore! She couldn't answer that one right now but what she could do was create a new belief.

Something like: 'It's healthy to express emotion and cry as well as to be open and honest about my feelings'. Catherine realised she had already had one experience of being open and honest with Gus as she recollected their conversation. She had felt really positive afterwards, as opposed to resenting him like she had Jack.

Next, men. *Is it true that men didn't want me? No, of course not! It is true that the men I've chosen to pursue didn't want a long-term relationship with me, but now I understand why. There have been plenty of men like Doug who do like me and would have a long-term relationship with me but I chose to reject them as 'too nice' instead of giving them a chance. If I'd given them a chance, I would have proven my belief wrong.*

So a new belief is: 'Men do want me.'

Friends. Catherine decided she didn't want to change this belief because it worked perfectly well for her. If anything, she could be more open and honest with everyone.

Work. Catherine decided this rule only needed a slight tweak because she liked that she did her best and succeeded at work. She liked her dogged determination. But what she didn't like was the stress and exhaustion.

So a new belief for work could be: 'Be the best that I can be but stop if it affects my health.' She felt pleased with this and moved onto the last one.

Body image. *Is it true that I have to be slim to be good enough? No, of course not! It's the person inside who counts.* But she argued with herself. *It's a difficult belief to shift when I'm bombarded by thousands of images of slim, stunning women on television, in newspapers and in magazine images. It puts a certain level of expectation on women. On me.* She wondered whether men ever felt such pressure.

A new belief could be something like, 'As long as I am true to myself, I am good enough.'

Satisfied that she had finished that latest task, it wasn't long before she drifted off, dreaming of being a slim and beautiful version of herself while surrounded by hundreds of gorgeous men vying for her attention. A wide smile spread across Catherine's face.

Chapter Thirty-three

When Catherine started to come round, she was still wearing a broad smile until she remembered where she was. Her grin turned into a grimace when her face felt burnt and sore to touch. She wondered how long she'd been asleep and exposed to the powerful sun's rays. She sat up and carefully opened her eyes, hoping the sun hadn't welded them together. It hadn't, but her eyes were sensitive to the sunlight so she used her hands to shield them. She noticed that Willow was lying next to her, reading *The Celestine Prophecy*.

'How long have I been out of it?' She sipped her cola lite and spat it out. It was warm and flat.

'A beautiful hour, man.'

'Does my face look as bad as it feels?' She placed her fingers over it to assess the damage. 'Ow!'

'Yeah, man. I've got some Aloe Vera cream in the room that'll give it some loving.' Willow passed Catherine an unopened bottle of water and she gulped it down greedily, realising how dehydrated she was.

'Thanks, I needed that.' Catherine paused and handed Willow the print-out of Step Eight. 'What do you make of this?'

Willow read it quickly. 'Light-fantastic!' Then stared at Catherine. 'How do you feel about the man who fathered you?'

Not what I was expecting! How weird. 'Why are you asking me about my dad?'

'Because every woman on this earthly plane was created from a male seed.'

Catherine was curious where this was going and she also saw an opportunity to find out what had happened to Willow's dad. 'You've only ever mentioned your mum. Where's your dad? If you don't mind me asking?'

Willow looked up to the sky and put her hands together as if she were praying. 'He floated away when I was five.'

'Oh Willow, I'm so sorry.' But she couldn't just leave it there. 'How did he die?'

Willow shook her head. 'He didn't. He left us. Maybe that's where I inherited my free-spirit and nomadic nature from. We never saw or heard from him again, man.'

Now it made sense why Willow never talked about him. Catherine considered how she felt about her dad. 'Angry. It's turning out that he's the cause of my unhappiness.'

Willow shaded her eyes with her hand. 'What beliefs might be causing you to feel angry, man?'

Catherine sat in the heat, blinking into the distance, pondering the question. 'I believe my dad doesn't care about me because he's emotionally detached.'

Willow switched hands to cover her eyes from the glare of the sun. 'Wow, man. And how might these beliefs be causing your reality?'

Catherine opened her mouth before she had time to think properly. 'If I feel that he doesn't care about me, it makes me feel bad and so I detach myself from him emotionally, which means that he emotionally withdraws further from me. And I get to be right! He's emotionally detached and doesn't care about me.' She threw her hands up in the air as if the penny had dropped.

Willow looked at the print-out. 'What could you think differently?'

'That he does care about me. This will make me feel better, which will make me act more compassionately towards him, which will draw him closer to me and, as a result, he will become emotionally closer to me. I get to be right.' Catherine paused. 'It sounds like your mum taught you well!'

Willow simply stared at Catherine with a neutral expression.

'Come on, I can't sit in this sunshine anymore or else my face is gonna burn to a crisp. Can we go back to the room while you tell me how your conversation went with your boyfriend?'

Willow followed Catherine's lead and stood up. 'We're no longer linked in loving union.'

Assuming she meant Willow had finished with him, Catherine pulled a sad face but winced in pain as she did so. 'You okay? What happened?'

Willow talked to the ground. 'Not really, man, but it's best for the love and light of the Universe.' Then she looked up and burst into tears.

Catherine's immediate reaction was to suggest going for a drink, but she needed to act as if she believed her new belief: 'It's healthy to express emotion and cry.' So, even though it felt alien, Catherine held out her arms. To her surprise, Willow fell into them and trembled gently as her tears flowed freely. Catherine wrapped her arms around

Willow and, to her surprise, it felt good: they were sharing an intimate moment and Catherine was honoured to be a part of it.

When Willow's tears subsided, she pulled away and wiped her eyes with her sleeve. 'Thanks man, that was emotional.' She placed her arm through Catherine's and they walked the rest of the way in silence. It wasn't long before they were back at their room, where Willow dug into her backpack and produced a tube. 'Here man, smooth this gently onto your face.'

'Thanks.' Catherine used the mirror above the sink, wincing with every touch as she dabbed the cream onto her face. 'What are you going to do about, you know, the pregnancy?'

Willow laid on her bed and placed her hands beneath her head. 'That insight is yet to manifest. Can we not talk about this now, I'm tired?'

Catherine smiled as she screwed the lid back onto the Aloe Vera cream and handed it back to Willow. 'Sure. Thanks. I'll leave you in peace and go check my emails.' And she left her friend to sleep. Or cry. Or both.

Catherine emailed The Bliss Expert with a summary of the work she had done in the park and awaited a response. It wasn't long before she saw a message ping in from him.

Well done, Catherine, you have been working hard! Your task is now to continue acting as if your new beliefs are true. Then I will send you the next Step. In the meantime, persevere with Willow. She needs your help and you'll be pivotal to her making a decision about what she is going to do next. Remember, it's all very well understanding what I'm teaching you on an intellectual level but it's a whole other ball game putting it into practice. Willow may need reminding of this!

As she wanted to give Willow more time on her own, she went to *Mickey's* for old time's sake. Catherine smiled when the waitress greeted her like an old friend and asked if she wanted a bottle of beer or a cola lite. She chose the latter, found an empty table in the corner away from the television screen, and watched the world go by.

It was dark by the time Catherine headed back to the room to find Willow reading *The Road Less Travelled*. She lay down on her bed and propped herself up with a pillow. 'You okay?'

Willow nodded.

'What's going on in that head of yours?' Catherine rolled over so she was facing Willow, no longer fearful of her unwavering stare.

Willow put her book face down on the bed. 'I'm feeling the opposite of my inspired, creative and conscious-living self.'

'How so?'

'I don't want to bring a new soul into this world but I can't manipulate the natural order of events. And I can't go home.'

'Why not?' Catherine was starting to get the hang of Willow-speak but wished she could speak as plainly as she had when she was helping her with the Steps.

Willow waved her hands from side-to-side over her head as if she were in a school play, pretending to be a tree swaying in the wind. 'I am free spirit wandering the Earth, a light worker passionate about birthing our new civilisation by vibrating at a higher frequency. I can't live with my mother; my light would be slowly starved of oxygen and I'd suffocate.'

Catherine was confused. 'What do you think will happen?'

She stopped swaying and slammed her hands onto the bed. 'She'll re-register me at medical school before my plane has landed back in the UK.'

Catherine sat up abruptly. 'What?! Back up there, you went to medical school?'

'Yeah, man. I was studying to be a doctor but I wanted to heal peoples' spirits, not their bodies. So I quit, changed my name, got myself a job in a New Age café, got my hair dreaded and dressed how I wanted to for the first time in my life. Mother said I was throwing my life away so I flew out here to escape. The rest you know.'

'So you assume your mum's going to dictate how you should live your life if you go home.'

Willow looked like she was about to cry again. 'Yeah, man. As long as I do what she wants me to do, I'll be hunky-dory. But, for me, it'll be like floating into a dark abyss of doom.'

Catherine thought about what The Bliss Expert had said about challenging beliefs to find out if they are really true. Maybe Willow had chosen to believe her mum was controlling. 'Perhaps you're making assumptions about your mum or you're misjudging her?'

Willow shook her head fervently. 'No way, man. Remember that cage I told you about? I'd be the bear. Trapped forever.'

Catherine let it slide for now. Maybe now wasn't the right time to talk about this but there was one thing she still wanted to know: 'What was your name before you changed it?'

'Hortense.' She shook her head. 'Courtesy of my conventional mother. No guessing what I was called at school. It was fierce, man.'

Catherine gave a sympathetic smile. *Poor thing, having 'whore' as a nickname must have been harsh.*

'What's worse is that my surname is Harrington-Hythe.' She shook her head again.

Catherine swallowed to contain the giggle bubbling up inside her.

'Hey man, can we leave it for now? Please?' Willow rolled over and pulled the sheet over her body. 'I'm tired.'

Catherine was tired too, but she was buzzing from having understood one of the Steps by herself. Even though Willow wasn't willing to listen, Catherine was proud that she'd tried to help her. It felt good to do something for someone else for a change. Despite the exhilaration, there was a nagging sense of sadness deep inside her gut. It was Christmas Eve the following day and she had the same feeling of dread every Christmas. She had assumed that, because she wasn't at home, it wouldn't surface this year. She was wrong. She wondered if her feelings were connected to The Bliss Expert's prophecy about her learning something huge at Christmas. If he was right like he had been several times before, she had no idea what it could be.

Chapter Thirty-four

Brown on Tour

Day 122: Antigua, Guatemala

Merry Christmas everyone! I hope you're opening your presents or stuffing your faces with a yummy cooked breakfast and Buck's Fizz to wash it down.

Save a thought for me as my breakfast was bread smothered in chocolate spread and washed down with water! And I didn't have any presents to open. Still, a group of us at the hostel are having a barbeque later so it's not all bad. Although, I'm not sure what I'm going to eat on a barbeque. Several corn on the cobs I suspect!

As you can see, I'm back in Antigua. I did go to a beautiful beach resort on the Pacific coast after the retreat for a couple of days but the sea had such strong rip tides that I couldn't enjoy it to cool off in the scorching heat. I was also a little bored. However, I'm glad I popped there because I met a cool girl called Willow who I'm now sharing a room with in Antigua.

Have a great time today everyone and think of me in thirty degree heat, partying with twenty strangers!

Catherine signed off and slumped back in her chair. Even though she knew she wasn't being honest in her blog, she had made a conscious decision to write an upbeat blog because she didn't want to bring everyone else down on such a special day. Despite not understanding why, the only thing that she could think of to do that might make her feel happier was phoning her family.

Dialling the number, Catherine expected to have a short phone call, partly due to the expense, but also because they were a family of few words. What she hadn't anticipated was that, within seconds of dialling the number, a lump would develop in her throat. In that instant, her nagging sense of sadness became clear. She missed her family and ached to be with them. She would give anything to be sitting at the dinner table, joining in with the banter, feasting on turkey and slowly getting sloshed with them. Thinking about the barbeque meal that Catherine had to look forward to with a bunch of relative strangers made her feel very alone.

Even worse was that she had created this distance. As a child, she had felt rejected, lonely and unloved by the very people who should make her feel wanted, connected and loved. So Catherine's way of dealing with the hurt this caused her was to detach herself emotionally from her family, which she had done with even more success this year by putting six thousand physical miles between them. But the only result of detaching herself had been to increase the level of rejection, loneliness and hurt she was feeling. Christmas, even though she had never realised it before, was a particularly painful period because it high-lighted how alone she felt. She wondered what belief might be lurking behind it. *Perhaps it's something like 'I'm not loveable?'* That made sense. *But is it the truth?*

Her mind was exploding as her mum switched on the speakerphone, and Catherine spoke to her entire family for a few minutes while desperately swallowing down the tears. She suddenly knew that the old belief she used to have wasn't the truth. She had chosen to interpret her family's inability to show emotion as meaning they didn't have feelings for her. But, as she said goodbye and put the receiver down, she slipped down the wall into a heap, realising she had been wrong all along. Just because they were not demonstrative of their love and didn't talk about it, that didn't mean the feelings were not there. Catherine had copied the same behaviour, and even though she knew she should tell them how much she loved them and missed them, she couldn't bring herself to do so.

Suddenly, she wanted to be surrounded by the people who loved her the most in the world. Through the tears and pain, she felt strangely elated. She knew she was homesick and had been for a long time. She felt like Dorothy in *The Wizard of Oz* and wanted to go home. It dawned on her that, as much as she knew Willow had been misjudging her mum, Catherine had been misjudging her own family. *They do care. They do love me. They just don't know how to show it.* She now wished Riley hadn't organised to fly out to see her or she could have got on the next plane home.

Willow appeared out of nowhere, like an angel, and hovered over Catherine. 'Come on, man, let's get you home.' She gently grasped Catherine's arm to pull her up. She grinned at Willow's usage of the word 'home' and wished she could tap her shiny red shoes together and be transported back to her real home in an instant, and tell her family how much she loved them and what a fool she'd been. Unfortunately, despite Willow's perception and kindness, even she didn't have that kind of power, so Catherine got up and followed her back to the hostel, where the party was in full swing. She explained to Willow what she had realised through phoning her family.

A couple of hours later Catherine had been enjoying herself at the barbeque meal so much that she hadn't noticed Willow disappear. She checked their room but there was no sign of her, so Catherine asked around but no-one had seen her. She began to worry but didn't know what to do. An hour later, Willow reappeared through the front entrance with eyes that looked like they'd been sprayed with tear gas.

Catherine ran up to her. 'Where've you been? I've been worried about you. Are you okay?'

Willow continued walking to their room. 'I've had a truth-seeking, magical moment with my mum.'

Catherine followed her into their broom cupboard-sized room. 'Willow, that's fantastic.'

Willow sat down on her bed with a big beaming smile. 'Yeah, man, I told her my news. You were right, I totally misjudged her.' She was silent while tears slipped down her cheeks. 'This little monkey,' she tapped her stomach, 'and what you'd told me about your family made me see her in a new cosmic light. She only ever wanted what was best for me, but I was too blind to see it. She'll support me in what *I* want to do.' She grabbed Catherine's hand. 'Thank you.

'Oh Willow, that's wonderful.' Instead of allowing her old habits to dictate her behaviour, Catherine sat next to her friend, pushed past her fears and hugged her. 'I take it you're going home then?'

'Yeah, man, but first I'm going to visit my monkey's seed-provider to say goodbye, and then fly back home a couple of weeks after.'

Catherine was devastated she would have to say goodbye to Willow and lose another person she could confide in, but she also felt happy for her. And she was glad to have had her in her life, albeit for a short amount of time. It would mean getting through just over two days on her own before Riley arrived. The thought of Riley conjured up butterflies as she wondered what that experience was going to throw at her.

Chapter Thirty-five

As Catherine sat on one of the orange plastic chairs in Arrivals, she wasn't sure what to expect when she saw Riley. Before she'd left England, she'd liked him enough that she'd considered cancelling her trip and, if it hadn't been for Rosie persuading her otherwise, she might have done so. But since she'd been away, she'd been unfaithful to him and had learnt a lot about herself. She'd even changed her name, kind of. Unsurprisingly, she was concerned how things would be between them. *Will I still find him attractive? Will he still find me attractive? Will we still get on? Will he guess I've cheated on him? Has he cheated on me?* She waited nervously in Arrivals.

When he walked through the door, her face turned the colour of crimson. *He's even more gorgeous than I remember!* She hoped her tan would cover up most of her blushing so she walked towards him and gave him a hug. He smelt really good. She withdrew from their embrace, kissed him on his lips then took a step back to take a good look at him. His shaved head, chiseled jaw and deep dark brown eyes reminded her of Jack, although there was one big difference: Riley was milk-bottle-white. She hadn't realised how bronzed she had gotten. 'Hi.'

He placed one hand gently behind her head, gripped her hair and pulled her back towards him. Then he kissed her properly. 'Alright babe.' His mischievous grin hadn't changed, nor had his cute Liverpudlian accent, and both drew her in like a groupie to a rock star.

Catherine felt right to be with him, even after just a few moments of his company. 'I've booked us an internal flight to La Ceiba so we can go to Roatán for New Year's Eve. It's supposed to be a great party place.'

'Nice one!' He took her spare hand and held it.

'The flight's in two hours' time. Are you hungry? Thirsty?'

Squeezing her hand he said, 'I could do with a bevvie, like.'

'Let's go through to Departures. There's a bar there.'

They walked towards Check-in, swinging their arms in unison and sneaking not-so-subtle peeks at each other. Once they were through passport control, they found a bar and chatted about life since they'd last seen each other. Catherine omitted to mention Jack, Erez or Gus but told him about some of her experiences on the retreat. In particular, she explained that she would like him to call her Catherine because this was more in keeping with who she wanted to be. He didn't say anything, which she took to mean that he understood. Riley told her what he'd been up to, about how Liverpool were doing in the Premier League, and about how excited he was to start his new job.

When they arrived in Roatán, it was dark and raining hard. To add to their misfortune, they couldn't find a vacant room for the night. The pair walked for over an hour before finally finding somewhere to stay. It cost four times as much as Catherine would normally pay, but at this point she didn't care.

They got to their room soaked through, and sober. And they were ravenous for food, or "scran" as Riley called it. So they quickly showered - separately - and put on the only dry clothes they could find in their sodden backpacks. For Catherine, that was a below-the-knee denim skirt and an over-sized, bright pink t-shirt she wore as a nightie. For Riley, that was a pair of navy shorts and a freshly-ironed, white Ralph Lauren polo shirt. Riley could not wipe the smirk off his face every time he looked at her fetching attire.

Catherine pretend-sulked by folding her arms tightly. 'Okay, it's not exactly what I had in mind for our first night out, either. Cut it out!'

'I'm loving this, like. We can't keep this,' he tugged at her t-shirt, 'proper nice outfit to ourselves.'

They held hands and ran to the nearest place still open for food, and by the time they were inside the timber shack they were soaked through again. They unravelled the cutlery to get to the paper napkins. Riley used his to dry his face while Catherine used hers to soak up some of the water from her dripping hair. 'Sorry about this.' Catherine felt guilty that Riley had come all this way to avoid the winter at home, only to be greeted with torrential rain. She listened to the rhythmic patter of the rain hammering down on the restaurant's roof as they sat down on wonky plastic chairs that threatened to collapse at any moment.

'Don't care, it was Arctic back home, like. At least it's warm here and I'm with you.' Catherine's face started to burn up again. She wished it wouldn't give her inner feelings away.

The restaurant was heaving with other Westerners with their waterproof jackets dripping wet on the back of their chairs. She also noticed two girls eyeing up Riley, giggling. She wondered if they were discussing what someone as good-looking as Riley was dong with someone like her. She felt her cheeks get even hotter as she looked down at her over-sized, bright pink t-shirt. *Probably.*

By the time they got back to their room, they were wet through again and Riley seemed as drunk as Catherine. 'Fancy a shower together, like?' She nodded enthusiastically and was glad she'd had a few drinks because the alcohol was giving her confidence. Without it, she might have suggested that they skip the shower and get straight under the covers with the lights out. Glad to get the unflattering clothes off, she was in her bra and knickers when she noticed Riley staring at her. 'You look great, you know.'

'What do you mean?'

'You've lost weight and that tan well suits you.' He wolf-whistled.

He just wants to get me into bed! Then she remembered that she had to think and act as if men did want her and, with this, she realised maybe he really meant it. After all, he didn't have to say anything. He knew he was going to have sex with her tonight. That much was obvious.

'Thanks. Not eating on the retreat must have helped.' But Riley wasn't listening. He was too busy stripping naked, grabbing her hand and leading her into the shower.

The heat of the water was a welcome change to the coolness of the rain and Catherine plunged herself under the powerful stream before Riley pushed her to the wall and starting kissing her. Just as she thought she might suffocate from a lack of oxygen, Riley moved away so his lips could explore every inch of her body. Then, he grabbed the shower head and directed the jet of water to her breasts.

The powerful spray ignited excitement which rushed through her body like electricity. He then spread her legs with his muscular thigh and aimed the shower head down there. The sensation was almost too much for Catherine and, despite feeling a longing for him to be inside her, the force of vibration sent her into a frenzy as her body gave in and she exploded in waves of ecstasy.

Riley laughed. 'You're clearly out of practise!'

'I've been waiting for you, of course!'

With that, Catherine squeezed shower gel into her hand and used it to lubricate her hand as she massaged it over his enormous organ. She could see from his face that he was close to coming, so she let the water rinse away the soap and then knelt down. She licked him seductively before taking him into her mouth fully and sucking hard. Catherine's jaw didn't even get a chance to ache before she felt shots of fluid squirt into her mouth.

Riley pulled Catherine up off her knees and led her back into the bedroom. He guided her hand to feel his excitement growing again and grinned. 'See what you do to me?'

Catherine took him in her hand and stroked him gently until he shook his head. 'No more playing. Lie on your front,' he ordered.

As Catherine obeyed, Riley pressed his saliva-wet fingers through the gap at top of her legs, lubricating her already moist groin, then replaced his hand with his erection and rubbed himself backwards and forwards, triggering Catherine's back to arch so she was in a prime position for him to pleasure her. His stiffness skimmed past her entrance and teased her pulsating button, enough to prime her but not enough to satisfy. Catherine had lost all sense of self and was focussed on only one thing: getting him to fill her completely. Instead, he stopped and got off her. *Uh oh. What's he doing?* Catherine strained her neck around to see him and sighed with relief when she saw him putting on a condom. 'All in good time, love.'

He climbed back onto her, distracting her with a kiss before plunging deep inside her. They gasped in unison at the relief and delight all mixed into one. Riley broke the silence, 'Ahhh, I've missed this.'

'Me too.' And she meant it, despite having been unfaithful to him. For a nano-second it occurred to her that she should be feeling guilty but she was so overwhelmed with the pleasure rippling through her body that it swamped any other thoughts or feelings.

As Riley thrust in and out, he altered the speed and force as well as how far he inserted himself, knowing he was toying with her. And it was working. Catherine could feel the vaguely familiar sensation stirring deep inside her; it was the appetiser before the main course and she was ready to explode. Riley must have sensed her imminent state so he maintained a potent yet constant stroke. The stirring intensified until it unfurled into a mind-blowing ecstatic peak.

Breathing heavily, Riley stopped momentarily. 'Better?'

'Oh yes! Now your turn!'

It took a total of three hard thrusts before Riley's body stiffened, followed by tiny convulsions and a grunt. He then collapsed onto Catherine and sighed. 'I *really* miss this!' After he got his breath back fully, he rolled off Catherine while pinging off the condom gently, careful not to let the contents splat out. As he lay with his arms rested behind his head, Catherine nuzzled up to him and nestled her head onto his chest. 'Wow!'

Riley smiled and kissed her forehead before closing his eyes. He was snoring within seconds.

Two days of rampant sex later, and Catherine had cabin fever as well as a sore nether-region. It had stopped raining for a couple of hours so they could go out without getting drenched.

'Come on, we haven't seen anything of Roatán yet!'

They walked along the muddy, pot-holed streets that were lined with wooden shacks, rustic bars and hotels, nosing inside each as they passed by. Catherine dragged Riley to a brightly coloured bar-come-restaurant and ordered two beers while Riley found a table. While the waiter pulled two bottles from the giant fridge, Catherine looked at her reflection in the mirror on the back wall and saw a dark brown face staring back at her with eyes shining through the darkness like sapphires. She'd never seen them look so striking. Tearing herself away from looking at her eyes, Catherine scanned the room and spied an enormous television screen suspended on one of the corner walls, showing highlights from that day's Premier League matches. Catherine smiled when she saw Riley twisting awkwardly in his chair and straining his neck to be in a position to see it.

When she returned to the table, Riley uncoiled himself and faced Catherine. 'Cheers.' They clinked bottles while he stroked her fingers with his free hand. 'Just let me know when Liverpool are playing, okay?'

Catherine was surprised he'd given her the seat that was facing the television but she was glad or she might not have got a sensible word out of him. They'd only managed a few sips of their refreshing drinks before she saw *Liverpool Vs Sunderland* flash up on the screen. 'It's on.'

Riley scraped his chair back and lifted it one-hundred-and-eighty degrees until he was facing the right direction. Catherine's heart was about to sink when he repositioned himself to look directly at her again. 'Only wanted to see the score.'

'What was it?'

He shook his head, grinning. 'Do you care, like?'

'No! But you do, so tell me.'

'Liverpool won 1-0.'

Catherine grinned from ear to ear. It had nothing to do with his team winning and everything to do with his choosing to pay her attention instead. She knew what football meant to him so this small gesture was enormous, for it meant he really did like her. Then, without warning, she was struck by panic as it gripped her insides and swelled like fog spreading through a menacing forest in a horror film. *I've got everything I've always wanted* so *why am I feeling so scared? How's it possible to go from feeling so good to feeling so bad so quickly?* Catherine wanted to bash her fists onto the table in frustration and wished she could email The Bliss Expert to find out what was happening.

Chapter Thirty-six

Catherine lay awake while Riley snored gently beside her. She hadn't slept much the night before, fretting about the unnerving feelings swirling inside her. She'd even avoided having sex with him when they'd come back at midnight, claiming that she was too sore, which wasn't too far from the truth. Carefully pulling on some shorts and a t-shirt, she crept out of the door and headed to a nearby internet café. She emailed The Bliss Expert asking for his help; she wanted to understand why she felt so scared at the very moment that love was becoming a reality with Riley. Then, to give him time to reply, she updated her blog.

Brown on Tour

Day 128: Roatán, Honduras

I said a sad goodbye to Guatemala and arrived at the Honduran border a few days ago. It was deserted when the minibus arrived, which was disconcerting to say the least! You'd think we should have breezed through, but no: we had to fill out several forms, pay unofficial taxes in cash, and watch while the bus was sprayed with insecticide.

As the Copán ruins were not far from the border, I decided to visit the Mayan archaeological site. I was surprised to see them set in thick emerald jungle, and equally surprised to be greeted by forty squawking macaws! I paid extra for a guide, who was worth every penny. He told me that the stonework was considered to be the best the Mayans had produced and he also told me about the famous ball court. Apparently there were two players to a team and the ball was made of rubber. No-one knows the exact rules but it is believed that the leader of the losing team was decapitated and his skull was used as the core around which a new rubber ball would be made!

Honduras has a serious problem with kidnapping, crime and violence, and homicide rates are some of the highest in the world. On the plus side, it's cheap! To be fair, I've not felt threatened since I arrived and, in fact, the people have been nothing but friendly and welcoming.

I'm now with Riley in Roatán, who's visiting me for just over two weeks. I can't say much about the place because it's been raining since we got here so I'll reel off a few facts for you.

Roatán is the largest of the Bay Islands which lie in the Caribbean roughly 30 miles from the northern coast of the Honduran mainland. Even though it's the largest island, it's only 48 miles long and less than 5 miles wide. It's surrounded by the second largest coral reef in the world, so it's a popular spot amongst divers. Not that I will be doing any diving!

I hope you're all out partying tonight. Have a good time and a very happy New Year to you all!!!

Catherine was relieved to see that The Bliss Expert had replied to her plea for help, so she clicked on his message straight away.

What you need to think about is what belief is playing out, and how you can change it? Ultimately, it depends how much you want a long-term relationship.

When you first met Riley, it was thrilling because it was more like a holiday romance than a real relationship. You didn't believe that someone as gorgeous as Riley could fall for you. By coming out to see you, he's proven to you that he does really like you and this is what's scaring you. The relationship feels too real and it's making you want to run away before you get in too deep. This is your pattern yet you must remember that "The definition of insanity is doing the same thing and expecting different results." If you want any hope of being in a long-term relationship, you have to do something different than you have to-date.

Why can't he just tell me what to do?! Catherine felt even more frustrated! She logged off, ordered a cola lite and stared into space, thinking about what The Bliss Expert had said. *He was spot-on about everything else he'd written, but what belief is playing out?* The first thing that sprang into her mind was that she was so used to chasing after men that when one actually liked her, she didn't know what to do. *That makes sense.* She continued with her line of thinking. *I'm so used to men finishing with me before I have time to develop my feelings, I don't know how to react when the relationship continues. On top of that, because I thought my dad didn't love me when I was a child, having a man love me is alien.* A tingling sensation rushed up and down her spine. *That'll be it then! But how do I change it?* The only idea she had was to push through the uncomfortable feelings and not allow them to dictate her behaviour.

Feeling happier and more optimistic than she had when she'd woken up, she went back to their room, climbed back into bed and snuggled up to Riley, doing her best to ignore the tension in her stomach. She stroked his chest, knowing her life could be different if she tried something different. She was sure she'd heard someone else mention the phrase about the definition of insanity before but she couldn't remember who.

'Everything okay, love?' Riley yawned and stretched his arms above his head.

'It is now. What shall we do today now that it's sunny? Fancy finding a beach? You do stand out like a typical British tourist!' She pretended to stifle her laughter.

'Go ahead, laugh at my expense. Just 'cause you've got a boss tan already!' He grabbed her hand and pulled her on top of him.

'If we spend all day in bed again, your new colleagues will wonder what you did on your holiday!'

He kissed her repeatedly all over her face. 'Well, let them wonder.'

Catherine pulled away, wiping her face with the back of her hand. 'Yuck! I need a shower now.'

'Not yet, you don't!' and he kissed her on the lips, which sent ripples of expectation throughout her body. 'There's something I want to show you, like.' He led her hand to his aroused state.

Chapter Thirty-seven

Catherine whispered into Riley's ear, 'Happy New Year, Baby.'

He prised one eye open and fake-smiled. 'Ouch, my head!'

Stroking his hair, she pulled an exaggeratedly sad face. 'Poor you.'

Catherine knew she should be feeling worse that she did after the amount of alcohol they'd consumed the night before. 'What do you fancy doing today?'

'Got any headache tablets? Can't think about anything else until I feel better.'

Catherine fumbled in her bag before producing some painkillers. 'Here.' She handed them to him together with a bottle of water.

Getting back into bed, she waited for Riley to swallow the pills and then she spooned him, feeling ridiculously happy. She remembered how Riley had not left her side all night: he'd been either holding her hand, caressing her back or stroking her hair. And it had felt good. Part of her still felt a little uncomfortable but she also felt needed and special.

Riley took her hand and squeezed it. 'How you feeling, love?'

'Surprisingly fine.' She hesitated for a couple of seconds before continuing, 'Shall we go to West Bay Beach today?'

'When I feel better and so long as I'm with you, 'course. Although...'

'What?'

'We're playing West Ham later.'

Catherine rolled her eyes playfully, then she kissed him. Thank goodness she hadn't let her old patterns get in the way of a great thing, even if she'd always be competing with Liverpool FC. She felt as connected as she had done in the retreat, only this time it was with one special person rather than with a group of people.

'Only joking. It's tomorrow.'

With this, Catherine play-hit him.

After getting a water taxi to West Bay beach, Catherine was stunned into silence by the paradise island: gorgeous white sand, crystal clear water and, best of all, warm sunshine brightening everyone's mood. There were Westerners sprawled out on the sand like a colony of seals, no doubt suffering from the ill-effects of the night before.

Riley pointed to the bars, 'Hair of the dog?'

'You're hardcore. But sure, why not?!'

He sauntered off with his pale back dazzling in the sun and returned clutching two ice-cold beers.

Feeling a little sozzled in the sun, Catherine suggested they grab some lunch before they passed out from drinking in the heat of the day. They sat in the shade and gulped down some water before they ordered. Not being very adventurous, Catherine went for boiled rice, chips and beans, while Riley opted for a seafood platter.

While they waited for their food to arrive, Catherine calculated that Riley had already used five days of his holiday, which meant that they had only fourteen days to get through two other countries on the way to Costa Rica, from where Riley was flying back to the UK. The thought of Riley leaving terrified her. Riley squeezed her hand gently. 'What's going on in that head of yours, love?'

'Nothing much.' She looked down and pretended to peruse the menu.

'Oh come on, I proper know you. What's up?'

Catherine smiled and looked up. Their eyes reconnected. She decided there was no point in making something up because he would know she was lying. 'I don't want my time with you, here, to end.' She held her breath, having no idea what reaction her words would trigger.

Riley released her hand, sat back in his chair, and folded his arms.

He smiled, leant forward again and took both her hands in his. 'You could come back with me.'

Catherine almost fell off her chair, metaphorically speaking. 'Do you really want me to?'

'Of course, like. That's settled then.' He twisted round to get the waiter's attention, signaling the end of their discussion, which irked Catherine. As much as she was happy that Riley wanted her to go home with him, she suddenly felt sick. She hadn't had time to think about it properly. Even though she didn't want him to go, she wasn't sure she was ready to end her travels yet.

The waiter came over and he ordered two beers, 'To celebrate!' Catherine clutched Riley's hand to get his attention back to her and to hint that, while he might have considered the topic closed, she had not, and she needed him to understand this.

'I worry that, if I went home now, everything would still be the same. Then I'd get depressed and ruin what we've got.'

'Don't be daft, we'd work things out. You could always come and live with me while you sort stuff out. Or for longer…'

Catherine swallowed hard.

Riley's face turned expressionless and his eyes dropped to the table. 'Thought you'd be happy, like.'

'Sorry, you took me by surprise. We've still got two weeks to go and, apart from changing my airline ticket, there's not much else to organise, so why don't we see what happens? Speaking of which, we need to decide where to go to next, or neither of us will make a flight out of Costa Rica!

Despite having come up with a solution, Catherine couldn't help but still feel sick. She knew by now that this was her body's warning signal so she wondered what it was trying to caution her about.

Chapter Thirty-eight

Brown on Tour
Day 135: Grenada, Nicaragua

After a week on Roatán, partying hard and sunbathing on idyllic beaches, we headed inland to the capital of Honduras, Tegucigalpa. Tegus for short. First impressions weren't great; it was heavily congested with traffic and the pollution was so high, I found it difficult to breathe. A stark contrast to what I'm used to!

The hostel was in an office block (?!) and our room was the size of a prison cell, and it felt like one due to its lack of windows. The receptionist told us to take extreme care wherever we went due to the likelihood that we would get robbed! She advised us to pay for a reputable taxi if we were to venture out anywhere and to stay in after dark (not a nice prospect given our accommodation!).

Put off from visiting any of the local sites, we opted to watch a film at the Multiplaza. The only film show-ing that we could agree upon was the remake of Point Break, which was difficult to understand given that some of it was in English with Spanish subtitles while the rest of it was dubbed in Spanish. Very confusing! It didn't matter anyway because we couldn't hear anything due to the audience's thunderous chattering. We have come to the conclusion that the locals go to the cinema to cool down as it was the only place where we found decent air conditioning.

I'm going to be the size of a house if we stay in Honduras for much longer. The only thing that I've found that doesn't contain meat or knock-your-socks-off spice is Tortilla con Quesillo, which is fried tortillas with cheese, served with a tomato sauce. While delicious, I dread to think how many calories each one contains.

Unsurprisingly, we got the first bus out of there and had a VERY long and boring bus journey to Nicaragua. We arrived in Grenada a few hours ago, which is on the north west side of the Lago Cocibolca – the largest fresh water lake in Central America. I'm really excited to explore Grenada as, from the little I've seen so far, it looks like an interesting and vibrant city what with its colonial buildings in pastel shades, and it's supposed to be steeped in colourful history.

Then it was time to tell the whole truth to Rosie.

A very happy New Year to you! I hope you had a good one?

Ever since Riley and I left Honduras, I've noticed a slight change in him - he's not quite as attentive as he was when he first arrived. Hopefully that's just because it has been a bit boring as we've done some quite hardcore travelling. Saying that, I thought he'd enjoy seeing the countries from a different perspective, meeting the locals on their transport and experiencing their culture, rather than hanging out in tourist destinations which have about as much charm as a flat bottle of bubbly.

He's asked me to fly back to the UK with him so you

might be seeing me sooner than you think! But don't get your hopes up just in case this changes, which it might if things continue the way they are between us. Wish me luck!

When Riley nodded to Catherine to indicate that he, too, had finished emailing, they went to a nearby café. Riley looked around to see where the waiter was while Catherine got out her *Lonely Planet* and read about the local area. 'Fancy climbing a volcano?'

Riley nodded again, but wouldn't look at her directly.

'There's one called Maderas and it should take about six hours.' Catherine rambled on, keen to keep the conversation on neutral ground. 'We could catch a bus to Rivas after we've eaten and get the last boat out to Ometepe.'

'Alright.' Riley sounded as interested as a priest being propositioned by a prostitute.

It took them most of the day to reach their destination. As they approached their accommodation for the night, Catherine could sense Riley stiffening up. The Finca – or farm – that was to be home for the night was a large wooden building in the middle of nowhere. It looked like something out of *Little House on the Prairie*. Catherine was too exhausted to find somewhere else and she didn't suppose there was anywhere else anyway. Riley hadn't said much for most of the journey and wouldn't look Catherine in the eye. The owner, a middle-aged man called Pedro who was permanently hunched over at an angle, welcomed them gleefully as if they were long-lost family and led them to their room for the night. Catherine snuck a peek at Riley to see his reaction when he saw the enormous room, with dirty and saggy mattresses of varying sizes covering the floor. Most of the mattresses already had backpacks on them to show they were taken.

Riley did not look happy. 'What the hell? Where have you brought me?'

She put her hands up as if defending herself. 'I'm sorry, I didn't know it'd be like this or I'd never have suggested it.'

He was gritting his teeth when he spoke. ''The beds look like they should be in a tip, like. Are you seriously suggesting I sleep here tonight? No way I'm spending the night with twenty strangers!'

Pointing outside, Catherine tried to placate him. 'I saw some hammocks on the veranda, so you could always sleep in one of those if you prefer?'

He shook his head, still not looking directly at Catherine.

As the light shone brightly through the window, Catherine checked her watch. It was six o'clock. The alarm was about to go off so she switched it off to prevent everyone else in the room from being woken up and nudged Riley with her elbow. 'Wake up, sleepy head!'

Catherine rolled to the edge of the mattress and sat up to see several other bodies in the room either snoring, fidgeting, or comatose. To avoid feeling exposed, she quickly got dressed before anyone else opened their eyes, and then she gently shook Riley who had not moved since she had first tried to wake him. He huffed, turned over and put his pillow over his head.

'Come on, you need to get up or coming here will have been for nothing,' she whispered into his ear.

He tore the pillow off his head and glared at Catherine. He didn't need to say how displeased he was; it was written all over his face.

They ate breakfast in relative silence and then Catherine frog-marched them to the start of the trek. For the first hour, Riley didn't talk except for a grunt in response to her questions, while Catherine tried to remain upbeat. However, once the gentle ascent soared to a steep incline, Catherine stopped talking. Instead, she was registering every one of the rocks they had to clamber up and over, the inches of thick mud they had to trudge through, and every single minute of the seven long hours of hell they had to endure. When they finally reached the top, Catherine felt exhausted and Riley looked thoroughly fed up. Not even the abseil into the centre of the volcano could brighten Catherine's mood, which was not helped by the fact that at the end of it, the only thing they could see in the middle of the crater was thick cloud.

Riley finally spoke. 'Well, that was worth it.' The sarcasm seeped out of his voice. Catherine chose to ignore him and started to climb back up the rope.

After a long and silent walk back to the farmhouse, Catherine cursed under her breath as they arrived five minutes too late to catch the last bus back to civilisation. *If Riley had got up straight away when I first woke him up, we wouldn't be spending another night in this hellhole.* Not only was she absolutely shattered and could barely move, but the drip that called itself a shower was cold. Riley spent all evening moaning about having to sleep on a dirty mattress in a room with twenty other people. Catherine's final thought before she fell into a deep sleep was that Riley would never survive as a backpacker; package holidays were more his thing.

Chapter Thirty-nine

As soon as they reached civilisation, Catherine rushed to the nearest internet café to escape Riley and to update The Bliss Expert on the confusion she felt.

Ever since Riley and I left Honduras and have been doing what I'd class as travelling rather than holidaying, things have been strained between us.

It started with him moaning about having to get up early. He said he was on holiday to relax and enjoy himself, not to be kept to a military regime. Then he moaned that it was too hot, that the road was too bumpy, the television was too loud and the bus too crowded or smelly. Nothing was ever right or good enough and it's getting on my nerves. We now seem to battle against each other. For example, I was telling him about my experiences of Astral Projecting and he told me it was a 'load or crock.' How rude! He's also started to call me Cath again, which I find disrespectful after explaining why I wanted to be called Catherine. And, to top it off, all he talks about is football. He doesn't mind getting up early when there's a live match on at nine o'clock in the morning! I used to find it endearing, but now it's just plain annoying.

Is this an example of the brain's filtering system at work? When Riley and I first met, was my internet search engine set to notice all of his good bits because we were in the honeymoon period? However, after spending time with each other, the gloss has worn off and is my search engine now registering the negative stuff?

While I'm not sure if I'm right and have understood Step Five correctly, I am sure that Riley is really irritating me. In fact, I can't wait for him to go home!

At least it means that I won't have a dilemma about what to do when he leaves. I will definitely be continuing with my travels. I am already feeling deprived of my personal journey, which I'm sure you'll be pleased about.

Catherine had time to update Rosie that she wouldn't be coming home any time soon and read all her other emails before an email pinged through from The Bliss Expert.

It would seem that you are having an interesting time with Riley. I could say I'm sorry that things haven't worked out, but you were never suited for a long-term relationship, so I won't! Don't regret your time with him because you've learnt a lot. I particularly like your observation about your internet search engine now paying attention to Riley's negative traits. I also wonder what negative traits Riley's search engine is now noticing about you?

If you're brave enough, why not ask him about his relationship with his boss? Don't be offended if the conversation doesn't turn out the way you expect, but if you do have the conversation with him, you might be surprised by what you notice. Just remember that not everyone is ready to hear this stuff.

As for why you're battling against each other, you're right in that you're not quite the match made in Heaven that you both wanted each other to be. That might explain the sick feeling you had when he first suggested going back to the UK together. I'm so glad you were aware of the sick feeling you get when something is not for your highest good. That's your intuition. Trust it and it will be there to guide you.

Catherine was curious about his comments on Riley's boss and on what negative traits Riley might be noticing about her now but she wanted to let The Bliss Expert know how grateful she was for his guidance, so she sent him an email saying simply,

'Thank you.'

That night over dinner, partly as something to fill the uncomfortable silence and partly to fulfil her curiosity, Catherine asked Riley about the situation with his boss, John. She knew he'd had ongoing issues with him but she was interested to find out what The Bliss Expert was referring to.

Looking away towards a table by the bar where two attractive girls were sitting opposite each other, he spoke, still without looking at her. 'He's a proper idiot, like.' Then, turning his attention back to Catherine he said, 'Why are you asking random questions? Don't analyse me again.'

Annoyed at his attitude, she pressed on. 'Just humour me. What did he do to make you think he was an idiot?'

He poured himself more wine, leaving Catherine's glass empty. She was sure he was doing it to wind her up. 'Nothing I did pleased him.'

Pouring herself some wine she asked, 'Can you give me an example?'

He rolled his eyes. 'In a team meeting, I made a proper good suggestion but he ignored me. Claire made the same suggestion and he congratulated her on coming up with a good idea, like.'

Catherine nodded. 'How does he make you feel when he does this?'

His fists tightened and Catherine wasn't sure if he was angry with her or his boss. 'Proper small, like, insignificant.'

Beginning to understand what The Bliss Expert was getting at she said, 'How did your dad make you feel when you were young?'

He frowned. 'What's me auld fella got to do with anything?'

Remembering how she'd reacted when The Bliss Expert had first asked her the same thing, she was empathetic. 'Please,' she touched his hand, 'Humour me.'

He tore his hand away. 'Do one, will ya,' Cath?' he said, his jaw tensing. Then he seemed to change his mind. 'Me auld fella always put me down. Ar kid, on the other hand, could do no wrong and everything he did was brilliant. We could climb up the same tree and me auld fella would say, "Well done ar Greg, you're proper good at that." If I did it, he would criticise me.' He took a swig of his wine. 'What do you say to that, Ms Freud?'

'Don't you see the connection between how your dad made you feel as a child and your relationship with your boss, a man in authority?'

Riley poured himself some more wine, having drained the previous glass. 'The only connection is that they're both dicks. Is this the mumbo jumbo you got from that retreat, like?'

'Yes,' Catherine answered, thinking it easier to admit to that than reveal the bizarre emails she'd been receiving from The Bliss Expert. 'But it's not mumbo jumbo. It makes perfect sense. Basically, we learn beliefs in childhood that form a template of how we behave and relate to others as adults.'

'Cath, you're doing my nut in. I don't give a rat's arse about this new-age, hippy stuff. Why not drink more and loosen up? You're proper serious.'

Catherine was taken aback by his reaction yet her interest was spiked by the fact he had just done to her what he claimed his father did to him. She chose to ignore his comment about loosening up because his revelation was far more intriguing. 'Okay, but one last thing. You've just belittled me! I'm really into this stuff yet you just dismissed it. You've also just insulted me by telling me to loosen up. Is it at all possible that you might have ever spoken to your boss in the same way without realising it?'

'Shut it. Now *you're* talking to me like I'm a child. You're being a dick like John! I'm going to the bar. Don't come.' He threw down a few *colones* on the table to pay for his share of the meal and skulked off like a petulant child to the bar. He stood next to the table where the two girls who he'd been eyeing up earlier were sitting.

Catherine was in a daze. The Bliss Expert had warned her that some people weren't ready to take responsibility for themselves, and he was right. They would rather point the finger at other people and blame them. It was a lot easier and renounced the accuser of any wrongdoing. She now knew why she'd had to wait so long for The Bliss Expert to send her the Steps. It had been frustrating but if he had have given them to her before she was ready, she may never have listened.

Catherine remembered something The Bliss Expert had said in Step Four. He had been right when he'd said that what he had been teaching her could be applied to any relationship with any other human being. Any relationship could be affected by the patterns laid down in childhood. She wished she could witness Riley interacting with his boss at work to see for herself whether John really did treat Riley in the way that he described, or whether it was just his perception based on his childhood experiences with his father, which then caused him to react in a certain way and caused John to treat him badly. If she'd been able to get through to Riley she could have told him to be aware of what information he was focusing on, and whether it was the truth or just his version of the truth based on what he expected it to be. While she would never know for sure, she had just witnessed him storming off like a child, even though she had only asked him a simple question. Unfortunately, he interpreted this as her belittling him. She smiled at how much she'd learnt, paid the bill, and went back to the room to read. She was fed up with drinking herself into oblivion.

Chapter Forty

Riley was lying next to Catherine but he was on one side of the bed while she was on the other. The three-inch gap between them spoke volumes. They hadn't touched, kissed or made love since leaving Honduras and the distance growing between them was palpable. She wanted to suggest they go their separate ways but she didn't want to be selfish because he had only five days left. *Five very long days.* She lay in bed immersed in her own thoughts while listening to the sound of howler monkeys on the roof chatting to each other. She could also hear the resident parrot throwing nuts onto the tin roof one after the other as if in a rhythmic attack on them. She popped to the bathroom and got involuntarily thrown around as a mild tremor ripped across the local area. She peeked round the bathroom door to check that Riley was okay. His snoring suggested he hadn't even noticed.

When Riley awoke, Catherine smiled at him and suggested going to the beach after breakfast.

'Can we chat?' He sat up and patted the bed to signal for her to sit down.

She complied. 'Sure.'

'I've only got five days left and I want to travel on my own, like.'

Catherine took a moment before responding. Cath would have smiled sweetly as if nothing was wrong while internally fuming because she would have interpreted his suggestion as rejection. Catherine, however, took time to process the reality of the situation and knew it was the best solution for them both and, in fact, it's what she wanted too. 'I think it's a good idea too.' She paused before blurting out her next question. 'Out of curiosity, why do you think we haven't been getting on?'

This time it was Riley's turn to pause. 'When we first met, you were fun, sexy and confident. We had a laugh. But you've proper changed.'

Catherine contemplated what he'd just told her and laughed.

'What's so funny? I thought you'd be proper gutted.'

The irony was not lost on Catherine. She had been trying to be more like Catherine in order to secure a long-term relationship. However, if she'd been more like Cath, they could have had a chance of staying together. 'I was thinking the same thing this morning. Only you were brave enough to verbalise it.'

After Catherine had stopped smiling, they went for breakfast and ate in silence. She would like to say they were each absorbed in their own thoughts but the truth was they had nothing left to say to each other and it was painful. Catherine subconsciously kept looking at her watch and berating herself each time she did so as it was obvious she was wishing time away.

Eventually they finished eating, and it was time to say goodbye. A part of Catherine was sad. Sad that all her hopes of having a normal adult relationship had been shattered, but relieved she'd found out that he wasn't the 'one' before she'd made a rash decision to go back to the UK with him. Even though Riley had thought he liked Cath and that they could have had a long-term future together, Catherine knew better. She didn't like Cath and so didn't want to be with someone who wanted her to be someone she wasn't. Cath was a façade, the glossy veneer created to cover up how lonely, sad and inadequate she felt inside. She couldn't be with someone who liked the crust. She wanted to be with someone who liked the whole loaf.

Catherine hugged Riley, knowing it would be the last time they'd see each other. As Riley strolled off, she felt strangely free as she realised she was better off on her own. It was time to concentrate on her real journey. *But where to?*

Unsure of her next steps, Catherine logged onto the internet and her heart skipped when she saw an email waiting from The Bliss Expert. *Perhaps he's got a suggestion for my next destination!*

> *It doesn't matter where you choose to go next, what's important is that you stay strong and keep putting into practice what you've learnt on your journey so far. Don't allow yourself to fall into your old patterns because you feel scared or uncomfortable. Good luck!*

A shiver ran down Catherine's spine as she vowed that Cath would never emerge again. *So why can I still sense her then?*

Chapter Forty-one

Catherine took a deep breath as she walked through Arrivals at Bogota Airport. Doug had said that Colombia was worth a visit so she hoped he was right. Then she remembered that she needed to have positive beliefs and tell her brain that this South American country known for being the Cocaine Capital of the World was a fun, friendly and welcoming country, so that this would become her experience. She didn't want to make the same mistake and think negatively as she had done when she'd arrived in Mexico City. *Look how that turned out!*

As the automatic doors glided open, Catherine was greeted by the cool night air and was delighted when she saw the Taxi Rank almost immediately. What's more, there was only one person queuing. His tailored dark denim jeans, check shirt and cowboy boots suggested that he was a local, so Catherine felt like an honoured guest when he offered for her to take the first taxi. *Wow! This stuff really works!* She thanked the man several times before climbing into the car and asking the driver – in her pidgin Spanish - to take her to a hostel that she'd pre-selected in her Lonely Planet guide on the flight.

As much as she wanted to stay positive, it was hard not to feel vulnerable when she was at the mercy of the stranger sitting behind the wheel.

I'll be fine, I'll be fine, I'll be fine.

About thirty minutes of heart-racing tension (that had been mildly moderated by positive thoughts), the taxi came to a halt in a residential street. Catherine's stomach tensed as the driver climbed out and opened the passenger door so she could get out. He said something she didn't understand so she just smiled and gave him enough money according to the amount indicated on the meter. Catherine scanned the street, which was devoid of any light, people or movement. The driver pointed to a doorway that was as dark as the rest of the street and pulled her backpack out of the boot but, instead of giving it to Catherine, he carried it for her while following her to the nondescript door.

The door didn't look like it was the entrance to a hostel and there was no signage to allude to the fact either. She looked up and down the street, which was in complete darkness and she didn't have a clue where she was. She realised she didn't have a choice other than to trust that the driver was a gentleman carrying her bag to a hostel that would look like a hostel once she got through the door.

The driver knocked on the front door of the alleged hostel and it seemed like an eternity before a lady in her mid-fifties opened the door with one hand while struggling to put the other one into the waving arm of a dressing gown. Her face said she wasn't pleased at being woken up, while her shaking head said there weren't any rooms available. The woman said something in Spanish but, seeing the blank look on Catherine's face, she turned to the driver and gestured wildly up the road. The driver looked at Catherine and said slowly, as if he were talking to a child, *'Ella tiene un hotel hermano en la carretera con las vacantes.'* Catherine looked at him blankly and so he said, *'Otro hotel alli.*' She jumped back into his taxi feeling relaxed that he was taking her to another hostel further up the road. A few seconds later they arrived at another nondescript doorway where the driver got out and knocked on the door again. This time Catherine stayed in the taxi while a woman who looked remarkably similar to the other lady talked to the driver. He turned around, smiled at Catherine, and beckoned for her to get out while he retrieved her backpack from the boot. He handed Catherine her bag and said, '*Buenas noches.*' Catherine walked through the door and was pleased when the woman was warm, friendly, and could speak English. 'Welcome.'

The woman led Catherine through the hallway covered in Art Deco pictures to a small hole in the wall, which Catherine assumed was the reception area. 'You try my sister's hotel?'

Catherine nodded. 'I guess I had a kind taxi driver.'

'Yes. He has daughter. No leave you in this neighbourhood. Not for girl alone.' She pulled a register out and asked Catherine to fill in her passport details. 'I show you to room. Breakfast at eight.' She then showed Catherine to a large but sparsely furnished room and closed the door on her way out. Left emotionally and physically exhausted, Catherine undressed, cleaned her teeth and considered how fortunate she'd been to have the taxi driver she had. She fell asleep thankful that someone was watching out for her.

When she woke up next morning it took Catherine a few moments to appreciate where she was, but once it dawned on her that she was somewhere new and would have to start all over again, her heart beat at a hundred miles an hour. She could hear voices outside her room so she forced herself up, got dressed, and went outside for breakfast. There was a communal area with a dozen or so people eating breakfast, so she found an empty table and helped herself to the self-service toast, jam and tea. It was problematic juggling her *Lonely Planet* and eating at the same time so she abandoned her research on Bogota until she'd finished eating. A fragment of her wished she'd gone home with Riley, where she would be surrounded by friends and family, instead of grappling for something to do in a new and unfamiliar place, again, alone. Usually she would feel excited about exploring a new place but today she just wanted to go home. She wanted familiarity. She wanted to be safe. She wanted her family.

When she was able to turn her attention to figuring out what she would do with her day, Catherine discovered that she was staying in a well-located hostel. La Candelaria district – where she was now – was the capital's cultural epicenter and was within walking distance of the Museo Del Oro, which housed the largest collection of gold from pre-Hispanic Colombia in the world. Catherine went back to her room, packed a small day bag which contained a bottle of water left over from the airport, her guide book, and a business card with the hotel's address on – in the likely event she would get lost – and headed in the direction of Plaza de Bolivar and towards the Museum of Gold.

On her way, Catherine's mind was in conflict. Given Colombia's reputation, she half expected to be kidnapped, caught up in the middle of a shoot-out between rival drug cartels or, at the very least, be mugged. At the same time, she knew that she needed to expect good things so that she'd experience good things. She had to over-ride her unconscious mind with conscious thoughts of safety, well-being, and friendliness. It seemed to be working because Catherine didn't notice anything remotely threatening. In fact, the only thing she noticed was that she was being stared at. A lot. They weren't staring in a mean way, but in a curious, amused way. Many of them spoke to her but having still not mastered Spanish, she didn't understand much beyond, 'Hello.' She even checked to find out if her skirt had wormed itself into her knickers. She tried to ignore the stares by focusing on the cobbled streets. They were lined with elegant, well-preserved colonial buildings which were a mixture of houses, restaurants, cafes, hotels, bars and churches. Bogota seemed to be as bustling and vibrant as any other city and the pigeons in La Plaza Bolivar even made her feel at home when they played a game of 'chicken' with her, flying straight for her face and redirecting seconds before they could hit.

Still being watched the entire way, Catherine reached the Museo del Oro and went straight up to the beginning of the exhibition on the first floor, relieved to be away from gawping locals. This floor was relatively quiet except for a group of school children that looked like they were about to head to the next floor. Finally Catherine could concentrate on appreciating the beautiful artifacts rather than worrying about why she was so interesting to locals. Relieved to see Spanish and English on the first display unit, Catherine became engrossed in the golden artefacts; in reading about their history and admiring their beauty. When she was about to move onto the second display cabinet, there was a swarm of over twenty ten-year-olds surrounding her. They weren't interested in the contents of the glass cabinets. Instead, they were focussed entirely on Catherine. She was imprisoned by a herd of little people. Their huge beaming smiles signalled they meant no harm but that didn't help Catherine's escape. Scanning the room, she spotted a harassed-looking middle-aged woman, presumably their teacher, and presumably pleading with the children to step away from the trapped tourist. Or that's what Catherine guessed her rapid commands in Spanish and arm movements were communicating to the children, who were far more interested in Catherine than in listening to what the mad, gesticulating woman was saying. Eventually the teacher gave up and marched towards Catherine, still shouting above the chattering children who seemed as excited by Catherine as if she were Father Christmas. 'Sorry! Children not, how you say, used to seeing foreign lady on own. They are curious. Want to ask you questions. It okay?'

'Sure, fire away.'

The teacher managed to hush the children into relative silence and began translating their questions one by one.

Teacher: 'Where are you from?'

Catherine: 'England.'

This was met with a chorus of 'Oooo!'s.'

Teacher: 'Are you alone?'

Catherine: 'Yes.'

Teacher: 'Why?'

A very good question indeed. Because all my friends are settled and happy. They don't need to escape reality to find happiness.

Catherine: 'Because I'm an adventurer.'

Teacher: 'Why are you in Colombia?'

Because I didn't know where else to go and Doug said it was great.

Catherine: 'Because I'd heard it was a beautiful country.'

Teacher: "Why aren't you married?'

Such great questions. Because I'm attracted to men who don't want me.

Catherine: 'Because I haven't met the right man yet.'

Teacher: 'Do you want children?'

Oh, come on!

Catherine: 'When I've met the right man, yes.'

Teacher: 'Do you work?'

Yes and I hated it so much. That's one of the reasons I left the UK.

Catherine: 'Yes, in sales.'

The question-and-answer session continued for fifteen minutes until the teacher read Catherine's face and saw she'd had enough. She managed to shoo the children away and as they left, they waved and said goodbye with their best English accents. It was nice to be able to move again. No sooner had she breathed a sigh of relief than a security guard approached her. Assuming he was just checking she was alright, she smiled until she realised he wanted to have a conversation too. She chatted with him for a couple of minutes and then raced up to the third floor, only to see the same group of school children. Catherine smiled and charged to the exit, leaving the museum without having seen more than one display of treasures.

Fed up with being stared at, Catherine headed back to the anonymity of the hostel where she sat in the communal area watching several other backpackers having fun; laughing and clinking glasses with each other. It made her feel left out and alone so she pulled out her book – *Tuesday's with Morrie* by Mitch Albom – and pretended to be absorbed in it. It wasn't long before she was interrupted by a guy with a slight Cockney accent.

'Hi, you a newbie?'

Catherine extricated her eyes from the book as if it was a great inconvenience to be disturbed. Inside she was jumping with joy. Examining the guy crouching down beside her, she observed brown hair and eyes, average build and mediocre looks that were neither alluring nor offensive. If she had to guess, she'd say he was in his mid to late thirties. There was nothing attention-grabbing about him, apart from his discernible confidence. Like Erez, Catherine wasn't sure if she found it attractive or off-putting. 'That obvious?'

He pointed at her book. 'You're either well boring or new.' He shot Catherine a smile to reveal a large dimple in his left cheek. Despite fighting every bone in her body, she found it charming. 'I'm hoping you're new.'

Catherine shifted in her chair and slowly placed her book on the table, using a napkin as a bookmark. 'That's for me to know and for you to find out!' As the words escaped, Catherine berated herself. *One hint of a confident man and Cath's back. He's not even attractive! Stop it, now.*

Still flashing a smile, he extended his hand. 'I'm Colin, 32, from Watford, on a month's holiday wiv me mates.' He turned round and pointed at a table of five other guys who chorused a loud cheer in return.

Catherine's cheeks were on fire. 'I'm Cath, I mean Catherine, 28, London. Away for a year. Probably.'

Colin furrowed his eyebrows. 'Okay. Sounds like you could be fun.' He flashed another smile and, with it, his dimple reappeared. 'You wanna join us?'

Catherine wavered. The Bliss Expert had warned her to stay strong so she knew she should politely decline and go back to reading her book. But that meant that she was on her own and she didn't want to be, not in this strange city. 'Sure.' Her stomach spun as fast as a fairground ride as she gathered her belongings and strolled over to the table of rowdy lads. As she joined them, she no longer felt mildly queasy but nauseous in titanic proportions. *Uh oh, what's that about?*

Chapter Forty-two

Brown on Tour
Day 146: Bogotá, Colombia

I'm now in Bogotá in Colombia having an amazing time. I'm a bit of a celebrity here because not many Westerners - and especially not Western women on their own - visit Colombia. Apart from being nosey, the Colombians I have met are incredibly welcoming, friendly and lovely. They seem genuinely happy that I'm visiting their country, of which they are extremely proud. And from what I've seen of the city, so they should be. I would love to explore other parts of the country but I'm a little scared after hearing all the stories of foreign tourists being kidnapped, so I'll just stay here, thank you very much.

I've been hanging around with a group of guys from Watford. We went to the best museum I've ever been to: the Museo Historico Policia, which as you can probably guess is the Police History Museum. The best bit was the exhibition about Pablo Escobar. His massive Harley-Davidson was there, a model of his bullet-ridden corpse, and most bizarre of all, a tile retrieved from the roof he was gunned down on. If you looked closely, you could still see his dried blood on the tile!

We also took the cable car to the top of Cerro de Monser-rate where there were breathtaking views of the city. I went to see a football match at the Estadio Nemesio Camacho, also known as El Campin, which I will never do again: Every time the local team scored a goal, the entire stadium on my side charged up to the front of the stand and I honestly feared for my life. Colombians are most definitely passionate about their football.

We've also been going to the best nightclubs in the Zona Rosa where the women are super-slim, have surgically enhanced huge boobs, endless locks of fake blonde hair and trout-pout lips. I fit right in with my vest top, flowing skirt and flip flops. It's very weird being a Westerner here; you can get into the most expensive, exclusive clubs looking like a tramp. You can't even get into a nightclub in London wearing £150 trainers!

Catherine then typed an email to The Bliss Expert.

I am so annoyed with myself. I have done it again. I've spent the last few nights fooling around with an English guy called Colin, who dumped me last night. His cruel parting words were, "Why would I want to be stuck with an English bird when there's all this hot Colombian totty about?"

And he's right! I feel so fat, ugly and unfashionable compared to the Colombian babes here. And they are babes, albeit artificial ones.

I know you're going to tell me to change my beliefs and act as if they're true but it's so hard. I would love not to be attracted to men I shouldn't be. I would love to feel so secure in myself that I don't need anyone else to make me feel happy. But it seems impossible!

I'm still hanging around with the boys from Watford - despite things being awkward between me and Colin - but I feel like I don't have a choice as they're the only people I know. I want to be happy but I am so bloody miserable. At the moment, it feels like attaining happiness is as elusive as diving to the bottom of the deepest ocean. Please help.

Catherine looked round to check no-one was watching and wiped the tears from her eyes. While she waited for a reply, she read an email from Doug.

I'm just heading to Quito and wondered if it's time for you to join me? I'm planning on going to a hostel called 'Equilibrium,' so come and find me. It would be great to see you.

It was as if Doug had read her mind. *That's the answer! I'll fly to Ecuador as soon as I can.* She was feeling a little happier when an email pinged in from The Bliss Expert.

Please don't give up. If the Steps were that easy, everyone would be doing them and would be happy. The crazy thing is that you know what to do, but you just have to persevere. Remember that you have the choice to react to your conditioned feelings. I know you feel lonely but finding comfort in a man – or Doug - is not the answer. Resist falling into your old habits and you will notice things change remarkably quickly. And then changing how you feel about the past will become easier and easier. Remember, you can do it.

Catherine wanted to punch The Bliss Expert. He was telling her to stay put and use this opportunity to choose her behaviour and reactions in order to feel better. *But it's so hard!* While she wanted to run away and join Doug, she knew she had to stay. She hoped that she had understood The Bliss Expert correctly and was doing the right thing. As she was gathering up her things, a local man got up from the computer next to hers and grabbed her bag on the floor next to her chair. He didn't make his escape quickly enough and Catherine caught hold of one of the straps. A tug-of-war ensued. The backwards and forwards tussling would have been comical had her passport, cash and credit cards not been in the bag. Panic-stricken, Catherine scanned the internet café, pleading with her eyes for assistance, but no-one moved. They either hadn't noticed or chose not to notice; either way, no-one was going to help her. Just as she was about to lose hope, Bez – one of Colin's mates who she hadn't seen in the café until now – sprang out of his chair, and pushed the thief with such force that he stumbled over before scuttling out of the door empty-handed. The last she saw of him he was bolting down the road.

She was still shaking as Bez positioned a chair behind her, took her arm and aided her into a seated position. 'My hero,' she said as she pretend-fluttered her eyelashes.

His cheeks flashed red, which clashed with his carrot-orange hair. 'Was nuffing. Loads of blokes would've done the same fing.'

Catherine looked around at the apathetic customers in the café. 'Clearly not. I can't thank you enough.'

Bez began kicking dust around on the floor like a football. 'Really, it was nuffing.'

'Seriously, it was. I would have been stuffed,' then in a hushed voice, 'Everything of value is in here. I won't make that mistake again.'

Then there was an awkward silence. Catherine had to break it. 'What are you doing now?'

Still avoiding eye contact, he answered. 'Not sure. You?'

Catherine knew she should listen to The Bliss Expert but the mugger had scared her. She no longer wanted to stay in Colombia and be forced to hang around with Colin. 'I want to book a flight to Quito, drop my bag off at the hostel, and then take you out for a drink.'

'Sure. I want to book a flight to Rio so I'll come wiv you.' He shuffled behind Catherine like a loyal servant.

Catherine hoped she wouldn't live to regret running to Doug because she needed to feel safe - and wanted - again.

At least I'm not going to get myself into any trouble tonight with Bez.

Chapter Forty-three

Catherine rested her head on the taxi window while massaging her forehead in the feeble hope that it might relieve her hangover, or at least erase the shameful memories from the previous night. Her plan had been to get a shuttle bus from Quito airport to *Equilibrium*, but she had felt so terrible – physically, mentally and emotionally – that the cost of a cab seemed a small price to pay.

When the taxi arrived an hour later, Catherine was still feeling nauseous when she caught sight of Doug sitting on a bench in the front garden of the hostel, reading a book. She gasped. *What's happened to him? He looks hot!* She clambered out of the taxi as elegantly as a newborn giraffe, and ran straight into his arms holding him tightly.

Doug almost ate her hair as he pulled away from the embrace. 'I wasn't expecting such a wonderful greeting.'

'You don't know how good it is to see you.' She eyed him up and down and wondered how he looked like Doug yet so different. His hair had grown and gotten blonder, so he was more like a cool surfer dude than a hippy, and he'd shaved off his beard and moustache so it was the first time she'd seen him without any facial hair. Finally, and probably most importantly, he looked plumper, as if he'd been eating a lot. But it suited him and had filled out his previously scrawny frame.

'I'm pleased to see you too.' He smiled but withdrew from her gawking as he took Catherine's bags from the cab driver. Then he looked her straight in the eyes. 'What's up? You don't seem yourself.'

She looked down and shook her head, recalling the events from the day before and replaying them like a movie in her mind's eye. Not wanting them to haunt her anymore, she pressed an imaginary pause button and shuddered. 'I'm ashamed to tell you. First, tell me about you and what you've been up to. Is there a bar or café we can go to? I need a cola lite.'

'There's a nice place around the corner. Give me a second and then we can go.' With that, he disappeared through the front door and reemerged a couple of minutes later holding a bag and a bottle of water.

The café was a short walk away, so after they'd ordered their drinks, Doug told Catherine what a wonderful time he'd had in Colombia and how he'd spent most of his time on Playa Blanca, a little island off the coast of Catagena, which had been paradise. He said it had been like the United Nations with a backpacker from every country chilling out in hammocks at a small beach resort. He'd met some interesting people and had managed to continue with his meditation, although he said practising yoga had proved difficult but he'd managed to do it most days.

Doug glanced at his watch. 'A couple of Danish guys and I are going to the Ciudad Mitel del Mundo this afternoon. Fancy coming?'

Catherine drained her drink and felt frustrated that Doug hadn't asked her anything about her adventures, and especially what she was ashamed of. But she decided to hide her irritation for now. 'What's that?'

Doug paid the whole bill. 'It translates as the "Middle of the World City" and marks the general location of the equator.'

Catherine shrugged and nodded. Doug led the way by crossing the road to where two Western guys were waiting with day packs on their backs. One of the Danes immediately stood out because his hair was bright white and he was so tall that he looked gangly and awkward. He stooped over as if he was embarrassed by his height. His friend was blonde – but a darker shade than his friend – and looked short in comparison but was actually the same height as Doug, who was over six-foot. Doug greeted them both with a handshake and introduced them to Catherine. The super-tall one's name was Andreas while Nicco was his shorter friend. The bus was on time so Catherine clambered onto the crowded transport first, squeezing in amongst the locals and grabbing an overhead handle whilst observing the locals finding Andreas' height and white hair enormously captivating.

One-by-one, seats became available until Catherine was able to sit next to Doug; the Danish guys had to settle for sitting next to locals. With a journey of 26 kilometres, Catherine wanted to tell Doug about her experience in Colombia. 'Do you want to hear about what happened to me in Colombia or not?' She didn't mean it to come out with quite as much sarcasm.

He tensed his forehead. 'You know I do.'

'In Bogotá, the nightclubs were so full of slim and attractive women that I felt fat, ugly and boring.' Something fired off in her mind that The Bliss Expert had taught her in one of the Steps: no-one can make anyone feel a certain way. But she was so keen to tell Doug about what had happened, she didn't have time to pursue her line of thought.

'There was a guy called Colin who was staying at the same hostel as me. I didn't fancy him, but I was flattered that someone would like *me* despite the overwhelming Colombian competition. Cutting a long story short, we got it together but he dumped me after a couple of days. Then...'

Catherine turned to Doug for dramatic effect but he seemed distracted. She followed the direction of his eyes and saw he was watching Nicco talking to a local guy sitting next to him.

Doug whispered to Catherine. 'Nicco looks worried.'

Oh right! I'm in the middle of pouring my heart out to him, revealing my vulnerability, and he's more interested in a guy he's known for a couple of days. Catherine folded her arms. 'He looks okay to me.'

Doug frowned as he strained to see around the mob of locals in constant flux every time the bus stopped. 'Maybe. But Nicco looks scared.' He shouted to Nicco but he didn't react so Catherine assumed Nicco couldn't hear over the general hum of the bus and chatting passengers. Doug gave up. 'What were you about to say?'

'I was nearly robbed but Bez – one of Colin's mates – saved the day. He was such a sweet, gentle guy and I took him out for a drink to say thank you. We got very drunk and joined the others, including Colin, at a club later. Something inside me snapped when I saw Colin make a beeline for a stunning Colombian woman. It made me feel this big.' Catherine put her thumb and forefinger together an inch apart. 'So I threw myself at Bez to make Colin jealous. When he laughed off my advances, I poured ice cubes down his trousers. He told me to F-off, which made me mad so I slapped him. I don't know if it was the force or the shock but he lost his balance and fell onto the filthy floor. To add insult to injury, I threw my drink at him and stormed out. The next morning, I got up early, packed my stuff and snuck out of the hostel. Luckily I'd already booked a flight to Quito so I just had to hang around the airport for a couple of extra hours. And here I am.' Saying out loud what she had done amplified how furious she was with herself. In a matter of hours, she had thrown away everything she'd learnt at the retreat, from Doug, The Bliss Expert and Willow.

Doug was grimacing.

Catherine nodded as if agreeing with his imagined assessment of her. 'Please don't hate me too.'

He shook his head. 'No, it's not that, I'm worried about Nicco. I would go over there but there are too many people in the way.'

What the...? I've just poured my heart out to him and he's still more concerned for some bloke he barely knows. 'You're obsessed. Do you fancy him or something?'

'What?! No! Something's not right.' He tried to gain Nicco's attention but couldn't so he shook his head and tutted before turning to face Catherine. 'Sorry. Where was I? Oh yes, I was going to ask you about your dad. On the retreat, you told me you didn't think you got much attention from your dad when you were little.'

Was he listening to a word I said? I wasn't talking about my dad.'

But Doug continued before she could argue. 'When our needs as children aren't met, we replay them as adults. For women, that usually plays out with their relationships with men.'

Catherine was flabbergasted as he had repeated what Step Three had explained.

'You thought your dad didn't pay you enough attention as a child and so it created a neediness within you. As an adult, you attempt to satisfy this neediness through male attention. So when you 'get' a man, you feel elated and as if you've won or conquered something. This feeling lasts until a man withdraws his attention from you. Then the years of pain, anger and frustration of not getting your needs met as a child snowball into a torrent of negative emotion aimed at the person you think is causing you the hurt. But it's never really about the men. They've just reflected back to you the pain you experienced as a child and are still experiencing as an adult. But remember, your thinking that you didn't get enough attention from your dad was only your perception, not the truth.'

The Bliss Expert had talked about there being no such thing as reality. How does Doug know about Step Five as well? And why do I need Doug to want me now? I need to change before I ruin this relationship too. 'But how do I change?'

Doug grinned and Catherine's heart almost melted. *How could Sophie see how hot he was when I couldn't?* 'First, do you see why your behaviour in Colombia makes perfect sense?'

'Yes but how do I change?'

Doug was about to answer when the bus came to an abrupt halt. A sign post outside the window that said *Ciudad Mitel del Mundo* provided a clue that they'd arrived at their destination. They tussled their way off the bus and caught up with Nicco who was looking rather pale.

Nicco flinched ever so slightly, then held up his hands to show them trembling. 'I was robbed at knifepoint.'

There was a chorused response. 'What?'

Nicco's voice continued to wobble as he spoke. 'The local next to me put a knife here,' he pointed to his left side just above his waist, 'and demanded my wallet and watch. He got off the bus at the next stop as if nothing had happened.'

Not wishing to experience something similar on the way back, Catherine suggested they get a taxi back. Nicco turned to his friend Andreas and they conversed in Danish before answering, 'Yes, I'd like that. Andreas can lend me money for taxi.'

The four companions were about to hail a cab when a gold-toothed woman offered them some bull's penis soup. Catherine declined on the grounds she was a vegetarian but the other three weren't quite so lucky in saying no to a determined octogenarian. As Nicco took a bite of the delicacy, Catherine saw he had done a better job of hiding his horror at being robbed than eating a bull's penis.

Later that night, at a cheap Pizza bar, Doug topped up Catherine's glass. 'It was a good suggestion of yours to get a taxi back. I think Nicco appreciated it.'

'No problem.'

He took a sip of his wine. 'So where were we? Oh yes, you asked how you can change your pattern with men. Before I answer that can I ask if you were drunk when you molested Bez?'

'I didn't molest him exactly! But, yes, I was wasted. But what's that got to do with anything?'

'A lot, but I'll explain later. The next time you fancy a guy, do a mental check and decide what specifically it is that you fancy. If it's his disinterest in you, then this is a sure sign to leave him alone. Or, if you're feeling needy, walk away.'

So because Doug doesn't seem as into me as before and because I'm feeling particularly needy after what happened in Colombia, it might explain why I'm finding him so attractive now? Whereas in San Marcos, he was like a dog on heat around me and I had Gus to keep my neediness at bay; that's why I wasn't interested in him then? But what he's saying is that I have to steer clear of him because I want him for the wrong reasons. Noted.

'Earth to Catherine!'

She apologised and asked him to continue.

'These men, or your dad, will never be able to make you feel better. Their attention would be like putting a plaster over a gaping wound. There's only one way to heal the neediness inside of you, but let's talk about that another time.' He finished his glass of wine and topped it up with the last dregs left in the bottle. 'Your biggest enemy at the moment is alcohol. Not that I'm against it; it's just that while you're trying to consciously change, it's difficult to do so when alcohol is involved.'

All the talk of alcohol was making Catherine thirsty so she sampled more of her wine. 'How come?' Catherine smiled at the irony of them polishing off a bottle of wine before their food had arrived.

'It takes away conscious reasoning, which means your unconscious mind will take over. At the moment, your unconscious mind is programmed to pursue men who don't want you because it thinks that will make you feel better about yourself. But imagine if you hadn't been drinking that night in Bogotá? If you'd seen Colin chatting up that attractive Colombian girl but you'd been drinking water, what do you think you'd have done?'

Catherine pondered for a few moments. 'I'd probably have left the club and gone to bed crying.'

'Now let's take it a step further. Imagine it's the same scenario but you know what you know now and you weren't drinking. What would have happened?'

She tapped her glass while she considered his question. 'I would have reasoned with myself that I didn't want Colin. I had only wanted him because he was a substitute for my dad's attention. So I wouldn't have been bothered by him flirting with someone else, and I wouldn't have needed Bez's attention to make myself feel better.'

Doug had a huge grin on his face. 'You're a quick learner! How does that feel?'

'Much better. Thank you. But in the club that night, I would have still felt bad about myself. I was surrounded by Colombian babes and then there was me. I would still have felt fat, ugly and boring. How do I change that?'

'That's for another time. I'm tired and hungry. Where's our food, by the way?' He looked round for a waiter. 'I'd like to add one more thing, though, and that's to be open to the nice guys out there. Give them a chance.'

Catherine's cheeks grew red. *I don't know what to do now! I fancy him but I'm afraid that's because I'm feeling needy, which means I should leave him alone in a romantic sense. Now he's saying I should give nice guys a chance. And he's a nice guy. This stuff is impossible!*

Their food arrived so Catherine gave up thinking about what to do. 'How do you know all of this stuff? Is it to do with NLP that you talked about in Guatemala?' She took a bite of her Llapingachos and loved the potato and cheese patties. Then she dipped them in their tasty peanut sauce called Salsa de Mani. 'Here, try some, they're gorgeous!' Catherine passed him her plate.

'Delicious! Much better than my bull's penis soup earlier.' He smirked. 'It's partly NLP, but not exclusively. I read a lot of self-help books and, if you take the main teachings from most of them, it's that *you* have the answers to everything.

Your outer world is a reflection of your inner world, so you need to heal your inner world if you want to change what's happening in the outside world. I was in a pretty dark place once and NLP helped me to understand that my negative thought patterns were causing me to do certain destructive things in my life. By changing my thoughts, I changed my life. I'm not heralding it as the be-all and end-all of transformation, but it helped me.'

'*You* had negative thoughts and did destructive things? No way! I don't believe you.'

'Well, believe it.'

Catherine let the silence hang in the air hoping Doug would fill it with further details but he didn't; he just stared at his plate. 'What should I do if I'm interested in learning more about NLP?'

He pulled his bag from the floor and onto his lap while he ferreted around in it for something. After a few moments he presented her with a book. The title was *Think and Grow Rich* by Napoleon Hill.

'It's not NLP, but I had a feeling you might be interested in it.' He handed the book to her.

She swallowed the last mouthful of food as she took the book from him. 'Wow, how did you know to bring it?'

'I just had an inkling I'd need it at some point today,' he said, not answering her question.

'Do you want to know something crazy? This book was published in 1937, yet even today very few people know about the power and impact of their thoughts. Just think how much better people's lives could be if they were aware of this stuff. I hope you enjoy reading it as much as I did.'

'Very odd,' she said, but she didn't press him further. They had finished their food and she was tired. 'Come on, let's get back before we get locked out of the hostel.' With this, they paid the bill and left the restaurant arm-in-arm, and Catherine felt a lot happier than when she'd woken up that morning. On the walk back, her mind was buzzing from their conversation about how she could change her pattern with men by using NLP and *Think and Grow Rich*. But most of all, she wanted to know what destructive things Doug had done in his life.

Chapter Forty-four

Catherine headed to the internet café feeling positive. She sent a quick email to The Bliss Expert updating him on her conversation with Doug and asking him why her default position was to feel fat, ugly and boring. While waiting for a reply from him, she read an email from Sophie.

So, you're off to be with Doug again; are you sure you're just friends? I'm in Isla Mujeres and you were absolutely right, it's gorgeous. I can't drag myself away from this place. Although that might also have something to do with a fella I've met...! He's a Brit called Henry, he's 22 and a good crack. We might go to Cuba together next week. I'm dreading the day we have to say goodbye to each other. I've fallen for him. Big time!

Give Doug a kiss from me when you see him and keep me updated with your news.

By the time she'd finished reading Sophie's email, there was one waiting from The Bliss Expert.

Even though I didn't want you to run into Doug's arms, you're there now and he'll be great for your learning. You've learnt so much and have come so far that it's time for you to discover more Steps that will help transform your life, and will answer your question as to why you feel fat, ugly and boring.

However, before we move on, Catherine, it's time to open your eyes. What happened in Colombia must never happen again. You need to integrate all of the Steps you've learnt up to now and acknowledge that, at an unconscious level, you have created your life. You must accept that there is no such thing as reality because what you are experiencing as reality is not a single, constant truth. There are only your perceptions and the meanings you assign to them that create your reality. These are based on your past experiences and your beliefs, which were predominantly established in your childhood. As a result, there is something deep inside you that needs to be healed. The next Step will reveal what that is and it is the key to finding true love, happiness and bliss.

Catherine held her breath and clicked onto the next section, excited to see what The Bliss Expert was referring to.

STEP EIGHT EXPLAINED: THE KEY

Millions of people around the world, including you, suffer from a disorder they are oblivious to. Yet it holds the key to transforming their lives for the better.

What is it? It's low self-esteem.

Self-esteem refers to the extent to which you like and accept yourself – warts and all - and how worthwhile a person you think you are. It is knowing that you're worthy of being loved, respected and accepted. Only when you know this, will you be loved, respected and accepted by other people. Only when you have healthy self-esteem will you attract a partner who loves and respects you as much as you do him. (Although the irony is that you won't feel the need for a partner when you truly love and respect yourself.)

The wonderful news is that your self-esteem can take as little as two weeks to change! The reason is because your recent thoughts, feelings and experiences tend to stay in your conscious mind for roughly a couple of weeks. So if you change your thoughts, they will start to change your self-esteem in roughly two weeks.

Do you remember all the way back to Step Two, when I mentioned that there is a Real Self beneath Cath and Catherine? This is the perfect you, the flawless diamond that I mentioned. Your true self has perfect self-esteem because it only knows self-love. This Step will help you to identify what level your self-esteem is at and what you can do to boost it. Step Nine will show you how to change the meanings you assign to your perceptions. Step Ten will show you a short-cut to improving your self-esteem so you can dust off the illusions you have mistakenly created about yourself and return to who you really are.

If you think about it, self-esteem is the sum total of the beliefs you have about yourself. As you already know, beliefs are not the same as reality; they might feel real but they are only your perceptions and interpretation of what's going on. Your beliefs about yourself exist because of the way you think and not because the world is that way. So you need you to be aware of the beliefs you have about yourself, replace the negatives with positive beliefs, and act as if they are true. Ultimately they will become true because, as you know, the belief cycle is a self-fulfilling cycle.

One way to identify your beliefs is to listen to how you talk to yourself because self-talk is a direct reflection of your beliefs about yourself. If you criticise yourself or say anything negative about yourself, stop it! Replace the negative thought with something positive and pretend it is true. Never again will you think of yourself as 'fat, ugly and boring;' instead you will only describe yourself as 'slim, beautiful and fun.' Watch what effect it will have in your life. In fact, listen to all your thoughts, and if they're negative, change them to something more positive. After all, who's in charge of your thoughts?! Remember, thinking something different will redirect your brain's search engine to find examples which will back up your new thoughts.

Summary of Step Eight:

1. Identify the beliefs you have about yourself. Words such as should/shouldn't, must/mustn't and can/can't are good ways to identify beliefs. Also listen to your self-talk and notice any negative things you say to yourself.

2. Think of a positive belief and/or thought that will counteract the negative belief and/or thought.

3. Act 'as if' it's true.

STEP EIGHT TASK:

1. What beliefs do you have about yourself? What negative things do you say about yourself?

2. What positive things can you say to yourself instead?

3. How can you act 'as if' they're true?

Catherine reread the email three times and typed her response straight away. She didn't need to think for long. She had heard herself repeatedly tell herself that she was an idiot, stupid, fat, ugly, and boring. And this might explain why she constantly compared herself to other girls and how she ended up feeling even worse about herself. *But how can just thinking 'I'm slim, pretty and fun' make me feel better about myself, stop me fancying unsuitable men and make my life better? I must talk to Doug about it and see what he says about it!*

Chapter Forty-five

Brown on Tour

Day 156: Baños, Ecuador

Today was one of my best days since I left England.

Doug and I are in Ecuador in a place called Banos. We went for a 20-kilometre bike ride along a hair-raising gorge. It culminated in crossing a kilometre-deep valley in a cable car that resembled a shopping basket in both looks and safety. We were slowly and precariously pulled across whilst we absorbed the most amazing views. I was scared out of my wits that we could fall at any moment. There was a river running beneath us but it was so far down that it looked like a stream.

Once we reached the other side we walked to a waterfall and abseiled down to the bottom, where we swam in clear, cool water. It was absolutely brilliant and I loved every minute of it. We then cheated by catching a truck back to Baños, where we felt we deserved to relax in the healing properties of the renowned, local, hot baths. Not only was the water cloudy and smelly like warm wee, every time I waded my hands through it, I came up with a clump of other peoples' hair. Yuck! We only lasted about five minutes in it before making a quick exit.

Catherine logged off and looked at Doug, who was standing in the doorway beaming a huge smile. 'Ready?' he asked.

'Yep.' Catherine locked the door to her room and joined Doug in the corridor. They walked through the village looking for somewhere to eat and agreed on a place that made oven-baked pizzas. They sat down and reminisced about the day's events.

'I honestly thought the cable was going to break,' Catherine said, now able to laugh with the knowledge they were still alive.

'Your face was a picture!' Doug formed his fingers into a square pretending it was a camera. 'I wish I'd captured the look of pure joy tinged with pure fear. It was priceless!'

After the laughter had subsided, they used the opportunity to peruse the menu and order. Then Doug asked Catherine how she was getting on with *Think and Grow Rich*.

'I'm enjoying it.' Catherine was momentarily distracted as the waiter delivered their drinks. 'It coincides with some emails I've been receiving, which I've been meaning to tell you about.' She gulped a mouthful of sparkling water and got a hit of bubbles like popping candy exploding on her tongue. 'A stranger called The Bliss Expert has been sending me Steps on how I can improve my life. And giving me advice about what to do, and what not to do, while I've been travelling.'

Doug seemed unperturbed. 'Such as?'

'He was keen that I travel with you when the time was right. He also knew things about my past. It's weird. I wish I knew who he was and what he gets out of our relationship, if you can call it that.' Catherine had already drained her glass and was about to pour herself some more sparkling water when the bottle slipped out of her hand and fell onto the table with a loud bang. Luckily, the cap was on or it would have spilled everywhere.

The vibration caused the straw from Doug's drink to flip out and tumble through the air onto the table, splashing Catherine in the face as it went. Doug stifled a chuckle. 'Sounds like you've got a Guardian Angel. But it is intriguing why he's helping you.' His question suggested he already knew the answer.

She dabbed the spray from her face using a paper napkin. 'I know, I've asked myself that same question. Maybe I'll start getting demands for money!' She laughed before turning serious again. 'The latest Step is about turning negative thoughts into positive thoughts.'

Doug picked up the fallen straw, sucked on it and placed it back into his glass of water. 'In general or about yourself?'

'Both. What do you know about it?' She fiddled with her straw and flicked water at Doug.

'Hey! Mine was an accident. That was not!'

'I would apologise but that would mean I'm sorry. But I'm not. Carry on.'

'Despite books like *Think and Grow Rich*, very few people understand the power of their thoughts. If they did, they'd never think another negative thought again.'

Catherine paused while the waiter arrived with their pizzas. 'Is that because thoughts, like beliefs, are a self-fulfilling prophecy?' She sawed at the pizza ferociously before a slice freed itself from the whole. Catherine gobbled it before the melting cheese could ooze down her chin.

'Ten out of ten. Absolutely.' Doug gave up using his knife and fork and ripped off a large slice of pizza with his bare hands, and devoured it in seconds. 'And it's exactly the same thing when it comes to self-esteem. Your thoughts about yourself create your reality.'

How does he do that?! I hadn't mentioned self-esteem. It's as if he's reading The Bliss Expert's Steps too. 'I kind of get it intellectually but I'm struggling to see how changing my beliefs about myself can change my reality.' Catherine chewed on her first slice of pizza slowly, savouring every flavor that lit up her taste buds.

After gulping down another mouthful, Doug pulled the straw out of his drink, licked the liquid off, and held it up. 'For arguments sake, think of this,' he pointed at the straw, 'as a cigarette. You told me you used to smoke, right?'

Catherine nodded, curious where this was going.

'When you were a smoker,' Doug coughed, 'what did you think of cigarettes?'

Catherine didn't need to think for long. 'They were a life saver. They helped me cope with stress and relax.'

Doug nodded. 'And now that you've given up, what are your thoughts about them?' He stuffed more pizza into his mouth.

'They're disgusting. They enslaved me for years, cost me a small fortune and affected my health so badly that I resorted to walking on a treadmill rather than running.'

'So what changed?' He placed his straw back into his water.

'My thoughts and feelings. When I thought positively, I felt good about smoking and so I smoked. When I thought negatively about smoking, I felt bad and stopped.' Catherine finished the last of her pizza and eyed the remaining chunk on Doug's plate.

As if reading her mind, Doug licked his fingers clean and wiped them dry on his jeans, signaling that he was full. 'Exactly. Now, moving onto self-esteem, how do you feel about yourself?' He pointed to the slice on his plate so Catherine grabbed it before he could change his mind.

She snuck in a mouthful of pizza but swallowed too quickly and choked. 'Honestly?' She coughed some more. 'That I'm fat, ugly and boring.'

Doug shook his head and appeared pained. 'Okay. If you believe these things about yourself, what are you likely to do?'

Catherine looked at the half-eaten piece of pizza in her hand as if it were a loaded gun and placed it back onto her plate. 'Comfort eat to make myself feel better.'

Doug grinned. 'And what happens when you comfort eat?'

'I get fat! And then I feel ugly. And because I want to hide from people, I feel boring.'

Punching his fist in the air, Doug whispered, 'And the penny drops!'

'But I still don't get it that suddenly thinking I'm slim, pretty and fun is miraculously going to change that?' As her hand landed heavily on the table in demonstration of her frustration, the cutlery hopped in the air and the rest of the diners turned to stare. Catherine blushed.

'By thinking about yourself more positively, it'll cause you to be mindful of what and why you're eating. If you lose weight, you'll feel better about yourself, and you might attract a long-term boyfriend. Or perhaps you won't feel the need for a boyfriend anymore because you'll feel happy by yourself.'

And he does it again! Repeating what The Bliss Expert had said. 'But I can't just suddenly believe it!' She was about to slam her fist onto the table again but stopped before she caused another scene.

'It doesn't matter whether you believe it or not. Yet. What matters is that you think something more positive about yourself because that will start to make you feel different and *that* is what will change your outcome. Remember, your conscious mind can only focus on a small fraction of the million bits of information that bombard your senses every second of every day. While you tell your conscious mind to focus on fat, ugly and boring, it'll only notice these things in you and other people.'

'You mean like putting fat, ugly and boring into an internet search engine and it only searching for items related to fat, ugly and boring?'

'That's exactly it! However, if you feed more positive data into your conscious mind – and to use your analogy, put slim, pretty and interesting into the search engine – you will start to see these things in yourself and others. One day, you will think positively about your beautiful, womanly curves, you will appreciate how attractive and fun you are and will understand how men would choose you over some skinny, boring thing any day.'

Catherine blushed scarlet. 'Thanks. Errrm…' Catherine sucked at her drink even though it was empty.

Doug took one of her hands and held it and electric sparks raced through her body. Then it dawned on Catherine that Doug hadn't been giving her a compliment; he had been offering a way for her to rethink about herself. Her cheeks burned a deeper shade of red.

Catherine removed her hand from beneath Doug's to order another sparkling water from the waiter who was rushing past their table.

Doug sat back and smiled as if nothing had happened. 'Until you *really* believe it, just 'fake it until you make it.' It doesn't matter whether you think you've got beautiful womanly curves or not. What matters is that you act as if you do because it'll become the truth. In the words of Henry Ford, "Whether you think you can or you think you can't, you're right."'

Hadn't The Bliss Expert used this quote too? Doug's uncanny ability to repeat stuff The Bliss Expert had explained was plain weird.

'And, for the record, you have got beautiful curves.' He placed his hand back on her hand and squeezed it. 'I wish you could see the person I see: the amazing person beneath both Cath and Catherine. She isn't down on herself. She loves and respects herself as much as she does everyone around her. She doesn't harshly judge herself or others. She doesn't need to accomplish or achieve anything — or pull men, eat junk food or drink alcohol — in order to feel good about herself. She doesn't need anyone to feel good about herself. She just feels good about herself and this reflects an inner beauty that will naturally attract positive people and situations to her.'

Catherine's cheeks were so hot they could have cooked marshmallows to gooey perfection.

Chapter Forty-six

Catherine headed to an internet café, even before having breakfast, and updated The Bliss Expert on her conversation with Doug. While she waited for a response, she emailed a few friends. By the time she'd finished, The Bliss Expert did not disappoint and there was an email waiting from him.

I'm so glad you've got Doug to help you understand the Steps. Remember to monitor how you talk to yourself and turn any negative thoughts into something more positive. Particularly watch how you call yourself idiot a lot. What could you say to be kinder to yourself?

Just a word of advice: if you are developing feelings towards Doug, keep them to yourself. I hope you trust me enough to listen. If you don't, you will mess up what you have together. Be open and honest with each other, stay just good friends, for now, and things will work out fine.

There's no way I'm going against his advice.

You are now ready for the next Step which will help you:

STEP NINE EXPLAINED: INFINITE MEANINGS

A direct consequence of self-esteem is how you perceive anything that happens in your life, because you process a situation as either positive or negative depending on the level of your self-esteem. If you have low self-esteem, you will see your life as a series of external disasters, where everything goes wrong and you always end up being the victim. Alternatively, if you have healthy self-esteem, you seize every situation as an opportunity to learn and become a stronger person.

Power Thinking is a technique which helps you alter the way you perceive an event and thus allows you to change the meaning you assign to it. If you change the meaning, you change your response and behaviour as well. It is not about ignoring problems, but about having sufficient flexibility to make your point of view work for you instead of against you.

STEP NINE TASK:

The next time you feel angry or annoyed about something, think about how you might think about it differently in order to make yourself feel better. Notice how your behaviour – and the outcome - changes as a result of this.

Catherine's thoughts immediately turned to her parents and how she had chosen to believe that they didn't care about her, which had led her to feel bad about herself, and to distance herself from them. However, the truth was that she loved them deeply and wanted to be close to them. *What can I think differently?* Nothing came to mind at first but then she remembered what she'd learnt at Christmas. They did love her, but their problem was they couldn't show it. Knowing this made her feel better but she wanted to take things a step further. Just because they were unable to express themselves, this didn't mean she shouldn't. It was at that moment that she decided to do something she'd never done before: to tell her parents she loved them.

I left Baños to travel to a place called Montanita (which is on the Pacific coast in Ecuador); it's a beautiful, rustic village that's famous amongst surfers. I gave surfing a go and really enjoyed it, despite not being very good at it!

Then we went to Peru to Trujillo, famous for its ruins of the great prehistoric Moche and Chimu cultures who had settled there before the Inca conquest. Unfortunately the rain had been so incessant that we had to spend the night on the floor of the bus station as there were no buses due to a flooded bridge. That had to be my worst night's accommodation to date! We didn't want to stay in the hustle and bustle of Trujillo so the next day we went to a nearby beach resort called Huanchaco where we found a plush hotel with a swimming pool for $10 a night! It's so nice to stay in relative luxury for a change that we're still here now. I'm gearing myself up for a LONG journey across Peru to a place called Huacachina, which is where it's possible to go sandboarding on sand dunes!

I hope all's well with you, and remember I love you very much.

Catherine pressed the Send button and wondered how her declaration of love would be received.

Chapter Forty-seven

Despite the tightness and pain in her muscles, Catherine was glad they'd decided to stay a few days in Huacachina, which was in the middle of the Peruvian desert. She turned around to look back at where they were staying and grinned. If she ignored the blight that was their hostel – which was more akin to a Club 18-30 hotspot than a destination for backpackers – the view of the mirror-calm lagoon ringed by palm trees and gigantic sand dunes (one of which she was currently attempting to climb) was utterly stunning.

'Come on!' Doug shouted as he grabbed Catherine's free arm to haul her up the steep incline. Her other arm clutched the plywood board firmly, not wanting to risk having to chase after it as it shot to the bottom in seconds.

'This is so difficult!' *If I tell myself it's difficult, then it will be difficult.* 'What I meant to say was, okay, I'm coming!' Catherine trudged up the hill one foot at a time, trying to ignore the pain coursing through her body as the talcum-powder-soft-sand sucked her feet down like an industrial-strength vacuum.

'Well done!'

'Thanks. I can do this, I can do this!'

By the time they reached the top of the dune an hour later, Catherine's face was as red as a beetroot. After securing the board deep in the sand, Catherine gulped down the rest of her water, wiped the moisture from her face with her already sweat-drenched vest top, and sat down to catch her breath. The spectacular 360-degree-view showed wind-sculptured dunes rolling into the distance in stark contrast to the clear blue sky. Goosebumps coursed up and down her back like a Mexican Wave.

'It's like a set from a Star Wars movie.'

But Doug didn't reply. Instead, he budged up next to Catherine, put his arm around her and kissed her shoulder. She didn't know if it was the mystical energy of the place, Doug's compassion or her growing feelings towards him but, whatever the cause, tears exploded out in a torrent.

'Go on, let it out,' Doug said as he kissed her shoulder again, this time his lips lingering long enough for it to signal that it was more than a friendly peck.

His soft lips on her exposed flesh stopped the flow of tears. Catherine turned to face him and their eyes locked, triggering a connection that felt so powerful it was as if nothing else existed around them. Moving his arm slowly yet deliberately from her shoulder, Doug trailed his index finger across the contours of Catherine's moisture-tinged back, sending shockwaves throughout her body. When he reached her jaw, he held it in his hand as delicately as if it were porcelain. His touch, together with the build-up from days of not knowing the boundaries of their relationship, meant Catherine was ready to surrender and plunge in despite her mind shouting otherwise: *No! What am I doing? The Bliss Expert warned me not to do this.* As she struggled with her thoughts, Doug inched his head forward until their lips were so close they were all but touching. Invisible sparks of electricity were flowing between their mouths as if there were communicating carnal messages with each other. As their lips made contact and their tongues were about to connect, the area around them went dark as a giant cloud passed in front of the sun. But before she could comprehend what had happened, Catherine heard a voice with a strong Birmingham accent. 'Hi. It's bostin' ain't it?'

'Eh?' It dawned on Catherine that the darkness had been, in fact, the shadow of a rather plump figure standing over them.

Catherine and Doug untangled their embrace and turned their attention to the stranger, who was sitting down and making herself comfortable inches in front of them, showing no regard for their personal space.

The girl repeated herself, 'I said it's bostin' ain't it?' Catherine vaguely recognised her from the hostel and looked at Doug in the hope he'd understood what the girl had just said.

Doug broke the awkwardness. 'Yes, it's stunning, isn't it? Are you staying at *Casa de Ambito*? I've seen you about.'

'Yeah, that's right. I'm Tracy.' She proffered her hand to Doug while completely ignoring Catherine.

Rude cow! I mean, there must be a reason why she's being so forward. Maybe she's lonely.

'Hi, good to meet you. I'm Doug and this here is the gorgeous Catherine.' He rested his hand on Catherine's knee, which helped to calm down her irritation.

Doug's suggestive move signalled to Tracy that she had to include Catherine in the conversation if she wanted to stay. Tracy semi-smiled at Catherine so the three of them engaged in the customary traveller-question-and-answer-session. From this, they found out that Tracy was thirty, she was from Birmingham, she'd been in Central and South America for a year and didn't have any plans to go back to the UK anytime soon. Catherine assessed her while she was chatting. Her face was pretty in a quirky, unconventional way, which reminded her of Jennifer Anniston in *Friends*. Her hair was also similar to Rachel's in the American sitcom. However, there were two big differences: Tracy had a strong Birmingham accent and was slightly overweight.

Only Doug had time to answer Tracy's questions before the sun dipped below the horizon and left a dramatic trail of orange, red and yellow whispers across the sky. It was so spectacular that none of them wanted to ruin the moment with words. During the silence, Doug clasped Catherine's hand and she gripped it back tightly, aware that Tracy was watching them with the intensity of a laser beam.

Tracy slapped Doug on the back as she stood up. 'Come on, we need to get down before it gets too dark.'

Who put her in charge? Stop it, Catherine! She's right, we need to go or we won't be able to see where we're going. 'Come on, let's go.' Catherine pulled her board from the sand's firm grip, placed it on the slope and stood on it, but the board had other ideas as it bolted forward, causing Catherine to face-plant the sand. She had visions of the board careering down the slope – on its own – but Doug managed to snare it with his foot just in time and handed it back to her.

He chuckled as Catherine stood up, covered from head to toe in sand. 'Why not lie face-down on your stomach like when you body surfed?'

Catherine did as he suggested and screamed as Doug took his foot off the board and she soared down the sand at breakneck speed like a bobsleigh. Before she had time to think another thought, she had arrived at the bottom of the dune. The descent had taken mere seconds.

By the time they walked to the hostel, the bar was already heaving with backpackers who looked like they were ready to party, which was standard fare at *Casa de Ambito*. As they got closer to the bar, Tracy moved her body provocatively in time with the music and tugged on Doug's arm. 'Let's get a drink!'

What's she playing at? How dare she try to muscle in on Doug! Catherine butted in before Doug had a chance to answer, 'Great idea, but I need to shower first. I've got sand in places it really shouldn't be! Doug, are you coming?'

'You go ahead. I'm famished and need a cold drink.'

'Okay, I'll be quick.' But Doug had already disappeared through the crowd and was headed to the bar, with Tracy close behind.

As the water's spray cascaded down her face, Catherine replayed the moment she and Doug had nearly kissed. The thought aroused a tingling sensation down below and she was tempted to pleasure herself with the shower jet but, knowing it would ruin her fun with Doug later if she climaxed now, she dismissed the idea. Then a strange thing happened when she switched off the water: a feeling of nausea snuck up on her like swirling sea mist and she suddenly felt afraid. The Bliss Expert had told her to remain just good friends with Doug, and Doug himself had cautioned her against chasing men for the wrong reasons. He'd also said drinking alcohol was a bad idea whilst trying to make conscious decisions so Catherine knew what she had to do. *I won't drink tonight, so my conscious mind can make rational decisions and, hopefully, I'll choose to do the right thing.*

Standing in front of the mirror, Catherine found herself scrutinising her body. Facing her reflection face-on, she prodded her flabby thighs. *Yuck! How did I let myself get so fat?* Then she turned to the side and pulled up the skin above her breasts to make them more pert. *When did they get so saggy?* As she heard her damaging thoughts, she stopped, shook her head as if ridding her mind of any negativity and turned to face the mirror again. *Look how much weight I've already lost. Well done! Look at my slim stomach, my thick, glossy hair and sparkling eyes.* She then turned to the side once more. *Look at my full breasts and voluptuous curves.* Feeling mildly better, she got dressed and sat on the bed before letting her body flop onto the hard mattress. Closing her eyes, she saw herself in her imagination standing in front of a mirror, admiring her body as if she were proud of her muscular, fit and curvaceous body. She visualised Doug commenting on her wonderful figure and felt the fantastic feelings associated with having the perfect physique.

By the time Catherine came round from a semi-conscious state, she realised she'd been gone a lot longer than she had intended. When she joined Doug and Tracy at the bar, it wasn't surprising that they were already drunk. The row of empty shot glasses suggested they'd been indulging in more than just beer.

Beaming a huge grin, Doug flung his arms open as if to embrace Catherine, causing him to lose balance and slip off the stool he'd been sitting on. From the floor he gazed up at Catherine through glassy eyes. 'Catherine! I've missed you!' As he hoisted himself up, he attempted to speak in a quieter voice meant only for Catherine, but his volume control wasn't working properly so everyone within a hundred yard radius heard. 'I'm drunk. Should have eaten something.' A hiccup slipped out as if to emphasis the point.

Tracy almost elbowed Catherine out of the way in an attempt to help Doug prop himself back onto his stool. *Calm down, don't react. I'm better than this.* Catherine chose not to react and signalled to the barman instead. 'Cola lite, please.'

Doug shook his head. 'You feeling,' hiccup, 'okay?'

Catherine smiled at him. 'I don't feel like drinking tonight, I...'

But before she could finish telling him that she was not drinking alcohol to ensure her conscious mind could think straight, Tracy interrupted. 'Oh Dougy, leave her be if she wants to drink pop like a baby.'

Drink pop like a baby? Dougy? Who the hell does she think she is? Catherine walked away before she could lose her temper and grabbed a menu from the bar as she headed to an empty table next to the swimming pool. *She's lonely, she's lonely.* It took Doug a few seconds to register what had happened before he stumbled after her and sat next to her on a plastic chair that would have looked more at home in a recycling centre.

He leant close to Catherine's face and the fumes from the alcohol were so strong they could have singed her eyebrows. If she had to guess, they'd been drinking white rum. 'What's up?' He hiccupped again and put his hand on hers.

Catherine was about to tell him how annoyed she was that Tracy was flirting with him when Tracy joined them.

Doug snapped his hand away from Catherine's. *Why'd he do that?*

Tracy rubbed Doug's back. 'Yow okay, Dougy? Then she turned her attention to Catherine. 'So why's the great Catherine got a cob on then?'

What the…? No, stop, act like an adult. 'I've not got a cob on! Do you have an issue with me, Tracy?'

Tracy nodded. 'Yow got a bob on yowself.'

'What does that even mean?' Catherine tried to keep her tone neutral and looked to Doug for support but his drooping eyelids indicated that he'd shortly be in Noddy land.

Tracy repeated the sentence slower and louder as if she were speaking to a foreigner.

Stay calm. 'You can repeat yourself as often as you like but I still don't know what you mean.'

Tracy reiterated what Catherine had said but did it by mimicking a posh accent, then added, 'Are yow thick or something?'

The penny dropped and Catherine realised Tracy was jealous of her. This change in thought transformed her irritation into pity. 'I think you've had enough to drink.'

'What?' Tracy stood up with such force that the chair flew back and landed in between a group of boys who told her to watch what she was doing, to which she told them to *piss off*. The she announced to the air, 'I've only just started!' before downing the rest of her drink and throwing the empty glass bottle into the swimming pool. Catherine noticed that people were staring at Tracy and whispering about her but she was oblivious as she flounced away to the bar. Catherine jostled Doug's shoulder in an attempt to wake him up but he just moaned and his head rolled to one side. Then Catherine heard Tracy before she saw her making her way through the crowd, parting them like Moses and the Red Sea as she jostled and shouldered people out of her way. It was a miracle there were no spillages from the two bottles of beer and six shots of clear liquid which she was balancing precariously on a tray.

After putting three shots and a bottle in front of Doug, it took Tracy a few seconds to register he wasn't going to be drinking any more that night, so she sat down with a huff and threw back all six shots in quick succession. 'Yow are annoying, yow know that?' Twisting around in her chair and pointing erratically at guys in the bar she said, 'They're all staring at yow. Yow are pretty, fun, cool and have a bostin' body. Why would they look at me when yow are around?' She slammed her bottle on the table with such force that it caused froth to ooze up and out of the top like lava from a volcano.

What's she talking about? The men are staring at her; because she's making an exhibition of herself! It struck Catherine that The Bliss Expert was right – there's no such thing as reality, only one's perception of it. Tracy clearly had issues and was projecting them onto Catherine. It suddenly struck Catherine that her own drunken behaviour in the past might not have been dissimilar to Tracy's.

'Doug's like Chris Hemsworth and he adores yow. But yow keep him trailing after yow like a puppy dog. Why yow leading him on?'

Catherine shook her head and asked, 'What *are* you talking about?'

'Doug said yow were a prick tease.'

Catherine's heart sank as she wondered if Doug had really said that. But before Catherine could quiz Tracy further, she stood up on her chair - which nearly toppled over in the process - and stepped onto the table, grinding her hips to the beats of the pumping dance music that was getting progressively louder as it was past nine o'clock. Then she started removing her t-shirt slowly, as if she were performing a striptease, which got her lots of wolf whistles from ogling blokes. Catherine shook her head and rolled her eyes but was secretly happy she'd decided not to drink or she might have been on the table with her. Tracy was about to untie her fisherman trousers when Catherine felt the plastic table legs shudder as if they were going to give way. It was a matter of seconds before the feeble legs buckled under Tracy's weight and she tumbled into the swimming pool. To Catherine, Tracy's unplanned belly flop seemed to be happening in slow motion and she was fairly certain she'd seen Tracy's head hit the side of the pool as she tumbled in. While everyone else lost interest and continued drinking and chatting with their friends, Catherine leapt up from her chair and knelt down by the pool waiting for Tracy to emerge. Time stood still. Catherine was about to jump in to rescue her when a bewildered and breathless Tracy bobbed to the surface flailing about. Catherine tried to grab her arm to help haul her up and out of the pool but Tracy pushed her away. 'Get off!'

'I'm trying to help you!' Catherine twisted around to see Doug slumped in his chair grunting. She was about to stand up to shake him awake when she heard a retching sound followed by a warm liquid feeling splattering on her foot. She looked down to witness Tracy – half in and half out of the pool – vomiting on her foot. Catherine flung her flip-flop off and hopped to the outside shower to wash the sick off her foot. Catherine was surprised to notice she wasn't angry with Tracy, she felt sorry for her instead. However, the night's events had jolted Catherine. She knew she couldn't be in a party place anymore, nor be surrounded by people like Tracy. What's more, she knew that she had to leave Doug if she were to complete her journey because it was time for her to be on her own.

Chapter Forty-eight

Catherine cursed when she saw the time. The bus for Ica was leaving in thirty minutes and it was the only one that day. She figured she'd make it if she left within fifteen minutes so she hurriedly got dressed and threw the rest of her belongings into her backpack, feeling sick about leaving Doug. But she had to do it. She had just written him a goodbye note when he stirred and mumbled, 'What time is it?'

She looked at him and her heart turned to liquid. His hair was disheveled, sticking out all over the place, and she could tell his stubble was a few days old because it had a ginger tinge to it while his eyes looked like pin holes. 'Nine o'clock.'

When he registered that Catherine had packed and saw the note on the bedside table with his name on, he suddenly became alert as if someone had switched his 'On' button on and sat bolt upright. 'What you doing?'

'I've got to go, Doug. I'm sorry.'

'What you talking about? Why?'

'Last night was an eye-opener for me. I don't want to be a party girl anymore. I want to make the most of my time away.'

'Without me?' He sounded so hurt, Catherine wanted to run over to him and fling her arms around him, but she couldn't. She needed to go.

'Tracy told me you said I'd been leading you on. She's right, I have, and it's not fair on you.'

'Bollocks! I never said that, I said we were leading each other on! I also said that I was so in love with you, I couldn't look at another woman, including her.'

That'll be why she was so mad with me then! Catherine couldn't deal with his last statement, so she ignored it. 'I'm sorry Doug, I've got to go.'

'But…,' was the last thing she heard him say before she shut the door behind her. She hurried to the bus stop, which was only at the end of the road and burst into tears.

The bus arrived but she stood there frozen, unable to climb on board. Hundreds of confused thoughts were zipping across her mind but the one that stood out was: *I can't leave Doug, not like this, it isn't fair.* So she waved the bus on and walked slowly back to the hostel, giving herself time to think. By the time she reached the entrance of *Casa de Ambito,* she saw Doug sitting at one of the tables next to the swimming pool. There was no sign of the table that had been crippled by Tracy. His head was in his hands and next to him was a steaming cup of coffee.

She approached him quietly. 'Hi.'

Doug looked up and his face broke into a wide grin. He stood and hugged her with such force they both nearly toppled backwards into the swimming pool. 'You came back!'

Catherine peeled off her backpack and propped it on one of the chairs. 'I couldn't leave you like that.'

'I thought I'd never see you again. You broke my heart.'

Catherine burst into tears again and Doug wrapped himself around her until she stopped.

'What on earth happened last night to make you want to leave me like that?'

She babbled on about how she wanted things to go further with him but she knew she wasn't ready because she still had work to do on herself. That she was still trying to find out who she was without a man. Then there was Tracy showing her that she didn't want to be like her – or like Cath – anymore and so she needed to get away from the party scene. And that she thought she'd been leading him on so decided the best solution was to disappear.

'But that's your old pattern, doing a disappearing act. You should've talked to me about it.'

Again, Doug was right. Catherine hadn't thought about another of her patterns playing out. Whenever things got painful or tough, she distanced herself just like she had with her own family. 'I'm sorry, you're right, I should have stayed and talked it through with you. I also shouldn't have believed what some drunken, deranged stranger had said you'd said. Again, I should have talked to you first. Sorry.'

He clasped her hand, 'I don't care; you're back so I'm happy.'

At the same time, they both noticed a very pale-looking Tracy scurrying past them to the bar, avoiding eye contact the entire way. She bought a bottle of water and darted back to her room as quickly as she'd appeared, without as much as a word. When her door shut, they burst into laughter.

Once the guffaws had subsided, Catherine needed to clear one last thing up. 'We need to discuss our relationship, Doug.'

'Go on.'

Catherine could sense him tensing up. 'I want to be with you, but I can't. If we're to continue travelling together, we can't be together in that way. I have to figure out who I am and what I want without you confusing me.'

Doug sighed, 'I understand.'

But Catherine could tell that he didn't. Not really.

Chapter Forty-nine

Brown on Tour

Day 172: Cusco, Peru

I love Peru; there's so much to do and see. I went sand-boarding on sand dunes, saw the Nazca lines from high above in a light aircraft (they're ancient drawings of enormous hummingbirds, spiders, monkeys, fish and lizards), and we trekked down Colca Canyon, which is deeper than the Grand Canyon! Then, after acclimatising to the altitude in Cuzco, we went white-water rafting on a grade 4+ river. I was even put on the front of the boat, given my "superior rafting skills". Get me! If that wasn't exhilarating enough, we then went abseiling down a 60-foot cliff.

Next, we walked for four days along the Inca Trail to Machu Picchu. It was really hard but I loved it. The views, the camaraderie and the food were wonderful, and then to arrive at Machu Picchu at sunrise was out of this world.

We're back in Cusco recovering from all the activity and to think about where to go next.

As Catherine finished typing, she saw that Doug had finished emailing too, so they decided to get some lunch. Cusco had the most magnificent array of restaurants so they were spoilt for choice. Doug suggested burgers and chips.

'No, I really should eat healthily...' As she was about to finish her sentence, she stopped and thought for a second, noticed the negative implications of the 'should' and thought something more positive. 'I mean, I'd like to continue eating healthily. How about that café with the salad bar buffet?'

Doug smiled. 'I'm impressed with how you're thinking much more positively, not only about yourself but about other stuff too.'

'Thanks. I've been shocked at the number of times I've caught myself saying something negative about myself or others. I've made a conscious effort to think more positively. It was hard to begin with but I'm getting the hang of it, and now – once I've noticed – I consciously think of something more positive.'

'What sort of things have you been doing?'

'Quite often when I'm naked and there's a full-length mirror in the room – and you're not around – I'll find myself bashing my thighs and having repulsive thoughts about my body, but I'm learning to stop and remind myself of the things I do like about myself. I tell myself I have *beautiful, womanly curves!*'

Doug smiled.

'The honest truth is that I don't really believe that I feel good about my body yet but I've noticed that I'm losing weight because of healthier food choices I'm making.'

'Great. Then one day you'll see what I see. And eventually you won't even care what you look like or how much you weigh.'

'What do you mean?'

'One day, what's inside will be the only thing that matters to you.'

'Okay, you're getting weird on me now. I'll stick to focusing on the aspects of my body that I like!'

'Good idea!'

As they entered the café, Catherine heard a girl's voice squeal, 'Hey you, Biscuit!' As she looked to where the voice was coming from, she immediately broke out in a huge smile as she saw Anna sitting by herself in the corner. The two friends embraced and held each other for a few seconds, really pleased to see each other.

Catherine loosened her grip first. 'How are you?'

'Good. Howzit with you?' Anna gestured for her friend to join her at her table.

'Not bad.' Catherine stopped. *That's not very positive!* 'No, I'm doing brilliantly.' Catherine sat down and realised she had forgotten that Doug was standing behind her. 'Sorry, Doug, this is Anna, a lovely friend I met in Antigua before I met you at the retreat.'

'Hi.' He shook her hand and sat down.

As Anna returned his grasp, she looked at Catherine and nodded approvingly. 'You two make a handsome couple, hey.'

Catherine answered quickly, 'Oh, we're not a couple, we're just travelling together.'

'Eish! I wish I'd met such a good-looking guy to travel with. I've been on my own for a month, bru, and I'm tired of it. Do you want to do the Inca Trail with me, hey?'

'Oh, I'd love to but we've already done it.'

'Ag no, shame. So tell me, what's happened since I last saw you?'

'Before I do, I want to apologise for leaving Antigua without saying goodbye. I felt really bad about it but I had to leave. Quickly.' Then Catherine gave Anna a brief synopsis of where she'd been since they last saw each other. 'How about you?'

'Fran went home, hey. Then I got with Yaniv. Remember him? Erez's mate with the spikey blonde hair?'

Catherine's flushed cheeks displayed her distress at the mention of Erez's name. It reminded her of the person she used to be. Anna continued. 'We travelled together for a month but, eish, he put his mates ahead of me. Got fed up with it. So I left.'

Anna either didn't notice or glossed over Catherine's obvious embarrassment. 'I've been on my own ever since.'

Doug looked at Catherine. 'Why've you gone so red?'

'Erez reminds me of a time I'd rather forget. Remember what happened to me in Colombia? Something similar happened before I came to the retreat. The same old pattern playing out.'

Anna leaned in, smiling. 'You two sound like a couple, hey. Sure nothing's going on?'

Catherine raised her hands like she was defending herself. 'Nope! Doug's like a big brother…'

Doug's chair screeched as he pushed his chair back with force. 'I'll leave you two to catch up. Good to meet you, Anna.'

Catherine was about to protest but he was out of the door before she had the chance to say anything. 'What was that all about?'

Anna raised her hands in frustration. 'You mean you don't know what just happened? Eish!'

'Nope!' Catherine shook her head to further emphasise her denial.

'He's crazy about you, Biscuit. And you said he's like a brother. That's an insult to any man!' She flicked Catherine's head with her fingers. 'Errrr, ja! What you going to do about it?'

'No idea!' After a short gap to gather her thoughts, Catherine asked Anna to fill her in on the rest of her adventures since they'd last seen each other.

As Catherine polished off the last of her salad, Anna commented on how different Catherine seemed.

'Good or bad different?' Catherine hoped it was the former.

'Good. Definitely good, hey.'

'In what way?'

'More relaxed and much more positive. Everything was gloom and doom before but you seem more optimistic. It's great, hey! I love it!'

'Thanks, I've been doing a lot of work on myself.'.

Anna crossed her arms and there were a few moments of silence while she considered what she was about to say. 'You know, I asked Yaniv why Erez was weird towards you.'

Catherine's smile evaporated. 'Mmmmm,' half wanting to know what he'd said and half not wanting to know.

'He thought you were a prick tease; chasing him one minute and backing off the next. He found your blend of confidence and shyness sexy in the beginning, but when you became needy and possessive, he'd had enough. He thought you were unhinged, hey!'

'Makes sense. I'm surprised he put up with me for as long as he did!'

'Izit? Not expecting you to say that. You really have changed!'

The girls continued chatting until it started to get dark and they decided it was time to say goodbye. They embraced each other and promised to keep in touch. As Catherine waved one last time, her heart felt heavy. It was time to find out whether Anna was right about why Doug had left so abruptly.

Chapter Fifty

'Are we okay?' Catherine asked as she filled her mouth with granola and yoghurt, eating as uncouthly as Sophie used to.

Doug concentrated on buttering his toast. 'What do you mean?'

'You've avoided me for two days. You're always too busy or tired. And you've not been your usual positive self. I've never seen you like this and I'd like to know what's wrong. You said we should always be able to talk to each other.'

'Everything's fine.' But he was still avoiding eye contact.

Catherine took a deep breath and gave herself time to consider what to do next. She could allow her old patterning to dictate how this was going to play out or she could choose something different. She thought the world of Doug; he was kind, thoughtful, giving, fun, and she really cared about him. He had also been instrumental in helping her to understand The Bliss Expert's Steps. She was a better person when he was around. But the same issue crept in between their friendship like a crack in a stone and was threatening to split it open if they didn't deal with it. Ultimately, it would always come back to him wanting more than she could give him. For now at least.

'Listen, Doug,' she said with as much kindness and concern as she could muster. 'We have to talk. We can't let anything fester and get in the way of the amazing relationship we have.'

Doug finally looked up at her and gazed into her eyes for the first time in days. 'Okay.' He seemed uncertain.

'You know I love being with you and I particularly love that I can be myself with you.' She stopped.

'I sense a "but"...'

'But... you know I can't be anything more than friends right now. I wish I could take things further, but I can't. Not now. I'm getting to know myself for the first time in my life and I can't let anything get in the way.'

'Oh come on, what you want to say is that you don't fancy me. The truth is, you see me as your brother, as you said to Anna the other day.'

There was venom in his voice and it scared Catherine. She'd never heard him angry before.

'Didn't you hear what else I said? "I love being with you."' Catherine saw there was no change in his expression so she decided to take a different tack. 'How interesting that you decided to take my "brother" comment as an insult?'

Doug's knife slipped out of his hand and clattered onto the plate, startling their neighbours in the café. 'How else do you expect me to take it?'

'As a compliment!'

'Catherine, I'm a man and it's insulting.' With that, he threw some money on the table and stormed off. Catherine couldn't believe what had just happened. And it frightened her. She had never thought Doug capable of such negative emotion, and what frightened her even more was that she found him even more attractive.

Catherine went to the local market for something to do. She needed to think because she didn't know what to do next. She and Doug were sharing a room and they'd made plans to travel to Bolivia together but, after this morning's outburst, she didn't think that would happen now. Her automatic reaction was to want to go back to their room, pack up her stuff and catch the next bus to Puno. But she knew that would be following her usual pattern of disappearing. Instead, she went to an internet café in the hope that The Bliss Expert might have answers for her.

The time has come for the final Step to Bliss. This is a short-cut to boosting your self-esteem and achieving everything you've ever wanted in your life!

STEP TEN EXPLAINED: PICTURE BLISS

Pictures are the language of the unconscious mind and allow you to use your imagination to bypass the conscious mind and speak directly to your unconscious mind. The brain does not know the difference between real and imagined, so visualising is a powerful way to create new neural pathways in your brain and stimulating new ways of thinking. The following exercise will help to re-programme your self-esteem, and the beliefs you have about yourself, quickly and efficiently.

STEP TEN TASK:

Repeat the following as many times as you wish. Mornings and evenings are best but you can do it anytime. The more, the better!

Close your eyes and see yourself in your mind's eye as the best version of yourself: the amazing person you know you really are. The Real You. Imagine yourself as your most confident, self-assured, fulfilled, loved and happy self. Make the picture big and bright, make the colours rich and vibrant and, if there's sound, make it loud and intense. If you're standing still in the picture, turn it into a movie.

Next, see yourself interacting with different people positively, confidently and full of love for yourself and others. Then, see yourself in different situations where you handle everything with ease and confidence and where the outcome is always positive. Now step into that person so that you feel what it's like to be that person. Then double and triple those feelings and allow them to surge powerfully through your whole body. Maintain these images, sounds and feelings for as long as you can (even a few seconds is better than nothing!). A few minutes would be ideal and you'll find it gets easier to hold the images, sounds and feelings for longer the more skilled you become. When you have finished, open your eyes. Good luck!

Catherine hoped that thinking about things in her mind could produce amazing results in her life. She couldn't understand how or why it worked but she was willing to give it a go. Everything else The Bliss Expert had told her had been correct so she printed off the email, then searched for a nearby clearing in the grassy area in the middle of the square. Catherine lay on the grass, closed her eyes and imagined Doug saying sorry and giving her a big hug. She hoped The Bliss Expert was right, and that visualising a positive outcome with Doug would work. She couldn't cope if it didn't.

Chapter Fifty-one

Doug was sitting on his bed with a big grin on his face. Catherine looked at him with a quizzical frown to indicate her confusion.

'I'm sorry.' He stood up and embraced her. Catherine reciprocated his hug and goosebumps raced up her back. After a few seconds, he let go and gestured with his hand for them to sit down. *Wow! This stuff really works.*

'Sorry for earlier. I overreacted. The connection we have is overwhelming, incredible and so extraordinary that I find it crazy we're not together. I've been patiently waiting and secretly hoping you'll realise you can be with me and still find out who you are but when I heard you say I was like your big brother, something inside me snapped. It occurred to me for the first time that you might be stringing me along and playing me for a fool. You reminded me of how my mother made me feel when I was younger.'

Catherine chose to gloss over this point for now. Doug had not opened up about his own past much so Catherine was desperate to hear more about his childhood. 'You've never said much about your past.'

It was Doug's turn to go red. 'That's because I'd prefer to forget it. My dad left me when I was little so I only had my mum, but she was more interested in finding a new husband than in looking after me. I took her disinterest in me as her not loving me. Your rejecting me triggered the old hurt, which explains why I exploded at you and blew everything out of proportion.'

'Oh Doug, I'm so sorry.' Catherine took hold of his arms and pulled him towards her in an attempt to hug him but he pulled away.

'Let me finish. Like you with men, I'm attracted to women who don't want me. In my teens I had a violent temper, which I now understand was because of all the anger I felt towards my mother. About four years ago I fell in love with a woman who I'd been with for about six months when, out of the blue, she finished with me. She told me she'd met someone else and I lost it. Literally. I couldn't control my emotions. I smashed up her flat and...' He stopped. 'I'm not sure I can, even now, bring myself to tell you this.'

'Please, Doug. You can tell me anything.' She squeezed his arm to encourage him to continue.

'I hit her. It was only once but I was appalled that I was capable of such violence towards a woman. She didn't call the police because I promised her I'd see someone about it. And I did. I saw an NLP coach and, as a result of its amazing effects, I decided to study NLP myself and that's when I started to make changes to the way I viewed the world.'

Catherine stared at him in disbelief. She would never have guessed in a trillion years that he was capable of hitting a woman. Granted, she'd seen him angry earlier at breakfast but she had not been scared he would turn violent. Even though she was stunned, she couldn't hold it against him. He had clearly changed and she had to take him for who he was now and not who he used to be.

'Say something please.'

She'd never seen him look so vulnerable. 'I can't deny that I'm not shocked but I feel honoured that you've told me. I'm also pleased in an odd sort of way because I thought you were Mr. Perfect, but you're not. Knowing you have flaws and you've had to work on yourself gives me hope that I can make changes to my life too. However, if you fancy me and I'm not reciprocating – for good reasons – doesn't it mean that you're still playing out your old patterns?'

'Yes. And that's why I got so angry with you when you said I was like your brother. But I wasn't really angry with you, I was angry at myself because it meant I hadn't changed as much as I thought I had. I needed to sulk for a bit before I could change my thinking.'

Catherine sat on the bed and patted the empty space next to her. 'To make you feel better, perhaps I should tell you that my old pattern played out a little this morning as well. When you lost your temper, I was even more attracted to you.'

Doug sat down. 'Don't say that or I'll get my hopes up again.'

'Sorry. Really, we should be happy that we're just friends. It means we're changing our old patterns.'

He touched her hand. 'I like how you're choosing to think positively about the situation.'

'Thanks.' Her face lit up as if the teacher had given her a gold star.

'While we're being honest with each other, did you know that Sophie tried it on with me at the retreat?'

Catherine's hand shot up to her mouth. 'No!' She said this with more surprise than she had at Doug telling her he'd hit a woman.

'She admitted it to me on the night of the Toy Fiesta. When I rejected her, she told me she couldn't understand why I fancied you when clearly you only had eyes for Gus. Of course, I knew exactly why I didn't fancy her and wanted you, but I couldn't tell her that!'

'I had no idea! But her behaviour makes perfect sense now. To make you feel better, I got an email from her the other day and she told me she's fallen for some guy so it looks like you're off the hook!'

The pair sat there in comfortable silence, lost in their own thoughts. Doug finally broke the quiet. 'Friends?'

'Definitely.' Catherine had her friend back and she felt closer to him than ever before. And, while she still regarded him as her guru, it helped to know he wasn't perfect.

Chapter Fifty-two

Catherine opened her eyes after her daily visualisation and nudged Doug to wake him up so they would have time to eat before catching the bus to Puno. They went to a small café, ate breakfast and then popped next door to an internet café. Catherine waited patiently while the connection whirred and kicked in slowly. She updated The Bliss Expert on what had happened between her and Doug, and read the emails in her Inbox while she waited for a reply.

I am so pleased for you, well done. Seeing as you're already putting into practise the art of thinking more positively and you're handling challenging situations like an adult rather than a needy child, I'd say you're well on your way to making constructive changes in your life, and so you will start to feel happier.

Remember though, that happiness is not an accident. It is created by behaving and thinking in certain ways. The more and more you do it, the better experiences you're going to have and the better you'll feel about yourself and others.

Catherine found it a little depressing that she would have to be disciplined with her thoughts all the time if she wanted to be happy. There had also been something troubling her for a few days, which she wanted to discuss with Doug. As they were getting the direct, non-tourist bus to Puno in about ten minutes' time, she would have six hours to broach the subject with him.

They joined the swarm of passengers shoving their way onto the bus, and Doug and Catherine jostled their way to the back and secured two seats before every other seat and inch of floor space were occupied by locals.

After an hour's worth of watching an endless expanse of arid farmland – speckled with mud-brick houses, distant hills, and occasional villages – Catherine was bored. She nudged Doug to get his attention. 'When you going home?'

Doug took a few seconds to come out of his trance and respond to what Catherine had asked. 'Why, do you want to get rid of me?'

She ignored his witticism and raised her eyebrows to indicate that she was waiting for a sensible answer.

'Not decided yet. I took a year's sabbatical from work so I've got...' He calculated something in his head, 'another eight months left, but I don't know what to do with it yet.'

There was a large pothole in the road and the pair were involuntarily thrown into the air. After their stomachs returned to their bodies, Catherine asked, 'How so?'

Expecting more jolts, Doug gripped the seat in front of him with both hands. 'I came away for adventure and to learn more about myself. I've had lot of fun but, apart from what's happened between us, I don't feel like I've been challenged much.' The road levelled off so he released his hands tentatively and placed them on his lap instead. 'For the last hour, I've been contemplating going home. I might be more challenged there.'

This is exactly what had been bothering her, and Doug was thinking the same thing. 'You think it'll be harder to change at home because your friends and family will push your buttons?'

'Absolutely. And I feel like it's time.'

'I've been thinking the same thing! I've got six months left but I'm homesick. And I'm intrigued to find out if I'll have a different perspective...'

Catherine was about to continue when the bus screeched to a sudden halt. Doug leaned over her to look out of the window to see why they had stopped in the middle of nowhere. There was nothing to see but never-ending stretches of flat grassland penned in by jagged grey mountains with fluffy white clouds hovering over them like smog. The doors to the bus flew open and a local woman in colourful traditional dress climbed aboard, balancing a large cardboard box on her head.

'What the...?' Doug untwisted himself and semi-stood up to see what she was doing.

'There's nowhere for her to go!' Catherine stared in amazement at the scene unfolding before her eyes. The lady waded through the bus, shouting an unfamiliar word, manoeuvred the box from her head and steadied it half on her knee and half on top of a local's head (who didn't seem fazed by having a stranger's box nestled on his hair). Next, she pulled an enormous machete from her belt and started hacking at the inside of the box. Bits of flesh flew out of the box like bullets from a machine gun and sprayed nearby passengers. Then she wrapped pieces of something pinky-brown from inside the box with crumpled brown paper and handed the package to a happy customer, who swapped it for cash. Catherine was not sure if she was more curious about what was inside the box or how the woman had materialised out of a massive expanse of nothing. As the woman got closer, this time it was Catherine's turn to lean over Doug in an attempt to see what was inside the box. She wished she hadn't. It was a pig's head.

She turned away. 'I feel sick!'

'Mmm, can't say I'm tempted,' Doug added. 'Anyway, what were you saying?'

'I'll tell you when I've stopped feeling ill.'

About half an hour later they reached the halfway point at La Raya, which was over four kilometres above sea level. Catherine wasn't feeling sick anymore but her eardrums were blocked by the dizzying altitude. As they clambered off the bus, she swallowed in quick succession to equalise the pressure in her ears. It worked but she had a sudden shock as the cold air slapped her in the face, neutralising the stench of dead pig that had worked its way into every pore and follicle of her body. She looked around and admired the snow-clad mountains in the distance. Closer by, a line of stalls selling colourful fabrics and knitted goods made by the indigenous locals disappeared into the horizon.

After a much-needed toilet break and a drink, it was time to get back on the bus.

'Where were we?' Doug asked as they settled back into their seats.

'We were talking about going home. The problem is that I don't know what I want to do when I get back. I did recruitment before but I want to do something I love rather than something just for the money. But I don't know what that something is. Will you go back to your old job?'

Doug nodded. 'Yeah, but not unless I have to. I'd like to be a coach rather than join the rat race again.'

'What kind of coach?' Goosebumps formed at the base of her spine.

'A personal development coach. A bit like what I've been doing with you, but more structured.'

'You should. I mean, you'd be brilliant. You've helped me more than you know. Hey, I could be your guinea pig,' she cleared her throat and added, 'I mean client. I could pay you.'

'Don't be silly. But you're making me think I'm wasting my time being here. I might look into flights home when we reach Puno.'

Catherine's heart did a free-fall into her belly. 'You can't do that! Not yet.' She stopped to allow herself time to think. 'Why don't we have a blow-out month of amazing adventure? Puh-leease!' She rested her head on his shoulder and looked up at him with puppy dog eyes.

'Okay, okay! Will you go home too?' He shifted his body so her head could no longer rest on his shoulder.

'Yes,' she said before she had the chance to change her mind. 'But you have to coach me so I know what to do when I get home. You've got a month. No pressure!'

'Deal.' Doug looked like a lottery ticket jackpot winner.

Catherine felt a bundle of nerves and dread but, above all, she felt excited and happy. Her journey had been full of adventure - with lots of learning as well as hardship and hurt - but it was time to go home and back to reality. Whatever that meant! Living out of a backpack was getting on her nerves, sharing bunkbeds with complete strangers and showering in communal blocks were wearing her down. She was craving normality and stability and she wanted to be surrounded by friends and family who loved her unconditionally, even if they didn't know how to show it. Despite knowing that she had made the right decision to go home, she couldn't understand why her heart was aching so badly.

Chapter Fifty-three

Brown on Tour
Day 190: Coroico, Bolivia

After Machu Picchu, we went to Puno where we visited the floating islands on Lake Titicaca. We stayed with a local family who, on our first evening, took us to a party. I use this word loosely because the 'party' involved trekking in pitch darkness to a small wooden hut in the middle of nowhere whilst wearing native costumes over the top of our normal clothes. Inside the hut, a few locals played instruments and sang while we had to dance. I'm not sure who was laughing at whom but it was highly entertaining in a wholesome kind of way!

Next, we headed to Bolivia. In La Paz we cycled down 'Death Road,' which earned the title of the World's Most Dangerous Road in 1995 because around two hundred people die along it every year. Every year! What were we thinking? That's what I asked myself when we set off in freezing cold temperatures and thick fog. The first few kilometres gave me a false sense of security because I remember thinking, 'This isn't so bad.' Then the smooth surface gave way to a dirt track which was carved into the side of a cliff with hairpin bends, and vertical drops of up to two kilometres. The stone and wooden crosses lining the way were a stark reminder of the level of concentration required to ensure I wouldn't join their fate over the cliff edge. I hurtled down the dusty and winding track for five hours, and by the time I reached the bottom I could barely peel my fingers off the handlebars. But it was mind-blowingly amazing and well worth every second of knuckle-clenching fear. At the end was an incongruous yet very welcome luxurious hotel where I could wash off the dirt and relax in the very unexpected yet very welcome swimming pool.

I'm off to the 'Gateway to the Amazon' tomorrow to explore the Pampas.

Chapter Fifty-four

Brown on Tour

Day 200: Rurrenabaque, Bolivia

After we left the luxurious hotel in Coroico, we travelled by jeep to Rurrenabaque, which is where civilisation ends and the jungle and pampas tours start. I won't mention the 12-hour back-jarring journey because it is now over. I also won't mention the intolerable humidity because right now I'm trying to imagine that it doesn't exist.

We were advised by our guide to buy secondhand light-coloured, long-sleeved trousers and shirts. It seemed I was the only person who'd listened because I was the only one who looked like a kid dressed up in her parents' work clothes. The long socks pulled-up-and-over-my-trousers look was particularly fetching.

The first thing we did was anaconda hunting, which involved trudging through six-inches of soggy, stinking mud. While everyone had been ridiculing my stylish outfit before the tour, they were now green with envy. There was not one speck of mud on my skin. The same could not be said for anyone else. Might I highlight that no harm came to any anacondas while we were hunting them. Our guide - or 'Pampas Man' as he called himself - found a baby three-metre long snake, which he said was very lucky. I'm not sure how lucky it was for the snake: being stroked and photographed by a group of over-zealous tourists wouldn't be my idea of lucky!

We then swam with pink dolphins but I was a little taken aback when I saw one. It looked more like ET when he was dying than the fuchsia pink I had envisioned it would be. We also went piranha fishing, but after hearing a story about the American President, Theodore Roosevelt, I wasn't so keen. Apparently, during a visit to Brazil in 1913 he'd witnessed a cow being savaged by a school of hungry piranhas in a matter of minutes.

At the campsite, Pampas Man entertained us with songs accompanied by his guitar playing. I think he was trying to calm us before he took us on a night boat trip to see crocodiles. This freaked me out somewhat and I wish I'd stayed tucked up in my sleeping bag, away from terrifying prehistoric monsters that would happily eat me as their hors d'oeuvres.

I'm now in town, thankful to be wearing my normal clothes again, which seem to have grown. Oh no! What am I talking about, it's me who's shrunk!

I have one day of sleeping in a comfy bed before we head off camping again, but this time to the Amazon Jungle.

Chapter Fifty-five

Brown on Tour
Day 205: Sucre, Bolivia

You'll be pleased to know that I now know how to survive if I ever get stranded in the Amazon jungle. While learning how to be Ray Mears, I also saw loads of cool tropical birds, flowers, reptiles, animals and insects; the best and scariest creature was a huge tarantula. There was also a crocodile that paid a visit to the campsite every night, which would have been scary had his nickname not been 'Toothless Pete.'

As much as I wanted to continue sleeping on rock-hard ground in a tent as hot as a sauna, whilst wearing all my clothes and stinking, and being surrounded by things that crawled, scurried and scrabbled all around me, Doug begged me to return to civilisation. Who was I to argue? What's more, the wimp couldn't bear the 20-hour bus ride back to La Paz so pleaded with me to fly instead. I reluctantly agreed to the one-hour flight.

After fully appreciating the luxury of sleeping on a mattress in a fan-cooled room with ensuite shower for a few blissful days, we travelled to Potossi, which is the highest town in the world. I didn't cope with the altitude very well and thought my head was going to explode. We visited a tin mine, which was harrowing. The workers have to work in appalling conditions for very little money. I felt very guilty but didn't know what to do about it.

On a happier note, I'm now in a place called Sucre where I'm about to go and see some giant dinosaur footprints!

Catherine deliberately signed off as if she was continuing her travels because, apart from her parents and Terence, she hadn't told anyone that she was flying home early. She wanted it to be a surprise when she turned up at Babushka's the following Saturday. Rosie's fiancé had organised a surprise party under the guise of special, invite-only pre-wedding drinks, so no-one suspected a thing. She couldn't wait. With this in mind, she thought she would send a quick reminder to Rosie's fiancé Terence.

Remember, don't breathe a word to anyone, most of all Rosie. I will meet you in the vodka bar as discussed at 7 p.m. on Saturday 26 March. Of course you remember that it's also my birthday on 28 March, so perfect timing! Can't wait to see you.

After she'd sent a message to The Bliss Expert telling him that she was going home, a message pinged in from him almost instantaneously.

I'm glad you're going home; now is a good time. You've had the adventure of a lifetime, but remember, it's just the beginning of your true journey. You must reread all of the Steps and continue to put them into practise every day. If you do, you will definitely find the fulfilment, happiness and bliss you're seeking.

What? That sounds like goodbye?! Catherine felt short-changed if it was, because she was desperate to know who The Bliss Expert was. She'd assumed he would reveal his identity once she was going home and that time was tomorrow, so she couldn't believe he'd leave her hanging like that. She typed an email asking when she was going to find out who he was and impatiently drummed her fingers on the table. Bored of waiting, Catherine clicked on an email from her mum, curious to see whether she would mention anything about her love comment.

> Thank goodness you were able to change your plane ticket without any extra charge. How fortuitous!
>
> We're so thrilled that you're coming home and we can't wait to see you and hear all about your adventures. Your dad and I will be waiting for you in arrivals at 9 a.m. We have taken the liberty of organising a family meal for Saturday night. We thought you'd like that but if you're too tired from the long flight, we can always postpone it to when you're feeling up to it.
>
> In the meantime, we hope you have a good flight and we look forward to seeing you very soon.

Catherine had to read the email twice as she couldn't believe her parents were going to meet her at the airport; she had assumed she'd have to get the train and they'd pick her up from their local station. She was grinning from ear to ear. She could sense her heart flutter with a gush of love for her parents and it didn't matter that her mum didn't mention anything about them loving her back. Their actions spoke volumes. She was also surprised they'd organised a family dinner for her first night home;

she couldn't remember a time when they'd ever gone to so much effort for her. No matter how jetlagged she felt when she got home, the dinner would go ahead. While she was brimming with happiness, another email from The Bliss Expert popped up so she clicked on it.

Patience, Catherine. As with everything else, all will be revealed when you're ready.

She logged off feeling more than a little annoyed.

Catherine saw that Doug was already nursing a coffee in the café opposite so she joined him and ordered a cola lite.

'You know, you'd be better off drinking water or the full-fat version?' He pointed at the bottle when it arrived.

Catherine poured the dark liquid and watched it glug into the ice-filled glass that the waiter had left moments before. She took a sip and enjoyed the sweet, bubbly coolness revitalising her dry mouth. 'But it's delicious!' She then took another hit of bubbles before adding, 'I think I'm addicted. If I don't have one by eleven-ish, I get moody and irritable.'

'Don't I know it?' He chortled before turning serious again. 'Isn't that enough to warn you off it?'

'Hmmm, maybe! I tell you what, I'll have this one and I'll stop tomorrow.' And she took another sip.

He clinked his glass of water with Catherine's. 'Said like a true addict!'

She leant forward and whispered so no-one else could hear her revelation. 'I reckon I've been addicted to something for most of my adult life. Alcohol, cigarettes, men, food, cola lite. It's time for me to stop relying on external vices and focus on healing myself from the inside out.'

Doug leant forward so that their faces were just a couple of inches apart. 'I *am* a good coach, aren't I?'

She rearranged a strand of his hair that wasn't out of place. 'Seriously, I don't know where I'd be now if it hadn't been for you. Thanks to your coaching, I now know what to do when I get home. That's a huge achievement, so thank you.'

Catherine realised she may have been too intimate with her body language and slouched back in her chair. Doug looked disappointed before signalling to the waiter for another drink and turning to face Catherine as if nothing had happened. 'Studying NLP won't be the whole answer but it certainly helped me.'

Catherine asked for a second cola lite when the waiter appeared with another water for Doug. 'Will we keep in touch when we get home?'

Doug screwed up his face as if she'd asked a nonsensical question. 'Why wouldn't we?'

She shrugged her shoulders. 'Don't know. I guess it's up to us to make the effort. Where'll you live?'

Doug didn't seem to be looking at Catherine but rather, through her. 'With my mum in Exeter until I sort myself out. You?'

Catherine tried to re-engage with him using humour. 'Same! Except I'll stay with *my* parents in Eastbourne.'

That seemed to work as Doug's eyes refocused. 'How are you feeling about going home now that it's time?'

She counted on her fingers as she listed her feelings. 'Really excited about seeing everyone. Scared about what I'll do after the NLP Practitioner course. Terrified that I'll find it hard being Catherine with my friends and family who know the old me. And sad about leaving South America as it means the end of my travels and my time with you.' She blushed.

'Yeah, but it had to end at some point. And anyone who can't accept the new you isn't worth knowing. You may end up culling a few people from your life. But so what? You have to let go of the old to let in the new.'

As Catherine finished the last dregs of her drink, she realised she had already moved the goalposts with regards to quitting because she was already planning to give up when she got home. She wondered how many more times she would postpone it.

Catherine touched Doug's hand to get him to look at her again. 'We should go out tonight, treat ourselves to a decent meal and get slowly sloshed on quality wine, maybe even champagne if we can find it. It's our last night together. Let's go out in style.'

'You make it sound very final.' Doug seemed sad.

'Well, it is for our travels, but not for us.'

That seemed to cheer him up. 'That's okay then!'

'I only have one request.'

'What's that?'

'No spaghetti.'

'Eh?'

'Long story. I'll tell you about it later,' Catherine silently reminisced about her first experience of farewell drinks with the Italian boys many months ago.

'Okay. Come on or we'll miss the Dinotour bus.'

With that they finished their drinks and headed to the big yellow bus that had just pulled up on the other side of the pavement, ready to take them to see the largest collection of dinosaur footprints in the world. Catherine felt mildly sick and excited as they were about to set off on their last adventure together in Central and South America before flying home the following day. She hoped it wouldn't be the last time she'd see Doug.

Chapter Fifty-six

Catherine was relieved to discover she was feeling relatively okay physically. She decided they should thank the quality of the sparkling wine they'd drunk the previous night because, by rights, the amount of alcohol they'd consumed should have left them feeling rotten. However, emotionally she felt a little wobbly. Doug stirred at about the same time as she was considering the prospect of packing, so she beamed at him across the room and checked he was feeling okay too. He was. They had an hour before the taxi was coming to take them to the airport so they hurriedly packed and went to a nearby café to line their stomachs for the long journey ahead.

The 40-minute internal flight from Sucre to La Paz was painless and they arrived with enough time to buy supplies from the overpriced airport shop for the onward journey. Then suddenly it was broadcast that Doug's flight was now ready for boarding, and with it came the realisation that it was time to say goodbye to each other. The two friends turned to face each other when they heard the announcement, and Catherine's bottom lip involuntarily started to tremble. She did everything she could to stop the tears but they flowed anyway.

'I'm sorry, I don't know where they came from,' she said in between gasps for air.

'Don't be so silly,' he said as he pulled Catherine close to him and hugged her tightly.

After a few minutes, he pulled away and said – with them standing but a few inches apart – 'Anyone would think we're never going to see each other again!'

'I know! But even knowing that I'll see you on Saturday night at my surprise birthday party, I feel gutted to be leaving you. I'll miss waking up with you and having our morning chats.'

'Me too. But it's farewell, not goodbye.' And, with this, he wrapped his arms tightly around her once again. They held each other for as long as they could before Doug needed to get to his departure gate. Catherine watched him walk down the long corridor and disappear around the corner. She sobbed like a baby, not caring who saw her.

Two hours later, her flight was ready for boarding so she strolled casually to the correct gate, looked back at Bolivia through the glass windows and said a silent goodbye. She climbed on board and was relieved that the seat next to her remained empty after the last passenger had boarded.

Relaxing into the flight, Catherine closed her eyes. She reflected on the incredible journey she'd been on physically, mentally and emotionally. There were the beautiful places she'd visited from tropical white sandy beaches, turquoise clear blue seas, volcanoes and jungles to Mayan ruins, bustling cities, colonial towns and remote villages. There were the people she'd met: some who she would rather forget, like Jack and Erez, but others who she never wanted to forget like Sophie, Doug and Willow. Then there were the Steps to Bliss from The Bliss Expert who had been pivotal to her feeling like a new person. Wishing that she could meet The Bliss Expert face-to-face to show her immense gratitude, Catherine vowed to email him to ask if they could meet up soon.

Six months ago an angry, lost, negative and pessimistic Cath had sat on a twelve-hour flight from London to Mexico City. Now, a happy, purposeful, positive and optimistic Catherine was looking forward to living her life. While everything at home would be the same on a physical level, she felt so different that she knew things were going to change. For the better. Catherine had all the tools available to create her own reality that she wanted to live in. With that in mind, Catherine envisioned her parents waiting for her in Arrivals, smiling in anticipation at seeing their daughter for the first time in six months. Catherine would run up to them and give them a big hug and they would hug her back. Tears of joy rolled down her cheeks before she fell asleep.

Chapter Fifty-seven

As soon as the automatic doors slid open, Catherine could see her mum and dad waving furiously at her from the gates. Her heart skipped a beat as she grinned. It was so good to see them. She sped up her pace to reach them faster. She noticed her dad looked somehow softer, kinder and gentler than she remembered. Like a giant cuddly bear. She almost crashed into him in her clumsy effort to hug him. But once she embraced him, she stood there clutching him, not wanting this moment to end. She felt warm, safe, and loved.

She realised in that moment how right Doug had been about the cigarette analogy. Her dad hadn't changed, but her thoughts and feelings about him had, and what she saw was wonderful. He was her dad and she loved him with all her heart. She never wanted old patterns to mask the truth again. As tears streamed down her face, she turned to her mum.

'Are you okay?' Her mum held her arms open ready for a hug.

Catherine nodded, unable to verbalise everything she was feeling in that moment. But her mum seemed to understand without words and drew her in for a hug. Catherine felt like she was wrapped up in cotton wool and it was wonderful. She knew in her heart that she was going to be okay.

Catherine sat in the back of the car, drinking in the lush, green countryside rushing past her. She'd never before appreciated how beautiful England was. It was so sad that she'd had to leave a place before she could see how amazing it was. *A bit like my family!* Catherine and her parents chatted for a while but mostly there was silence and Catherine was fine with that, because she no longer needed words to reassure her that her parents loved her and were glad to have her home. She just knew.

When they arrived home, Catherine couldn't decide what she wanted more: a cheese and pickle sandwich, cornflakes with proper English milk, or Marmite on toast? So she opted for a bit of everything. But only after she'd had a cup of tea. It struck her that she didn't crave food in the same way as she had before. She still loved the taste but she didn't need food to replace the unhappiness in her life. After eating her fill, she took a long, hot soak in the bath, looking forward to seeing the rest of her family for dinner.

Chapter Fifty-eight

Hi Doug,

I wanted to update you on how last night's meal went with the family. It was brilliant! Both my sisters came with their husbands, and my parents cooked me my favourite dinner: lasagna with garlic bread and salad, and for pudding, syrup sponge pudding with custard. I only ate until I was full and I didn't feel guilty about eating it at all. It was lovely to see everyone and to feel part of a family again. I know it's because I've changed my perception but they seem different: more open, warm and loving. Even though I was knackered, I could have stayed up all night with them, which I never thought I'd hear myself say!

Best of all, after many a morning spent imagining it (you remember don't you?!), my dad asked me if I wanted to go with him to the pub at lunchtime today! Can you believe it? I'm so happy!

Anyway, I hope you are enjoying being home as much as I am and I can't wait to see you next Saturday.

Catherine was frustrated to see that The Bliss Expert still hadn't sent her an email so she spent an hour researching NLP Practitioner courses in London before she was due to go out with her dad.

The clock struck twelve, announcing to Catherine that it was the moment she'd been waiting for since she'd turned eighteen. It wasn't about the trip to the pub; it was the fact her dad wanted *her* to go with *him*. When they got to *The Horse and Hare*, her dad held the door open for her and she ducked under his arm to access his sanctum. It was the stale smell of hops that first hit her, followed by the sticky carpet that attached itself to her shoes as she sauntered to the bar. She grinned, because nothing had changed: the oak panels and lurid red swirling-patterned carpet were still there, as were the usual regulars propping up the bar and sipping their favourite tipples. Low murmurs and the clanking of knives and forks as the waitress set the tables up for lunch created an atmosphere that only a real English pub in England could create. Her dad interrupted her thoughts and asked what she wanted to drink.

'A pint of lager, please.'

While her dad chatted to the barman and bought the drinks, Catherine secured a small round table in the corner under a bay window and sat down.

It wasn't long before her dad joined her. 'Here you go.' He placed her pint on a mat and raised his glass. 'Cheers!'

Catherine picked up her glass, to which the cardboard beer mat was clinging. 'Cheers, Dad.' The clinking of glasses seemed symbolic of a fresh start. Even though she'd consumed a lot of lager while she'd been away, the taste of this pint was the best she'd ever had. The amber liquid slipped down her throat and relaxed every muscle in her body.

Her dad cleared his throat. 'It's good to have you home, love.'

With a lump in her throat, Catherine looked into her pint as if she were having a conversation with it. 'It's good to be home, Dad.'

Then there was silence apart from the chitter-chatter of other patrons. Catherine felt awkwardness creep up inside her but it was a ghost of old feelings rather than real emotion. To give herself time to think, she sipped on her lager, but not too much, as she recalled Doug's advice about alcohol affecting conscious thought. She decided she had a choice: she could either continue allowing her old patterns to haunt her like a recurring pimple or she could choose to perceive what was happening in a new light. *Maybe my dad likes silence? Maybe silence is his way of showing he cares?*

Before she could come up with more alternatives, her dad interrupted her train of thought. 'What's on your mind, love?'

Catherine wanted to get the words out but they were stuck in her throat. It dawned on her that her pattern had been to ignore her dad, not have an adult conversation with him.

'Another one?' she asked, pointing to his near-empty glass. She knew she'd chickened out but maybe a little Dutch courage would help at this point.

Two pints and three packets of crisps later, Catherine felt more confident. 'Can I ask you a question?'

'Depends on what it is. If it's can you borrow some money for the next round, the answer's no.' He chuckled at his own joke.

'Very funny.' Catherine concentrated on using her finger to rub the condensation off the glass. 'It's why you've never asked me to go to the pub with you before?' Her heart was pounding as hard as her first night in Mexico when she was being led down a dark alley by the so-called taxi driver.

'Haven't I?' He seemed momentarily distracted as he nodded to a friend at the bar.

Catherine tried to keep calm but her voice was wavering. 'No, never.' She shook her head, emphasising that he hadn't.

Her dad leant back and stared at the sporadically worn carpet. 'I haven't thought about it before. Why do you ask?'

Catherine felt able to look at her dad because he was still concentrating on the carpet. 'I've always wondered why you haven't.'

'Oh.' He took a big gulp of his drink and made direct eye contact with Catherine. 'I didn't think you'd want to come. You didn't show any interest in me or in what I was doing, so I assumed you wouldn't want to come to the pub with your old man.'

Catherine glanced away as her face flashed crimson. She mentally stepped into his shoes and considered how he saw her behaviour. What he'd said made perfect sense, based on the self-fulfilling cycle. 'Oh, I thought it was because you didn't like me.'

He smiled. 'You're my daughter. Of course I like you.'

Catherine shifted in her seat. She felt hot and uncomfortable. 'I thought you didn't like me so my way of dealing with it was to ignore you. But because I ignored you, you thought I didn't like you!'

Her dad didn't say anything.

'Can I ask you another question?' Catherine pressed on while she was on a roll. 'Why was I never good enough for you?'

He shook his head and stared at his half-full glass. 'What do you mean, Love?'

Trying to keep emotion out of the words, Catherine continued. 'When I got my GCSE results, I was over the moon with my three A's, three B's and three C's but, when I told you, you said,' in a put-on deep voice to mimic her dad, '"Make sure they're all A's next time." I took it to mean you were disappointed in me.'

'Not at all. I was really pleased. I thought you knew that.' He paused. 'You always were a sensitive soul.' There was another pause. 'I did the best I could with what I was given in life so I wanted you to always do your best.'

Idiot! No, I mean, here's another example of me allowing my negative perceptions to interpret a situation incorrectly. She wondered on how many other occasions she might have misinterpreted something.

Catherine drained the last dregs of her lager. 'Can we start over?'

Her dad nodded slowly. 'Start what over?'

'Us. Our relationship. Fancy another one?' She gestured to his now empty glass.

'One more but that's it or you'll have to carry me home. We'd better phone your mother to get her to pick us up. I'm in no fit state to drive now!'

'Okay.' Then she shuffled out of the seat and was about to march over to the bar but stopped. She turned and faced her dad and looked him directly in the eyes. 'I love you, Dad.' Even though he didn't say it back to her, his smile said that he loved her too.

Catherine woke up with a mild hangover but she was buzzing from the conversation she'd had with her dad at the pub the day before.

After a cooked breakfast that her dad had prepared for them, she had time to check her emails before Lou was due to arrive with her two girls, Catherine's nieces. She sipped a glass of water, missing the sweetness of cola lite, but she had to quit drinking it. While she read emails from friends updating her on their lives, she was eager to get to the one from The Bliss Expert. She hoped that now was the time he would reveal his secrets.

Welcome home!

I know you're burning to know who I am. But before I answer that question, I ask that you suspend your disbelief because the truth might be difficult for you to swallow.

I am you. Catherine Brown. Or, to be more accurate, I am me! I am the future you / me.

That is why I've wanted to help you. In my timeline, it took me twelve painful years of difficult experiences, arduous studying and reading - as well as encounters with a whole host of wonderful teachers - before I started to feel happy and fulfilled. At that point, I wished someone had handed to me on a plate everything that I'd learnt in one go, rather than my having to experience twelve long, hard years. I decided I would find a way to do that for you. I wanted you to be able to take a fraction of the time it took me by having the information at your fingertips, so I packaged my key findings and used your trip to Central and South America as the vehicle to get the Steps to you.

Don't worry too much about the mechanics of how I got them to you because it would literally blow your mind. What I will say, however, is that one day you will understand that time, like everything else in the world, is just an illusion. The past, present and future exist all at once, which enables me to communicate with you from the future. But really, it is now. There's no point trying to comprehend it with your current level of awareness but one day you will understand.

Finally, I know you're desperate to know what your life has in store for you but, ultimately, it depends on the choices you make. If you choose the same path as I did, you will find true love with a wonderful man who you will marry, and you will have his child (although not necessarily in that order!), and you will have a great relationship with your parents. In addition you will have purpose and meaning in your life as well as a fulfilling career that you will love so much you'd do it for free if you could. But you don't need to worry about that because it pays incredibly well too!

The last message I have for you is to stay focused, determined, and true to yourself, and be the best version of YOU possible, and you will have all these things too. Keep practising the Steps and, when you're ready, I'll send you some more to take you to an even higher level of bliss. Good luck!

What the...?! Catherine sat there in utter bewilderment. She couldn't wait to tell Doug so she forwarded the email to him and hoped she wouldn't have to wait long for a reply. Sitting back in the chair, Catherine realised she was feeling the most optimistic and happiest she had for as long as she could remember. Even though she didn't know how she would find a job she felt passionate about and a career that would fulfil her and earn her lots of money, she felt excited about finding it. She had already signed up to an NLP Practitioner course in London that was due to start the following week and, assuming she could stay with Rosie and Terence for a while, she had time to figure out where she wanted to live permanently. It felt thrilling to be at the beginning of a new chapter in her life. While she still didn't know how things would develop between her and Doug, if at all, she had no anxiety about whether it would or wouldn't happen. She felt content to be on her own. Ultimately, she understood that she had control over her life and destiny. *If I don't like it, then it's up to me to change it. I have the strength, power and know-how!*

Catherine powered off the computer and joined her mum and dad in the conservatory for lunch, her stomach fluttering with excitement for life. As her mum reeled off a list of tempting sweet things she had in the kitchen, Catherine knew she didn't need any external vices to keep her emotions down because she was okay with expressing how she felt. 'No thanks, Mum, I'm sweet enough as it is.' With that, Catherine knew she was on the way to finding her bliss.

The End

Personal Study

Here are the Steps again should you wish to revisit them:

STEP ONE TASK:

1. *From your perspective, what positive and negative characteristics would you attribute to your mum and dad?*

2. *Write down a list of positive and negative characteristics you would attribute to yourself. Do you have a Cath and Catherine inside yourself?*

3. *Compare and contrast the lists from 1 and 2. What do you notice?*

STEP ONE EXPLAINED: MODEL PARENTS

How is it possible to be your parents' traits? Partly, your parents passed on their genes to you, but also your parents were the people who you were exposed to the most, certainly until you went to school, so they were your role models on how to behave. The good news is that, because many of the traits and behaviours you developed were created by observing your parents, not inherited from them, you can change them.

STEP TWO TASK:

1. *Who are you when you're totally alone?*

2.

    a. How do you like others to see you?

    b. If you were trying to prove something to other people, what would it be?

3. How do you think these traits connect with your parents, and the two aspects of you?

STEP TWO EXPLAINED: BURIED BEAUTY

Step Two is about understanding that there are two parts that make up 'you':

Your Real Self.

    This is who you were born to be before you were influenced by anyone and anything. Your Real Self is perfect, like a flawless diamond.

Your Ideal Self.

This is who you decided you wanted to be.

    From a very early age, you received explicit and implicit expectations from others who put unrealistic demands on you. You also got your first messages of non-acceptance and criticism. Of course, much of this was unintentional from your well-meaning parents, but it happened nonetheless. Even the word No, which your parents said to you to keep you safe, led to you receiving the message that you were wrong or not good enough. As a result, you learnt how to fit into your family environment and how to protect yourself by covering up your Real Self. Often, the only choice you think you have is to be like your mum or dad and how you decide which one to emulate.

    Your Ideal Self takes up a lot of time and energy to maintain and it can be exhausting. And it means that the core of the Real Self is so far hidden beneath the Ideal Self that the Real Self is lost. It is like layers of dirt are covering a flawless diamond within and, eventually, only the dirt and not the brightness of the diamond can be seen because it is buried so deeply beneath.

STEP THREE TASK:

1. List the last five men you've dated, and describe their characteristics in terms of how you perceived them in the relationship with you?

2. What happened in each of the relationships? What pattern do you notice?

3. How did each relationship make you feel when it ended?

4. How did your father make you feel when you were a child?

5. What conclusions can you draw from this?

STEP THREE EXPLAINED: AUTO PILOT

In terms of your relationships with men, you are likely to be replaying patterns from your childhood, particularly to do with your father. But you may want to explore how your mother made you feel too. The answers to the questions in Step Three should help you to work out what patterns you are playing out.

The challenge many people face is that they use so much energy in recreating their patterns from childhood that it is exhausting. It can even dominate their life. The good news is, it is possible to change these patterns. And you will find out how by following all Ten Steps. Sometimes the realisation of what you have already learnt is enough to make a shift in your old patterns.

Before you continue, you need to decide whether you want your life to change. How much do you really want it to? On a scale of 1 – 10, how much do you want it to change? (1 being not bothered - 10 being more than anything.)

Please note that you are only going to make an effort to change if you answer 10/10.

STEP FOUR TASK:

1. *When your last boyfriend finished with you, you felt...?*

2. *When you're with a beautiful friend, you feel...?*

3. *When you're with a sensible friend, you feel...?*

STEP FOUR EXPLAINED: RESPONSE-ABLE

Did you know that no-one can 'make you feel' anything. No-one can make you feel angry and hurt, no-one can make you feel insecure, and no-one can make you feel like a naughty schoolgirl. Unfortunately, the English language would make it seem that they can. But it is literally not possible for one human being or a situation to create an emotion in another human being. If I laughed at you for having purple feet, it wouldn't provoke a reaction in you. However, if I laughed at you for being overweight, I'd make you feel bad about yourself - but only because you already feel sensitive about your weight.

What's actually happening is that one person is assigning responsibility for their emotions to someone else who, or something else that, is outside of their control. Put another way, the person is taking no responsibility for the way they react and act.

As a controversial but powerful example, think of a piece of white paper with a black shape drawn on it: an equilat-

eral cross with four legs bent at ninety degrees. Show this to a young child and they might say, 'That picture reminds me of helicopter blades.' Hence their interpretation will cause little or no reaction.

Show this picture to an Israeli and they might say, 'It makes me feel sick,' because it reminds them of a Swastika and the atrocities that were forced upon their Jewish grandparents. It might cause them to retaliate or seek revenge.

Show the picture to a member of a neo-Nazi group and they might say, 'It makes me feel proud,' because, for them, it represents the symbol of a great leader. It might cause them to attack someone who is different to them.

Show it to someone who practises the Hindu religion and they might say, 'It makes me feel lucky,' because it's a sacred and auspicious symbol. It might cause them to apply for a job they might otherwise have ignored.

Ultimately, the picture of the shape in itself means nothing but it's how the perceiver interprets it that causes them to feel something (or not). As you will also see in Step Seven, how someone feels then creates their reality.

So if you are interested in creating a happier and more fulfilled life, you must accept this one fundamental fact: once you leave childhood, there will never be anyone who can make you feel better. Apart from you. The only way is to let go of the past, take responsibility for yourself, and focus on the here and now. The past is in the past anyway, so why hold onto it and allow it to affect the here and now?

The next time you hear yourself blaming someone or something else for the way you are feeling, stop and ask yourself the following:

- *What is happening to cause you to feel that way?*

- *How are you choosing to perceive a person or situation that is making you feel that way?*

- *How could you choose to react differently in order to create a different outcome?*

All of these insights can be applied to any relationship that you have with another human being – people you work with, your siblings, friends, as well as your lovers. Remember that not everyone is ready to hear that they're responsible for how they feel and act.

STEP FIVE EXPLAINED: TUNNEL VISION

Did you know that there is no such thing as reality? There is only what your brain chooses to let you see and experience?

Every day, your senses are exposed to millions of bits of information, yet only a fraction of these get through to your conscious mind. This means that there is a lot of information that goes missing between what goes in and what gets through for you to experience as reality. How this works is that the brain has a highly sophisticated filtering system that automatically sifts through the information and decides which data does and doesn't get through. Think about what an anorexic person 'sees' in the mirror. When they 'see' their grotesquely fat body staring back at them, is this the 'truth' when they weigh barely five stone?

Did you wonder why, as soon as you decided you wanted to buy your Mazda MX-5, you saw this model of car everywhere? Or, when you decided to give up smoking, why everyone seemed to smoke?

This is an example of your brain's filtering system at work. Once you consciously set your mind to something – rather like an internet search engine – your filtering system hunts those millions of bits of information for anything that matches and brings only those items into your conscious awareness. This filtering process of information is what creates your reality. The Mazda MX-5s and smokers were always there, but your brain chose not to bring them to your attention because it deemed them unimportant. Then, when you identified them as being important, they were allowed through into your conscious awareness and you saw them everywhere.

In essence, we don't see the world as it is, we see it the way we think it is. Like with knowing you have a choice about how you react to certain people and situations, you also have a choice about how you perceive situations and how you interpret experiences. How you perceive and interpret an experience will cause you to feel a certain way and, as you will see in Step Seven, this will create your reality.

STEP FIVE TASK:

What experiences in the outer world match your expectations, beliefs and assumptions in your inner world?

STEP SIX EXPLAINED: MIND INTO MATTER

The brain filters what information gets through to the conscious mind, and influences what an individual experiences as 'reality.' But how does the brain know what to filter in and what to filter out? One answer is beliefs. But what are beliefs, and why are they important?

Beliefs are often said as statements of fact – 'I am fat,' 'I am intellectual,' 'I am good at drawing,' but they are actually just personal viewpoints which provide a set of rules by which we live our lives. They are created out of a need to organise and store experiences in a way that helps us to make sense of the world.

Most beliefs are formed between the ages of zero to seven, which means the beliefs will have been shaped by parents, siblings, teachers and peers, who have all inadvertently passed their beliefs and their versions of the truth onto the innocent child: you. These beliefs become hardwired into your own brain and become your 'truths.'

As it is bombarded with new information all the time, the brain needs to be able to process this data efficiently so it compares new information to what it already knows. A belief is nothing more than a thought we keep on thinking.

What is particularly important for you to understand is that your beliefs are a self-fulfilling prophecy:

*Your **beliefs** cause you to **think** a certain way.*

*What you **think** determines how you **feel**.*

*How you **feel** determines what you **do** in terms of your behaviour.*

*What you **do** has a direct impact on what you **get** (your outcome).*

*What you **get** reinforces your **beliefs**.*

*Your **beliefs** impact what you **think**.*

*What you **think** impacts how you **feel,** and so on.*

*For example, if you **think** that men don't want you, that they'll leave you after a short period of time, you'll **feel*** *insecure. If you feel insecure, you'll be needy (**do**). If you are needy, many men will find that off-putting, so they will finish with you (**get**). And that reinforces your belief that men don't want you and that they'll leave you after a short while. And so it goes on.*

While you will have many beliefs which are positive and will create conditions of success, you will also have beliefs that are limiting and will hold you back from success. And as beliefs are just thoughts you keep on thinking, you can change them.

STEP SIX TASK:

1. *What beliefs do you have about:*

   - *Family?*

   - *Men?*

   - *Friends?*

   - *Work?*

   - *Body image?*

2. *How do these beliefs play out in the belief cycle?*

3. *Which beliefs are positive (empowering), and which are holding you back (limiting)?*

STEP SEVEN EXPLAINED: CHANGING FORTUNES

The key to changing limiting beliefs is to become conscious of them. Once a belief is drawn out from the unconscious mind and into the conscious mind, you have the power to change it, so the process of detecting your limiting beliefs can be very powerful.

The next step is to challenge them. Are they really true or did they just become so because of the self-fulfilling cycle? (The answer will be Yes because, "Whether you think you can or you think you can't, you're right.")

The final step is to think of a new positive belief that will reverse the limiting belief. Then you need to act 'as if' you believe in this new belief, because changing the way you think will reverse the self-fulfilling cycle from vicious to virtuous. It works because it creates new neural pathways in your brain, which will replace the old ones when you've done it enough times.

The good news is that by being conscious of your limiting beliefs, you can change them. The not-so-good-news is that it takes a lot of consistent effort until the new positive belief becomes so habitual that it can go to the unconscious mind where it can be left on automatic pilot.

In Step Three, the reason I needed to hear you say that you wanted to change 10/10 was because it is going to take effort – consistent effort – to create the change you want. But if you are willing to put in the effort, you will reap huge rewards.

Here's a summary of how to change limiting beliefs:

1. Be aware of your beliefs and the effects they're having on your life.

2. For beliefs that are having a negative impact in your life or are preventing you from getting what you want, challenge them. Are they really the truth?

3. Assuming they are not the truth, think of a new positive belief and act 'as if' it is true, and it will become so.

STEP SEVEN TASK:

1. Challenge the beliefs you no longer want. Look at them from an objective viewpoint: are they really the Truth? Or did you choose to believe them?

2. What new positive and empowering beliefs could you have with:

   • Family?

   • Men?

   • Friends?

   • Work?

   • Body image?

3. Act 'as if' it is true and it will become so.

STEP EIGHT EXPLAINED: THE KEY

Millions of people around the world suffer from a disorder they are oblivious to. Yet it holds the key to transforming their lives for the better.

What is it? It's low self-esteem.

Self-esteem refers to the extent to which you like and accept yourself – warts and all - and how worthwhile a person you think you are. It is knowing that you're worthy of being loved, respected and accepted. Only when you know this, will you be loved, respected and accepted by other people. Only when you have healthy self-esteem will you attract a partner who loves and respects you as much as you do him. (Although the irony is that you won't feel the need for a partner when you truly love and respect yourself.)

The wonderful news is that your low self-esteem can take as little as two weeks to change! The reason is that your recent thoughts, feelings and experiences tend to stay in your conscious mind for a couple of weeks. So, if you change your thoughts, they will start to change your self-esteem in roughly two weeks.

Do you remember all the way back to Step Two, when I mentioned that there is a Real Self? This is the perfect you, the flawless diamond that I mentioned. Your true self has perfect self-esteem because it only knows self-love.

If you think about it, self-esteem is the sum total of the beliefs you have about yourself. As you already know, beliefs are not the same as reality; they might feel real but they are only your perceptions and interpretation of what's going on. Your beliefs about yourself exist because of the way you think and not because the world is that way. So you need you be aware of the beliefs you have about yourself, replace them with positive beliefs, and act as if they are true. Ultimately, they will become true because, as you know, the belief cycle is a self-fulfilling cycle.

One way to identify your beliefs is to listen to how you talk to yourself because self-talk is a direct reflection of your beliefs about yourself. If you criticise yourself or say anything negative about yourself, stop it! Replace the negative thought with something positive and pretend it is true. Never again will you think of yourself as 'fat, ugly and boring;' instead you will only describe yourself as 'slim, beautiful and fun.' Watch what effect it will have in your life. In fact, listen to all your thoughts and, if they're negative, change them to something more positive. After all, who's in charge of your thoughts?! Remember, thinking something different will direct your brain's search engine to find examples which will back up your new thoughts.

Summary of Step Eight:

1. Identify the beliefs you have about yourself. Words such as should/shouldn't, must/mustn't and can/can't are good ways to identify beliefs. Also listen to your self-talk and notice any negative things you say to yourself.

2. Think of a positive belief and/or thought that will counter-act the negative belief and/or thought.

3. Act 'as if' it's true.

STEP EIGHT TASK:

1. What beliefs do you have about yourself? What negative things do you say about yourself?

2. What positive things can you say to yourself instead?

3. How can you act 'as if' they're true?

STEP NINE EXPLAINED: INFINITE MEANINGS

A direct consequence of self-esteem is how you perceive anything that happens in your life because you process a situation as either positive or negative depending on the level of your self-esteem. If you have low self-esteem, you will see your life as a series of external disasters, where everything goes wrong and you always end up being the victim. Alternatively, if you have healthy self-esteem, you seize every situation as an opportunity to learn and become a stronger person.

Power Thinking is a technique which helps you alter the way you perceive an event and thus allows you to change the meaning you assign to it. If you change the meaning, you change your response and behaviour as well. It is not about ignoring problems, but about having sufficient flexibility to make your point of view work for you instead of against you.

STEP NINE TASK:

The next time you feel angry or annoyed about something, think about how you can think about it differently in order to make yourself feel better. Notice how your behaviour – and the outcome - changes as a result of this.

STEP TEN EXPLAINED: PICTURE BLISS

Pictures are the language of the unconscious mind and allow you to use your imagination to bypass the conscious mind and speak directly to your unconscious mind. The brain does not know the difference between real and imagined so visualising is a powerful way to create new neural pathways in your brain, stimulating new ways of thinking. The following exercise will help to re-programme your self-esteem, and the beliefs you have about yourself, quickly and efficiently.

STEP TEN TASK:

Repeat the following as many times as you wish. Mornings and evenings are best but you can do it anytime. The more, the better!

Close your eyes and see yourself in your mind's eye as the best version of yourself: the amazing person you know you really are. The Real You. Imagine yourself as your most confident, self-assured, fulfilled, loved and happy self. Make the picture big and bright, make the colours rich and vibrant, and if there's sound, make it loud and intense. If you're standing still in the picture, turn it into a movie.

Next, see yourself interacting with different people positively, confidently and full of love for yourself and others. Then, see yourself in different situations where you handle everything with ease and confidence, and where the outcome is always positive. Then step into that person so that you feel what it's like to be that person. Then double and triple those feelings and allow them to surge powerfully through your whole body. Maintain these images, sounds and feelings for as long as you can (even a few seconds is better than nothing!). A few minutes would be ideal and you'll find it gets easier to hold the images, sounds and feelings for longer the more skilled you become. When you have finished, open your eyes.

Now you have all the tools needed to change your life, and be far happier and healthier. So get to work, and Good Luck!

Letter From The Author

This story is inspired by true events (but not the rude parts, of course, Dad!). The characters are based on real people but the majority of them are a combination of the traits of several individuals I met on my travels.

I really was dumped by a boyfriend on my birthday and I'm thankful now for the experience, because it was the catalyst for me taking steps to discover how I could change my life.

Throughout my twenties and early thirties, I was always single, felt I had no passion or direction in my life, and I was pessimistic, not believing that anything could change. I piled on weight whilst drinking too much in an attempt to drown out my unhappiness. I was desperate for change and would have swapped a kidney for a boyfriend if he would stay with me for more than a month. But I didn't know what to do or where to start.

I would settle into a job until I got fed up, which is when I would disappear for months on end to far-flung places. Anything to escape. At the time, I thought I could outrun the negative things in my life. What I didn't appreciate was that no matter where I ended up, I was always there. It eventually dawned on me that maybe it was me that needed to change, not my environment.

What I couldn't understand was why I was so miserable. I had an ordinary and stable upbringing with both parents and two sisters. My dad was a solicitor and my mum was a stay-at-home-mum for most of my childhood, we had family holidays, and lived in a sedate seaside town in the South of England. What I'm saying is that there was nothing in my childhood that warranted me feeling so miserable. Yet I did and it didn't make sense. As I got older, I became increasingly bitter and jealous that my friends were being promoted at work, buying houses and settling down with lifelong partners. I had none of those things. I found it easier to blame others for my misfortunes rather than to look at how I was creating my unhappiness.

It took me ten long years to start feeling happy and positive. Over that period, I met a variety of inspirational teachers, I read every self-help book I could lay my hands on, and I studied everything I could – from NLP and psychology to life coaching and spiritual counselling – until I learnt how to change my life for the better. This book contains the main lessons I wish I had known when I started out on my journey.

I am now in my forties; happily married to a wonderful man, and we have a gorgeous son, I'm a healthy size twelve, optimistic, and I love life. I also have a fantastic relationship with my parents (we go on holiday together most years now).

I also love my job so much, I'm not sure I can call it a job. I am a skills trainer who wears two hats. One hat involves